American Children's Folklore

"This is a well-rounded collection of the folklore of American children, showing both their good sides and their nasty ones—which is just what it is intended to be."

THE CHATTANOOGA TIMES

"It belongs on every folklorist's bookshelf but also will appeal to a general audience."

NORTH CAROLINA FOLKLORE
SOCIETY NEWSLETTER

"Earns straight A's in the Nostalgia Test...All the terrible beauty of childhood is here."

WASHINGTON POST BOOK WORLD

AMERICAN FOLKLORE SERIES

This title is part of the
American Folklore Series,
which also includes the
following works:

Mexican-American Folklore
John O. West

American Foodways
WHAT, WHEN, WHY AND HOW WE EAT IN AMERICA
Charles Camp

German-American Folklore
Mac E. Barrick

Native American Legends
THE SOUTHEASTERN TRIBES
George E. Lankford

The Oral Tradition of the American West
Keith Cunningham

Southern Folk Ballads, Volume I
Southern Folk Ballads, Volume II
W. K. McNeil

Ozark Mountain Humor
W. K. McNeil

American Children's Folklore

Compiled and edited by

Simon J. Bronner

This volume is a part of
The American Folklore Series
W.K. McNeil, General Editor

August House / *Little Rock*
P U B L I S H E R S

Printed in the United States of America

10 9 8 7 6 5 4 3 2

LIBRARY OF CONGRESS CATALOGING-IN-PUBLICATION DATA

American children's folklore
compiled and edited by Simon J. Bronner. — 1st ed.
p. cm. — (The American folklore series)
Bibliography: p.
ISBN 0-87483-068-0 (alk. paper): $9.95
1. Children — United States — Folklore. 2. Folklore — United States.
3. United States — Social life and customs — 1945-1971.
4. United States — Social life and customs — 1971-
I. Bronner, Simon J. II. Series.
GR105.3.A44 1988   88-23469
398'.0973—dc19   CIP

Cover illustration by Bill Jennings
Production artwork by Ira L. Hocut
Typography by Diversified Graphics, Little Rock, AR
Design direction by Ted Parkhurst
Project direction by Hope Norman Coulter

This book is printed on archival-quality paper which meets
the guidelines for performance and durability of the Committee
on Production Guidelines for Book Longevity of the Council on
Library Resources.

AUGUST HOUSE, INC.   PUBLISHERS   LITTLE ROCK

*A book for parents, teachers, counselors,
and all those adults who were once children*

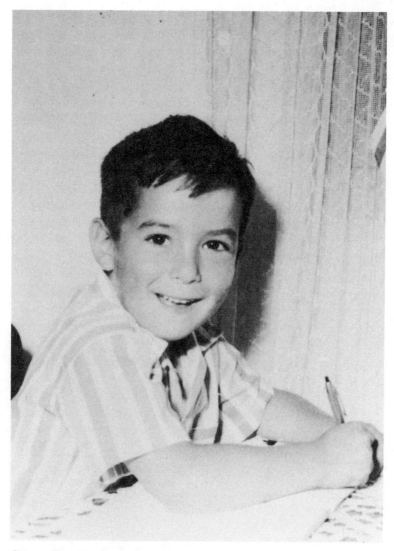

Simon Bronner, age 5.

Contents

Happy Birthday to You
Here Comes the Bride
How Dry I Am
Popeye the Sailor Man
McDonald's Is Your Kind of Place
Chiquita Banana
I Don't Like Navy Life

Séances
Mary Worth Rituals
Initiations
Customs

Introduction

WRITING OVER A century ago William Wells Newell commented that "the existence of any children's tradition in America, maintained independently of print, has hitherto been scarcely noticed."[1] This statement was among the prefatory remarks to Newell's *Games and Songs of American Children* (1883), a book that was his first and most important folklore study and one that marks the beginning of serious investigation of American children's folk traditions. A native of Cambridge, Massachusetts, Newell (1839-1907) was, in effect, the founder of the American Folklore Society and a major figure in American folklore circles from the 1880s until his death. At one time a Unitarian minister, Newell spent a decade running a private school in New York City. During this time he observed and collected children's street games, material he utilized in his book. Contemporaries recognized his volume as a significant work, and more than a hundred years later it is still of much more than historical importance.

Prior to 1883 English children's games had received considerable attention, but those found in the United States had been almost totally ignored. Judged by what preceded it Newell's research must have seemed gigantic and even today is still impressive. Whereas previous collectors gathered material haphazardly, the onetime schoolteacher set about systematically compiling and presenting on a large scale the games and game songs of English-speaking children. Moreover, he offered the first annotated comparative study of such data and demonstrated that these games and their texts were part of an international tradition. He combed through collections of children's lore in many languages and the literature of many ages and so was able to provide not only a geographic but also a historical account of these games. By this means he also demonstrated that games, songs, and rhymes moved across linguistic and geographic barriers just as easily as folktales and legends. Considering that in 1883 it was not common practice to print melodies with folksong collections, Newell was a pioneering scholar in that he provided tunes for several of the songs in his book. Equally farsighted was the arrangement of games into categories of use (e.g., "Love Games," "Playing Work," "Guessing Games," "Games of Chase"), a tactic suggesting an early approach towards what later came to be called functionalism.

Not everything about *Games and Songs of American Children* is admirable. There is a feeling of nostalgia and lament about the book, for Newell held the belief common to many early collectors that traditional lore was waning and would very soon be extinct. Thus, in his introductory comments he talks of how "the vine of oral tradition, of popular poetry . . . is perishing at the roots; its prouder branches have long since been blasted, and children's song, its humble but longest flowering offshoot, will soon have shared their fate." The numerous collections of children's lore that have appeared in the years since 1883 prove that Newell was wrong and that the traditions were not dying but constantly changing. His belief that children's lore was dying probably explains why he gathered much of his collection not from children but from adults "who remember the usages of their youth."[2] In the initial version of *Games and Songs of American Children* Newell maintained that the children's lore he reported had survived better in America than in England. When the second edition appeared in 1903 he reversed this earlier opinion, noting "that the stream of childish tradition continued to flow abundantly in England."[3] This change of view was precipitated by Alice Bertha Gomme's *The Traditional Games of England, Scotland, and Ireland*, a two-volume work issued in 1894 and 1898 that generally corroborated Newell's views about the distribution and diffusion of children's games and songs. Gomme's mammoth collection also offered proof of the thoroughness of Newell's research, for while her book contained many more variants it reported only a few games not in his earlier work.

Much of the comment in *Games and Songs of American Children* is aimed at proving that diffusion, rather than polygenesis (independent origin at several different places) or racial migration, is the only tenable explanation for similarities in rhymes and games found in widely separated lands. Cognizant that some readers might find his resolution of the problem of parallelisms uninteresting, Newell adds that "the interest of their resemblance is hardly diminished by this consideration." If anything, this fact heightened enthusiasm, for in order to prove diffusion of certain games one had to go back to the early Middle Ages, and this led to continual surprise regarding "the extent of the identity of our American . . . child's lore with the European."[4] Only by taking each individual game and tracing it through space and time could one arrive at sufficient data to make definite conclusions about such lore.

In this, his first folklore book, Newell reveals a common link with most other scholars of his day who regarded oral traditions as basically items of the past. In discussing the games and rhymes he collected, he always finds them survivals of the long ago and often the far away. For Newell, popular lore "invariably came from above, from the intelligent class" and by a form of cultural decay sifted down to the folk level.[5] This concept of cultural decline has come to be known as *gesunkenes Kulturgut* (literally "sunken good culture"). Who were the people that preserved such traditions now? Newell's answer coincided with an attitude common among folklorists, for he found that children's lore now lingered on mainly in rural surroundings. Only in the past three decades has this rustic stereotype of folklore been widely refuted on the scholarly level, and it still reigns unchallenged in popular thought. Newell considered those who preserved and propagated oral traditions as highly inventive persons who inherited their amusements only because of the necessity of general currency.

> If a sport is familiar only to one locality or one set of children, it passes away as soon as the youthful fancy of that region grows weary of it. Besides, the old games, which have prevailed and become familiar by a process of natural selection, are usually better adapted to children's taste than any new inventions can be; they are recommended by the quaintness of formulas which come from the remote past, and strike the young imagination as a sort of sacred law.[6]

Newell reiterated his ideas concerning folklore primarily in the pages of the *Journal of American Folklore* from 1888 until 1907. Although a major voice in the study of children's traditions, he commented little on the subject after 1883. His survivalist views and the emphasis on games and songs were echoed by most of those who immediately succeeded him in the study of children's folklore. Some scholars, however, refined Newell's views; chief among these is the little known William Henry Babcock. Often overlooked in discussions of the history of American folklore studies, Babcock was an American Indian specialist who should also be recognized as one of the pioneers of urban and children's folklore studies.[7] Like Newell, Babcock dealt mainly with children's games, but unlike the earlier scholar he demonstrated that children's games and lore thrived in big cities as well as in rural areas. With three articles, two of them published in *Lippincott's Monthly Magazine* in 1886 and one in *American Anthropologist* in 1888, Babcock proved his viewpoint.[8] These works, apparently, attracted little notice at the time and have been almost totally overlooked since. Babcock published nothing more in this area, concentrating on American Indian studies. His later attention to other concerns perhaps explains partially, but certainly not fully, why his early contributions to the study of children's folklore are rarely noted.

Getting much greater attention at the time was a slender volume titled *The Counting-Out Rhymes of Children: Their Antiquity, Origin, and Wide Distribution, A Study in Folk-Lore* (1888). Its author, Henry Carrington Bolton (1843-1903), was a chemist by profession with degrees from Columbia University and colleges in Paris, Heidelberg, Berlin, and Göttingen. He published several articles in the *Journal of American Folklore* and was one of the charter members of the American Folklore Society, which was founded in 1888. In December 1887 he completed the manuscript for his volume on rhymes, his only book on a folklore topic.

Although Bolton previously published articles on counting-out rhymes based on his own collecting, his book was primarily a second-hand work utilizing the contributions of several correspondents who sent him texts in response to published appeals. As might be expected, such a method of gathering data resulted in a very uneven body of material. Eight hundred and seventy-seven rhymes are present in nineteen languages and dialects, but a sizeable number of entries appear only in German and English. While touching upon a topic partially considered by Newell, *The Counting-Out Rhymes of Children* is not equal to the earlier work. Bolton conceded that *Games and Songs of American Children* "has been of service to us"[9] but he did not follow that model closely enough.

Like Newell, Bolton set out to demonstrate that the material he presented was part of an international body of tradition of great antiquity, but, unlike his predecessor, Bolton sought to prove that all the rhymes had a single origin "in the superstitious practices of divination by lots."[10] Whereas Newell arranged his data functionally, Bolton admitted that his scheme was "perfectly arbitrary" and "by no means ideal."[11] Newell attempted to describe in full the manner in which all the games and songs he reported were used, but Bolton provided such information for only a few rhymes. He voided Newell's mistaken assumption that British items survived better in the New World than in their homeland, but in collecting primarily "memory lore" from adults rather than from children currently using the rhymes he followed Newell's lead. Like most writers of the day Bolton paid no attention to the informant except as a person from whom texts could be collected, and this attitude prevented his gaining important insights into how a person uses and reshapes a text. Of course, the second-hand manner of collecting data also removed Bolton from the possibility of making such perceptions.

Many other names in nineteenth- and early twentieth-century American folklore studies made small contributions to the field of children's folklore, most of them following Newell's lead and focusing on games. For example, Robert Stewart Culin (1858-1929), an authority on games primarily remembered today for his mammoth *Games of the North American Indians* (1907) but known in his own time also for studies of Asian games, produced one article on street games played by boys in Brooklyn, New York.[12] Fanny Dickerson Bergen (1846-1924), primarily known for her two compilations *Current Superstitions* (1896) and *Animal and Plant Lore* (1899), contributed a brief essay on pigments used by children at play.[13] However, she diverged from the path charted by Newell to produce two articles dealing with children's foodways, folk cures and beliefs, toys, instruments, and constructions from nature. Some lesser lights, such as Talcott Williams, also assisted in the amassing of game texts.[14]

During the first half of the twentieth century, publications on children's games and songs continued unabated, although most of them were on the order of Mari Ruef Hofer's *Children's Singing Games Old and New* (1901) and Albert Ernest Wier's *Songs the Children Love To Sing* (1916).[15] That is, they were primarily recreation books designed for children, not books of scholarship. A few individuals did take a more academic approach, but in most cases these authors did little more than present texts without contextual information or historical perspective. One of the most active collectors didn't even do this much. Frank Clyde Brown (1870-1943), a long-time professor at Duke University, began collecting various types of folklore, including children's games, in 1912. His massive archive, consisting of items collected by himself and his students, was published posthumously in seven volumes from 1952 to 1964. The section on children's games and rhymes, edited by Paul Brewster, contained in the first volume is an excellently annotated and broad-ranging collection but contains little contextual data or information about collecting situations or informant backgrounds.[16] Mellinger Edward Henry, a

New Jersey schoolteacher who specialized in collections of southern Appalachian ballads, also published a collection of game songs from Georgia.[17] Dorothy Howard (1902-   ), later known for her studies of children's lore in both Australia and America, began her work in this area with an Ed.D. dissertation at New York University on folk jingles used by American children.[18] Her most recent contribution to the study of children's folklore is her autobiography, *Dorothy's World: Childhood in Sabine Bottom, 1902-1910* (1977), which includes considerable information on children's games in turn-of-the-century Texas.[19]

One of the most valuable articles on children's games published during the first half of the twentieth century was Leah Rachel Clara Yoffie's "Three Generations of Children's Singing Games in St. Louis," which appeared in the sixtieth volume of the *Journal of American Folklore*.[20] Yoffie departed from her usual field of Yiddish folklore to produce this study of change in games played by St. Louis children over a fifty-year period. She concluded "that the children of fifty years ago played more of the traditional games of England than children do to-day."[21] Instruction in games and dances by kindergarten and elementary schools helped preserve some of the older games; others of similar antiquity that were not sustained by such influences fell into disuse and were forgotten. New song-games, either derived from old ones or newly created and reflecting changed environmental conditions, replaced those games that died out. Thus, in contrast to many folklorists of her time who found education inimical to the propagation of folk tradition, Yoffie found it not only beneficial but even essential to the perpetuation of traditional children's games. Yoffie's essay is an important illustration of the value of collecting material over an extended period of time in a relatively small area.

Carl Withers (1912-1970), originally acclaimed for his study of an Ozark community in *Plainville U.S.A.* (1941), initiated a series of popular publications on children's folklore in 1946 with a book on counting-out rhymes, concluding with the posthumous *A Treasury of Games, Riddles, Mystery Stunts, Tricks, Tongue Twisters, Rhymes, Chants, Singing* (1974). Though popular in intent, Withers's books on childlore were based on considerable fieldwork. Such volumes as Fred Ferretti's *The Great American Book of Sidewalk, Stoop, Dirt, Curb, and Alley Games* (1975) are seemingly of the same order but they are too often based on nostalgic reminiscences of the author than on fieldwork. Ferretti's book, however, is one of a host of similar works, including but not limited to John and Carol Langstaff's *Shimmy Shimmy Coke-Ca Pop: A Collection of City Children's Street Games and*

Rhymes (1973) and James Wagenvoord's *Hangin' Out: City Kids, City Games* (1974), which have looked at city streets as settings for folk traditions.

An enigmatic scholar, Paul G. Brewster (1898-   ) is one of the most important twentieth-century scholars of children's games. An Indiana native who is known to American folklorists by name but rarely personally, Brewster is noteworthy for both his ballad scholarship and his work on games. His *American Nonsinging Games* (1953) contains descriptions of 150 children's games and is significant for several reasons. One, it is the first major work dealing with non-singing games. Two, it is based on extensive fieldwork, albeit not necessarily all by Brewster. Third, Brewster has comparative skills in this area second to none and provides good annotations. But the book also has its flaws. As much as by actual fieldwork, Brewster did work by correspondence — certainly an acceptable method, if not the most desirable one. That approach, however, does not excuse his failure to identify informants or even to give dates of collection. Considering his thorough grounding in the demands of European comparative folklore scholarship, it is also incomprehensible why Brewster says nothing about local changes in games. For example, names of some games differ from region to region and it would be helpful to know what these differences are, but unfortunately they are not detailed in Brewster's book.

Although Brewster was only in his mid-fifties when *American Nonsinging Games* was published, the 218-page compilation of material recorded from 1939 to 1952 marked the culmination of his work on children's games. He remained in academe for another fifteen years, finishing up his teaching career at Tennessee Technological University in 1968, but his later years were devoted to ballad studies. His one book on the subject of games is still important and is among the handful of worthwhile volumes on this specific aspect of children's lore.

One of the most entertaining recent volumes on children's games is *Step It Down: Games, Plays, Songs, and Stories from the Afro-American Heritage* (1972), which also happens to be one of the few extensive works on the subject of Afro-American children's lore. Based on an M.A. thesis by Bess Hawes at the University of California, the book is essentially made up of reminiscences of Bessie Jones (1902-1984), a Georgia native who became widely known as a folksinger. The seventy items in the book are broken down into nine categories: baby games and plays, clapping plays, jumps and skips, ring plays, singing plays, dances, house games and plays, outdoor games, and songs and stories.

Introductory material discusses the historical meaning and context of each item, giving the reader a good idea of how those traditions were generally used. Annotations, musical transcriptions, discography, and a bibliography are all provided. Some notes are vague, but in general this is an enjoyable and valuable introduction to Afro-American children's lore.

Counting-out rhymes, which formed the basis of Bolton's study, have also received frequent attention from American folklorists, although the number of publications on this aspect of children's lore do not rival those dealing with games. Like the research on games, most of the early publications on counting-out rhymes were collections rather than analytical works. Typical is the work of Emelyn Elizabeth Gardner (1882-1967), for many years a member of the Wayne State University faculty, who is primarily remembered today for her groundbreaking book *Folklore from the Schoharie Hills* (1937). While a few examples of children's lore are scattered throughout that book, Gardner's main contribution to the study of children's folklore is a brief article on counting-out rhymes in Michigan.[22] This one-page piece is a collection gathered mainly by Gardner's students. Other collections of counting-out rhymes that merit mention are Florence Maryott's lengthy selection of texts from Nebraska and Ruth Ann Musick and Vance Randolph's collection of 93 items, many of them counting-out rhymes but also including rope-skipping rhymes, riddles, and other materials.[23] To date, the most extensive work on this aspect of children's lore is *Counting-Out Rhymes: A Dictionary* (1980). This compilation, edited by Roger D. Abrahams and Lois Rankin, provides representative texts for 582 separate rhymes with an extensive listing of sources and variants for each one, along with information about the provenance, date, and use. In addition, Abrahams and Rankin provide cross-references for variants whose first lines differ from those of the representative texts, and Abrahams gives an introductory discussion of the significance of counting-out rhymes in children's play.[24]

Abrahams also provided a similar work for another type of children's rhyme with his *Jump-Rope Rhymes: A Dictionary* (1969). Until the 1920s the pastime of jumping rope was exclusively a boys' activity, but since then it has been almost exclusively one for girls. Abrahams includes 619 rhymes dating from the nineteenth century to the late 1960s, drawing on the work of several earlier collectors such as Babcock, Brewster, Howard, Randolph, and Charles Speroni.[25] Three of the earlier works utilized by Abrahams deserve special mention because they are attempts to classify or analyze jump-rope rhymes and games. The earliest of these, Sue Hall's "That Spring Perennial — Rope Jumping," proposes six categories of games based on the style of jumping.[26] Bruce Buckley's 1966 article also takes the same approach to the classification of rhymes, while Ruth Hawthorne's essay of the same year is an attempt to delineate the variables of jumping rope rather than to establish categories.[27] Abrahams, however, followed none of these authors but rather catalogued rhymes alphabetically by keyword.[28]

Although the earlier collectors of children's lore evinced little interest in narratives told by youngsters, the subject has been of increasing significance to recent American folklorists. John Vlach, primarily known for his studies of material culture, used stories told by students at an Indiana school to make a case for what he called the "humorous anti-legend," a term borrowed from European folklore scholarship.[29] A decade later Brian Sutton-Smith published narratives collected from children ages two to ten in a New York City school in *The Folkstories of Children* (1981). Approximately 500 texts are given primarily for the purpose of making a large collection of children's stories available to a wider public. Even so, the book does have some analytical comments, primarily plot analysis modified for this particular work from Russian folklorists Vladimir Propp's structuralist approach. Sutton-Smith's discussion demonstrates how the stories reveal an imaginative process by which children cope with matters of great concern in their lives. This book is certainly an important addition to the body of literature on children's folk narratives.[30]

Most studies of American children's folklore have focused on Anglo-American or European-American traditions. Very few have paid attention to narratives, or other folklore, passed along by American Indian children. One scholar who has is Margaret K. Brady, whose *"Some Kind of Power": Navajo Children's Skinwalker Narratives* (1984) is an eloquent argument not only for the study of Navajo children's narratives but for the serious study of children's folklore as well. Based on a collection of 100 narratives about the skinwalker (a human witch that wears coyote skins and travels at night), the volume is an exploration of "the ways in which these stories operate both within Navajo traditional culture and within the culture of a specific group of Navajo children."[31] Brady draws on the comments of the tradition bearers in examining the narratives, thereby avoiding a pitfall common to many earlier scholars of children's lore — namely using the traditions to bolster a theoretical view rather than examining the material on its own terms. Brady's volume is a milestone work providing ample evidence that children are highly articulate and utilize narratives in making sense of the cultural worlds around them.

Jokes are one aspect of traditional narrative that is usually slighted by students of children's folklore. Martha Wolfenstein (1911-1976) is the most important person who has specialized in this area of scholarship, producing two important articles and a book on the subject.[32] Her *Children's Humor: A Psychological Analysis* (1954) is a significant, yet often overlooked, study of the meaning of wit and humor as well as a classic work on children's folklore.[33] Based on jokes related to her over a school year by children aged from four to twelve in a New York City private school, the book contains much contextual data and biographical detail concerning informants. Those features alone are unusual in books on jokes but the volume is also noteworthy for Wolfenstein's attempt to demonstrate that different age groups have different concepts of humor. This last point has only recently come to be widely appreciated and in the early 1950s must have seemed innovative indeed. Wolfenstein not only did extensive fieldwork but did field experimentation as well, testing many of her hypotheses by intentionally introducing material to her informants. Such details make *Children's Humor* of enduring value despite its many flaws, such as the author's evident ignorance of some previous collections of jokes and her strict, almost stodgy, Freudian interpretations.

Most collections and studies of American riddles, such as Archer Taylor's mammoth and essential *English Riddles from Oral Tradition* (1951), are not confined just to material related by children. One, however, that is so restricted is John Holmes McDowell's *Children's Riddling* (1979), which is based on two large bodies of riddles, one collected by McDowell from Mexican-American children in Austin, Texas, and a second group recorded in an Austin studio as part of a Texas Children's Folklore Project.[34] McDowell excludes from consideration non-oral riddles and verbal sequences such as knock-knock jokes that do not attempt to deceive, confining his attention to question-and-answer routines that contain an identifiable block element. McDowell's concept of riddle is more narrow than that of many modern researchers, but his book is both impressive and important. He covers, among other matters, the linguistic structure of riddles, characteristic subjects, etiquette and rules of riddling, structure of riddling sessions, and cultural factors shaping the riddling of ethnic and class groups, matters rarely treated in most studies of riddles, be they told by children or adults. Unfortunately, an unnecessarily jargon-laden, pedantic style of writing makes the volume less accessible than it might be.

Some studies of American folk tradition are invariably classified as publications on children's folklore despite the fact that their subject matter is not necessarily correctly catalogued under that heading. For example, the numerous articles and books on "play-party" games are usually cited in bibliographies as works on children's folklore, even though "play-parties" were actually attended by persons young and old.[35] Similarly, in the early nineteenth century, when the tradition of autograph albums began in the United States, inscriptions were made by both children and adults, but were definitely more popular with the latter group until about 1900. Nevertheless, essays on the subject are usually referred to as articles on children's folklore.[36] Some other aspects of children's folklore have been slighted, getting at best little more than passing attention. Schoolboy slang is one subject that still awaits definitive treatment, though it has been treated by A.W. Eddins, a collector of Texas Negro lore; Eddins's article on slang appeared in 1916 in *Round the Levee,* the first volume of the Texas Folklore Society Publications.[37] A 1937 article in the *American Journal of Psychology* called attention to the magical behavior of children concerning school, while in the journal *Sociology and Social Research* M.W. Cramer discussed the leisure activities of privileged children, a group rarely considered in folklore studies.[38] In an essay in *Western Folklore* Norris Yates called attention to children's folk plays; an interesting article by Norine Dressed in *New York Folklore Quarterly* noted the folklore qualities of telephone pranks.[39] David Winslow gave serious attention to children's derogatory epithets and Bess Hawes treated from a scholarly standpoint a subject that had previously been given short shrift — the lullaby.[40] This list could be extended almost indefinitely, for despite the considerable amount of work done in children's folklore the field is really in its infancy (no pun intended).

One indication that relatively little work has been done in American children's folklore is that only in the last two decades have any volumes purporting to cover the entire field been produced. Actually, the late Peter Opie and his wife Iona compiled a valuable work of this type which is sometimes used by teachers of courses on children's folklore. However, *The Lore and Language of Schoolchildren* (1959) is based on data recorded from approximately 5,000 schoolchildren in the British Isles and therefore, except in instances where the same traditions are found in the United States, does not deal with American children's folklore at all.[41] The same cannot be said about Mary and

Herbert Knapp's *One Potato, Two Potato ... The Secret Education of American Children* (1976), which includes folk traditions gathered from children in 43 states, some United States territories, and a few foreign countries. Geographically this collection is the most wide-ranging body of children's lore yet published, but it is not entirely satisfying as a scholarly work. Although the Knapps used a variety of methods — observation, interviews with children, adolescents, and young adults, and questionnaires — in obtaining material, they fail to indicate which items were elicited by specific techniques. In fact, beyond mention of the methodologies employed, no comments about the manner or circumstances of collection are offered. Very little data is given about informants, not even their ages or the places of collection. Thus, it is impossible to utilize this material in comparative analyses of childlore or in studies of change and diffusion of these traditions. Moreover, the Knapps insist that children live in isolation from the adult world, an idea with which many, if not most, folklorists would disagree. They do attempt some analysis, but frequently their comments of this type seem naive or simplistic. For example, they suggest that a traditional saying in which blacks and whites are mentioned owes its popularity to the limited successes of the civil rights movement, an explanation that ignores historical realities or the traditional contexts in which the saying is used. Thus, despite the relatively recent publication of the Knapps' book, it already appears very dated.[42]

Despite its limitations *One Potato, Two Potato* is important, even if only because of the vast collection on which it is based. A more modest collection is included in Jack and Olivia Solomon's *Zickary Zan: Childhood Folklore* (1980), whose title suggests the possibility of a book about the entire field of American children's lore. Actually, the book deals solely with folk traditions of Alabama children, the traditions presented being collected primarily by students in an introductory folklore course taught by the Solomons. Texts are given here unencumbered by any of the contextual or informant data most contemporary folklorists consider essential. A list of "contributors" is appended to the end of the book, but readers are left to their own devices to ascertain what specific items they contributed. The main value of *Zickary Zan* is a useful bibliographical essay included near the end of the book.[43]

While the preceding pages by no means include references to every worthwhile publication on American children's folklore, they do indicate the general nature of the work that has been done. Paradoxically, there has been intensive study over a long period of time and simultaneously inadequate investigation of the topic. Examples of some genres have been collected extensively, while many others have been virtually ignored. Too often folklorists have been guilty of being text-hungry but have spent little time telling us what the texts mean or how they are used traditionally. The biggest problem is that there has been no adequate attempt to survey broadly the field of American children's lore, one that would demonstrate the value of such material and the reasons why it should receive serious scholarly attention. A hopeful sign is the establishment of an active Children's Folklore Section of the American Folklore Society, one of its former presidents being Simon J. Bronner. Among the planned projects of this organization is a book on issues in children's folklore, a work that, apparently, will be aimed primarily at an audience of professional folklorists. The present volume by Simon J. Bronner is designed for a much wider audience consisting of academics and the lay public as well. It covers the field broadly, adding new material to the consideration of the children's folklore field; shows changes and continuities in children's folk traditions; includes variants; cites informants and settings; and connects the material to the realities of modern society. Hopefully, it will become the model by which other books on the subject will be judged.

W.K. McNeil
OZARK FOLK CENTER
MOUNTAIN VIEW, ARKANSAS

Notes

[1] William Wells Newell, *Games and Songs of American Children* (New York: Dover Publications, Inc., 1963; reissue of a work originally published in 1883), xix.

[2] Ibid., p. 1.

[3] Ibid., xv.

[4] Ibid., p. 4.

[5] Ibid., p. 7.

[6] Ibid., p. 27.

[7] See, for example, Babcock's article "The Nanticoke Indians of Indian River, Delaware," in *American Anthropologist* 1 (1899): 277-83, for one of his articles on American Indian folklore. He also published *Legends of the New World* (Boston: R.G. Badger, 1919), a collection of poetic renderings of Indian legends.

[8] The articles are "Song Games and Myth Dramas in Washington," *Lippincott's Magazine* 37 (1886): 239-57; "Carols and Child-lore at the Capitol," *Lippincott's Magazine* 38 (1886): 320-42; and "Games of Washington Children," *American Anthropologist* 1 (1888): 243-84.

[9]Henry Carrington Bolton, *The Counting-Out Rhymes of Children: Their Antiquity, Origin, and Wide Distribution, A Study in Folk-Lore* (Detroit: Singing Tree Press, 1969; reprint of a work originally published in 1888), p. 47.

[10]Ibid., "Preface."

[11]Ibid., p. 62.

[12]The article is "Street Games of Boys in Brooklyn, N.Y.," *Journal of American Folklore* 4 (1891): 221-37.

[13]The article is "Pigments Used by Children in Their Play," *Journal of American Folklore* 8 (1895): 151-53. The other articles mentioned are "Nibblings and Browsings" and "Pandean Pastimes," which appeared in *Atlantic Monthly* in 1893 and 1896 respectively. These two essays are reprinted in Simon J. Bronner, *Folklife Studies from the Gilded Age* (Ann Arbor, Michigan: UMI Research Press, 1987), pp. 119-33.

[14]Talcott Williams, "A Game of Children in Philadelphia," *Journal of American Folklore* 12 (1899): 292.

[15]Hofer's book was published in Chicago by A. Flanagan & Company while Wier's was published in 1916 by D. Appleton and Company. He also published a similar work in *Songs to Sing to Children* (New York: Harcourt, Brace and Co., 1935).

[16]The section "Children's Games and Rhymes" appears on pp. 29-219 of vol. 1 of *The Frank C. Brown Collection of North Carolina Folklore* (Durham, North Carolina: Duke University Press, 1952).

[17]The article is "Nursery Rhymes and Game-Songs from Georgia," *Journal of American Folklore* 47 (1934): 334-40.

[18]The dissertation is *Folk Jingles of American Children: A Collection of Rhymes Used by Children Today* (Ed.D. dissertation, New York University, 1938).

[19]*Dorothy's World: Childhood in Sabine Bottom, 1902-1910* (Englewood Cliffs, New Jersey: Prentice-Hall, 1977).

[20]Leah Rachel Clara Yoffie, "Three Generations of Children's Singing Games in St. Louis," *Journal of American Folklore* 60 (1947): 1-51.

[21]Ibid., 51.

[22]Emelyn E. Gardner, "Some Counting-Out Rhymes in Michigan," *Journal of American Folklore* 31 (1918): 91.

[23]Florence Maryott, "Nebraska Counting-Out Rhymes," *Southern Folklore Quarterly* 1 (1937): 39-62; Ruth Ann Musick and Vance Randolph, "Children's Rhymes from Missouri," *Journal of American Folklore* 63 (1950): 425-37.

[24]Roger D. Abrahams and Lois Rankin, *Counting-Out Rhymes: A Dictionary* (Austin: University of Texas Press, 1980).

[25]The work of the other scholars mentioned here is discussed elsewhere in this essay. Speroni contributed "Some Rope-Skipping Rhymes from Southern California," *California Folklore Quarterly* 1 (1942): 245-52.

[26]Hall's article appeared in *Recreation* (1941): 713-16.

[27]Bruce R. Buckley, "Jump-Rope Rhymes: Suggestions for Classification and Study," *Keystone Folklore Quarterly* 11 (1966): 99-111; Ruth Hawthorne, "Classifying Jump-Rope Rhymes," *Keystone Folklore Quarterly* 11 (1966): 113-26.

[28]Roger D. Abrahams, *Jump-Rope Rhymes: A Dictionary* (Austin: University of Texas Press, 1969).

[29]John Vlach, "One Black Eye and Other Horrors: A Case for the Humorous Anti-Legend," *Indiana Folklore* 4 (1971): 95-125.

[30]Brian Sutton-Smith, *The Folkstories of Children* (Philadelphia: University of Pennsylvania Press, 1980).

[31]Margaret K. Brady, *"Some Kind of Power": Navajo Children's Skinwalker Narratives* (Salt Lake City: University of Utah Press, 1984), p. 11.

[32]Martha Wolfenstein, "A Phase in the Development of Children's Sense of Humor," *Psychoanalytic Study of the Child* 6 (1951): 336-50; ———, "Children's Understanding of Jokes," *Psychoanalytic Study of the Child* 9 (1953): 162-73; ———, *Children's Humor: A Psychological Analysis* (Glencoe, Illinois: Free Press, 1954). Another scholar who has written a book on children's jokes is Sandra McCosh, whose *Children's Humor* (London: Granada Publishing/Panther Books, 1979) is not discussed here because it deals primarily with British material. Mac E. Barrick is among the very few who have published worthwhile articles on riddling questions and ethnic jokes, two types of humor perpetuated by children. See, for example, his "The Shaggy Elephant Riddle,"

Southern Folklore Quarterly 28 (1964): 266-90, and "The Newspaper Riddle Joke," *Journal of American Folklore* 87 (1974): 253-7.

[33]The book was reprinted in 1978 by Indiana University Press with a foreword by Alan Dundes.

[34]John H. McDowell, *Children's Riddling* (Bloomington: Indiana University Press, 1979).

[35]See, for example, the listings in Charles Haywood, *A Bibliography of North American Folklore and Folksong* (New York: Greenberg Publishers, 1951), especially pp. 160-68.

[36]See, for example, Sylvia Ann Grider, "A Select Bibliography of Childlore," *Western Folklore* 39 (1980): 248-65, especially p. 259.

[37]A.W. Eddins, "The State Industrial School Boy's Slang," *Texas Folklore Society Publications* 1 (1916): 44-46.

[38]S. Blackowski, "The Magical Behavior of Children in Relation to School," *American Journal of Psychology* 50 (1937): 347-61; M.W. Cramer, "Leisure Activities of Privileged Children," *Sociology and Social Research* 34 (1942): 440-50.

[39]Norris Yates, "Children's Folk Plays in Western Oregon," *Western Folklore* 9 (1951): 55-62; Norine Dresser, "Telephone Pranks," *New York Folklore Quarterly* 29 (1973): 121-30.

[40]David J. Winslow, "Children's Derogatory Epithets," *Journal of American Folklore* 82 (1969): 255-63; Bess L. Hawes, "Folksongs and Function: Some Thoughts on the American Lullaby," *Journal of American Folklore* 87 (1974): 140-48. Actually, there have been a number of publications on the lullaby, but all of those prior to Hawes's article were in the nature of collections or books intended for parents looking for songs to sing to their children. Winslow also contributed several other works on children's folklore, including "An Annotated Collection of Children's Lore," *Keystone Folklore Quarterly* 11 (1966): 151-202; "The Collecting of Children's Lore," *Keystone Folklore Quarterly* 11 (1966): 89-98; and "An Introduction to Oral Tradition Among Children," *Keystone Folklore Quarterly* 11 (1966): 43-58.

[41]Iona and Peter Opie, *The Lore and Language of Schoolchildren* (Oxford: Clarendon Press, 1959). The Opies also published several other works on children's folklore that have some relevance to American traditions. These include *The Oxford Dictionary of Nursery Rhymes* (Oxford: Clarendon Press, 1952); *Children's Games in Street and Playground* (Oxford: Clarendon Press, 1969); and *The Oxford Book of Children's Verse* (Oxford: Clarendon Press, 1973).

[42]Mary and Herbert Knapp, *One Potato, Two Potato: The Secret Education of American Children* (New York: W.W. Norton, 1976).

[43]Jack and Olivia Solomon, *Zickary Zan: Childhood Folklore* (University, Alabama: University of Alabama Press, 1980).

Acknowledgments

I am grateful for the helping hands that made this book possible. I want to give special acknowledgment to the archivists, assistants, and professors who opened files and troves galore for me: Camille Bacon-Smith at the University of Pennsylvania; Barre Toelken, Mary Kay Peterson, and Barbara Walker at Utah State University; William Wilson at Brigham Young University; Marsha MacDowell and Kurt Dewhurst at Michigan State University; Margaret S. Mims and Janet Langlois at Wayne State University; Edward D. Ives at the University of Maine; Joe Hickerson, Marsha Maguire, and Gerald Parsons at the Library of Congress; Vicki L. Slocum and Patricia Hodges at Western Kentucky University; Robert Bethke at the University of Delaware; Michael Owen Jones at the University of California at Los Angeles; Peggy Brooks and Richard Bauman at Indiana University; Mac Barrick at Shippensburg University; Roderick J. Roberts at the State University of New York at Oneonta; Michael J. Dabrishus at the University of Arkansas; and Esta Lou Riley at Fort Hays State University.

I am also grateful to the individuals who aided my local collecting and interviewing: Carolyn Henry, Hannelore Wertz, Jerrold Stouder, Rich Bowra, Nancy Dewald, Mark Cislo, Charles Spillar, Eileen Franz, Martha Detweiler, and Pamela deWall. Others kindly supplied helpful references: Alan Mays, Jay Mechling, Tom Johnson, Priscilla Ord, Sue Samuelson, Mac Barrick, Danielle Roemer, Gary Alan Fine, Phillips Stevens, Chip Sullivan, Richard Meyer, Tara Tappert, and Bill McNeil. Bill McNeil also deserves credit for his editorial advice, not to mention his saintly patience.

At Penn State Harrisburg, where I study and teach, I was blessed with wonderful support. I thank Jacqueline Guida, who sorted things out at the archives; Carol Kalbaugh, who transcribed tapes at the Center for Research and Graduate Studies; Joanne Meinsler and Michael Kalbaugh, who prepared graphics at Instructional Services; Ruth Runion Slear, who worked on my interlibrary loan requests; Henry Koretzky, who helped with my periodical searches at the Heindel Library; Thea Hocker, who made connections and gave advice at Community Relations; Darrell Peterson, who printed the photographs for the Humanities Division; Division Head William Mahar, who encouraged my work; and Division secretary Donna Horley, who handled my correspondence. I also want to recognize here the many students over the years enrolled in my American folklore class. Their enthusiasm and their involvement enlivened my work.

Most of all, I thank the kids. And I am thankful for the kids in all of us.

CHAPTER ONE

An Overview

TOO OFTEN, WHAT children are told to express by teachers and authors is recorded out of proportion to what they themselves have to sing and say. When children's folk expressions are transcribed, they are commonly distilled into a romanticized, antiquated vintage. Thus, despite its artistry and historical relevance, much authentic modern children's folklore has escaped preservation. To be sure, the preservation of this lore is challenging because of its communal, sometimes rough-hewn, and often evanescent nature. We take the everyday experience of folklore for granted, even though its very worldliness makes it especially significant to our lives.

Therefore my purpose in this book is to present and preserve a representative, but not comprehensive, sample of children's folklore in modern American life. This collection reports what children really have to say, and not necessarily what we like to hear. No, children's folklore is not all the sweetness and light of "Ring around the Rosies." And no, it is not stuck in a past golden age. Yes, it thrives in the city as well as the country, in our modern times much as it did in pioneer days, among rich children and poor, girls and boys, of all ethnic groups and religions. It adapts to changing times and comments on them. It works hard for its living.

This book brings children's folklore up to date. It covers the era after World War II when much changed in the way children played and adults worked. The one-room schoolhouse was fading from the scene, while playgrounds and centralized schools became second homes for most children. With new labor laws, children were free to play and learn, and with an expanding middle class, children became consumers — indeed harbingers — of fads and trends. The cities of the nation increasingly housed the population, and returning veterans helped swell that population to new heights. Expanding technology opened new communication wonders from the telephone to the television in almost every corner of the country. The country seemed a smaller place, but not a more tranquil one. Raging issues of civil rights, sexual freedom, and moral responsibility swept through adult consciences and children's lives.

Folklore reflects these changes and provides hedges against them. Concerned, as we should be, with the changing character of American life, we can look at folklore particularly to interpret where our culture has been and where it's heading. As part of our national tradition, as part of every person's experience, folklore preserves part of the past and responds to the needs of the present. The customs, games, and verses of childhood remind us of society's cherished values and attitudes. Folklore is part of the learning that prepares children for life in society. The frequent repetition of folk expressions instructs children in the time-tested ways they are expected to act, or not act, and think.

This book not only brings children's folklore up to date, but brings it back to reality. The examples here are not rewritten and bowdlerized. As much as possible, I retain the sound and spirit of children's experience, and identify real-life sources. In doing this, I offer a portrait of children in all their beauty and harshness. Portraying American children demands a variety of textures, for they and their expressions display ethnic, regional, religious, and racial diversity. And there are differences of age and gender to consider. Different children may call the same game "Cowboys and Indians" or "Cops and Robbers" or "SWAT Team." In a counting-out rhyme, they can "catch a tiger by the toe," "catch a nigger by the toe," or "catch Tojo by the toe." Each variation expresses an attitude unique to a certain time and place.

Still, my observations from one end of the country to the other impressed upon me the continuity among American children. In 1980, one-half of all Americans were living in a home or apartment different from the one they occupied in 1975; the largest rise in home sales (88 percent) in that period was in mobile homes. Moving around as much as their parents do, most American children have a basic repertoire of lore that can be employed in different places. Therefore the examples I have provided in the book present a mix of what connects and separates us in America. The book presents the unity within the diversity of American experience.

The children in this book range in age from four to seventeen, from pre-school to high school. Granted, there are many divisions to be made within this span. Today we are familiar with categories within childhood of infancy, early childhood, pre-adolescence, and adolescence. Teachers say that there can even be sharp distinctions between grades. The perception of an encompassing childhood in American society is nonetheless significant. It identifies a division between adulthood, where authority resides, and childhood, where individuals are still under parental control. It is a powerful division that is reflected in the lore itself.

For children, we must remember, do not simply ape the mores of adults. They want to declare their own identity, and lore is their protected expression of cultural connection to one another. Secret languages and private verses offer an index to the rise of a child's world within the larger one we know. Increasingly independent, children fiercely hang on to their cultural property to express their distinct personality and social separation from other ages. Increasingly left to themselves, they use folklore to help them grow.

At close to 30 percent of the population, children compose America's largest semiliterate group. Thus folklore flourishes among them, because it is transmitted by word of mouth, imitation and demonstration, and custom. Through word of mouth, children learn a vocabulary not found in the dictionary; they readily pass along stories, riddles, puzzles, and rhymes, each conveying a lesson. Through imitation and demonstration, they learn the native crafts and gestures of childhood. They instruct one another in the making of spitball-shooters and love chains; they master hand-clapping and ball-bouncing moves. Through custom, or ritualistic repetition, they learn what to do and say on holidays; they perform initiations and ceremonies from the snipe hunt to the album-signing rite. The three types of informal learning are not easily separable, and can be seen complementing one another in the development of a child's folk game repertoire. Tradition emerges from this learning, especially when expressive forms repeat and vary over time.

Folklore, being a familiar and creative way for people to relate to one another, also provides a social cohesiveness. In childhood, the segregation of children by school grades allows for the easy transmission and development of distinct cultural expressions. The same children see one another almost every day, and their largely oral culture promotes the kind of variation and repetition of expressions characteristic of the structure of folklore. Back at home, children seek out groups for play, and in these social situations they use folklore to organize games and usher creativity. In the intensive experience of camp, another common childhood institution, folklore provides the parables that help children adjust to a new natural environment and the company of strangers. Wherever they are, children rely on formulas of rhyme and meter that enable them to remember and improvise folklore easily and pass it on quickly. As adults, we may forget the names of our camp, school, or play mates, but we are likely to remember the scary story we heard that reminded us to stay out of the woods, or the games that separated the boys from the girls.

For children growing up, folklore is the backdrop for much socializing and communicating. They go through a rapid succession of physical and emotional changes — perhaps the most rapid in their lives. Folklore responds with many rituals and lessons to ease the passage through these early years and to provide benchmarks for growth. With each year, children pick up new lore and discard old lore as "babyish." Rhymes give way to stories, beliefs give way to customs. As they age, games signify children's growing independence. Many of the early childhood games call for children to flee a "home base" and then seek their way back to the safety of home. As children age, the games themselves take them farther and farther away from "home" and back again. Some early childhood games force children to say "Mother may I?"; later in preadolescence, other rituals call for them to declare their independence by cutting down one another's mothers with insults. Birthday customs, camp initiations, and game preferences announce how old they are and with whom they belong.

Children's folklore has styles and themes that distinguish it from lore of other ages, despite the fact that many of the forms that children hear are inherited from adults. Children establish their cultural independence by employing techniques of parody, antithesis, and nonsense. In parody, popular songs and sayings suffer indignity in the mouths of children. They delight in manipulating the sacred texts of adult-minded popular culture into a child's-eye view. In the technique of antithesis, children deliberately oppose norms. When a child suddenly shouts "tons and tons of tightly twisted turtle turds," it is possible to recognize in the tradition the license of alliterative speech play. But more so, the antithesis of speech norms tests the limits of social control. Much of children's lore thus deals with subjects that are sensitive to control: profanity, bodily taboos, food habits, sexual manners. In using nonsense, children can go one step further, especially in their early years, by creating a unique, even disordered, sound and spirit out of the apparently strict speak-right rules and precedents of adult society. "Icka Backa Soda Cracker" or "Eeny Miney Moe" are clarion calls for children to gather because they establish a children's cultural code out of ordered nonsense. Many of the forms of folklore that children learn are put in the context of play, within which they can say things that cannot normally be said in conversation. In folk riddles, rhymes, jokes, and stories children can tease, fantasize, protest, and symbolize freely. In games they have license to run wildly, even flirt with the opposite sex.

Besides rebelling against adult norms, children's folklore reflects children's concerns about their rapid growth, the appropriate responses to adult society, and traditional roles and values in a nation being modernized. The themes of maturity, rationality, identity, power, and curiosity run throughout the examples in this book.

Maturity is a strong theme because of the great power held by adults in our society. In the United States it often seems that reaching adulthood, rather than understanding adulthood, is the goal of childhood. Children can be heard performing folklore to demonstrate their advancement beyond babyish behaviors, or childish behaviors, or those of sixth grade. The elaborateness of speech play and narration, or the complexity of hand movements in clapping games, can be signs of advancement. An off-color parody of a nursery rhyme reminds others that the teller no longer is connected to the innocence of the nursery, and what's more can understand the harsh images he or she has created. Calmly telling horror stories, and scaring someone younger, is another sign of maturity, as children define it. An especially important measure of maturity is knowledge of sexual information, especially as children's bodies develop. Children declare this measure by the kinds of jokes they tell, the language they use, the customs they enact.

The theme of rationality comes out in the ways that children explain, and relate to, their environment. They explore nature freely, making whistles out of grass and divining love with daisies. To them the natural world is also a spiritual place, where events are predicted, prevented, and explained by supernatural references. The dark has its boogeymen, the woods their scary figures, and the hills their ghosts. Pulled teeth bring fairies and Halloween raises goblins. The existence of jinxes, cooties, and sidewalk cracks demands one's prudence and alertness. Then as children advance in school, science becomes more than a subject for homework; it becomes a formula for living. Every marvel, students learn, has a rational scientific explanation. But children question this drummed-in message through rituals, and in their folklore re-establish the mystery of life. Séances, levitations, and scary stories — so much a part of children's culture — serve to comment on and adapt to modern rationality.

Much of growing up is about gaining an identity comprising one's expression of ethnicity, religion, gender, region, and family, to name some. Folklore, a communally shared expression, thrives because it offers a sense of belonging so important to children. Some of this theme is evident in friendship tokens, food customs, and ethnic games. But as this kind of folklore defines a group by what it shares, another kind of folklore separates a group by what makes others different. Jokes, especially — ethnic, handicapped, sexual — seem to serve this function. Other folklore forms remind us of what is considered important in the United States in judging identity. Just read an autograph album and take note of the significance placed on appearance, on family, and on popularity. Listen to a ritual-insult session and interpret the apparent premium placed on wealth, looks, and male values in acquiring a successful character. Folklore does allow for individuality; since much of it is performed, it invites individual flair and accomplishment. Children can distinguish themselves by possessing an extensive storytelling or paper-folding repertoire, or being able to improvise in the ritual-insult game of Dozens. And since much of folklore has a recognizable structure which allows creative license, children can substitute names, places, and times to satisfy their personal and local tastes. "Roses are red, violets are blue," we all remember easily — and we can finish the phrase with many variations, invented or traditional.

The theme of power pervades children's folklore because, first, children compose a subordinate group in relation to adults, and second, to raise their own prestige children often try to subordinate others, especially younger children. This flexing of symbolic power can lead to distortions of reality to turn the tables on the authority of parents, teachers, and counselors. "On top of Old Smoky," children sing, "All covered with blood, / I shot my poor teacher / With a forty-five slug." In jokes, teachers and counselors are embarrassed, controlled, and eliminated, while children disobey and triumph. In playful horror tales, the youngest children are the bravest and most worldly. Even in the making of folk toys by children there is an exercise of power, because children control the processes of construction from collecting raw materials to completing the product. Other constructions such as the treehouse circumscribe territory as well as process to be controlled by children outside the view of and regulation by adults.

Folklore is frequently a medium for the exercise of power by older children over younger children, or those deemed "First-grade babies, second-grade tots, / Third-grade angels, fourth-grade snots, / Fifth-grade peaches, sixth-grade plums, / All the others dirty bums." To show superior strength or knowledge, children will also subject their younger mates to pranks. Or they will taunt: "Baby, baby, stick your head in gravy; / Don't take it out until you join the Navy." Folklore further shows children's power as a group when it communicates their internal code of unwritten laws — laws of loyalty to other children and mutual protection from the adult world. Accusations of "tattle-tale," "momma's boy," or "teacher's pet" can stigmatize a child. On the other hand, reminders like "Keep your nose out of my beeswax" and "Finders keepers, losers weepers" assert proper behavior among peers; because of folk forms children remember to share, or else face the accusation of being an "Indian giver," and to be truthful, or else face the disgrace of being told, "Liar, liar, pants on fire, hang them up on telephone wire."

As children age, curiosity grows about the adult world they are about to enter. Although eager to be "grown up," they express anxiety about the prospects of sex, marriage, work, and mortality. When reality blends with imagination in folklore, children may confront uneasy situations before they happen; they learn by symbol and parable from stories heard from a friend of a friend, who heard it from his second cousin. An effective way to prepare for what lies ahead is to contemplate the meaning of adult experiences through legends and customs. In legends can be found the cautions to be taken in courtship down lover's lane or the responsibilities of taking a job — symbolized by babysitting — or owning and driving that socially potent symbol, a car. Because folklore supplies a context in which to predict and talk about momentous events to come, children may gain confidence about their future. They may fold papers and burn matches to divine their future fate, not to mention their future mate. Customs from inscribing yearbooks to initiation ceremonies to graduations ease their social transitions to adulthood.

As they mature, children also learn that the world's news affects their lives. Adults often try to shelter children from the harshness of news, but children have the outlet of folklore to discuss the meaning of issues of the day. The increasing closeness of death, the moral debate over abortion, the meaning of child abuse, the changes brought about by the civil rights and women's movements, the role of privacy and humanity in the wake of technological expansion, the adjustments forced by mainstreaming of the handicapped, and fear of sexually transmitted diseases have all found their way into children's lore. Often humor is used to relieve some of the anxiety raised by these issues, and within the content of the humor is often a commentary on the sides taken. In an era of change, folklore can be a stabilizing, conservative force, because it represents the power of tradition. By allow-ing outlets for expression and interpretation, folklore oils the gears of change.

Once grown, we don't do away with the use of folklore. But different conditions alter its role and shape. In adulthood, folklore often revolves around work rather than play. It more frequently appears in conversation and custom rather than in playful performance, and it frequently serves to maintain family traditions. Yet this is not to suggest a sharp break with our childhoods. Lore, customs, and games have helped shape who we are, and the values and attitudes they foster take us through our lives. The models of narration and art we learn feed our creative efforts, and models of gamesmanship are evident in various arenas from politics to relationships.

Still, we often remember childhood as the period when tradition governed our lives. Our everyday experience with schoolmates, and the play that resulted, fostered an intense and exciting sense of cultural transmission and creation. Children's folklore is significant because it has touched all of us. In the texts presented in this book, we read ourselves.

The sampling in this book emerged from more than a decade of collecting children's folklore in Indiana, Michigan, Mississippi, New York, and Pennsylvania. To this collection I added well-documented examples from folklore archives around the country. Most of the examples are collected from children themselves, and are supplemented by selections drawn from adult recollections to cover the period after World War II. My choices reflect what is typical and interesting, rather than what is unprecedented and unparalleled, in American children's lore. These choices are then presented in an organization that moves from chapters on verbal lore to social and material genres.

In this book, the lore is meant to be read, although a full appreciation requires hearing and seeing the lore performed spontaneously. Still, separating the texts and printing them for consideration has some benefits. The form, whether in story or structure, is the durable and comparable portion of the lore. Once it is recognized, we may then consider more carefully the enactment, setting, and performers of the lore. Toward this end, photographs and illustrations in the book add something of the look of folklore in action.'

'Readers who are interested in further historical, psychological, and social information and documentation are referred to the annotated edition of this book.

Having presented what has been collected from the last forty years, this book will, I hope, lead to contemplation on what the future holds for children's culture. It can attune us to the sounds of tradition emerging around us, especially as our society increasingly places cultural significance on the division of age. The growing adult regulation of children's play and learning has led many observers to bemoan the loss of children's spontaneous expression. More children submit to adult supervision in after-school centers and playgrounds than ever before. Is it the role of adults to entertain and regulate children while they passively await our cues? Or will children continue to rely on their own stock of lore to actively socialize and communicate?

Before answering, consider what has happened to Halloween, to name one changing custom discussed in this book. Once a children's folk celebration, the holiday has been restricted by some town councils to a few hours prior to the last day of October. This has been in response to their fears of criminal tampering of Halloween treats. With television sensationally reporting this rare danger to every living room, and with the modern-day reality of communities that have more strangers than neighbors, other forms of regulation have followed. In many towns, the community play of children on the holiday has been legislated almost out of existence, while adults in a kind of parody play have usurped much of the holiday for themselves. Children still need the functions of traditional Halloween to bear on their lives. They used to rely on the customs associated with the season for adjusting to the dark, cold nights; they used the occasion for creative outlets in response to adult control; they ventured out on their own to relate to, and to create, a community. Children may no longer rely on Halloween to serve these functions, but they will likely find, or create, some other folk practice to satisfy the same needs.

In the changing customs for Halloween, we can see the protective concern for children today. Sometimes this concern takes the form of legislation, in an attempt to compensate for decreased parental and community involvement with children. It is often protection from a distance, because another trend is toward greater segregation and independence for children. More and more, children spend time away from their parents, as the spread of two-income households and variable workdays has changed the patterns of child care prevalent in America. At the same time, growing institutions of day-care and after-school centers have fostered more cultural unity among children, a unity which has helped preserve old, and perpetuate new, folklore. Contributing to the unity is greater integration of the sexes at these centers, evident as a result of the movement away from children's playground and school activities restricted by gender.

Other social changes affect children where they live. The United States Census shows a trend of the nation's households out of large cities, often across great distances, to suburbs and the countryside. The size of American families, on average, is decreasing. Children have fewer brothers and sisters than they used to, but the number of out-of-household chums is likely to be larger. The landscape of children's groups is leveling out, giving rise to more interconnections among children across the street and across the country.

These trends promise an impact on American culture, and folklore can reveal it. For now, the folklore in my collection will provide one reference for our times. Still more collection is needed among America's more than 60-million-strong youngsters to chart the continuing flow of tradition. This collection will tell us of the directions of life as we contemplate the end of one century and the beginning of a new one. The collection of American children's folklore, often neglected because of the preoccupation of adults with the study of other adults, broadens our understanding of the nation from the events that influence us to the culture that inspirits us. With children's folklore, we anticipate our future by realizing our legacy.

"Who Says?": Speech

FROM THE MOUTHS of babes come some amazing sounds. With the encouragement of adults, infants mature quickly to form words and make themselves known to other children as well as to their watchful parents. For many years, children primarily rely on oral rather than written communication, and with their peers establish what could be called speech communities. By sharing words with special meanings known particularly to them and by expressing themselves with predictable phrases, children connect socially. Even before books are put in their laps and they are taught to vary and manipulate language, children have engaged in speech play. But while their books display a standard form of language on the printed page, children recognize their friends, their neighborhood, and their age group by the special vocabulary and pronunciation they utter. Meanings for children become expressive and collective through the sharing of sayings, nicknames, routines, and other traditional forms of speech play.

Through oral tradition, children have learned the power of words to endear, tease, and insult. They have recognized the appropriateness of certain sayings to special situations. Confronted with a challenge from another child, for example, a child might easily reply, "Who says?" To which the answer, if the confrontation is to continue, is "I says. What do you make of it?" Here speech is being tested, its meaning evaluated. Tradition helps to frame this process; it provides a structure within which children learn the flexibility of language and its role in social relations. The examples of folk speech in this chapter demonstrate even further the forms of language shaped by children. They show the ways that children relate to one another and separate themselves from adults through the power of oral tradition.

VOCABULARY

Children's folk vocabulary often flaunts adult taboos on direct sexual and scatological references. As a result, a long list of words replaces terms for genitals and excrement. Children in their social development are also particularly sensitive to nonconformity, and many words comment on stupidity, ugliness, and weakness. The aggressive nature of children's play, especially among boys, comes out in a host of words for fighting and beating. Children want to be clear, too, about their reactions, especially of disgust, and terms such as "icky," "gross," and "yukky" unequivocally express feelings in the child's vernacular.

1. bag	*vt*	to ignore or forget, as in "I decided to bag it"
bean	*vt*	to hit someone
birdbrain	*n*	stupid person
bite	*vi*	insult, with homosexual implications, as in "you bite"
booger	*n*	nasal mucus
clobber	*vt*	to beat someone badly
cooties	*n*	lice-like insect, dirt, or disease, which a person can contract. Often used to identify a disliked, ugly, or nonconforming child, as in the taunt "Oh, you've got cooties"
copy cat	*n*	person who imitates another
creepy	*adj*	scary, disgusting
cruddy	*adj*	unsatisfactory, poor
crummy	*adj*	unsatisfactory, poor
cry-baby	*n*	epithet for a sensitive child
cut the cheese	*v*	release flatus, fart (also "cut one")
dog-doo	*n*	excrement from a dog
doo-doo	*n*	feces
doofy	*adj*	foolish, awkward
dork	*n*	disliked boy; especially boy who is considered boring or who acts inanely
drip	*n*	boring; see "dork." See also reply to being called "drip" under section on taunts and replies in this chapter
ear bender	*n*	someone who talks too much
fag	*n*	effeminate boy; homosexual
goober	*vi*	drool
goody-goody	*n*	someone who does everything he or she is supposed to, with the implication that this behavior is an affectation
gross	*adj*	disgusting, crude
gunk	*n*	filthy or slimy substance

heinie	*n*	buttocks
ick, icky	*interj*	exclamation of disgust
jollies	*n*	fun, laughs (often with the implication that the fun is inappropriate; one boy says of an umpire: "He gets his jollies out of calling strikes")
klutz	*n*	uncoordinated awkward boy
log	*n*	flat-chested girl; feces
mental	*adj*	irrational, wild, as in the taunt "that boy is mental"
nail	*vt*	hit, as in "nailing" a car by throwing an egg at it; also can indicate being caught and punished, as in "I got nailed for acting up"
noogie	*n*	the act of putting a bruise in a person's arm or head by pressing the joint of the index finger into the victim's body; also called a "noogie shot"
pee	*vi*	to urinate
poop	*vi*	to excrete feces; *n,* feces
potty	*n*	toilet
privates	*n*	genitals
scaredy-pants	*n*	fearful child
screwball	*n*	child who acts silly. See also reply to being called "screwball" under section on taunts and replies in this chapter
sleazy	*adj*	lucky, often with the implication that the luck was undeserved (as in "sleazy catch"). Sometimes "sleaze" will be used as a noun to describe a boy who is undeservedly lucky; also can be meant in the sense of sly or deceiving person
slide	*vt*	to beat, punch, or hurt someone, as in "I'm going to slide that guy!"
smarty-pants	*n*	term for condescending or arrogant child
smear	*vt*	beat badly
snag	*vi*	to spit; *vt,* to catch
snot	*n*	nasal mucus
spaz	*n*	awkward, uncoordinated boy
suck	*vi*	be of poor quality, no good; stink; reek
swift	*adj*	good, excellent

tattle-tale	*n*	a child who informs authorities (parents, teachers) about misbehavior of other children
tinsel teeth	*n*	someone who wears metal braces on his or her front teeth
tough	*adj*	unfortunate; "too bad," as in the phrase "That's just tough" or "That's just a tough situation," or the wellerism "'Tough titty,' said the kitty, 'but the milk sure tastes good.'" When used more aggressively, the word is followed by "shit"
turd	*n*	disliked boy; excrement
unreal	*adj*	unbelievable in a negative way, bad, stupid
wedgie	*n*	prank which involves sneaking behind a boy and yanking or tugging at his underwear (also called "snuggie")
wuss	*n*	effeminate boy
yuk	*interj*	expression of dislike
yutz	*n*	stupid person

TAUNTS AND REPLIES

Tradition teaches the child to use sayings in certain situations to make a point emphatically. Such sayings can provide a quick and easy response to the taunt of another child, or a powerful demonstration of the child's stand. The sayings contain a collective wisdom that exerts a certain amount of pressure on children. In other cases, sayings offer a form of play with words; children use the traditional structure of such sayings to play with the rhythm, rhyme, and meaning of words to draw attention to themselves. (See next chapter for more attention to the rhyming taunts.) Especially evident in these sayings is the use of metaphor and simile in children's speech; children are learning to become more emphatic by relying on the emotional appeals of nonliteral references.

2. Liar, liar, pants on fire, hang them up on telephone wire. *(Said to lying child)*

Cross my heart and hope to die, stick a needle in my eye. *(Swearing the truth)*

Finders keepers, losers weepers. *(Said when picking up an item, such as a coin)*

Dare, double dare you. *(Said to make someone do something)*

Last one in (there) is a rotten egg. *(Said to start race to water or other place)*

You're all in the mustard, and you can't ketchup. You're all in the dip without no chip. *(Said to taunt opponent in race or game)*

3. You're losing altitude. *(To a boy with an open zipper)*

Close your barn door before the horses get out. *(To a boy with an open zipper)*

Do you have a license to sell hot dogs? *(To a boy with an open zipper)*

It's snowing down South. *(To a girl with a slip showing)*

4. Make like a drum and beat it. *(Telling someone to leave)*

Make like a banana and split.

Make like a tree and leave.

Make like a ghost and vanish.

This is an A and B conversation; C your way out.

Move out of the way. Your dad ain't no glassmaker.

5. Who cut the cheese? *(Said in response to flatulence)*

Who let one go?

Who cut one?

Who teed off?

P.U.! *(Said to identify bad smell, as in flatulence)*

The one who smelt it, dealt it. *(Said in response to question about flatulence)*

6. What time is it? Two hairs past a freckle, half past a monkey's ass, a quarter to his balls.

What time is it? Same time as yesterday, only a day later.

7. What's your name? Puddin-tame. Ask me again, I'll tell you the same.

What's your name? Buster Brown. Ask me again, and I'll knock you down.

8. What happened? None of your B.I. business.

What happened? None of your beeswax.

What happened? For me to know and for you to find out.

9. Sticks and stones may break my bones, but names will never hurt me. *(Reply to insulting epithet)*

I'm rubber, you're glue. Everything you say bounces off me and sticks to you. *(Reply to insult)*

10. Drip's a drop, drop's water, water's nature, nature's beautiful. Thanks for the compliment. *(Reply to being called a "drip.")*
Screwball's iron, iron's ore, ore's nature, nature's beautiful. Thanks for the compliment. *(Reply to being called a "screwball.")*

11. Is water wet? *(Emphatic affirmative reply)*
Is the sky blue?
Do birds fly?
Is the Pope Catholic (Polish)?
Does a bear shit in the woods?
Is a pig's ass pork?
Does a hobby horse have a hickory dick?

12. Does a chicken have lips? *(Emphatic negative reply)*
Does a snake have knees?
Does a cow meow?

INSULTS

A common form of speech play among children, especially boys, is to hurl insulting barbs at one another. In this play children use insults to test verbal skills. For the insults to be effective, the participants require quick thinking and fast talk; the insults need to be creative as well as expressive. Children have to be adept at manipulating simile, rhyme, and metaphor, as well as timing and tone. The insults also take a composer's touch. The insults rely on speech formulas such as "Your mother's so ——— , she ——— " within which children freely improvise.

Although black and white children draw on a shared repertoire, among white children the insulting is often referred to as "cutting" and "ranking" and relies especially on the uses of metaphor and simile. Among black children the insulting is often known as "dozens," "sounding," and "joning," and relies especially on the use of rhyme.

The content of the insults often declares independence from parents (especially the apron-strings of one's mother), yet the insults ironically force the participants into the position of defending their parents as well. The insults also indicate the importance of peer pressure to conform among children as they mature. This is especially true for matters of physical appearance, gender distinction, and intellectual ability.

13. Your teeth are like stars, they come out at night.
Your nose is like a faucet — drip, drip, drip.
Does your face hurt? It's killing me.
I heard the Army uses your face for target practice.
If I had a face like yours, I'd sue my parents for damages.
Your ass is grass and my fist is a lawn mower.
Let's play horse. I'll be the front end, you be yourself.
If brains were dynamite, you couldn't blow your nose.
If you had brains, you'd be dangerous.
You're so low that if someone said, "Your fly is down" you would have
     to look up and say, "Where, where?"
You are really funny, but your looks aren't everything.
You are so weak, you couldn't kill a dead army ant.
You're so dumb, when they were handing out brains, you thought they
     said "trains" and said "I'm not going anywhere."
You're so ugly that when you were born, the doctor slapped your
     mother.
You're so ugly, when they were handing out looks, you thought they
     said "books" and said "I don't read much."
If ugliness were judged by sidewalks, you'd be a boulevard.
You're so ugly, when you were a kid your parents fed you with a sling-
     shot.
You're so ugly, when you were a kid your parents had to tie a pork
     chop around your neck just to get the dog to play with you.
When you were born your mother said "Oh treasure," and your father
     said, "Yeah, let's bury it."
When you were born, your dad took one look at you and ran down to
     the zoo to throw rocks at the stork.

14. Your mother's so ugly, when she moves in next door, your lawn's
     going to die.
Your mother's so fat, they had to widen the doorways in your house.
The only difference between your mother and an elephant is five
     pounds.
The only difference between your mother and my asshole is about an
     inch and a half.
Your mother wears combat boots.
Your mother wears a jock strap.

Your mother got crabs (cooties, worms).
Your mother's so skinny, you could crack her in half.
Your mother's so heavy, she could crack me in half.
Your mother's so low, she could play handball on the curb.
Your mother's so low, she could walk under a pregnant ant.
Your mother's so low, she has to look up to see the curb.
Your mother's tits are so big, they drag the floor.
Your mother's so flat, every time she gets a pimple, she tries to put a
    bra on it.
Your mother's like a birthday cake, everyone gets a piece.
Your mother's like a merry-go-round, everyone gets a turn.
Your mother's like a doorknob, everyone gets a turn.
Your mother's like a lollipop, she gives everybody a lick.
Your mother's like a railroad track, she gets laid all over.
Your mother's like eggs, she gets laid all over.
Your mother's like a revolving door, everybody going in and out.
Your mother's like the sun, she goes down at night.
Your mother's like the phone company, her rates go down at night.
Your mother's like a fan, turn her on, she blows.
Your mother's like a nail, always getting banged.
Your mother is like peanut butter, always getting spread.
Your mother's like the margarine, so spreadable it's incredible.
Your mother's like a bus, guys getting on and off all night.
Your mother's like a board — flat.
Your mother's like a pirate — sunken chest.
Your mother's like a dollar: wrinkled, green, and spent.
Your mother's like a dollar: wrinkled, green, and used.
Your mother's like a dollar, everyone's had it once.
Your mother's like an old Ford: used, rusty, and easy to get.
Your father isn't half the man your mother was.
I went to your house, but they said you moved two sewers up.
I went to your house, but they said you moved two cans to the right.
I went to your house, but the garbage man already emptied it.
I walked in your house, I stepped on a cigar butt, and your mother
    said, "Who turned off the heat?"
That's a low blow. Speaking of low blows, how's your mother?
That's a dirty crack. Speaking of dirty cracks, how's your mother?

15. Dozens

Your momma, your daddy, your greasy granny,
got holes in her panties.

Bullfrog, bullfrog, bank to bank,
your momma built like an Army tank.

I can tell by your knees,
your momma eats surplus cheese.

I can tell by your knees,
your momma climbs trees.

I saw your momma flying through the air,
I hit her in the ass with a rotten pear.

I saw your momma down by the river,
I hit her in the ass with two pounds of liver.

I fucked your momma in New Orleans,
her booty turn red on First and Green,
behind started popping like a sewing machine.

I fucked your momma between two cans,
she jumped up and yelled Superman.

I hate to talk about your momma, but you talk about mine,
She's got ring-ding titties and a rubber behind.

I hate to talk about your momma, she's a good old soul,
She's got a rubber titty and a ten-ton asshole.

I hate to talk about your momma, she's a good old soul,
She got a humpback boodle like a G.I. Joe,
She got nipples on her titties as big as plums,
She got a ass make a dead man run.

TONGUE-TWISTERS

If the performance of insults teaches something about composition, then tongue-twisters provide a playful lesson in diction. The "coincidence of sound" in these phrases and sentences makes them difficult to pronounce. Children challenge one another to "say it three times fast" or else to get through a long twister without making a mistake. Sometimes children take glee in the mistakes made, because they lead to a risqué announcement.

16. Rubber baby buggy bumpers.

Sally sells seashells by the seashore.

How much wood would a woodchuck chuck if a woodchuck could chuck wood?

I'm a sheet slitter and I slit sheets. I'm the fastest sheet slitter that ever slit sheets.

17. Betty Botter bought some butter. "But," she said, "this butter's bitter! If I put it in my batter, it will but make my batter bitter. But a bit of better butter would but make my batter better." So she bought a bit of butter, and made her bitter batter better. So 'twas better Betty Botter bought a bit of better butter.

18. Moses supposes his toes-es are roses.
But Moses supposes erroneously,
'Cause Moses he knows-es his toes-es aren't roses,
As Moses supposes his toes-es to be.

SECRET LANGUAGES

A child's world can appear ever so private and just a bit convoluted when one hears the sounds of Pig Latin or Bop Talk. These traditional secret languages demonstrate the elaborate ways that children can manipulate the English language to communicate in a special way. Here, for example, are interviews with children about their languages.

19. Pig Latin

Q. How does this language work?
A. If you want to say a name like Michelle you say Ichelle-may. You take the first letter of the word, bring it to the end, and add *ay*.
Q. What do you do at the end of words and sentences?
A. You just pause like in regular talking.
Q. How would you say "Secret languages are fun" in this language?
A. Ecretsay anguageslay . . . areay unfay.

20. Bop Talk

Q. You say you know three secret languages. Let's start with Bop Talk. When did you learn it?
A. Last year when I was ten.
Q. Who taught it to you?
A. My friends Debby and Merrill. We were talking. They wanted to tell

me something without another person knowing about it.

Q. How does it work?

A. If you have a name or something, to all the consonants you add *op (ap)*. Like *top (tap)* for *t*.

Q. Say a sentence like "Speaking Bop Talk is fun."

A. Sop pop E . . .

Q. E?

A. Oh yes, you don't do anything with the vowels. You just say them.

Q. Okay. Sop pop E . . .

A. Sop pop E A kop I nop gop bop O pop top A lop kop I sop fop U nop.

Q. How does a person know when a word is finished?

A. I guess you pause between words.

Q. When do you use Bop Talk?

A. When I'm talking to friends and I don't want anyone to understand.

21. G-Talk

Q. How does it work?

A. I don't know how to explain it. I think you put a *g* sound before each syllable.

Q. Say "Speaking G-Talk is fun."

A. Gitaspeak gita-ing gita-G gita-talk gita-is gita-fun.

Q. So you're really putting *gita* before each syllable?

A. Well yes, but you say the sentence very fast.

Q. From whom did you learn G-Talk?

A. From my friends Wendy, Lisa, and Laurie. They go to P.S. 268.

Q. How old were you at the time?

A. I think six years.

Q. How does G-Talk work?

A. If you have the word *no* you say *geno*. You add *ge* before every word unless it begins with a *g*. Then if it begins with a *g* you just say it.

Q. How would you say "Secret languages are fun" in G-Talk?

A. Gesecret gelanguages geare gefun.

22. Girl and Boy Talk

Q. How does it work?

A. Say you want to say *and*. For *a* you would say a girl's name like Ann, for *n* you would say a girl's name like Nancy, *d* like that letter. After every word you clap your hands. That's it.

Q. Say "Secret languages are fun," in Girl Talk.

A. Sally Ellen Carol Robin Ellen Terry *(clap)* Lisa Alice Nancy Gail, uh I don't know a name that starts with *u (someone volunteers "Ulisa")* — Ulisa Alice Gail Ellen Sally *(clap)*. You're supposed to say them fast.

47

Alice Randi Ellen *(clap)* Frances Ulisa Nancy.
Q. How about a word like *exit?*
A. Ellen . . . uh . . . We never use words like that. And Boy Talk is the same. Just use boys' names. I learned it the same time as Girl Talk.
Q. Which do you use more often?
A. Girl Talk.
Q. What do you do at the end of a sentence?
A. Make a fist and turn it.

23. Egg Talk

Q. How do you speak Egg-Talk?
A. Before every vowel in the word you put the word *egg* and pronounce it that way.
Q. How would you say "Speaking Egg-Talk is fun"?
A. Speggeakegging eggegg teggalk eggis feggun. You're supposed to say it rapidly.

24. Barracuda

Q. When do you use Barracuda?
A. When I talk to other friends, and I don't want another person to understand what I'm saying.
Q. How does this language work?
A. Drop the first letter of every word and put a *b* instead. If a word starts with a *b* you change the *b* into an *r*. If the word starts with an *r* you change it into a *b*.
Q. This is a bit confusing. How would you say "Secret languages are fun" in Barracuda?
A. Becret banguages bare bfun.
Q. Did you say *bfun?*
A. Yes, if there is a possibility that the word can be confused by dropping the first letter, you leave the first letter and just put a *b* in front. Even if a word starts with an *r,* like the word *run* becomes *brun.* If the word can't be confused, you just add *b* instead of the first letter. Like *happy* becomes *bappy.*
Q. I was thinking of that. Dropping the first letter of a word might leave you without any idea as to what it was originally.
A. Well, you can understand from what you're saying. Also if a word has some silent letters you pronounce them. Like *bomb* becomes *romb* (*b* is pronounced).
Q. How about a one-letter word like *I?*
A. You would say *bi-I.*

Q. This is certainly not easy. How fluently can you speak it?
A. I can't speak it quickly. No one can. It's hard to speak and even harder to write. You have to get used to it and it takes a lot of practice.

"And That's The Way My Story Goes": Rhymes of Play

FOR MANY ADULT observers, rhymes are the essence of a child's trove of lore. Children's lore is more diverse than that, but rhymes have drawn a lion's share of attention because the rhymes can appear especially playful and colorful. And there's something endearing, many observers might say, in the innocence with which real-life issues are raised in rhyme. There's also something instantly recognizable and memorable in familiar rhymes. Many rhymes have kept their basic forms for hundreds of years, yet with each new generation, and indeed with each play group, they can display inventive changes wrought by creative children.

Rhyming is an effective childhood strategy of fashioning oral tradition. The rhymes are, after all, an effective aid to memory. And within the easily comprehensible rhyming structure, a child can improvise, thus commenting on local conditions and personal preferences. For five-year-old Sara Gochnaur of Harrisburg, Pennsylvania, handclapping is accompanied by:

> I have a boyfriend and his name is Harry
> And he came from Cincinnati
> With a pickle on his nose and forty-eight toes
> And that's the way my story goes.

For little Jeannie High of Bloomington, Indiana, the verse is:

> My boyfriend's name is Davy
> He's in the U.S. Navy
> With a pickle for his nose, cherries on his toes
> And that's the way my story goes.

The "story goes" in rhyme, and moreover, the rhythm created by the coupling of rhymes in different lines can advance various childhood activities involving repetition and precision such as counting-out, hand-clapping, and ball-bouncing.

Knowing these rhymes qualifies children for membership in a play group. But on a larger scale, the rhymes often suggest social problems that children will encounter with maturity. Behind the smokescreen of playful rhyming, children can raise touchy subjects. In Sara Gochnaur's little verse cited above, for example, the reference to her boyfriend (at the age of five no less) continues with what many analysts interpret as a veiled suggestion of pregnancy:

I love you very dearly
I love you most sincerely
So I jumped in a lake
To swallow a snake
And came out with a bellyache.

Sara's verse, as other examples in this chapter will show, is not unusual. Courtship, childbirth, violence, and children's relations to parents, teachers, and siblings are among the delicate subjects frequently covered in children's rhymes. In many cases, rhymes on these subjects offer children opportunities to test the limits of social appropriateness, to violate norms expected of them, and to interpret developing social values. So while the structure of rhymes may make them appear innocuous, they often deal with serious matters. And by dealing with them in rhymes, children often defuse the explosiveness of these matters, and indeed often appear to have "fun" with them. They take advantage of the chance to work through the complexity of their small community in relation to the greater society through play and lore.

My outline of the uses to which rhymes are put helps to explain the sequence of rhymes in this chapter. To begin, counting-out rhymes organize children through the mandate of tradition. The next four categories of ring-game, hand-clapping, ball-bouncing, and jump-rope play are activities commonly accompanied by rhymes (many of which are used for all three activities) and commonly bring up matters of courtship along with relations to parents and siblings. Although associated with the play of girls, these rhymes are frequently familiar to boys as well. The next three categories are rhymes that test or enforce limits. Children use derisive rhymes, the first of these categories for instance, to point out what they consider to be irregularities in other children's behavior, whether it be affection, obesity, or lying. They can also be used to bring down authorities a notch or as a release for frustrations, as in the case of rhymes about teachers. Parody is a common technique in children's creativity, as will be seen later in the chapter on songs, and the next category here explores parodies of nursery verse and commercial jingles, among other rhymes. Following the parodies are what I call "gross" rhymes — taking their name from the folk speech of children — which are intended to "gross out" listeners and develop ideas of social appropriateness.

COUNTING-OUT RHYMES

Counting-out rhymes help children choose up "sides" or decide who will be "it" for many kinds of games engaging them typically between the ages of five and twelve. The rhymes appear to offer a random way of choosing players, but observation shows that the reciter can alter the rhyme's start with a certain player or alter the rhythm of the rhyme to ensure a desired outcome. In the counting-out ritual that typically accompanies the rhyme, children stand in a circle and point to players as they chant. Otherwise, they will stretch out their fists (sometimes called "the potatoes") to be counted out, or they will place a foot into a circle and have it touched by a counter, usually the leader of the child's play group. Counting-out rhymes have drawn a great deal of attention because they are among the oldest, most universally recorded examples of children's folklore, and they draw on a variety of sources including nursery rhymes, game rhymes, and singing games.

1. One potato, two potato, three potato, four,
Five potato, six potato, seven potato, more.

2. Bubble gum, bubble gum in a dish
How many pieces do you wish?
Five — One, two, three, four, five, and out goes you.

3. Blue shoe, blue shoe
How old are you?
1, 2, 3 . . .

Children counting out with their feet to determine who will be "it"

A threesome saying a counting-out rhyme, with their "potatoes" extended

4. Inka bink, a bottle of ink
The cork fell out, and you stink.

5. One, two, three, four, five, six, seven
All good children go to Heaven
When they get there they will shout
O-U-T, and that spells out.

6. Eenie, meenie, miny, moe,
Catch a tiger by the toe
If he hollers, make him pay
Fifty dollars every day
My mother says to pick the very best one.
Y-O-U spells you and you are not it.

7a. Engine, engine, number nine
Going down Chicago line
If the train falls off the track
Do you get your money back? *(Child answers yes or no)*
Y-E-S spells yes and you are not it (*or,* N-O and out you go).

7b. Engine, engine number nine
Running, running on the Chicago line
The line broke, the monkey got choked
And they all went to heaven
On a streetcar L-I-N-E.

8. Monkey, monkey bottle of beer
How many monkeys are there here?
1, 2, 3, mother caught a flea
The flea died and mother cried
O-U-T spells out.

9. One, two, three, four
Mary's at the kitchen door
Five, six, seven, eight
Eating cherries off a plate
O-U-T spells out goes she.

10. Wire, briar, limber lock
Three geese in a flock

One flew east, one flew west
One flew over the cuckoo's nest
O-U-T spells out goes he
Old dirty dishrag you.

11. My mother and your mother were hanging out clothes
My mother punched your mother right in the nose
What color of blood came out of her nose? *(Child answers a color)*
G-R-E-E-N and you will be the one.

12. Johnny rode a bike over the sea
Johnny rode a bike under the sea
Johnny broke the bike, blamed it on me.
I told Ma, Ma told Pa,
Johnny got a whipping
And a ha, ha, ha. How many whippings did he get?
One, two, three . . .

13. One, two, button my shoe
Three, four, shut the door
Five, six, pick up sticks
Seven, eight, lay them straight
Nine, ten, a big fat hen
Eleven, twelve, mind yourself
Thirteen, fourteen, maids are sporting
Fifteen, sixteen, maids are kissing
Seventeen, eighteen, maids are waiting
Nineteen, twenty, maids are plenty
Twenty-one, twenty-two
If you love me as I love you
No knife can cut our love in two
Twenty-three, twenty-four
Mary at the kitchen door
Eating apples by the score.
One, two, three, four.

14. Ibbity bibbitty sibbitty sab
Ibbitty bibbitty canal boat.
Dictionary down the ferry
Out goes you.

15. Ippity, bippity, zippity, zak
Ippity, bippity, zippity, zak
Kinoba in, kanoba out
Kinoba over the water spout.

16a. Hacker packer soda cracker
Hacker packer too
Hacker packer soda cracker
Out goes you.

16b. Hacker packer soda cracker
Does your mama chew tobacker?
If your mama chew tobacker
Promenade in green.

17. Eenie Meenie Cafateenie,
Ala bama boo.
Ootchie kootchie ala mootchie
I choose you.

RING-GAME RHYMES

Sung or chanted, the words "London Bridge is falling down, falling down, falling down, / London Bridge is falling down, my fair lady" remind us of early childhood play. But today, classics such as "London Bridge" and "Farmer in the Dell" do not generally come out of the folk expression of children. They are more often associated with the organized activities supervised by playground instructors and early childhood teachers. But there are still ring-games that come from the spontaneous play of children. Sometimes the folk expression began as a school text, as evidenced by "Punchanella," but the others listed here have a long history in oral tradition. Like counting-out rhymes, the ring games draw children to a circle and often draw someone out from the circle. Unlike other games in America, especially those played later by boys, this activity tends to be non-competitive. The goal is the cooperation of the group, accented by the frequent hand holding that occurs in the rings. In the rings, children delight in the chance to literally be "the center" of attention within the group, and find aesthetic appeal in the precise repetition demanded by the game.

18a. Little Sally Ann, crying on a pan
Rise Sally rise, wipe your dirty eyes
Turn to the east, turn to the west
Turn to the one you love the best.

18b. Little Sally Ann, sittin' in the sand
Weepin' and cryin' for a nice young man.
Rise, Sally, rise, wipe your weeping eyes
Put your hands on your hips
Let your backbone slip
Ah, shake it to the east,
Ah, shake it to the west,
Ah, shake it to the one
You love the best.

19. I'm going to Kentucky
I'm going to the fair
I met a senorita
With flowers in her hair

Shake it senorita, shake it all you can
So all the boys around you
Can see your underwear.
Rumble to the bottom, rumble to the top
And turn around and turn around
Until you make a stop.

20. Pretty little shoe, punchanella, punchanella
Pretty little shoe, punchanella in the shoe.
Now what can you do punchanella, punchanella
Now what can you do punchanella in the shoe.
We can do it too punchanella, punchanella
We can do it too punchanella in the shoe
Now who do you choose punchanella, punchanella
Who do you choose punchanella in the shoe.

HAND-CLAPPING RHYMES

Girls in particular are familiar with rhymes that accompany hand-clapping routines involving two participants. The routines stress repetition and precision; uttering the rhymes at the same time provides a rhythm for the play, and it also insists on coordination between verbal and motor skills. A model of this kind of play is "Patta-Cake" (Patta-cake, patta-cake, / Baker man, / Make me a cake / As fast as you can), which is often introduced to youngsters by adults. But children go on to vary greatly the content of hand-clapping rhymes within the rather stable structure established by hand-clapping rhythms (many of the hand-clapping rhymes are also used in ball-bouncing and jump-rope activities discussed in the next sections). The themes of the hand-clapping rhymes notably dwell on maturation, courtship, and pregnancy, and the characters, especially the boys, do not act particularly kindly.

21a. I'm a little Dutch girl
As pretty as can be
And all the boys around the town
Are chasing after me
I have a boyfriend, and his name is Harry
And he came from Cincinnati
With a pickle on his nose and forty-eight toes
That's the way my story goes
One day when I was walking
I heard my boyfriend call
With lily on the bed
And this is what I said to him
I love you very dearly
I love you most sincerely
So I jumped in a lake
To swallow a snake
And came out with a bellyache.

21b. I am a pretty little Dutch girl
As pretty as can be
And all the boys in all the world
Are crazy over me
My boyfriend's name is Davy
He's in the U.S. Navy

With a pickle for his nose, cherries on his toes
And that's the way my story goes.

21c. I am a pretty little Dutch girl
My home is far away
And when the boys start kissing me
I always run away
My boyfriend's name is Sunny
He comes from the land of honey
With a pickle on his nose, three black toes
And that's the way my story goes
Shave and a haircut, two bits
Who you gonna marry, Tom Mix
What you gonna feed, buckbones
Who you gonna marry, Spike Jones.

22. I met my boyfriend at the candy store
He bought me ice cream
He bought me cake
He brought me home with a bellyache
Mamma, mamma, I feel sick
Call the doctor
Quick, quick, quick
Doctor, doctor will I die?
Count to five and you'll be alive
1, 2, 3, 4, 5, I'm alive.

23. Miss Susie had a baby
His name was Tiny Tim
She put him in the bathtub
To see if he could swim
He drank up all the water
He ate up all the soap
He tried to eat the bathtub
But it wouldn't go down his throat
Miss Susie called the doctor
The doctor called the nurse
The nurse called the lady with the alligator purse
Out ran the doctor
Out ran the nurse
Out ran the lady with the alligator purse

And now Tiny Tim is home sick in bed
With soap in his throat and bubbles in his head.

24. Lulu had a steamboat
The steamboat had a bell
Lulu went to heaven
The steamboat went to
Hello operator
Please give me number nine
And if you disconnect me I'll kick you up
Behind the refrigerator
There was a piece of glass
Lulu sat right on it
And bust her silly
Ask me no more questions
And I'll tell you no more lies
And that is the story
Of how Lulu died, died, died, died, died.

25a. Playmate, come out and play with me
And bring your dollies three
Climb up my apple tree
Slide down my rain barrel
Climb down my cellar door
And we'll be jolly friends
Forevermore.

Playmate, I cannot play with you
My dolly has the flu
Boo hoo hoo hoo hoo hoo
Ain't got no rain barrel
Ain't got no cellar door
But we'll be jolly friends
Forever more.

25b. Playmate, come out and play with me
And bring your tommy gun three
Climb up my poison tree
Drown in my rain barrel
Fall down my cellar door
And we'll be enemies
Forever more, more, more, more, more.

25c. See see my playmate
I can't go out to play
Because of yesterday
Three boys came my way
They gave me fifty cents
To lay across the bench
They said it wouldn't hurt
They stuck it up my skirt
My mother was surprised
To see my belly rise
My father was disgusted
My sister jumped for joy
It was a baby boy
My brother raised some shit
He had to babysit
The end.

26a. My mother gave me a nickel
My father gave me a dime
My sister gave me a lover boy
Who loved me all the time
My mother took her nickel
My father took his dime
My sister took her lover boy
And gave me Frankenstein
He made me do the dishes
He made me mop the floor
I got so sick and tired of him
I kicked him out the door.

26b. My mother gave me peaches
My father gave me pears
My boyfriend gave me fifty cents
And kissed me up the stairs
My mother took my peaches
My father took his pears
My boyfriend took his fifty cents
So I kicked him down the stairs

26c. My mother sent me to the store
To buy some food one day

I fell in love with the grocery boy
And there I stayed all day
He gave me all his peaches
He gave me all his pears
He gave me fifty cents
And chased me up the stairs
I ate up all the peaches
I ate up all the pears
I held on tight to the fifty cents
And kicked him down the stairs.

26d. My boyfriend gave me peaches
My boyfriend gave me pears
My boyfriend gave me fifty cents
‚And I kicked him down the stairs
I gave him back his peaches
I gave him back his pears
I gave him back his fifty cents
And he kicked me down the stairs
My mother needed peaches
My brother needed pears
My father needed fifty cents
To buy a pair of underwear.

27. When Billy was zero
He went to be a hero
Here Billy oh la
Here Billy oh la
Half past two, cross down

When Billy was one
He learned to suck his thumb
Thumb Billy oh la
Thumb Billy oh la
Half past one, cross down

When Billy was two
He learned to tie his shoe
Shoe Billy oh la
Shoe Billy oh la
Half past two, cross down

When Billy was three
He learned to climb a tree
Tree Billy oh la
Tree Billy oh la
Half past three, cross down

When Billy was four
He learned to shut the door
Door Billy oh la
Door Billy oh la
Half past four, cross down

When Billy was five
He learned to seek a hive
Hive Billy oh la
Hive Billy oh la
Half past five, cross down

When Billy was six
He learned to pick up sticks
Sticks Billy oh la
Sticks Billy oh la
Half past six, cross down

When Billy was seven
He learned to go to heaven
Heaven Billy oh la
Heaven Billy oh la
Half past seven, cross down

When Billy was eight
He learned to clean his plate
Plate Billy oh la
Plate Billy oh la
Half past eight, cross down

When Billy was nine
He learned to break his spine
Spine Billy oh la
Spine Billy oh la
Half past nine, cross down

When Billy was ten
He learned to start again
Again Billy oh la
Again Billy oh la
Half past ten.

28. Ronald McDonald a biscuit
Ronald McDonald a biscuit
Oh she she wa wa a biscuit
I got a boyfriend a biscuit
He's so sweet a biscuit
Like my cherry tree a biscuit
Ice cream soda oh cherry on eve
Ice cream soda oh cherry on eve
Down, down, baby
Down by the rollercoaster
Sweet, sweet baby, I'll never let you go

Shimmy ko-ko pop
Shimmy shimmy pow
Shimmy ko-ko pop
Shimmy shimmy pow
Please Mr. Postman I don't wanna sock you.

29. Oh Mary Mack, Mack, Mack
All dressed in black, black, black
With silver buttons, buttons, buttons
All down her back, back, back
She asked her mother, mother, mother
For fifteen cents, cents, cents
To see the elephant, elephant, elephant
Jump the fence, fence, fence
He jumped so high, high, high
He reached the sky, sky, sky
And never came down, down, down
Till the fourth of July, ly, ly
Her Uncle Ned, Ned, Ned
Fell out of bed, bed, bed
And cracked his head, head, head
On a piece of cornbread, bread, bread
She called the doctor, doctor, doctor

Sisters engrossed in the hand-clapping rhyme "Ronald McDonald a biscuit" (See no. 28)

And the doctor said, said, said
That all he needed, needed, needed
Was a piece of cornbread, bread, bread.

BALL-BOUNCING RHYMES

These rhymes typically accompany the bouncing of a rubber ball on the ground or wall. The object of the exercise is to complete the rhyme and various tricky moves with the ball without making a mistake. In one common ball-bouncing ritual called "Alerio," for example, the child recites, "One, two, three, alerio." On "alerio," the child bounces the ball under her leg. She continues, "Four, five, six, alerio, seven, eight, nine, alerio," and when she says, "Ten-alery postman," she passes the ball to a playmate who goes through the routine. In other ball-bouncing rituals, the child is required to clap her hand or spin around before catching the ball in time to the rhythm of the sharply articulated rhyme.

30. A, my name is Alice
And my husband's name is Al
We come from Alabama
And we sell apples.
B, my name is Betty
And my husband's name is Bob
We come from Boston
And we sell bananas.

31. Hello hello hello sir
Are you coming out sir?
No sir
Why sir?
Because I've got a cold sir
Where'd you get the cold sir?
From the North Pole sir
What are you doing there sir?
Catching polar bears sir
How many did you catch sir?
1 sir, 2 sir, 3 sir . . .

32. Ordinary secretary
No moving
No talking
No laughing
One hand, the other hand
One foot, the other foot
Front claps, back claps
Front and back
Back and front
Tweedle, twaddle
Courtesy salute-sy
Cross your heart
And away she goes.

33. Bounce and catch
And reach for the stars
Here come Jupiter
There goes Mars.

34. Oliver Twist
You can't do this
So what's the use
Of trying
Touch your toe
Touch your knee
Clap your hands
And away we go.

35. Claimsies, clapsies
Rollie, pollie
Crossies
Backsies, frontsies
Telephone answer
Stamp your foot
Wave goodbye
Highsies tootsies
Lowsies tootsies
This hand
The other hand
Wave goodbye.

JUMP-ROPE RHYMES

While two children threateningly twirl a rope, a child evades the rope by rhythmically jumping over it. Making the task more difficult and creative is the rhyme that the child shouts out to the delight of her playmates. As she offers her rhyme, passersby may hear within this playful setting rhymes that direct her action within the rope's cage or that keep count of her successful jumps, and many not-so-veiled references to courtship, sexuality, and violence. This scene repeats in schoolyards all over the United States, and the rhymes that are part of this activity are among the most familiar in children's folklore.

36a. Not last night, but the night before
Twenty-four robbers came knocking at my door
As I ran out, they ran in
I asked them what they wanted
And this is what they said
Little Orphan Annie jumping one foot, one foot
Little Orphan Annie jumping two feet, two feet
Little Orphan Annie jumping three feet, three feet
Little Orphan Annie jumping four feet, four feet
Little Orphan Annie get out of town.

36b. Not last night but the night before
Two little rats came knocking at my door
I went up to let them in
And this is what they said
Butterfly, butterfly, turn all around
Butterfly, butterfly, touch the ground
Butterfly, butterfly, throw out a kiss
Butterfly, butterfly, get out before you miss.

37a. Cinderella
Dressed in yellow
Went upstairs
To kiss a fellow
Made a mistake
And kissed a snake
How many doctors did it take?
1, 2, 3, 4, 5 . . .

37b. Cinderella
Dressed in yellow
Went downtown to see her fellow
On the way her girdle busted
How many men were disgusted?
1, 2, 3, 4, 5 . . .

38. Teddy bear, teddy bear
Turn around
Teddy bear, teddy bear
Touch the ground
Teddy bear, teddy bear
Go upstairs
Teddy bear, teddy bear
Say your prayers
Teddy bear, teddy bear
Turn out the light
Teddy bear, teddy bear
Say good night.

39. Gypsy gypsy please tell me
Who my husband is going to be
Rich man, poor man, beggarman, thief
Doctor, lawyer, merchant, chief
Butcher, baker, candlestick maker
Tinker, tailor, cowboy, sailor
Gypsy gypsy please tell me
What my dress is going to be
Silk, satin, calico, rags
Gypsy, gypsy please tell me
What my ring is going to be
Diamond, ruby, sapphire, glass.

40a. Fudge, fudge
Call the judge
Mother's had a newborn baby
It isn't a girl, it isn't a boy
It's just a newborn baby
First floor miss
Second floor miss
Third floor miss.

40b. Fudge, fudge, tell the judge
Momma's gonna have a newborn baby
Wrap it up in tissue paper
Send it down the elevator
Boy, girl, twins, triplets
Boy, girl, twins, triplets.

41a. Policeman, policeman
Do your duty
For here comes Delinda *(or other child's name)*
The bathing beauty
She can wiggle
She can waddle
She can do the kick
And I bet you all the money
She can do the split.

41b. Here comes *(child's name)* with the tight skirt on
She can wiggle
She can wobble
She can do the split
But I bet you five dollars
She can't do this
Lady on one foot, one foot, one foot
Lady on two foot, two foot, two foot
Lady on three foot, three foot, three foot
Lady on four foot, four foot, four foot.

42. Shirley Temple went to France
To teach the girls the hootchie-kootchie dance
First on heels, second on toes
Do the split and away she goes.

43. Blondie and Dagwood went to town
Blondie bought an evening gown
Dagwood bought the evening news
And this is what it said
Blondie jump on one foot, one foot, one foot
Blondie jump on two feet, two feet, two feet
Blondie jump on three feet, three feet, three feet
Blondie jump on four feet, four feet, four feet
Blondie jump out.

44. Mother, mother I am ill
Send for the doctor
Over the hill
First comes the doctor
Then comes the nurse
Then comes the lady
With the alligator purse
Didn't like the doctor
Didn't like the nurse
Didn't like the lady
With the alligator purse
Out went the doctor
Out went the nurse
Out went the lady
With the alligator purse.

45. Down in the meadow
Where the green grass grows
There sits *(boy's name)*
Sweet as a rose
Along came *(girl's name)*
And kissed him on the cheek
How many kisses did he get?
1, 2, 3, 4 . . .

46. House for rent, inquire within
Where the people moved out
For making gin
And if they promise to make no more
Here's the key to Sally's *(name of child who will be next to jump in)*
    back door
How many bottles did they make?
1, 2, 3, 4, 5 . . .

47. Bluebells, cockleshells
Eevy, ivy, over
Here comes the teacher with a big bad stick
Now it's time for arithmetic
One and one are two
Two and two are four
Four and four are eight

Now it's time for spelling
C-A-T spells cat
D-O-G spells dog
H-O-T spells hot!

DERISIVE RHYMES

One of the powers of lore, children quickly learn, is to direct attention. Often that attention is thrust upon another child in the form of teasing. Although frequently thought of as speech play, the teasing may be functional as well. It can point out expected norms of the child's world (camaraderie, conformity, cooperation, cleanliness); it can have the effect of drawing out information or emotional response from the teased child; and it creates a social drama enacted before the child's peers. In addition, some of the rhymes, such as ones dealing with the sight of underwear, seem to provide younger children with titillation. Children also use derisive rhymes to comment on the immature behavior of younger siblings, thus emphasizing the maturity of the teaser.

Besides being aimed at other children, derisive rhyming forms are directed at authority figures. The largest assortment of this type is aimed at schoolteachers, who are in the strange position of being in charge of children for many hours of the day without the bond of parenthood. Further, teachers are temporary authorities in children's lives, for children know that they will start over with a new teacher before long. This situation makes teachers natural targets for many children, and the rhymes take aim without directly attacking the authority.

48. Fatty, fatty, two by four
Can't get through the bathroom door
So he went all over the floor
Licked it up and went some more.

49. Baby, baby, suck your thumb
Wash your face in bubble gum
Baby, baby, stick your head in gravy
Don't take it out until you join the Navy.

50. *(Girl's name)* and *(boy's name)* up in a tree
K-I-S-S-I-N-G
First comes love
Then comes marriage
Then comes *(girl's name)* with a baby carriage.

51. *(Name)* is mad and I am glad
And I know how to please her *(or* him)
A bottle of wine to make her *(or* him) shine
And a great big kiss from *(name).*

52. Tattletale, tattletale
Hanging on a bull's tail
When the bull has to pee
You will get a cup of tea.

53. Mary, Mary, is no good
Chop her up for firewood
If the fire does not burn
Throw her in a butter churn
If the butter turns to cheese
Georgie, Georgie, will give her a squeeze.

54a. I see London, I see France
I see someone's underpants
They are purple, they are pink
O my gracious do they stink.

54b. I see London, I see France
I see someone's underpants
Not too big, not too small
Just the size of a cannonball.

55. There goes *(name)*
Walking down the Delaware
Chewing on her underwear
Can't afford another pair
Six weeks later
Bitten by a polar bear.

56. Georgie is a nut
He has a rubber butt
And every time he wiggles it
It goes putt putt.

57. Going down the highway 57-4
(Name) lit a fart and blew me out the door
The brakes couldn't hold her
The engine fell apart
All because of *(name)*'s supersonic fart.

58. Gene, Gene made a machine
Joe, Joe made it go
Art, Art let a fart and blew it all apart.

59. Mama, mia
Papa, pia
Ump's got the diarrhea.

60a. I made you look
You dirty crook
You stole your mom's pocketbook
Turn it in, turn it out
Now you know what welfare's all about.

60b. I made you look
You dirty crook
You stole your momma's food stamp book
Turn it in, turn it out
Now you know what welfare's all about.

61. April Fool's
Go to school
Tell your teacher
He's (she's) a fool
If he (she) smacks you
Don't you cry
Pack your books and say good-bye.

62a. School's out, school's out
Teacher let the monkeys out

One went east
One went west
One went up the teacher's dress.

62b. School's out, school's out
Teachers let the monkeys out
One went in
One went out
One went in the teacher's mouth.

63a. Hi ho, hi ho
The teacher bit my toe
I bit her back, that dirty rat
Hi, ho, hi ho, hi ho.

63b. Hi ho, hi ho
It's off to school we go
With tommy guns to shoot the nuns
The teachers look like Frankenstein
The milk tastes like terpentine
The principal drinks token wine.

63c. Hi ho, hi ho
It's off to school we go
With razor blades and hand grenades
And BB guns to shoot the nuns
Hi, ho, hi ho, hi ho.

PARODY AND NONSENSE RHYMES

From nursery rhymes to television commercials, adults feed children messages. The barrage of repeated, adult-controlled messages is grist for the child's imaginative mill. Children are fond of parodying the standard and familiar, especially when in the process of doing so they can establish that they have a world of their own making. Besides mocking nursery rhymes and television commercials, children are fond of parodying popular culture figures such as Tarzan and Superman, bringing them down to earth, and making nonsense out of the dry recitations of church and school, rendering them a bit juicier.

64a. Ladies and jellybeans
Reptiles and crocodiles
I stand before you to sit behind you
To tell you something I know nothing about
There will be a meeting tomorrow evening
Right after breakfast
To decide which color to whitewash the church
There is no admission
So pay at the door
There are plenty of seats
To sit on the floor.

64b. Ladies and gentlemen,
Hobos and tramps,
Cross-eyed mosquitoes,
And bow-legged ants
I come before you to stand behind you
To tell you a story
I know nothing about
Late Thursday night, early Friday morning
An empty truck full of bricks
Pulled into my front yard
Killing my cat in the back yard
That same night two boys got up to fight
Back to back they faced one another
A deaf policeman heard the noise
Came and shot the two dead boys
If you don't believe this lie is true
Ask the blind man
He saw it too.

65a. Tarzan, Tarzan, through the air
Tarzan lost his underwear
Tarzan say, "Me don't care —
Jane make me another pair"
Jane, Jane, through the air
Jane lost her underwear
Jane say, "Me don't care —
Boy make me another pair"
Boy, boy, through the air
Boy lost his underwear

Boy say, "Me don't care —
Monkey make me another pair"
Monkey, monkey, through the air
Monkey lost his underwear
Monkey say, "Me don't care —
Me don't need no underwear."

65b. Cheetah, Cheetah, flying through the air
Cheetah, Cheetah, lost his underwear
Cheetah said, "Ugh, me no care —
Tarzan make me new pair"
Boy, Boy, flying through the air
Boy, Boy, lost his underwear
Boy said, "Ugh, me no care —
Tarzan make me new pair"
Jane, Jane, flying through the air
Jane, Jane, lost her underwear
Jane said, "Ugh, me no care —
Tarzan like me better bare."

66. Tarzan the monkey man
Swinging on a rubber band
The band broke
He fell on a bump
And skinned his rump
And landed in the city dump.

67a. Now I lay me down to sleep
With a bag of peanuts at my feet
If I should die before I wake
I leave them with my Uncle Jake.

67b. Now I lay me down to sleep
I parked my Ford out in the street
If it should roll before I wake
I pray thee, Lord, put on the brake.

67c. Now I lay me down to rest
I pray I pass tomorrow's test
If I die before I wake
That's one less test I'll have to take.

67d. Now I lay me down to sleep
A bag of candy at my feet
If I die before I wake
You'll know I died of stomach-ache.

68. I'll do my duty, I'll do my best
To help the Girl Scouts get undressed.

69. Trick or treat
Smell my feet
Give me something good to eat
If you don't I don't care
I'll pull down your underwear.

70. Comet, it makes your teeth turn green
Comet, it tastes like Listerine
Comet, it makes you vomit
So get some Comet, and vomit, today.

71. Mary had a little lamb
She tied it to a heater
Every time it turned around
It burned its little peter.

72. Old Mother Hubbard
Went to the cupboard
To get her poor dog a bone
But when she bent over
Old Rover drove her
And gave her a bone of his own.

73. Jack and Jill went up the hill
To smoke some marijuana
Jack got high and zipped his fly
But Jill said, "I don't wanna"

Jack and Jill went up the hill
Looking for some fun
Jill forgot to take the Pill
And now they have a son

Jack and Jill went up the hill
To fetch a pail of water
Jill forgot to take the Pill
And now they have a daughter.

GROSS RHYMES

Some children intentionally shock their listeners by offering
"gross" rhymes, which are especially popular, it seems, at summer
camps and school lunchrooms. These rhymes comment on children's
growing understanding of taboos on certain images and words, as
well as their realization of norms placed on cleanliness and dining. As
one child told me poignantly, "They're sickening but neat." With
responses of disgust gained from listeners, children dramatize with
one another the purposes and limits of these taboos.

74. The night was dark
The sky was blue
Down the alley
A shit wagon flew
A bump was hit
A scream was heard
A man was killed
With a flying turd.

75a. Never laugh when a hearse goes by
For you may be the next to die
They wrap you in a big white sheet
And throw you down about fifty feet.
The worms crawl in
The worms crawl out
The worms play pinochle on your scalp
They scoop up the pus and put it on bread
And that's what you eat when you are dead.

75b. The worms crawl in
The worms crawl out
The worms play pinochle on your snout
Your face turns a ghastly green
Your eyes pop out

Your cheeks cave in
And pus runs out like whipping cream
And me without a spoon.

76a. Great big globs of greasy, grimy gopher's guts
Mutilated monkey's meat
Little birdie's bloody feet
All whipped together in penetrated porpoise pus
And I forgot my spoon.

76b. Great green gobs of juicy, grimy gopher guts
Mutilated monkey feet, chopped-up parakeet
Eagle eyes in a great big bowl of pus
And me without a spoon.

76c. Great green gobs of greasy grimy gopher guts
Mutilated monkey meat even while the birdies tweet
Over great pink pools of pink and purple pelican puke
And I forgot my spoon.

"Remember Me": Autograph Album Inscriptions

CHILDREN'S AUTOGRAPH ALBUMS recall the common bond of school-days passed together, the friendships gained, the lessons endured. In our mobile society, when we can't very well expect to see one another again after leaving school, the autograph album has taken on even more significance as a keepsake. It looks back, to be sure, but it also prepares the child by looking ahead to adult-sized problems of courtship, career, and marriage. "Remember me," an album calls out, "when far away / And only half awake, / Remember me on your wedding day, / And send me a piece of cake."

The album tradition has endured for several centuries, although its use as a schoolchild activity has been most pronounced in this century. In the fifteenth century, German university students had mentors sign their books to present as letters of introduction. During the nineteenth century, keeping autograph albums was a sign of Victorian gentility. British and American ladies had their friends inscribe sentimental and homiletic bits of poetry in the albums. By the late nineteenth century, children began taking up the tradition and called on a host of nursery and valentine verse for their inscription. At first discouraged, then condoned, autograph-album writing became a regular part of the school-leaving ritual at eighth grade (for the old "grammar school"), and later for sixth (for the progressive "elementary school") and eighth or ninth grades (for the "junior high" or "middle" school). By the time high school rolled around, students had advanced to yearbooks which they inscribed with prose rather than formulaic verse.

Today, verses found in autograph albums are often playful and impudent. The irreverent tone of so many of them reflects the release of rules that children associate with leaving school. The album-writing tradition today looks like sanctioned mischief, yet children's album writing is played with its own set of unwritten rules. A child will exchange a book with another child, and they will simultaneously write a

DATED TILL
LIP STICKS

Dear Simon,

The owner of this book
has asked
A word or two of me
But being in a generous
mood —
I've written twenty-three
Lots of luck in everything
Luv
Marsha

Page from eighth-grade autograph album (Brooklyn, New York, 1967)

verse in each other's book. But it is unwise to look at what the other person is writing if you finish first. The expression is savored after the writing. A certain premium is placed on the number of inscriptions one accumulates, indicating one's popularity. Another premium is placed on the variety of verses found in one's book. As a result, children call on an assortment of verses in their repertoire, so as not to repeat themselves in someone's album. Especially in the younger grades, the rhymes are humorous and formulaic; often they are parodies of simple rhymes such as "Roses are red, violets are blue." They commonly dwell in parody on matters of appearance and intelligence. Later, one can detect more involved verses which touch comically on courtship, marriage, sex, and career. It is also an observation that boys and girls commonly express themselves differently, with girls expected to provide more sentimental verse. In short, children use the playful setting of the album to express themselves in a number of ways — as friends and classmates to one another, as maturing individuals leaving a familiar setting, as learning students applying the creativity and knowledge they have gained.

Although albums sometimes make available published verses for the child to use, children usually prefer to rely on the font of tradition. This font is represented here with a sampler of commonly reported rhymes from the last three decades. The rhymes generally fall into categories of opening lines which are then elaborated, parodied, and altered. For example, there are the most common formulas of "Remember . . .," "Roses are red . . .," and "When you . . ." A second set offer witticisms in the form of simple arithmetic (2 young / 2 go / 4 girls"), personal testimonies ("I saw you in the ocean, / I saw you in the sea, / I saw you in the bathtub, / Oops! Pardon me"), and humorous bits of advice ("Beware of boys with eyes of brown"). And to round things out are the inscriptions that accompany many of the verses, like "Dated till butter flies," which remind us of the lasting quality of this tradition.

"REMEMBER . . ."

A series of modern verses of remembrance are a carry-over from the nineteenth century when they were the most popular category of verse. Often they were extracted from longer complex sayings suggested by formal album advisers, or varied from popular valentine verses. The essential use of the albums for remembrance has preserved them, although modern albums often parody the sentiment involved.

1a. Remember M
Remember E
Put them together and remember me.

1b. Remember A
Remember B
Remember the day we both made D.

2. Remember Grant
Remember Lee
The heck with them
Remember me.

3. Remember the city
Remember the town
Remember the girl
Who ruined your book by writing upside down.

4. Remember the North
Remember the South
Remember me and my big mouth.

5. Remember Jack
Remember Jill
Remember the girl
Who writes downhill.

6. Remember the moon
Remember the stars
Remember the day
We smoked cigars.

7. Remember the tests
Remember the fun
Remember the homework
That never got done.

8. Remember the fork
Remember the spoon
Remember the fun
In Andrea's room.

"ROSES ARE RED . . ."

In modern autograph albums, by far the most common formula for the child's inscription is a take-off on "Roses are red, / Violets are blue, / Sugar is sweet, / And so are you." As early as the eighteenth century, adults used the verse as a valentine rhyme and later introduced it to the nursery as a child's play rhyme. Today, children delight in the many variations possible on the verse's simple meter and rhyme, and find humor in offering the antithesis of the verse's sentiment.

9. Roses are red
Violets are blue
Sugar is sweet
And so are you.

10. Roses are red
Violets are blue
There has never been a friend
That's better than you.

11. Roses are red
Violets are blue
Flowers smell good
And so do you.

12. Roses are red
Violets are blue
Sugar is sweet
It's nothing like you
The roses are wilted
The violets are dead
The sugar is lumpy
And so is your head.

13. Roses are red
Violets are black
You'd look better
With a knife in your back.

14. Roses are red
Violets are blue
Monkeys like you
Should be in the zoo.

15. Roses are red
Violets are blue
You've got a nose like a B-52.

16a. Roses are red
Violets are blue
Garbage stinks
And so do you.

16b. Roses are red
Violets are blue
Pickles are sour
And so are you.

16c. Roses are red
Violets are blue
The sidewalk is cracked
And so are you.

17. Roses are red
They grow in this region
If I had your face
I would join the foreign legion.

18. Roses are red
Cabbage is green
My face is funny
But yours is a scream.

19. Roses are green
Oranges are blue
If you had 10 drinks
You'd think so too.

20. Roses are red, so is wine
I wish your pajamas were next to mine
Now don't get excited and don't get red
I mean on the clothesline not in bed.

"WHEN YOU . . ."

Autograph verse commonly looks into the future. The verse offers advice, for example, on married life, but often with a cynical twist. During the nineteenth century, someone might have written, "When you a husband have / He these lines shall see, / Tell him of our school-days / And kiss him once for me." Children today remark, "When you're married and have twins, / Don't come to me for safety pins." The "When you" opening can also comment on the friend that the album holder will always have, even if space and time separate them. During the nineteenth century one wrote, "When you are sitting all alone, / Thinking of the past, / Remember that you have a friend / That will forever last." Now one might read from a child's pen, "When you grow old and ugly / As some folks do / Remember you have a friend / Who's old and ugly too."

21. When you get old
And think you're sweet
Pull off your shoes
And smell your feet.

22. When you get old
And out of shape
Remember girdles are $2.98.

23. When you grow old and ugly
As some folks do
Remember you have a friend
Who's old and ugly too.

24. When you get old
And cannot see
Put on your specs
And think of me.

25. When you get married
And live across the lake
Send me a kiss by a rattlesnake.

26. When you get married and live in a tree,
Send me a coconut C.O.D.

27. When you get married and have twins
Don't come to me for safety pins.

28. When you get married and live in a home
Teach your children to leave me alone.

29. When you are married and have 25
Don't call it a family, call it a tribe.

30. When you get married and live far from a phone
Shout me a message by a megaphone.

31. When you get married and live on a hill
Send me a kiss by a whippoorwill.

32. When you get married
And have two boys
Don't ask me
To buy them toys.

33. When you get married
And live in a hut
Send me a picture
Of your first little nut.

34. When you get married
And live in a truck
Order your children
From Sears and Roebuck.

35. When you get married
And live by a jail
Put up a sign
Kids for Sale.

36. When you get married and live by the river
Send me a piece of your old man's liver.

37. When you get married
And go out West
Send me a man
By Pony Express.

38. When you and your boyfriend
Are standing at the gate
Remember love is blind
But the neighbors ain't.

ARITHMETIC

Creatively mocking the fundamental lessons of their education, children form messages out of the familiar sights of 1 + 1 and 2 + 2. Offering the inscription as a playful puzzle, children turn the numbers into words, and use letters as well for words, that fill out a code tailor-made for the autograph album. There is a sense, too, in which the structure of the inscription parodies the impersonal drilling that accompanies these lessons. The message of the child's inscription converts them into a more humane statement.

39. U R 2 good 2 be 4 gotten.

40. 2 young 2 go 4 boys.

41. 2 hugs 2 kisses 4 you.

42. 2 in a car 2 little kisses 4 weeks later Mr. and Mrs.

43. 2 young 2 drink 4 roses.

44. 1 and 1 = 2
2 and 2 = 4
If the bed collapses
Continue on the floor.

45. 2 yy u r 2 yy u b
I c u r 2 yy 4 me.

46. 2 lovers
  2 be
  2 gether
  4 ever
  ——————
  10-der lovin' care

PERSONALLY SPEAKING

Many verses work around, or mock, emotions by appearing to speak from the heart but end instead with a rude twist. Although serious expressions of love and friendship were regular parts of the nineteenth-century autograph album kept by adults, children today have difficulty with such sentiments. But the sentiments can still be used to provide humor, breaking up the tension of being "mushy," as some children like to say, and to remind them of the emotions they can later expect to feel.

47. I love you a little
I love you big
I love you like a little pig.

48. I saw you in the ocean
I saw you in the sea
I saw you in the bathtub
Oops! Pardon me.

49. I love you I love you I love you, I do
Don't get excited I love monkeys too!

50. It's hard to lose a friend
When your heart is full of hope
But it's worse to lose a towel
When your eyes are full of soap.

GIVING ADVICE

Because autograph albums mark a transition from one stage to another, they are often filled with humorous bits of advice for traveling the road ahead. Judging from the content of the albums, however, new schools on the road are of less concern than courtship and related experiences along the way.

51. There's a meter in the basement
There's a meter in the park
But the best place to meter
Is to meter in the dark.

52. Twins are bad
Triplets are worse
Sleep by yourself
And play safety first.

53. Twinkle, twinkle, little star
Eyebrow pencil, cold cream jar
Powder puff and lipstick too
Will make a beauty out of you.

54. Beware of boys with eyes of brown
They kiss you once and turn you down
Beware of boys with eyes of black
They kiss you once and never come back
Beware of boys with eyes of blue
They kiss you once and ask for two
You will meet boys of all kinds
So beware of boys.

55. Be a good girl
Live at your ease
Get a good husband
And do as you please.

56. You can fall from a tree
You can fall from above
But wait a few years
Before you fall in love.

57. Don't worry if your job is small
And your rewards are few
Remember that the mighty oak
Was once a nut like you.

"DATED TILL . . ."

To let the owner of the autograph album know that the message inscribed will last forever, writers will often "date" their verses with creative reminders. These phrases are stated in tradition as "Dated till . . ." or "Yours till . . ."

58. Dated till the side walks.
Dated till the board walks.
Dated till the toilet bowls.
Dated till the kitchen sinks.
Dated till door steps.
Dated till butter flies.
Dated till horse flies.
Dated till bacon strips.
Dated till lip sticks.

Dated till bobby pins.
Dated till the bees get hives.
Dated till dill pickles.
Dated till Soupy Sales.
Dated till Gregory Pecks.
Dated till Don Drys Dale Evans.
Dated till Niagara Falls.
Dated till Catskill Mountains.
Dated till Bear Mountain gets dressed.
Dated till France fries Turkey in Greece.
Dated till the Hudson River uses diapers to keep its bottom dry.
Dated till Hell freezes over and little devils go ice skating.
Dated till the undertaker undertakes to take you under.

CHAPTER FIVE

"Our Gang Goes Marching On": Song Parodies

BY THE TIME children are past the early grades, they have taken in a host of songs and hymns. Drummed into their heads, the songs bear adults' sanction all too plainly to the children, who before long turn the tunes to their own purposes. In today's schools, for example, children regularly pledge allegiance to the flag of the United States and they also gain allegiance to the values of American society, or so we think, by singing songs that are given a kind of sacred status. Most notably, there are the "Battle Hymn of the Republic" and the "Marines' Hymn," which are among the most frequently parodied. Besides these are the folk and popular songs that children invariably learn. "On Top of Old Smoky" and "Yankee Doodle" give them a sense of Americana, while "Row, Row, Row Your Boat" is one of those elementary songs used to teach harmony. Children parody these songs in fun or disrespect, or both.

Why does so much of children's folklore consist of parody? Parodies of such songs are powerful instruments in the child's social tool-kit. The tunes are familiar, often too familiar, and because they are so well known they invite a twist of novelty. Being sacred texts of society, typically learned at school, the songs once parodied afford children a chance to stretch the limits of childhood control and to flex some playful protest. In songs like "Battle Hymn of the Republic" turned into "My eyes have seen the glory of the burning of the school," for example, a measure of allowable protest is apparent. In the song, children attack teachers and principals with often gruesome results. Putting these attacks in traditional song gives their message a cutting edge, a chance to be heard, and a connection to other children, but it also makes it all seem unreal and playful. Yet being able to turn the song into this mythical power statement, and get away with it, provides the shouts of youthful glee that have encouraged the song to be a child's standard, a sacred text of the child's world. After all, neither school nor popular song is within the control of young children, and parody, operating in an oral tradition, offers them some scope of autonomy. Parody also comments on other institutional and authoritarian settings besides school, most notably the camp. Children like to share these songs in places where they have school and camp on their mind but where they feel some immunity: on the bus, on the playground, in the lunchroom.

Underlying many of the parodies is the adult expectation that children as they grow older will conform quickly to a set of manners showing social respectability. Children especially feel these pressures about dining, and in several songs, such as "On Top of Old Smoky" and "McDonald's Is Your Kind of Place," the abuse of food flies in the face of grown-up rules.

The "McDonald's" song is only one of several commercial jingles that children parody. Watching television avidly and listening to radio, children are more familiar than most with the commercial songs, at least in part because the jingles are often based on children's rhyme forms. The parodies suggest on the part of children a healthy skepticism about commercial claims and a willingness to mock institutions and media that loom large in their lives. Parody brings the jingles back into the oral tradition on which children primarily rely for this purpose.

Children also take popular songs that express innocence or sentimentality and turn them into announcements of their growing sexual awareness. "My Bonny Lies Over the Ocean," for example, is changed to tell the real story of "how they got little me." Children also sing to say that they know what the adult world is really about and can handle it. Another parody of "My Bonny Lies Over the Ocean" contains some apparently stomach-turning images, while a parody of "Rudolph the Red-Nosed Reindeer" includes references to marital violence hardly expected of children.

"Rudolph" is one of many Christmas carols that invite parody. Christmas carols are texts which take on a sacred character because they are associated with special, or even religious, occasions. For children, the strong element of many of these occasions is celebration, despite adult pronouncements to the contrary, and children's parodies invoke a playful sentiment. Besides the carols, for example, one can regularly hear parodies of "Happy Birthday" and "Here Comes the Bride." In the case of these parodies, not only is there celebration but also the suggestion again that parodies bring those on a pedestal down a notch.

I have selected for this chapter some of the most common parodies sung by children. The heading for each section announces the song that children are parodying, and of course the tune that is used for the words.

Parodies are our modern children's folk songs. Spreading quickly across the country in many versions, the songs freely comment on children's joys as well as their frustrations. The songs are creative, assertive work within the structures that adults have given children. And so "our gang goes marching on," to the sound of parodies that bond it together.

BATTLE HYMN OF THE REPUBLIC

The most commonly reported parody sung by children changes "Mine eyes have seen the glory of the coming of the Lord" to "My eyes have seen the glory of the burning of the school." These words take off on the spirited Civil War vintage song "Battle Hymn of the Republic" attributed to the singing of fighting Union troops. The parody also appears to rally the troops, divided into grades and classes, and equally imagines a miraculous victory, a victory of usually powerless children over their educational authorities. This expression of things that couldn't happen, especially sung to such a sacred text, gives the song its humor and gives children a certain release singing it. The song is found in a number of variations, and children often compare the versions they know with others to revise their arrangements.

1. Mine eyes have seen the glory of the burning of the school
We have tortured every teacher and we've broken every rule
His truth is marching on.
Glory, glory hallelujah, teacher hit me with a ruler
Met her at the door with a Colt .44
The truth is marching on.
Glory, glory hallelujah, teacher hit me with a ruler
I hit her on the butt with a rotten coconut
Our gang goes marching on.
Glory, glory hallelujah, teacher hit me with a ruler
I hit her in the bean with a rotten tangerine
Our gang goes marching on.

2. My eyes have seen the glory of the burning of the school
We have tortured every teacher, we have broken every rule
We have stood in every corner of that cotton-pickin' school

97

Our fame is marching on.
Glory, glory hallelujah, teacher hit me with a ruler
I stood behind the door with a loaded forty-four
And that teacher don't teach no more.

3. Mine eyes have seen the glory of the burning of the school
We have tortured every teacher and have broken every rule
We have hung — — *(principal's name)* on the flagpole of the school
As the brats go marching on.
Glory, glory hallelujah, teacher hit me with a ruler
I hit her on the bean with a rotten tangerine
As the brats go marching on.

4. Mine eyes have seen the glory of the burning of the school
We have tortured all the teachers and we have broken the Golden Rule
We tore into the office and we tickled the principal
Our truth is marching on.
Glory, glory hallelujah, teacher hit me with a ruler
'Cause I bopped her on the bean with a rotten tangerine
And the juice came running down.

5. Glory, glory hallelujah, teacher hit me with a ruler
So I met her in the attic with a semi-automatic
Now she ain't my teacher no more.

6. Mine eyes have seen the glory of the coming of the Lord
He is driving down the alley in a green and yellow Ford
With one hand on the teacher and the other on the sword
His truth is marching on.
Glory, glory hallelujah, teacher hit me with a ruler
Met her at the bank with a loaded army tank
And she ain't my teacher no more.

7. Mine eyes have seen the glory of the burning of the school
We have tortured all the teachers and we hung the principal
We have written in the books and we've broken all the rules
Then we've beaten all the dumb aides in a game of dirty pool
Our gang is marching on.

8. Glory, glory hallelujah, glory, glory hallelujah
Got there just in time to see the burning of the school

Stripped every teacher, broke every rule
Going to hang the principal tomorrow afternoon.
Glory, glory hallelujah, teacher hit with a ruler
Bopped her on the beam with a rotten tangerine
Now she's buried six feet deep.

ON TOP OF OLD SMOKY

Second in popularity to parodies of the "Battle Hymn of the Republic" is the popularized old folk song "On Top of Old Smoky." The mountain "all covered with snow" becomes a schoolhouse covered with sand or blood. The violent imagery in the parody is similar to that in "My eyes have seen the glory of the burning of the school" but in "Smoky" children add a graphic funeral scene. A distinctive second type of "Smoky" parody revolves around food: spaghetti all covered with cheese or bread all covered with seeds. This is especially popular at summer camp where a great deal of children's attention is paid to a regulated amount and variety of food, and the often difficult negotiation of manners exhibited by so many children with different backgrounds.

9. On top of old Smoky all covered with sand
I shot my poor teacher with a red rubber band
I shot her with pleasure I shot her with pride
I couldn't have missed her, she's forty feet wide.
I went to her funeral, I went to her grave
Some people threw flowers, but I threw grenades.

10. On top of old Smoky all covered with blood
I shot my poor teacher with a forty-five slug.
I went to her funeral, I went to her grave
Some people threw roses, I threw a grenade.
The grenade went boom! and that was the end
Of my poor teacher who was not my friend.

11. On top of spaghetti all covered with cheese
I had a meatball until somebody sneezed
It rolled onto the table and onto the floor
And my poor meatball rolled out of the door
Into the garden and into a bush

My poor meatball was nothing but mush.
So if you like spaghetti all covered with cheese
Hold onto your meatball when somebody sneeze. Ahchoo!

12. On top of old Smoky all covered with cheese
I lost my true lover when I had to sneeze.
On top of old Smoky all covered with hair
Of course I'm talking of Smoky the Bear.

13. On top of old rye bread all covered with seeds
I lost my dill pickle when somebody sneezed
It rolled off the table and into the jar
And then my poor pickle was saved from devour.

MARINES' HYMN

The words to the standard "Marines' Hymn" reflect the toughness
and readiness of the Marines. They thus become a natural vehicle for
mockery by children who within the institutional structure of the
school feel neither tough or ready. Rather, most children, subject to
rules of order, are put into a passive position. But they imagine equal
status with authority, and fight in a spirit of camaraderie for their
"rights." To assure these rights, assumedly as our armed forces do, in
their childhood arsenal is an assortment of weapons including
"spitballs, mud, and clay."

14. From the halls of Montezuma
To the shore of Bubble Gum Bay
We will fight our teacher's battles
With spitballs, mud, and clay
We will fight for lunch and recess
And to keep our desks in a mess
We are proud to claim the title
Of "Teacher's number-one pest."

15. From the halls of Edith Fritch school
To the chain fence over there
We will fight our classroom's battle
Anyway, anytime, anywhere
First to fight for longer recesses

And to keep our desks a mess
We are proud to claim the title
Of the teacher's rough tough pests.

ROW, ROW, ROW YOUR BOAT

This popular song dating from the nineteenth century is commonly given as a round and is often used today as an elementary tune to teach music to children. The first two lines remain in the most common parody, but instead of life being a dream in the "straight" version of the song, life is quite difficult if you're a teacher in the parody.

16. Row, row, row your boat
Gently down the stream
Throw your teacher overboard
And listen to her scream.

TA-RA-RA BOOM DER-É

Similar to the sentiment expressed in "Row, Row, Row Your Boat" is a parody of the popular minstrel-styled hit "Ta-Ra-Ra Boom-Der-É." The frolicking tone of the song undoubtedly makes the song appealing as a take-off on the enthusiastic death and dumping of a teacher. There's no mourning here, only celebration for a day off from school.

17. Tra la la la boom de-ay
There is no school today
Our teacher passed away
We threw her in the bay.
Tra la la la boom de-ay
The teacher passed away
We threw her in the bay
The sharks had lunch today.

YANKEE DOODLE

The catchy tune and words of "Yankee Doodle" have been readily interpreted comically from its first appearances on the stage during the eighteenth century. In children's performances today, the tune and words again have a comical air, and remind listeners how children are titillated by pointing to the private realm of undergarments and the body parts they surround. As children sing in this parody, propriety comes fully into view.

18. Yankee Doodle came to town
Riding on a turtle
Turned the corner just in time
To see a lady's girdle.
Yankee Doodle keep it up
Yankee Doodle Dandy
Turned the corner just in time
To see another panty.

19. Yankee Doodle came to town
Riding on a turtle
Hit a hump and skinned his rump
And landed in the city dump.

MY BONNIE LIES OVER THE OCEAN

This popular nineteenth-century lament lives again in the form of children's parody. Similar to the gross rhymes and gross jokes, one of the parodies of this song tests the listener's ability to take it, or shows the singer's willingness to dish it out. The sentimental tone of the original is given an ugly twist, which of course lends a certain amount of humor as children see it. Singing the parody violates norms and thus also announces a performer's sense of power or emotional wherewithal. The exploration of real life's gritty details also shows in another form of the "Bonny" parody, "My Mommy Lies Over the Ocean." Again children are singing their own praises, announcing that they deserve more credit than they normally get for being aware of what life is all about.

20. My Bonnie has tuberculosis
My Bonnie has one rotten lung
She spit up a bloody solution
Right up on the tip of her tongue.
Come up, come up, come up, dear dinner, come up, come up

Come up, come up, come up, dear dinner, come up.
I'm coming, I'm coming for my head is hanging low,
I hear the old-time voices saying,
Hasten Jason, bring the basin
(Spoken) Whoops, slop, get the mop.

21. My Bonnie has tuberculosis
My Bonnie has only one lung
My Bonnie spits blood in a bucket
And dries it and chews it for gum.
(Spoken) Dentyne, Dentyne, that wonderful, wonderful gum.

22. My mommy lies over the ocean
My daddy lies over the sea
My daddy lies over my mommy
And that's how they got little me.

I'M LOOKIN' OVER A FOUR-LEAF CLOVER

This song dates from 1927, when it was written by Mort Dixon and Harry Woods. Its merry message and catchy tune have made it a popular standard. But out of the mouths of children the song is brought back down to earth.

23. I'm looking over my dead dog Rover
That I ran over with the mower
One leg is missing, another is gone
The third one is scattered all over the lawn
There's no use explaining, the one remaining
Is stuck in the front screen door
I'm looking over my dead dog Rover
That I ran over before.

24. I'm looking under a two-legged wonder
That I underlooked before
First come the ankles, and then come the knees
Then comes the knockers that swing in the breeze
And there's no need explaining, the one remaining
Is something that I adore
I'm looking under a two-legged wonder
That I underlooked before.

25. I'm looking under a green cucumber
That I underlooked before
The first one was sour, the second one sweet
The third one was the one that I couldn't eat
No use explaining, the one remaining
Is the one that I dropped on the floor.
I'm looking under a green cucumber
That I underlooked before.

JOY TO THE WORLD

If "Mine Eyes Have Seen the Glory" has sparked many a children's parody about the burning of the school, then it follows that "Joy to the world, the Lord is come" should also produce its share, and that's exactly the case. Indeed, the violent imagery of "Joy to the World" parodies is similar to that of "Battle Hymn of the Republic," although the singing of "Joy to the World" is more often inspired by winter vacation from school.

26. Joy to the world, the school burned down
And all the teachers died
We're looking for the principal
He's hanging on the flagpole
With a rope around his neck
With a rope around his neck
With a rope, a rope around his neck.

RUDOLPH THE RED-NOSED REINDEER

Since the 1950s "Rudolph the Red-Nosed Reindeer" has been a pop favorite, and it has been especially evident among songs typically performed for children. The original recording by cowboy singer Gene Autry is one of the all-time best-selling records. That might explain the conversion of this song in the most common parody of "Rudolph" to a cowboy song with a soap-opera twist.

27. Randolph the six-shooter cowpoke
Had a very shiny gun
And if you ever saw him

You would turn around and run
All of the other cowpokes
Used to laugh and call him names
They wouldn't let poor Randolph
Play in any poker games.
Then one foggy Christmas Eve
The sheriff came to say,
"Randolph with your gun so bright
Won't you shoot my wife tonight?"
Then how the cowpokes loved him
And they shouted with glee,
"Randolph the six-shooter cowpoke
You'll go down in the penitentiary."

JINGLE BELLS

"Jingle Bells" is an enduring Christmas song that resembles many of
the rhymes with which children are already familiar (see Chapter
Three). Parodies of this tune offer an antithesis of the serene surroundings suggested by the original. In the "Jingle Bell" parodies is found
the violent lashing-out at the teacher found in many children's parodies, and some cynical statements both about Christmas mythology
and the comic-book world of crime.

28. Jingle bells, shotgun shells
— — *(name of teacher or principal)* on the run
Oh what fun it is to shoot — — with a gun.
A day or two ago I thought I'd take a ride
And take my father's gun and shoot — — in the hide.
Jingle bells, shotgun shells
— — 's on the run
Oh what fun it is to shoot — — in the bun.

29. Jingle bells, shotgun shells
Santa is dead
Someone stole my .30-.30
And shot him in the head.

30. Jingle bells, Batman smells
Robin laid an egg

Batmobile broke its wheel
And Joker got away.

DECK THE HALLS

The appearance of "halls" in the words of this song no doubt inspired the burning desire expressed in this parody for doing in the halls of school.

31. Deck the halls with gasoline
Fa, la, la, la, la, la, la, la, la
Light a match and watch it gleam
Fa, la, la, la, la, la, la, la, la
Watch the teacher burn to ashes
Fa, la, la, la, la, la, la, la, la
Aren't you glad you play with matches?
Fa, la, la, la, la, la, la, la, la.

WE THREE KINGS OF ORIENT ARE

In this Christmas carol, a favorite of children's choirs across the land, the words gloriously announce "We three kings of Orient are / Bearing gifts we traverse afar." But the parody, intended as well for group singing, ignobly announces disaster from an ill-starred cigar.

32. We three kings of Orient are
Tried to smoke a rubber cigar
It was loaded! It exploded! Boom!
We two kings of Orient are
Tried to smoke a rubber cigar
It was loaded! It exploded! Boom!
I one king of Orient am
Tried to smoke a rubber cigar
It was loaded! It exploded! Boom!
(Sing first line of "God Rest Ye Merry, Gentlemen" or "Silent Night")

TWELVE DAYS OF CHRISTMAS

This song is especially prevalent in parody form at summer camp. With a twist of the words, the familiar inventory of treasured gifts lends itself to contrast to the novel situation of camp and its special demands for ignoble items. Campers will take a shot at substituting items in the list, thus giving the parody the feeling of a game.

33. On the first day of girls camp my mommy sent to me
A box of oatmeal cookies.
On the second day of girls camp my mommy sent to me
Two T-shirts and a box of oatmeal cookies.
On the third day of girls camp my mommy sent to me
Three pairs of socks, two T-shirts, and a box of oatmeal cookies.
(*Song continues with the following:* four woolen caps, five underpants, six postage stamps, seven nose-warmers, eight Archie comic books, nine bars of soap, ten cans of Right Guard, eleven shoestrings, twelve cans of blood-sucking helicopter repellent).

HAPPY BIRTHDAY TO YOU

"Happy Birthday to You" may just be the most frequently sung song in America. It is a required part of any birthday party, which children indulge in even more than adults. "Happy Birthday" parodies might be expected in the playful atmosphere of children's birthday parties. But there is a sense, too, that children are sensitive to any special attention given to, or change in status of, another child, and they use "Happy Birthday" parodies to affectionately keep the celebrated child in line with them.

34. Happy birthday to you
You belong in a zoo
You look like a monkey
And act like one too.

35. Happy birthday to you
You live in a shoe
You look like a monkey
And smell like one too.

36. Happy birthday to you
You belong in the zoo
With the lions and tigers
And the baboons like you.

HERE COMES THE BRIDE

Almost as familiar as "Happy Birthday" is another special occasion tune, "Here Comes the Bride." In the most common parody, children turn the somber occasion into a comical drama.

37. Here comes the bride
Big, fat, and wide
See how she wobbles from side to side
Here comes the groom
Skinny as a broom
He had to use the side door
Because there wasn't room.

HOW DRY I AM

Adults usually offer the song "How Dry I Am" to comment on drinking, but for children "dry" and "wet" have connections to bathroom habits. Self-control and public behavior, a constant theme in American child-rearing, is the prevalent subject in the parody.

38. How dry I am
How wet I'll be
If I don't find the bathroom key.
I found the key
But not the door
It's too late now
It's on the floor.

POPEYE THE SAILOR MAN

The catchy musical theme to "Popeye" cartoons has given rise to a parody that exaggerates the rough-hewn attributes that the Popeye character suggests. Children play up this exaggeration in their singing, and in doing so, the song resembles other parodies that challenge the limits of propriety.

39. I'm Popeye the sailor man, toot-toot
I live in a garbage can, toot-toot
I eat all the worms
And spit out the germs
I'm Popeye the sailor man, toot-toot.

MCDONALD'S IS YOUR KIND OF PLACE

During the 1970s, McDonald's Hamburgers, the largest of the fast-food burger chains, used "McDonald's Is Your Kind of Place" in television and radio commercials. McDonald's had previously reached out to children with their use of Ronald McDonald, a clown figure, in advertising, and their placement of playgrounds and special attractions for children at their stores. The restaurant, it seemed to children, was a playful place. Children soon came up with a parody that provided a natural play on food and dining behavior (see parodies of "On Top of Old Smoky" and "Twelve Days of Christmas") and brought a large institution into their all-knowing, cynical perspective.

40. McDonald's is your kind of place
Hamburgers in your face
French fries up your nose
Ketchup between your nose
McDonald's is your kind of place
Ain't got no parking space
McDonald's is your kind of place

McDonald's is your kind of place
They serve you rattlesnakes
They throw them in your face
McDonald's is your kind of place
Next time you go up there

They'll serve you underwear
McDonald's is your kind of place.

41. McDonald's is your kind of place
Hamburgers in your face
French fries between your toes
Two pickles up your nose
Ketchup running down your back
I want my money back
Before I have a heart attack.

CHIQUITA BANANA

Another popular commercial featured the Latin-style music of the Chiquita Banana jingle. It was an appealing image to children: a banana coming to life and singing its own praises. In the children's parody, the banana offers advice on a subject repeated often in the child's singing repertoire: doing in the teacher.

42. I'm Chiquita Banana and I'm here to say
If you want to get rid of your teacher today
Just peel a banana and throw it on the floor
And watch your teacher go flying out the door.

I DON'T LIKE NAVY LIFE

Returning servicemen helped to spread the popularity of a humorous ditty about the trials of military life called "I Don't Like Navy Life." "They say that in the Navy, / The biscuits are so fine," they sang, "But one dropped off the table / And killed a pal of mine." The rousing chorus then declared "I don't like Navy life, / Gee Mom, I want to go / Right back to Quantico, / Gee Mom, I want to go home." Children's camps, with their barracks, food services, and hierarchies that raise images of military regimen, have taken up the chorus of "I Don't Like Navy Life." It is a campers' song, meant to unite strangers, release tension and a laugh, and provide a mischievous, human touch away from home.

43. The biscuits up at camp they say are mighty fine
One fell off the table and killed a friend of mine.
Oh Gee, I want to go to Porcupine
Gee Dad, I want to go, oh how I want to go
Gee Dad, I want to go to camp, camp, camp, camp
Camp, camp, camp, camp.
The drivers up at camp they say are mighty great
They drive around a corner and end up in the lake.
The boys up at camp they say are mighty fine
Most are over eighty, the rest are under nine.
The leaders up at camp, they say are mighty fine
With hair like Phyllis Diller, and a face like Frankenstein.
The trails up at camp, they say are mighty great
Walk a half a mile, and get bitten by a snake.

CHAPTER SIX

"Mommy, Mommy, Why Do I Keep Going Around in Circles?": Riddles and Jokes

THE ANSWER TO the question in the title of this chapter is "Shut up or I'll nail your other foot to the floor." It is one of many so-called cruel jokes that have become standard fare in children's humor. Such jokes tend to burst on the scene and circulate quickly, only to be replaced in popularity by new cycles. Why should these cycles draw our attention? Many of them respond to disaster, death, prejudice, and disturbing moral issues of the day. What people laugh at is often what they take very seriously. Humor provides indexes to values, attitudes, and biases of a society. For children, humor plays a special role because children normally do not have outlets to resolve issues. Adults often assume that children are oblivious to problems they debate, but indeed children are quite vocal, if symbolically, about the society they are growing into.

Many of the jokes are outgrowths of riddling forms that for generations provided a test of wits. They were timeless wisdom builders, brain teasers, poetic puzzles. Children recognized their formulas, their use of comparison, symbol, and metaphor. Children parodied them for a laugh, dramatized them for effect, and molded them into commentaries on the modern day.

The oppositions and contradictions of riddles and joking questions work well in the overall speech play of children. While depending on tradition and formula, they provide ample opportunities for variation and improvisation. They invite manipulation and parody. They involve children in a vocabulary of jests and witticisms that can be shared in play with one another.

That vocabulary also finds its way into a narrative tradition of jokes. The jokes poke fun at the central figures in the child's life — teachers and parents. They humanize them, and bring them down to the child's level. At the same time, the jokes also deal with issues of the child's maturation, for they often bring out the quickly growing sexual awareness and rapid physical development that adults, so children say, do not adequately take into account.

The jokes are sometimes shocking, more often telling. Only hesitantly picked up by media, the jokes testify to the power and persistence of children's oral tradition. But as they are shocking, they thus serve the purpose of reminding us of social limits that children in every generation want to explore, to test. And on the near side of those limits, where the chapter opens, we can find what children are learning, what they are expressing, through their changing poetic puzzles and parodies.

DESCRIPTIVE RIDDLES

The classic kind of riddle, sometimes called the "true riddle," is posed as a series of enigmatic statements which provide clues to the identity of an object or event. These kinds of riddles test the wits of the listener as well as demonstrate the wisdom of the riddler. They are among our most ancient forms of folklore; in many traditions, they were set within games or contests aimed at raising children's thinking. With their creative use of metaphors, oppositions, and comparisons, such riddles have the air of playful poetry. Today, American children are less familiar with them than they once were, but many collections still attest to the hardiness of this traditional brain-teaser.

1. A box without hinges, key, or lid
Yet golden treasure inside is hid. — An egg.

2. There was a green house. Inside the green house was a white house. Inside the white house was a red house. Inside the red house were many black and white people. What am I? — A watermelon.

3. Round as an apple
Deep as a cup
All the king's horses
Can't pull it up. — A well.

4. Round as a biscuit
Busy as a bee

Prettiest little thing
You ever did see. — A watch.

5. Go all around the house
And make but one track. — A wheelbarrow.

6. I'm Tillie Williams from Walla Walla
I'm odd and queer but not peculiar
I like pepper but not salt
I like walls but not ceilings. — Double letters.

7. There was a man who had no eyes. He went outside to view the skies. He saw an apple tree that had apples on it. When he got through, there were no apples on the tree. He had eaten no apples. What happened? — He didn't have *eyes,* but he had one eye; the apple tree had two apples, he ate one, and left one apple on the tree.

8. Whitie went into blackie
And whitie came out of blackie
And left whitie in blackie. What happened?
— A white hen went into a black stump and laid an egg. The white hen came out of the stump and left the white egg inside the stump.

9. There was an old man walking across the bridge
He tipped his hat and drew his cane
And in this riddle I've told his name. — Andrew.

RIDDLE PARODIES

Parodies of the ancient descriptive riddle defy expectations of the old standards. In one form, the riddler goes through a long, involved description, giving the listener the idea that the answer is rather tricky to figure out. But instead, the answer requires simple common sense. Another common form uses wordplay, usually comical puns, to make light of the heavy riddle.

10. Three men walked into a restaurant. One man ordered an egg with a piece of bacon on either side. The second man ordered an egg on the right side and two pieces of bacon on the left side. The third man ordered an egg on the left side and two pieces of bacon on the right side. How could the waitress tell which one was a sailor? — She looked at his uniform.

11. A dime and a nickel were on the top of the Empire State building. The nickel jumped. Why didn't the dime jump? — He had more cents.

12. A banana, an apple, and an orange stood on a bridge. The apple jumped, the orange jumped. Why didn't the banana jump? — He was yellow.

13. You go into the bathroom American. You come out of the bathroom American. What are you in the bathroom? — European.

RIDDLING QUESTIONS

A "short" form of the descriptive riddle directly asks the listener for an answer to a question. This form emerged especially outside the riddle "contests" where the context which normally supplied the "question" is not as apparent. These riddling questions thus can pop up in children's play among other forms of children's lore.

14. What has legs and cannot walk? — A table.
What has one eye and can't see? — A needle.
What has eyes and can't see? — A potato.
What has four eyes and can't see? — Mississippi.
What's black and white and read all over? — A newspaper.
What's black and white and red all over? — An embarrassed zebra.
What has a head and can't think, has legs and can't walk? — A bed.
What goes through the door but never out? — The keyhole.
What goes up to the house, but never goes in the house? — The sidewalk.
What has a tongue but cannot talk? — A shoe.
What has ears but can't hear? — Corn.
What has feet but can't run? — A yardstick.
What has one horn and carries milk? — A milk truck.
What's black and white with a cherry on top? — A police car.

JOKING QUESTIONS

Children often use the riddling question to set up a humorous punch-line. They follow some standard patterns. A favorite is "What did one —— say to the other —— ?" In the descriptive riddle, we may be given the dialogue and asked to figure out the speakers. Here the reverse is true, and the answer typically uses a play on words to provide humor. Other joking questions reverse the usual composition of the riddle. A question such as "Why is the grass dangerous?" with the answer "It's full of blades" gives the description (the "clue" in the descriptive riddle) as its answer. Where descriptions are given (What's purple and conquers the world?), the answer often twists a name or word to give an absurd, punning, colorful, or off-color-ful result (Alexander the Grape).

15. What did one wall say to the other wall? — I'll meet you at the corner.

What did one wall say to the other wall? — Don't lean on me, I'm plastered too.

What did the wallpaper say to the wall? — Don't move, I've got you covered.

What did one strawberry say to the other strawberry? — If you weren't so fresh we wouldn't be in this jam.

What did the picture say to the wall? — First they frame me, then they hang me.

What did one tonsil say to the other tonsil? — Put on your hat and coat, the doctor is taking us out this morning.

What did one chimney say to the other chimney? — You're too young to be smoking.

What did the salad say to the refrigerator? — Shut the door, I'm dressing.

What did the mother bullet say to the father bullet? — We're going to have a BB.

What did the mommy pill say to the baby pill when the guests arrived? — Aren't you going to vitamin?

What did the teacher pill say to the student pills? — Get out your tablets.

What kind of pills do astronauts take? — Capsules.

What did the father pill get when he sat on the hot burner? — Aspirin.

What did the mother hen say to her baby chicks when they were bad? — If your father could see what you've done, he'd turn over in his gravy.

Why did the golfer bring two pairs of pants to the golf course? — He was afraid he'd get a hole in one.

Why did the baby shoe run away? — His father was a loafer and his mother was a sneaker.

What did the burp say to the other burp? — Let's be stinkers and come out the other end.

Why did the rocket lose its job? — It got fired.

Why did the boy put ice in his father's pockets? — He wanted a cool pop.

Why is the grass dangerous? — It's full of blades.

What sits in a tree and is dangerous? — A sparrow with a machine gun.

What's the difference between a snow man and a snow woman? — Snow balls.

What's purple and conquers the world? — Alexander the Grape.

What's purple and lives in the jungle? — Tarzan the Grape Man.

What's brown and sits on a bench? — Beethoven's last movement.

What's brown and sits in a cave? — Winnie's pooh.

KNOCK-KNOCK JOKES

"Knock-Knock" jokes are essentially dramatic routines that two children act out. Indeed, the questioner in this routine is not the riddler, and is put in the position of receiving a comical answer. The script of these routines is set (Knock knock, who's there?), but the effectiveness of the joke depends on the questioner's not knowing the last line. So the burden of wit is put on the person who initiates the routine. The wit is typically placed in the form of some kind of wordplay, which often results in a line embarrassing the questioner. Some adults wonder whether there's "anything to" these popular routines beyond their involvement of speech play. One might point to modern notions of privacy that are demonstrated by these jokes. In a mobile, urban society, one encounters more strangers than ever before. Children are especially vulnerable, and are reminded to be cautious. The object of the knock-knock routine is essentially a reminder to press strangers for their identity. The humor is a break to what appears as a routine, but potentially tense, situation.

16. Knock, knock. — Who's there? — Lenny. — Lenny who? — Lenny in, it's cold out here.

Knock, knock. — Who's there? — Harry. — Harry who? — Harry up and open the door, it's cold out here.

Knock, knock. — Who's there? — Turnip. — Turnip who? — Turnip the heat, it's freezing in here.

Knock, knock. — Who's there? — Doughnut. — Doughnut who? —

Doughnut talk to strangers knocking at your door.

Knock, knock. — Who's there? — Oh lady he. — Oh lady he who? — I didn't know you could yodel!

Knock, knock. — Who's there? — Dishes. — Dishes who? — Dishes the last knock-knock joke I'm telling.

Knock, knock. — Who's there? — Chesterfield. — Chesterfield who? — Chesterfield my butt and ran away.

Knock, knock. — Who's there? — Senior. — Senior who? — Senior dog digging in the trash yesterday.

Knock, knock. — Who's there? — Handsome. — Handsome who? — Handsome pizza my way, I'm starved.

Knock, knock. — Who's there? — Sarah. — Sarah who? — Sarah doctor in the house?

Will you remember me in a week? — Yes. — Will you remember me in a month? — Yes. — Will you remember me in a year? — Yes. — Knock, knock. — Who's there? — You forgot me already!

Knock, knock. — Who's there? — Banana. — Banana who? — Knock, knock. — Who's there? — Banana. — Banana who? — Knock, knock. — Who's there? — Banana. — Banana who! — Knock, knock. — Who's there? — Orange. — Orange who? — Orange ya glad I didn't say banana?

MORON JOKES

One of the developments of children's language is the acquisition of metaphoric language. A child who does not understand the nuances and idioms of the language produced by metaphors can appear dumb. This is brought home by "little moron" jokes. The questions in these jokes ask explanations for absurd behavior, and the answer lies in a misunderstanding of metaphoric language. The moron takes a ladder, for example, to get to high school; he takes a cow to hear the new pastor. The moron is "little," the jokes emphasize, and assumedly the little moron is not mature enough to know better.

17. Why did the little moron bring his ladder to the beer parlor? — Because the beers were on the house.

Why did the little moron take a ladder and briefcase to court? — He wanted to take his case to a higher court.

Why did the little moron take a ladder to school? — He heard it was high school.

Why did the little moron take a ladder to a baseball game? — He heard the Giants were playing.

Why did the little moron take a ladder to church? — He heard there was going to be a high mass.

Why did the little moron take a cow to church? — He heard there was going to be a new pastor.

Why did the little moron throw the butter out the window? — He wanted to see the butterfly.

Why did the little moron throw a quarter off the mountain? — He wanted to see the eagle fly.

Why did the little moron throw a match out the window? — To see a firefly.

Why did the little moron bury his car? — He heard his spark plugs were shot.

Why did the little moron bury his car? — Because he heard his battery was dead.

Why did the little moron take his ruler to bed? — He wanted to see how long he slept.

Why did the little moron walk softly past the medicine chest? — He didn't want to wake the sleeping pills.

How did the little moron get his name? — He had rushed to catch the bus at the bus stop. Many people boarded the bus and when his turn came, the bus driver called "Sorry, no more on."

Why did the little moron sit on the stove? — He wanted to ride the range.

Why didn't the little moron get hurt when he jumped from the Empire State building? — He had on his safety pin.

Why did the little moron take his spoon, bowl, and milk to the movies? — He heard a new serial was starting.

Why did the little moron jump off the Empire State Building? — He wanted to make a hit on Broadway.

MARY JANE JOKES

A particular brand of the moron joke tells about Mary Jane, or Little Audrey, or Little Emma. Mary Jane is unaware of how the world works; she can be innocent to the point of being abused or destructive. In the telling, innocence means immaturity, a child who hasn't grown up, and older children especially have told this joke to remind others that they themselves are well aware of reality.

18. One day Mary Jane was walking down the street and a carload of guys yelled out the window: "Hey, pick-up." Mary Jane just laughed and laughed because she knew she weren't no truck.

Mary Jane went to the doctor and he told her that she was going to have twins. She laughed and laughed, because she knew she didn't do it twice.

Mary Jane was walking through a field and she saw this fly on a pile of manure. She laughed and laughed because she knew the fly couldn't do all that.

Mary Jane was playing with matches and burned the house down. Mary Jane and her mother were looking at the ruins. Mary Jane's mother said, "Mary Jane, your daddy is going to kill you when he gets home." Mary Jane laughed and laughed, because she knew her daddy was asleep on the couch.

ETHNIC JOKES

America has welcomed to its shores diverse peoples and also exposed them to prejudice. One group often puts down others by laughing at their physical appearance or supposed lower intelligence. Many of the barbs were based on the traditional form of the moron joke. In this form, the newcomer finds it difficult to fit into society. The newcomer butchers the language, batters logic, and bounces off. Jews, Italians, Scandinavians, and Irish have all fallen prey to this humor in their immigration history. Immigrant groups are not the only ones to bear the brunt of this kind of humor. Many of the same jokes find their way in the humor of neighboring states (Hoosiers, for instance, tell Kentucky jokes and Kentuckians tell Hoosier jokes), and sometimes even neighboring counties.

The debate over the causes and functions of this humor rages on, especially when ethnic jokes are gleefully offered by children. Today, an assortment of ethnic-styled jokes can be heard on the lips of children. Most notable of these is the Polack joke, which became popular after World War II when jokes playing on the moron joke arose about the backwardness of Poland's military response to German attack. Performance in war became a test of national character. Jokes were humorous releases from a war-torn chapter of history, one that brought the world into conflict as well as bringing soldiers from different countries into uneasy alliance. Especially during the 1960s, however, the jokes became symbols of America's visible ethnic tensions. The "Polack" played the part of the rube in ethnic America.

Jokes about blacks took a slightly different turn, deriding stereotypical physical features and cultural patterns. Many saw in the humor not a release of ethnic tension, but a hold on prejudice in changing times. In the last decade, new groups have taken the heat in children's humor. Iranians, for example, a group that didn't show up in collections of the 1960s, appear conspicuously in this recently collected list. The new notoriety of Iranians comes from the events surrounding the taking of American hostages in Iran during the late 1970s. The name of the group was grafted onto several existing forms of children's joking questions. One was the question of how many of a group it takes to screw in a light bulb. Whereas performance in war had been the test of character for mid-century America, the new test was in the handling of energy technology, so significant to the nation in the late twentieth century. In ethnic humor, then, we can see the continuities and changes of folklore responding to the biases of the American experience, and we can hear children expressing them lest we become complacent.

19. What are the famous words of the Polish war hero? — I surrender.
What's a Polish tank? — It has one forward gear and three reverse gears.
How did the Polack break his arm raking leaves? — He fell out of the tree.
How many Polacks does it take to change a lightbulb? — Eleven: one to hold the lightbulb in place, and ten to turn the chair.
How do you drive a Polack crazy? — Put him in a round room and tell him to go to the bathroom in a corner.
How many Polacks does it take to make popcorn? — Seven: one to hold the pan, and six to shake the stove.
How many Polacks does it take to paint a house? — Five hundred. One Polack to hold the brush and 499 to move the house back and forth.
Why do they use only two Polack pallbearers to carry a coffin? — Because there are only two handles on a garbage pail.
What is a Polish seven-course dinner? — A ring of sausage and a six-pack.
What do you get if you cross a Polack and a one-legged mongoloid? — A Polaroid One-Step.
How many cops does it take to arrest a black guy? — Three: one to hold him, and two to hold his radio.

What is a Negro hitchhiking in the South? — Stranded.

What is a Negro who doesn't have legs or arms? — Trustworthy.

How do you babysit ten black children? — Wet their lips and stick them to the wall.

What is black and brown and looks good on a colored person? — A Doberman.

What do you call a twelve-year-old black child in kindergarten? — Gifted.

What do you call a black on a brand-new ten-speed bike? — A thief.

What do you get when you cross a groundhog and a Negro? — Six more weeks of basketball.

What does it say on the inside of a black man's lips? — Inflate to seventy pounds.

What is black and white and rolls down the boardwalk? — A black man and a seagull fighting for a french fry.

What do you get if you cross a black man with an Irishman? — An Irish jig.

How many Iranians does it take to screw in a light bulb? — One to screw it in, and ninety-nine to hold the house hostage.

Why do Iranians carry shit in their back pocket? — For identification.

How do you get a one-armed Iranian out of a tree? — Wave to him.

How do you save an Iranian from drowning? — You don't!

How many Iranians does it take to catch a possum? — Four: one to catch it, the other three to look out for cars.

What did the Mexican do with his first fifty-cent piece? — He married her.

How many Jews can you fit in a German car? — Four in the seats and thirty in the ash tray.

How do Italian tires go? — Dago fast, dago slow, dago flat, denn dago wop, wop, wop.

CRUEL MOMMY JOKES

During the 1950s much attention was given to "cruel" or "sick" jokes, and the jokes still surface in children's joking repertoire. Although much of children's humor deals harshly with cruel tricks, this cycle drew laughter from the usually hushed-up misfortune of child abuse at the hands of an unfeeling mother. The jokes are given as two-part dramatic routines. The child imitates a whining infant in the opening line, and with the second line the child switches to the role of the mother. The mother provides the cruel action that in essence answers the riddle of the infant's descriptive whine. The humor comes from the fact that the second line appears so incongruous with the expected treatment of children as to appear absurd.

20. Mommy, Mommy, I'm tired of running in circles! — Shut up or I'll nail your other foot to the floor.

Mommy, Mommy, I don't want to see Grandpa! — Shut up and keep digging.

Mommy, Mommy, why does Daddy look so pale? — Shut up and keep digging.

Mommy, Mommy, why is Daddy running so fast? — Shut up and keep shooting.

Mommy, Mommy, Daddy threw up on the floor! — Shut up and get me the big chunks.

Mommy, Mommy, come here quick, Daddy's bleeding all over the place! — Don't just stand there, stupid, go get the flavored straws.

Mommy, Mommy, what's a vampire? — Shut up and drink your soup before it clots.

Mommy, Mommy, I don't want to go to Paris! — Shut up and keep swimming.

Mommy, Mommy, little brother just got run over by a steamroller! — I'm taking a bath, so just slip him under the door.

Mommy, Mommy, why are we going across this bridge? — Shut up and get back in the bag.

Mommy, Mommy, can I play with little brother? — Absolutely not! You've already dug him up three times this week.

But Mommy, I don't like little brother. — Shut up and eat what's put before you.

Mommy, Mommy, I'm tired of spaghetti. — Shut up or I'll take out the veins in your other arm.

KIND MOMMY JOKES

Another cruel joke series revolves around a kind-sounding mother who reminds children of their physical deformity or handicap. While such handicaps were kept out of the spotlight for many years, after World War II a barrage of visual reminders evoked sympathy for the problems of disabled children. "Poster children" stared sadly out from walls, and celebrities asked for collections of dimes to help eradicate the crippling scourge of polio and later, after that was accomplished, to combat birth defects.

21. Mommy, Mommy, why can't I go horseback riding? — Honey, you know your wheelchair won't fit the saddle.

Mommy, Mommy, why can't I go skating at the new roller rink? — Darling, you know your crutches won't fit the skates.

Can we go to the drive-in tonight, Mommy? — No, Son, you know we can't get your iron lung in the back seat of the car.

Mommy, Mommy, why can't I jump rope? — Darling, you know your stubs always bleed.

Mommy, Mommy, why do the kids call me "werewolf"? — That's all right, dear, just go comb your face.

Mrs. Johnson, can Billy come out and play ball with us? — Now you know Billy doesn't have any arms or legs. — We know, we wanted to use him for first base.

ELEPHANT JOKES

The world presented in elephant jokes is topsy-turvy. Elephants go through refrigerators, sneak across pool tables, and hide in strawberry patches. But while the jokes appear to be an extension of children's fondness for creating whimsy out of constructions of nonsense, some observers have noted possible underlying meanings that might explain their sudden rise to prominence. Even nonsense purposely selects its symbols. As they were particularly popular during the civil rights struggle of the 1960s, one interpretation suggests, elephant jokes became a symbol for the movement for black equality. And in the jokes, an ambivalence toward the success of the movement is expressed. The elephant is a dark powerful character from the jungle in an alien setting. In many of the jokes, the elephant is virtually ignored, despite its conspicuous presence; it appears awkward or naive in its various modern settings; its attempts to hide appear comical. During the late 1970s and 1980s, the tone of the elephant jokes changed. Many of the jokes presented the elephant as a woman, and this time extended feminine characteristics such as menstruation into signs of awkwardness. The circulation of these jokes coincided with the rise of the women's movement, and suggests a connection.

22. How do you tell if an elephant has been in your refrigerator? — By the footprints in the butter.

Why do elephants paint their toenails green? — So they can sneak across the pool table.

What time is it when an elephant sits on a fence? — Time to get a new fence.

Why do elephants have flat feet? — From jumping out of palm trees.

Why does an elephant wear three white sneakers and one yellow sneaker? — He forgot to lift up his leg.

Do you know what is four feet long, and hangs in the trees in Africa? — Elephant snot.

What's green, slimy, and looks like an elephant? — Ellamucus.

How can you tell if an elephant is in bed with you? — By the peanuts on his breath.

Why did the elephant take toilet paper to a party? — He wanted to be a party pooper.

Why did the elephant paint himself all different colors? — So he could hide in a package of M&Ms.

Why did the elephant paint his toenails red? — To hide in the strawberry patch.

Why does an elephant want to get in a cherry tree? — Because the cherries match his toenails.

How does an elephant get out of a cherry tree? — Sits on a leaf and waits for it to grow.

How does an elephant get out of a cherry tree? — Sits on a leaf and waits for it to fall.

How do you shoot a red elephant? — With a red elephant gun.

How do you shoot a blue elephant? — You hold the elephant by his nose, wait until he turns blue, and then shoot him.

What did the grape say when the elephant sat on it? — Nothing, it just let out a little wine.

How do you get 100 elephants into a Volkswagen Beetle? — With a blender.

How do you get the same 100 elephants out? — With a straw.

Why did the elephant lie in the middle of the sidewalk? — To trip the ants.

What's gray on the inside but clear on the outside? — An elephant in a Baggie.

Why can't an elephant ride a bike? — He has no thumb to ring the bell.

Why aren't elephants allowed on the beach? — They can't keep their trunks up.

What did Tarzan say when he saw the elephants coming? — Here come the elephants.

What did Tarzan say when he saw the elephants wearing sunglasses? — Nothing. He didn't recognize them.

What did Tarzan say when he saw twelve elephants coming over the hill? — Here come twelve elephants coming over the hill.

What did Jane say when she saw twelve elephants coming over the hill? — Nothing. She was blind.

How do you know elephants were having sex in your backyard? — All the trash can liners are gone.

What's the sexiest part of the elephant? — Her foot; if she steps on you, you're screwed.

Why did the elephant paint her head yellow? — To see if blondes had more fun.

What does an elephant use for a tampon? — Sheep.

What does an elephant use for a vibrator? — An epileptic.

How do you know when an elephant has her period? — You find a quarter on your dresser and your mattress is missing.

How do you know when an elephant has her period? — You find a bunch of red sheep running around.

DEAD BABY JOKES

During the 1970s, many children shocked the sensibilities of adults by offering up dead baby jokes as the latest youthful laugh craze. In these jokes, babies are mutilated and maligned. Not a pretty picture. But children enjoyed the typical oral response of "Oh, how gross." The sickening answer violated the expectation of a "normal" riddling question like "What's red and white and sits in a corner?" Indeed, the dead baby joke goes beyond the norms of the joking questions (see item 15) and appears to parody them. One interpretation of the underlying meaning of these jokes is that they were a response to the issue of abortion which had been thrust into the spotlight by the media. According to this interpretation, the jokes turned humor into a release for the disturbing moral dilemma of a baby's death or a way just to comprehend its significance. "Oh, how gross" tells the child that it is indeed a horrible sight. Still another thought that some had was that graphic coverage of the Vietnam War during the 1970s, which often featured bleeding infants, influenced the circulation of the dead-baby jokes.

23. What's red and white and sits in a corner? — A baby chewing on razor blades.

What's red and green and sits in a corner? — The same baby, two weeks later.

What's red and swings back and forth? — A baby on a meathook.
What's blue and sits in the corner? — A baby in a Baggie.
What's red and white and spins around? — A baby in a blender.
What's red and has wrinkles? — A baby in a microwave oven.
What's a little black thing tapping on a window? — A baby in a microwave.
How do you make a baby float? — A bottle of 7-Up and two scoops of baby.
What's more fun than nailing dead babies to a wall? — Ripping them off.
What's more fun than shoveling dead babies on a cart? — Using a pitchfork.
What is easier to unload: a truck full of dead babies or a truckload of flour sacks? — A truck full of dead babies, because you can use a pitchfork.

HELEN KELLER JOKES

Helen Keller's life was often given as a lesson of how one woman's personal determination helped her overcome handicaps and led her to become a celebrated member of society. But it was not an easy lesson for many to swallow, especially because the handicapped presented new challenges to Americans for adjustment and tolerance. During the 1960s, Helen Keller jokes appeared to reflect some of these tensions. Keller in these jokes independently takes up everyday activities taken for granted by able-bodied people (using a waffle-iron and fork, for example), but she ends up hurting herself. In many of the jokes, there is a resemblance to the cruel jokes where someone abuses Keller's innocence or cynically comments on vain attempts to engage in able-bodied activities (see items 20-21). With Keller, a name became attached to many of these kinds of jokes. Keller's fame made her an easy target for such commentary, and a choice symbol for the changes that were occurring in society.

24. What's punishment for Helen Keller?—Change the furniture around.
Why is Helen Keller's leg always wet?—Because her dog is blind too.
Why did Helen Keller burn her fingers?—She was trying to read a waffle iron.
Why does Helen Keller have holes in her face?—She tried to eat with a fork.
What happened when Helen Keller fell down a well?—She screamed her hands off.

What did Helen Keller do when she fell off the cliff?—She had to feel
   her way down.
How do you torture Helen Keller?—Put a plunger in the toilet.
Why does Helen Keller wear tight pants?—So you can read her lips.
Did you hear about the new Helen Keller dolls?—You wind them up
   and watch them bang against the walls.
Did you hear about the Helen Keller concert?—Everyone came to
   watch.
Have you seen Helen Keller's house?—Neither has she.

DOLLY PARTON JOKES

Sometimes we treat celebrities as one of the family. Through the
wonders of mass media, they are with us daily, and we are familiar
with their most intimate secrets. Dolly Parton's fame as a singer and
actress has made her name a household word and her chesty figure a
regular sight to behold. To children becoming aware of developing
parts of their bodies, Parton's appearance invited joking comment on
the problems that this full condition presents.

25. Why doesn't Dolly Parton drive a 280-Z?—She wears one.
How can you tell Dolly Parton's kids in a crowd?—By the stretch marks
   around their mouths.
Why are Dolly Parton's feet so small?—Nothing grows in the shade.
Have you seen Dolly Parton's new shoes?—Neither has she.
How do you catch Dolly Parton in a forest?—Set a boobie trap.
How did Dolly Parton kill herself?—She stood on her head and was
   smothered.
What do cough syrup and Dolly Parton have in common?—44D.
What do you call sweat on Dolly Parton's chest?—Mountain Dew.

CHRISTA MCAULIFFE JOKES

On January 28, 1986, a stunned audience saw the *Challenger* space-
ship explode with seven astronauts on board. One of those killed was
Christa McAuliffe, a teacher by trade. In the days that followed, jokes
about the *Challenger* arose, apparently to break the tension of a disturbing event, and a major portion of those jokes concerned
McAuliffe. In collections among children, she was especially evident.

Even before the flight, her role as the first schoolteacher in space coupled with her bubbly personality and all-American values assured her a memorable place in America's heart. In the jokes, her background in the teaching of schoolchildren provided opportunities for humorous wordplay; other jokes brought out her neophyte status on the flight. Some of the jokes borrowed from other celebrity jokes having to do with death. For example, when Natalie Wood died on a boating trip, children asked, "Why didn't Natalie Wood take a shower on her yacht?" and answered, "Because she figured she'd wash ashore." And we find McAuliffe fitting into a version of this joke.

26. Where did Christa McAuliffe take a vacation?—All over Florida.
What were Christa McAuliffe's last words?—What does this button do?
What were Christa McAuliffe's last words to her class?—I'll be back in a flash.
What were Christa McAuliffe's last words at home?—You feed the dog and I'll feed the fish.
Why was Christa McAuliffe such a good teacher?—She only blew up in front of her kids once.
How do you know that Christa McAuliffe wasn't a good teacher?—Good teachers don't blow up in front of their class.
What did Christa McAuliffe teach?—She taught English, but now she's history.
What is Christa McAuliffe doing now?—Teaching schools of fish.
Why didn't Christa McAuliffe take a shower on the flight?—She figured she would wash ashore.
What color were Christa McAuliffe's eyes?—One blew here, one blew there.
How did they know that Christa McAuliffe had dandruff?—Her head and shoulders were on shore.

NAMES-OF-THE-DEFORMED JOKES

If it wasn't enough that the problems of the handicapped became the subject of often derisive humor (see items 21, 24), a lurid cycle of humor followed about the names given to amputees. This cycle of the 1980s may also be a sign that public tolerance of the handicapped has improved, but tensions still exist in the extent of acceptance. Another interpretation is that the jokes took the fad of changed names and vanity plates to its absurd limits. The play on names characteristic of these jokes is hardly new to children. Children are known for their derogatory epithets to describe unusual appearances (Fatty, Stringbean, Shorty) and constantly comment on appropriate nicknames (see items 35-37 for narrative jokes about names). The knock-knock jokes also involve the manipulation of names, and the familiar cruel joke of "Can Billy come out to play?—You know he doesn't have arms or legs.—We know, we want to use him for third base" (see item 21) earlier brought the paraplegic up as a joking subject.

27. What's the name of a man with no arms and legs in the water?—Bob.

What's the name of a man with no arms and legs hanging on a wall?—Art.

What's the name of a man with no arms and legs lying on the floor?—Matt.

What's the name of a man with no arms and legs coming in the mail?—Bill.

What's the name of a man with no arms and legs in the leaves?—Russell.

What's the name of man with no arms and legs in a hole?—Phil.

What's the name of a man with no legs?—Neil.

What's the name of a woman with one leg?—Eileen.

What's the name of a Japanese woman with one leg?—Irene.

What's the name of a woman with no arms and legs on the beach?—Sandy.

WHAT'S-GROSSER-THAN-GROSS JOKES

The sick jokes of the past might appear mild by comparison to those of today. Many observers argue that the limits of decency have steadily become more extreme and ever more hazy. With the standards of taste appearing ambiguous, children of the 1980s interpreted social limitations with the pointed joking question, "What's grosser than gross?" And in some versions of this cycle, the question ultimately became "What's grossest of all?" Many of the jokes made direct reference to other sick joke cycles such as dead-baby jokes. Others refer to food contamination, especially of concern to children who normally do not prepare their own foods, and a sign of maturity which is often treated as one of contamination (menstruation). The jokes have a youthful stamp on them, both because their use of children's folk speech "gross" and repeatedly test social limits.

28. What's grosser than gross?—Throwing your underwear against the wall and it sticks.

What's grosser than gross?—Being joined to your Siamese twin and he brings it up.

What's grosser than gross?—Kissing your grandmother and she slips you the tongue.

What's grosser than gross?—Biting into a hot dog and it has veins.

What's grosser than gross?—Two vampires fighting over a bloody tampon.

What's grosser than gross?—Finding a wad of hair at the bottom of a glass of tomato juice.

What's grosser than gross?—Finding a tampon at the bottom of the tomato juice can.

What's grosser than gross?—Eating a bowl of rice and the last kernel crawls out.

What's grosser than gross?—Finding birdshit at the bottom of your soup bowl.

What's grosser than gross?—One dead baby in seven trash cans.

What's grosser than gross?—A truckful of dead babies and one live one at the bottom.

What's grosser than that?—One eating his way out.

What's grosser than gross?—A baby sliding down a razor blade and landing in a pool of alcohol.

What's grosser than gross?—Falling off a fifty-foot building and catching your lip on a nail.—What's grosser than that?—Falling off the Empire State building and catching your eyelid on a nail.—What's grosser than that?—A baby falling off the Empire State building and catching his eyelid on a rusty nail.

What's grosser than gross?—Babies chopped up and put in a jar.—What's grosser than that?—A man at the bottom that has to eat his way up to the top.—What's the grossest of all?—He made it!

What's grosser than gross?—A cheerleader doing the split and sticking to the floor.—What's grosser than that?—A cheerleader doing the split and ten minutes of rocking her back and forth to get her unstuck.—What's grosser than that?—A cheerleader doing the split and sticking to the floor, and when she gets up you hear a loud pop.—What's grossest of all?—A cheerleader doing the split and sticking to the floor, when she gets up you hear a loud pop and five class rings fall out.

TEACHER-PUPIL JOKES

Some of the most common narrative jokes that children tell concern a fact of their daily life—their relations with the teacher. In these jokes, the teacher is typically one-upped. The teacher's control of the class is challenged or her wisdom is derided. The classroom in these jokes has a recurrent cast of characters. There is the innocent child who takes the teacher's instructions to learn three words literally, and ends up using them impudently. And there is the smart-aleck or vulgar child, sometimes taking the name of Dirty Ernie or Dirty Willie, who threatens the teacher's respectability.

29. It's the first day of school and the teacher is asking the children the alphabet by calling on various children. It becomes Johnny's turn and the teacher asks Johnny to stand up and recite the whole alphabet. Johnny replies: "A, B, C, D, E, F, G, H, I, J, K, L, M, N, O, Q, R, S, T, U, V, W, X, Y, Z." The teacher asks, "Where's the P?" And Johnny says, "Running down my leg!"

30. There was this little boy in school and the teacher knew better than to call on him because he was such a vulgar kid. Well, one day the class was saying their ABCs and making words with each alphabet as they said it. First, the teacher called on Suzy. She said, "A for apples, they grow on trees." They were going on through the alphabet and Willy was having a fit wanting to answer. They got to R and the teacher thought to herself, There's not anything dirty Willy can make of R and since he wants to answer I'll let him. Dirty Willy got up and said, "R for rats, big fuckin' ones with tails this God-damn long!"

31. There was this class and the teacher was asking the kids questions. She asked one little boy, "What's round and red and grows on a tree and has green leaves?" Little Johnny says, "The pear." The teacher says, "No, Johnny, it's an apple." But since he said it was round it does grow on a tree, she said, "That just goes to show you that you're thinking right." She goes on and asks a few more students the same question. Well about that time Peter, who was a smart-ass, sitting in the back of the room, yells out, "Teacher, I've got one for you. What do I have in my pocket that I've got my hand a hold of that's long, white, and thin, and has a red head?" And the teacher says, "Oh Peter!" And he says, "No teacher, it's not, it's a matchstick, but that just goes to show you you're thinking right."

32. There's this boy and his teacher told him to remember three good words for homework. And so he asks his sister, he said, "Do you have any good words I can write?" She said, "Shut up." So he remembered that one. Then he was listening to the radio and he heard someone say, "Yeah, yeah, yeah." So he remembered that one. Then he was watching TV and he saw Superman, so he remembered that one. And he goes to school the next day and the teacher says, "Do you have any of the words?—He says, "Shut up." And the teacher says, "Really! Do you want to go to the principal?" And he says, "Yeah, yeah, yeah." And the principal says, "Who do you think you are?" And he says, "Superman."

33. One day Johnny Deeper stayed after school. The teacher said, "What's wrong, Johnny?" He said, "Teacher, teacher, will you take your dress off?" "Well, no." "Please, please," Johnny pleaded. "Well, okay." So she took off her dress. Johnny then said, "Teacher, teacher, will you take off your bra?" "Well, no." "Please, please," Johnny pleaded. "Well, okay." "Teacher, teacher, will you take off your underwear?" "Well, no." "Please, please." "Well, okay." "Teacher, teacher, will you lay down on the table?" "Well, no!" "Please, please." "Well, okay." And Johnny's mother came in the school then looking for Johnny, and she yelled, "Johnny Deeper, Johnny Deeper!" And he yelled back, "Mommy, I am as deep as I can go!"

34a. There were these little kids at school and the teacher was having them go up to the front of the room blindfolded and having them guess what kind of candy they were eating, and if they could, the teacher gave them a whole box full. A lot of kids had gone up and guessed candy, like Clark Bars, Paydays. Well this little girl goes up and she was eating candy Kisses and she couldn't guess what it was, so the teacher says, "I'll give you a hint, your mommy and daddy do it every night before they go to bed." Well Billy, the little smart-aleck in the back of the room, yells out, "Spit it out, it's a piece of ass!"

34b. There was a schoolteacher who was testing her group of children on some different types of candy. She passed around some butterscotch drops and a little boy said, "Teacher, that's a butterscotch drop." "That's right," she said. Then she passed out gumdrops and the little girl said, "Teacher, that's a gumdrop." "That's right," said the teacher. Then she passed out Hershey Kisses and nobody knew what they were. So, she hinted, "What is the first thing your mother gives your dad every morning and the last thing every night?" A little boy in the back of the room yelled, "Spit it out, spit it out! It's a piece of ass!"

35. It was the first day of school and the children filed into the classroom and took their seats. Teacher says, "All right, boys and girls. Now I want you all to stand up one at a time and tell everybody here your name, so we will all get to know each other." First little boy stood up and said, "My name is John Brown." "Very good, John, you may be seated." Next a little girl stood up and said, "My name is Nancy Jones." "Very good, Nancy, you may be seated." Next a little girl stood up and said, "My name is Pissy Smith." The teacher said, "You mustn't talk that way. We're in school, you know. Now tell us your real name." "My name is Pissy Smith," the little girl said. The teacher again reminded the little girl where she was and again asked her to give her real name. The little girl for the third time said, "My name is Pissy Smith." "Okay," the teacher said, "one more chance to tell us your real name or leave." The little girl again said, "My name is Pissy Smith." "Get out," the teacher said, "until you can learn to talk right." As Pissy left the room, she said to a little boy in the back row, "Come on, Shit Head, she won't believe you either!"

36. There was this kid whose name was "Shit," and one day at school they were having a spelling bee, and the principal of the school stepped in to watch. He didn't know anybody's name in the room. And so the word "substantial" came up and nobody could spell it. Finally it was Shit's turn to try and the teacher said, "Shit, you can't spell 'substantial.'" And the principal jumped up and yelled, "Well Jesus Christ, you could at least let the boy try."

37. There was this boy that was born, and his mother and father didn't know what to name him, so they finally decided to name him the next commercial that came on TV, and the next commercial that came on was "Mountain Dew" so they named him Mountain Dew. And he kept growing and growing until he got to the first grade, and his first-grade teacher said that "If you give me something that rhymes with your name or a hint of your name, then I'll guess your name and tell you where to sit." And this little girl said, "A flower." And the teacher said,

"Rose, you sit there." And this little boy said, "Tiny." And the teacher said, "Tim, you sit there." And then it finally came along to Mountain Dew, and Mountain Dew said, "It'll tickle your innards." And the teacher said, "Peter, you sit there."

PARENT-CHILD JOKES

An oft-told tale among pre-adolescents concerns the child's discovery of adult sexuality. The vehicle for this discovery is a shower with each parent. Despite conditions set by the parents for looking at their naked bodies, the child disobeys and pointedly asks for information about developed adult genitals. But the parent still hides the identity of sexual organs from the child by offering innocent metaphors such as headlights or grass. In the end, the child exposes the parents and embarrasses them. In its various forms, the story speaks powerfully about growing childhood awareness of sexuality and the fallibility of adult guidance.

38a. One day a boy said to his dad, "Can I take a shower with you?" "Okay, but don't look down." So, of course he looked down at his dad and he said, "What's that?" And his dad said, "My snake." So then he went to his mom. So then he said to his mom, "Can I take a shower with you?" And she said, "Yes, but don't look up or down." So he looked up and he said, "What's that?" She said, "My headlights." And he looked down, and said, "What's that?" She said, "My grass." So then that night the boy was scared of monsters and so he said, "Can I sleep with you, Mom and Dad?" And they said, "Okay, but don't go under the covers." So he went under the covers, and he said, "Mommy, Mommy, turn on your headlights, Daddy's snake is in your grass."

38b. One day a boy took a shower with his dad but his dad said, "Don't look down." So the boy looked down and he said to his dad, "Daddy, what's that?" And his dad said, "That's my Z-28." So he dried himself off and got dressed and he took a shower with his mom then. And his mom told him not to look up or down but he did anyway. And he said, "Mommy, what's that?" She said, "That's my gate." And then he said again, "Mommy, what's that?" She said, "They're my floodlights." So that night he was afraid of the thunder and he said, "Mommy, Daddy, can I sleep with you?" They said, "Yes, but don't look under the covers." Being a curious child he did and he said, "Mommy, turn on your floodlights, open up your gate, because here comes Daddy with his Z-28."

38c. There's this boy, he's about six years old. He goes in and he asks his father, "Can I take a bath with you?" He says, "Okay, but don't look down." He takes a bath with him and looks down. "Daddy, what's that?" "Oh, that's my submarine." And so, he says, "Mother, can I take a shower with you?" And she says, "Okay, but don't look up or down." And he looks up and down. First he looks up and he says, "Mother, what are those?" She says, "Oh, those are my bombs." And so, he looks down and he says, "Mother, what's that?" "That's my tunnel." And then, he says, "Daddy, Mommy, can I sleep with you?" And they said, "Okay." And so, they were sleeping and the little boy's awake, and he says, "Mommy, Mommy, drop your bombs, Daddy's submarine is going into your tunnel!"

39. Billy went into the bathroom when his mother was taking a bath. Looking down, Billy said, "Mommy, what's that?" Mother answered, "That's my sponge." Billy returned to the bathroom five minutes later with his friend Johnny. Billy asked his mother to show Johnny her sponge. And she said, "Well, I lost it." A little while later, Billy returned and said, "Mommy, I found your sponge. The maid is using it to wash Daddy's face!"

40. A little boy caught his mom and dad doing it. The little boy says, "What's that?" The dad says, "That's my car, and I'm trying to drive it into your mommy's cave." Well the little boy went outside, found the little neighbor girl and they started doing it. About that time, there was a big scream from the little boy. So the man runs out of the house and he says, "What's the matter?" And the little boy says, "I tried to drive the car in and it didn't fit so I cut off the back tires."

41. There was this little boy and he was peeing out the window. When his mother saw him she said, "Johnny, if you do that again I'm going to cut it off." Not too much later, his mother caught him again, peeing out the window. And she said again, "Now Johnny, I mean it. If I catch you do that again, I'm going to cut it off." Again it happened. His mother said, "All right, it wouldn't be too bad of an idea. The little girl across the street had hers cut off and it looks rather nice, neatly folded under."

BOY-GIRL JOKES

The changes brought about by puberty and growing sexual awareness are the subject of another common series of jokes about the lost
innocence of boy-girl relations. In many of the stories, the little girl is
especially vulnerable to the boy's advances or sensitive to the changes
occurring to her body. She is beginning to be noticed sexually, but is
not always aware of the attention and its implications. Tellers of these
jokes often convey a mature awareness of sexuality, and occasionally
will also bait the listener into an embarrassing admission (see item
44).

42a. There was this little girl coming home from school and this little
boy goes to her, "I'll give you ten cents if you climb the flagpole." So,
she did. She went home and told her mom that a boy gave her ten
cents to climb the flagpole. Her mom goes, "Why did you do that?—He
just wanted to see your underpants." On the way home the next day,
the same boy asked her to climb the flagpole again, but this time for a
quarter. So, she did. She went home and told her mom that she got a
quarter this time. Her mom goes, "Don't you ever climb the pole
again. He just wants to see your underwear." On the way home the
next day, she sees the same boy again and he goes, "I'll give you fifty
cents this time if you climb the flagpole." So, she did. She went home
and told her mom that she got fifty cents this time. Her mom goes,
"What did I tell you about climbing the flagpole. All he wants to do is
see your underwear." And the little girl goes, "Well, he didn't get what
he paid for, because I didn't wear any."

42b. Once this little boy and girl were playing out in the yard, and the
little boy said, "I'll give you a cookie if you'll stand on your head." So
she took the cookie, stood on her head, and told her mother about it
later. Her mother scolded, "You mustn't do that. He will see your panties." The next day, the little boy tried to bribe the little girl with a cookie, but she refused, so he offered her two cookies if she would stand
on her head. So she took the cookies, stood on her head, and told her
mother about it later. Her mother scolded, "But I told you not to do
that. He will see your panties." The little girl said, "Oh no, this time I
fooled him. I took them off first."

43. This little girl and boy were taking a bath together. The little boy
asked if he could put his finger in the little girl's navel. She said, "No,"

but finally consented. She screamed, "That isn't my navel." The little boy answered, "And that isn't my finger."

44. A little boy asked a little neighbor girl to go for a walk with him, but she said, "Oh, I can't do that. It's dirty!" He answered, "Oh, no, it isn't." So they went for a walk. Pretty soon, he said, "Let's hold hands while we walk," but she answered, "Oh, I can't do that. It's dirty!" He said, "Oh, no, it isn't." So they held hands and walked on. The little boy said, "Oh, let's go in the barn over there," and the little girl answered, "Oh, I can't do that. It's dirty." But he said, "Oh, no, it isn't." So they went over and into the barn. They looked around, and the little boy said, "Let's go into the, uh, uh—" (At this moment, the storyteller points up and stammers as though he cannot remember the words he is trying to say. When the listener helps him by saying, "The hay loft," the storyteller brings his finger down pointing to the listener and says, "Oh, you're experienced. You know the rest of the story!")

45. Once upon a time there was a boy and he was thirteen. He went to a girl and all of a sudden he said, "You wanna do it?" And she said, "No, I have my period." And he said, "I don't believe you." And she says, "Okay, I'll show you." And she went to the store and she got some red paint and painted her panties red and he said, "Okay." And he asked a girl who was younger. And it was the same thing. And he asked a girl who was about eleven. And she said the same thing and she did the same thing. There was a girl who was ten, and he asked her and she said, "No, I have my period." And he said, "I don't believe you, you're too young." And she said, "Okay, I'll show you." And she went to the same store that everyone else did. And she said, "You have any red paint?" And he said, "I'm out. You know, people have been buying a lot." And he said, "The only colors we have left are purple, yellow, green, and yellow." And the girl said, "I'll take green." And she painted her pants green. And the boy said, "That's not the color it's supposed to be." And she said, "Can I help it?—Mine hasn't ripened yet."

THREE (OR FOUR) GUYS JOKES

A formula that children often employ in jokes is to contrast the response of three characters, often given national or ethnic titles, to a stressful situation. A car breaks down in the desert, a plane is about to crash, a firing squad takes aim, and God confronts mortal men. In some punchlines, a "little moron" type of character draws humor by missing an opportunity through his lack of quick thinking. Several of the jokes take place at a cliff, at the edge of disaster, where one meets his maker and his true colors stereotypically come through. In several of these jokes, for example, the American ignobly displays racial or ethnic prejudice. In others, a childhood character such as the supposedly naive Boy Scout ends up out-tricking the deceivingly wise adults who have made an early quick escape. As many of these jokes take on some of the character of a fable with interpretations of human character for their moral, parodies arise of the moral itself. The punchline becomes an ironic twist on an old proverb or commercial jingle, or a *spoonerism*—a humorous interchanging of the sounds of words in sayings. And thereby hangs a tale, or as some would have it, tangs a hale.

46. There was a Polack, a Chinese, and an American and they were in the Sahara Desert and the car broke down, so they had to walk. And the Chinese took the trunk cover off and the Polack said, "Why are you taking that?" And he said, "In case I get hot I'll have something to shade me." And the American took the seat cushion out and the Polack said, "Why are you taking that?" And the American said, "So I can sleep on it." So the Polack took the car door and the other two said, "Why are you taking that?" And he said, "In case I get hot, I'll roll down the window."

47. There were two American prisoners and one Polish prisoner. When it was time for them to be executed they were led outside. The first American was being aimed at when he yelled, "Hurricane!" And the soldiers ran and hid. The American soldier got away. When it was the second American's turn, he yelled, "Tornado!" And the soldiers ran and hid and he got away. Next it was the Polish prisoner's turn. While the soldiers aimed, he yelled "Fire!" and they shot him.

48. There were these four guys in an airplane. There was the pilot, smartest man in the world, a priest, and a Boy Scout. And the plane was going to crash, and there were only three parachutes. The pilot says, "I'm not going to die," and he takes a parachute and jumps out. Then the smartest man in the world goes, "Well, got to deliver these things to the Russians," so he took one parachute and he jumped out of the plane. And then there was the priest and the Boy Scout left. And the priest said, "Well, you go ahead, you have your life to live." And the

Boy Scout goes, "Don't worry, Father, that smartest man in the world jumped out with my backpack."

49a. There are these three guys, right. And they come to a stop and they are on a cloud and God tells them, "You can make any wish you want if you jump off the cloud." And this first guy he said that he wanted to be a motorcycle rider, so he jumped off the cloud and he turned into a motorcycle rider down there. And then the second guy said, "I want to work as a carpenter," and he jumped off the cloud and he got on earth and he worked as a carpenter. The third, he didn't say nothing, he just jumped off the cloud and then he says, "Uh oh, my radio," and he turns into a radio and it all smashes.

49b. An American, Frenchman, and Polack had died and were standing at the edge of a cliff. The American said that if you jump off the cliff you will be reincarnated as anything you want. The American jumped off while saying "airplane" and he turned into an airplane and flew away. The Frenchman jumped off and said "eagle" and flew away. The Polack forgot what he wanted to be as soon as he jumped off. In his excitement and desperation, he couldn't remember what he wanted to be, he swore and said "shit."

49c. There was this black man, white man, Chinese man, and an angel. The angel said whatever you want say it and it will fall from the sky. The white man said he wants money and that dropped from the sky. The Chinese man said he wants rice and that dropped from the sky. Then something hit the black man and he said, "Oh, shit." And horse poop dropped from the sky.

50. There's a Polack, a French guy, an American, and a black guy by the cliff. The French guy goes, "I'm going to do something for my country," so he jumps off the cliff. And the Polish guy goes, "I'm going to do something for my country," so he jumps off the cliff. Then there's the black guy and the American left. And the American guy goes, "I'm going to do something for my country," so he pushed the black guy off the cliff.

51. There were three people: a Hindu, a Jew, and a Polack. They were walking down a road when they came to a farm. They went to the farmer's house to ask if they could stay for the night. The farmer replied that he had room for only two in the house and that one would have to sleep in the barn. The Hindu offered to sleep in the barn. He came back a few minutes later, and the Jew and the Polack wanted to know the reason. The Hindu said that there was a cow in the barn and his religion considered cows to be sacred; so he could not sleep in the barn. The Jew then offered to sleep in the barn. A few minutes later he also came back. The Jew said that there was a pig in the barn and his religion forbade him to sleep with a pig. The Polack was the only one who could sleep in the barn, so he went out. A few minutes later there was a knock at the door. There stood the cow and the pig claiming they could not sleep with the Polack.

52. Once there was a white man, a black, and a Puerto Rican man. First the white man went to this hotel and the lady said, "We're full, but there's one room and it's haunted." The white man said, "That's okay." So the man went up to the room and the ghost said, "Sit in my hands and you will melt away." So the man did and he melted away. The Puerto Rican rented it out and the ghost said, "Sit in my hands and you will melt away." So he did and melted away. The black man came and rented it out and the ghost said, "Sit in my hand and you will melt away." The black man said, "Milk chocolate melts in your mouth and not in your hands."

53. These three guys went to Africa on a safari. Each of them wore a big, broad hat. Their guide told them if the fou bird shits on them not to wipe it off. They went out on the hunt, and a fou bird shit on the one guy's head. He wiped it off without thinking anything of it. Five minutes later, he died unexpectedly. Now, the second guy was just about to shoot a lion when a fou bird shit on his head. He got scared and left it on. A week later, it started stinking. He figured there was no curse and wiped it off. Five minutes later, he died unexpectedly! The next day, the third guy went out and a fou shit on his head. He kept it on when he went back to America and he never wiped it off. Thirty years later, he was looking at his trophies and his hat was lying there. He figured the curse would never last that long, so he wiped off the hat. Five minutes later, he died unexpectedly. The moral: when the fou shits, wear it.

CHAPTER SEVEN

"And Then He Heard These Footsteps": Tales and Legends

THE CHILD'S WORLD is a storied place. Mysterious houses, dark woods, and murky rivers invite exploration, and stories about them summon caution. The dangers of the night, as well as the busy street, and a child's wanderings into both, bring up stories that have more than a hint of the bizarre, but are sworn to have happened — or at least that's what the child has heard. Brought up on fantasy, children as they grow out of infancy look for supernatural realms closer to home. Stories help to explain the strange sights and sounds that lurk outside the house, the camp, the car.

Parents, camp counselors, and babysitters have helped to stock children's world with stories in order to warn them about potential dangers and to exert some control over their wanderings. Many remember, for example, the scary figure of the boogeyman who would "get you" if you were bad or left your bed at night. Parents slept a little sounder knowing that the story kept their children in line when they were out of earshot.

Children take in the stories and try them out on one another. In the telling, the raconteur gauges reactions: Are the listeners scared? Is anyone acting "like a baby"? Maturing involves courage to face the night and other dangers; reactions to stories provide a test of that maturity. And it might not be long before children check the stories out, using them as road maps to confront the mysteries around them. They look into a haunted house far from home, go to see the nearby hill's fabled "spook lights," listen for the crying heard at the haunted bridge, and watch for strange goings-on at the graveyard.

From what they've taken in, children themselves become adept at creating a scary story. In addition to explaining strange things that have happened by spinning a tale, they can also use the drama of the tale to create humor. There are stories that could be called "playful horror tales" or "hoax tales" because the listener expects a spooky outcome, but is instead caught flatfooted by a silly or catch ending. An imposing ghost screams "I am the ghost of the bloody fingers" and scares to death the big, brave adults, only to be told by a impudent child, "Well, put on a Band-aid then." Or as the climax approaches, the teller grabs the listener and forces a jump and scream that brings mirth to the rest of the audience. The tales make listeners feel a little foolish for being scared, in some cases, or else if they sense the catch ending coming on, the message of the child's control of the real world comes through loud and clear.

There are as many ghost stories as there are places, it seems, and as many hoax stories as there are ghosts. But I have selected legends (based usually on a core of belief and intended to be serious) and hoax tales (recognized as fictional and intended to be humorous) widely known to children that represent the kinds of stories steeped in tradition heard across America.

GHOST STORIES

Around the world ghost stories about unnatural deaths have long circulated, and today, grisly death caused by cars and planes — to name two common wonders of technology — inspire legends of noises, lights, and curses that remain at the spots of death. Youths cut down prematurely by death, especially, return to continue their journeys. A commonly heard story that takes many forms is of a girl going to a party (or home) who is picked up by a driver. But when the driver arrives at the girl's destination, she disappears, and the driver later discovers that she had died years before on that night. This story is given legendary status by being attached to a girl's name, a specific place, a recent place in time, or a real-life source (such as a friend of a friend).

To be sure, ghost legends raise a finger of mystery and caution as they bring reality into question, and often the telling of ghost legends serves to provide transcendent moral lessons. Many spiritual "ladies in white," particularly, walk the earth in story to remind others of the heartbreak of disregarding the maternal commitment to children, the misery that can result when couples disregard parents' wishes, or the anguish of love forsaken.

1a. There was this man, a little man, he was supposed to have his head chopped off by a jealous lover or evil men. And they never found out why they done it. And a lot of people have seen him roaming around looking for his head. And no one knows how to figure it out.

1b. Out around the bridge, there was a lady whose husband cut off her head. And this lady came back from the dead and found a lantern with a red light, and she's holding the light looking for her head. They say they've taken wire around the lantern and there is nothing holding it up.

2. This man and lady were riding down the street, this old couple, and they had a car wreck in this one place, and the lady turned into a white ghost. And then about three days later this teenager was riding down the street, and he had an accident in the same place and killed himself. And the next night it happened at the same time, and everything. And the next night it happened at the same time again. And then, this next night, my friend's mother, she was riding down the street, and she saw á streak of white go across the street.

3a. The street in front of a school had not been covered with tar or cement. It was a dirt and gravel road. Every time you drove over it, the gravel would fly up and hit under your car. One gloomy, muddy day, a man was carelessly driving down this road. He had not noticed this sweet little girl running across the street just as he was passing her, when her coat got caught on his car's front bumper. He had heard a thumping noise, but he thought it was just the gravel. He had driven a couple blocks when some people were waving him down. He stopped. He realized when he saw the little girl that it wasn't the gravel knocking from under car, it was the little girl pounding on his car to tell him to stop, that he was dragging her. And from this day, they say, that the people who know of this will not drive across that gravel road, because if they do the spirit of the little girl returns and pounds from under your car.

3b. One day a little boy was playing near the street. He was sitting on the curb near a car. The little boy was playing with something he found in the street and did not hear a lady get in the car. She was taking off when the little boy started to knock for the lady to stop but she didn't and drove off with his hand stuck to the car. Beware, because in Warren (or some other city), Knock-Knock Street is still around. Watch out when you drive over it, you may hear a knock.

4. There was a girl who hung around with a group of kids. They were all talking about this graveyard outside of town that was real spooky. She said she wasn't afraid and to prove it she would go out and stick a knife in one of the tombstones. She got out there and stuck the knife in and when she turned to get up, she thought a ghost or something was holding her and she died of fright. The next morning, when they found her, they found the knife stuck in the edge of her skirt.

5. One night a man who lived in the country was walking back from town. The way he went led him by a graveyard. As he was walking by the graveyard, he noticed a man sitting on a tombstone. The man got up and walked toward him. As he got closer, he saw that it was an old friend of his. He invited the friend to come home with him and have a drink of tea. The two men started walking, and as soon as they walked, they talked of old times. When they got home and started to drink tea, they lost track of time because they were talking and drinking tea until the first streak of dawn had appeared. When the friend noticed that it was the morning, he got up and left. After the man had left, the other man realized that the friend he was just talking to had been dead for five years.

6a. There was a girl walking to a party. She was wearing a pretty dress. And two boys picked her up. And after the party, they took her home. While she was riding, she said she was cold so the boy gave her his coat to wear. When they dropped her off, she forgot to give him back his coat. So the next day, the boys went back to get his coat. They asked the people if the girl with this kind of dress lived here. They said that that was their daughter and she was killed five years ago in an automobile accident while on the way to a party. So the boys went to the graveyard nearby and found the grave and on the grave was his coat.

6b. There was this man driving down the road, and he saw this girl, and she wanted a ride. So he asked her where she lived. And she told him where she lived. And so, he was driving down the road, and she had on this purple dress and also a white hat. And then, they crossed this cemetery. And all of a sudden, she disappeared. Only she left her hat on the seat. So he went to the house where she said it was and knocked on the door. And some lady answered, and he asked if a girl with a purple dress lived there. And she goes, "No, because she's been dead for years."

7. A young couple in their late teens or early twenties were in love and wanted to get married, but neither of the two parents would permit them to get married. On a cool and rainy night the two decided to run off and get married. The young couple's travels away from home brought them to the Buckhorn Mountain, on which there is a very steep and winding road that is known for its extensive accidents. Traveling down the mountain on a very dark and foggy night caused them to lose control of their car and crash into the valley below, killing them both. After the crash the boy's body was the only one found; the girl's body was missing and never found. The girl is now believed to haunt the mountain on dark and rainy nights in her white wedding dress that she never got to wear.

8. There was this house and it was haunted. It really was. This is why. There was a girl lived there with her mother and dad. Well she had a boyfriend and he wanted to marry her but she would not. So one night he went and knocked on her door. Her mother came out and he asked for her. So she came to the door. Well this boy just took and cut her head off with a big knife. Well ever after that this girl would appear at night carrying her head in her hands out of the door where he killed her. No one will move in that house now. It has been empty for years.

9a. There is a white lady, a lady in white, and at night you can sometimes hear her crying. She cried because when her kids were born she drowned them; there were four of them. God sent her back to pick up every single kid. Today she goes around looking in every mud puddle looking for her kids. God told her that she couldn't come back to heaven until she picked up her kids.

9b. One time there was a girl she was lonesome because she killed her kids and her husband. Every night she would sit on a gate and would start crying for her kids and husband. Sometimes when you're walking at night you can see the white woman. She doesn't have no face. When you see her, she disappears.

HORROR LEGENDS OF KILLERS AND CARS

Automobiles have an allure for children. They promise mobility and independence, and they symbolize maturity and arrival into society. But with these temptations come dangers, and the dangers escalate, legends emphasize, when young couples stray from home. These legends of parking couples, then, caution young listeners, at the same time that they anticipate the independence of adolescence. Related to such stories are legends about vulnerable women behind the wheel, who are beset by killers hiding in the back seat or dressed as old ladies, but are rescued by police or another driver. These legends, too, advise caution, with a stress on the special vigilance needed by independent women.

10. There was this boy and this girl. They were driving along this back country road. They were lovers trying to find a place where no one would see them kissing. Pretty soon the boy's red Corvette broke down. They waited for awhile but no one came along so the boy said he would go get some help. He told the girl to crawl into the back seat, get down on the floor so no one could see her, and lock all the doors. The boy was gone a real long time and the girl was beginning to wonder what had happened when she heard a scratching noise on top of the car. She thought it was only a branch from the tree at the side of the road. Pretty soon she heard a "drip — drip — drip." She looked out the window and saw a car coming which had its headlights on. A policeman got out of the other car and told the girl to come in with him and not to look back. But she did and saw her boyfriend hanging from a tree by the car with his head cut off.

11a. One night two teenagers were up in the canyon sitting on the grass listening to the car stereo when an announcement came on. It said that a very dangerous murderer had just been seen in the canyon. The murderer, on foot, had a very distinguishing feature — his right hand was a very sharp hook. He was wanted in many states for using that hook to kill people. One of the teenagers wasn't very concerned. "He's probably miles away," he told the girl, but she was still too nervous and insisted they go. She was laughing at herself for being so silly when they pulled into her driveway. She said goodnight and got out of the car. Suddenly, she felt something fall on her foot. She slowly looked down to see a bloody hook.

11b. There was a guy and a girl, and they were out on a date. They were having a great time. Then they drove into the country to park. They had the radio on. A special broadcast came over the radio, and it said that a mad killer escaped from prison. He had been seen in that area. You could recognize him by a hook on one hand. They got scared, so they drove home. The guy stopped at the girl's house and walked around to the girl's car door to let her out. There on the handle was a hook with blood dripping off of it.

12. One dark night, a girl walked quickly to her car. She had worked late, and it was just about 1:00 a.m. She quickly got in the car, started it, and pulled away from her reserved parking place. Not too many people were out that late, she noticed, as the only car she could see was the one behind her. Suddenly, she was nearly blinded as the car behind her flashed their brights in her mirror. She swerved slightly but was fine. Slowly, the car behind crept up behind her and flashed his brights again. This kept up all the way home. By the time she finally did reach home, she was terrified! She was out of her car almost before it stopped. She was in her house with the door locked no more than a moment when she heard a voice through the door tell her to call the police. When the police arrived, they found the man waiting outside her house. He led them to her car where they found a wanted murderer with a long steel dagger in his hand. The murderer was quickly arrested and the man explained. "I was driving along behind the car when I saw something move in the back seat. At first, I thought it was a kid or a dog, but it moved so slowly. It was strange. I made out a head, then an arm, then I saw something in the hand as it was brought slowly up. Suddenly, I realized what was happening and did the first thing I could think of. I flashed my brights to warn her. I saw the figure quickly disappear. I followed the car home and flashed my brights each time I saw the figure. After she ran in the house, I told her to call the police and then waited to make sure the figure didn't try to go anywhere. I'm glad things worked out."

13. A girl was going to get some groceries. She parked far away because she wanted to protect her new car. She locked the doors and went inside. She got her groceries, came outside and looked towards her car. She thought she saw a shadow in her car. Walking closer, she noticed a little old lady sitting in her back seat. As she approached the car, she asked the lady, "What are you doing in my car?" "I've been walking so long, and my feet are very tired. Would you be so kind as to drive me home? I just live up the street." The girl thought, "Well, sure, I could do this for this poor old lady," when suddenly she remembered that she had locked her car doors, and there was no way she could have gotten in there. Remembering this, she replied, "Sure, just a minute. I forgot my keys. Let me go get them. I'll be right back, and then I'll give you a ride home." She went into the store and got the store's security men. They came out, but the little old lady was gone! After searching her car, they found a hatchet in her back seat. Later on, she found about a man who was supposed to have been wanted in California for murder believed to be dressed up like a little old lady.

HORROR LEGENDS OF BEING LEFT ALONE

For many children, the first jobs they receive are as babysitters. To work and make money is a sign of maturity and a status symbol, but the fears of being alone in a house at night with the responsibility of watching infants can weigh heavily on young babysitters. A host of legends revolves around the babysitting experience and the dangers that exist. The stories serve to remind youngsters about their responsibility. "Check the children," one popular story states, as the baby-sitter prepares to raid the refrigerator or watch television. Sitters told of the "worst possible scenario" found in these legends either are persuaded to keep on their guard or reminded that the problems on the job that they inevitably face, which threaten to unnerve them, actually pale by comparison.

When the story is not about babysitting, it still appears to focus on a teenage girl alone in a house. The scene shifts from someone else's house to her own. The story reminds listeners that as they age, they are more frequently left on their own or in charge of the house. But with this independence comes dangers worth watching out for. A lingering message is not to take things for granted. The harsh outside world becomes confused with the tranquil domesticity of childhood in the story's use of a human attacker who imitates the faithful dog.

14a. There was a girl who had a dog that would lie under her bed. Whenever she wanted to know if everything was okay, she would put her hand under the bed. If the dog licked her hand, that meant everything was all right. One night the girl was home all alone, and she was in bed. She heard a noise like a dog panting. She put her hand under the bed and the dog licked it. Later that night she wanted to get something to eat. She went down to the kitchen. When she got to the kitchen she heard, "Drip, drip, drip." She went over to the sink but the tap wasn't dripping. In the sink, though, there was a bloody knife. After she saw the knife, she backed up and backed into the fridge. Again she heard, "Drip, drip, drip." She opened the fridge door and out swung her butchered dog. On the dog there was a note that said, "Humans can lick, too."

14b. A girl was babysitting the three children of her neighbors. Before the mom left, she told her to keep the doors locked and the family dog close to her all the time they were gone. The dog would protect her and lick her hand from his regular spot behind the couch. The babysitter put the three little children to bed, went to the kitchen to get a snack, and returned to the living room to watch TV. She then noticed that the back door had been blown open which scared her because she thought the mom had locked her in. Nothing seemed out of the ordinary so she went back to wait for the kids' parents. Then the phone rang. A man on the other end said, "You better go check the kids." She thought it was a prank call, but she checked to see if the guard dog was still with her to protect her. He was. The call came three more times, and finally, the girl decided to check the kids. When she reached the top of the stairs, there were the three children mutilated, the dog was butchered, and a bloody axe was there beside them. When she ran downstairs to call the police, "Humans can lick, too" was written in blood on the glass coffee table right in front of where she had been sitting. The murderer had been licking her hand ever since she had gone to the kitchen to get her snack.

15a. There was a girl who was babysitting and she had just put all the children to bed. She was sitting on the couch watching television and the phone rang. She answered it and a man said, "Check the children." The babysitter hung up the phone. She was scared but thought the call was just a prank. The phone rang again and a man's voice said, "Check the children." The babysitter hung up the phone again and went back to watching television. Soon the phone rang again and for the third time the man said, "Check the children." This time she decided to check on the children. She climbed up the stairs. At the top of the staircase all the children were lined up. Each of the children had been hit several times with the blade of an ax.

15b. There was a babysitter one night and she was babysitting in a two-story house. It was about 11:30 p.m. and the baby was sleeping and the phone rang. She picked it up and some guy was breathing real hard and then he hung up. The guy called about ten minutes later and he said that he was going to kill her so she ignored the call. About a half-hour later the guy called again and said that she was going to die that night. The girl called the operator and told her what happened. The operator told her to keep him on the phone as long as possible. So he called back and said that he was going to kill her. The operator called and told her it was a crazy man calling from upstairs and told her to get right out of the house.

15c. There's this babysitter and the parents leave and she puts the kids to bed. And she turned the TV on and she got this phone call and she hears this guy and the guy goes, "You just turned the TV on." And she is sitting there and says, "What is this, what is this." And she hangs up real quick, you know, and she's really scared because she thinks someone's looking in the window. So she shuts the drapes and she gets this other phone call and the guy goes, "You just shut the drapes." And she hangs up and she's getting really scared and so she calls the operator and she goes, "Can you please trace this phone call, because someone keeps calling me up and telling me what I've been doing after I've done it." And the operator said, "Well you do something that will make him call again, and I'll try and trace the line." And so she throws a newspaper across the room and she gets this phone call, "You just threw the newspaper across the room." And the guy has to be on a certain amount of time for them to trace it. And so she keeps on saying, "Who are you? What are you doing, and why are you doing this to me?" And he just laughed and hung up, and it's about five minutes later and the operator calls up and says, "Lady, you'd better get out of your house, because these calls are coming from your upstairs phone." And then the police came over and they found all the kids upstairs with their throats cut.

CAMP LEGENDS

Summer camps are usually located in rustic, often isolated settings. For many, the camp presents a first-time experience with a strange environment of woods, lakes, and mountains to fathom. Away from the restrictions of parents and teachers, and far outnumbering counselors, children at the camps at the same time often feel a streak of independence and mischief. Almost every camp responds to these conditions with a share of stories that speaks about figures who lurk outside the camp and keep mischievous campers in line. Campers meanwhile use the stories as well to comment on the fate of evil counselors.

16. There's this man and he goes around, and he's kind of loony, and whenever people go on campouts and stuff that are far away from, like, civilization, if he's around there, he'll go up and the person that's the farthest away from all the rest of the people, he chops their head off. And so, one of the counselors at camp was out on a camping trip. He had a couple boys out and there was this one kid that got mad at the rest, so he slept about thirty feet away and the next morning they woke up and his head had been chopped off.

17a. Three-fingered Willy got his name by being buried alive while in some sort of trance or fit. Upon awakening he found himself in a coffin underground and in frenzied fear began to scratch away at the coffin lid. In digging his way out, he wore away all but three fingers of one hand. Following his escape, he roamed the woods near the Y camp. He catches campers who wander away from where they should be, misbehave, make noise after taps, and so on.

17b. There was this mean old counselor, I mean really terrible to the kids. The kids wanted to get even. One night when everyone was camping, he was escort counselor, they all ganged up on him when he was sleeping and threw him over the cliff. He lost all the fingers on his left hand and all but three on his right hand. A country doctor saved him. The bang on his head affected him so that he grew to be ten feet tall and the hair on his body grew long and red. He vowed vengeance on all little campers.

17c. A counselor who was not liked went on a date [and] had just taken his date home. There was a full moon and it was a Saturday night about 3:00 a.m. He fell asleep in his car on a ridge because he was tired. Five or six boys saw his car and decided to push the car over the cliff. Willy was able to escape and swim across the lake. He went through the woods for two miles and found a doctor in the vicinity. Willy had lost his left hand in the accident, and only a stub remained. He had just three fingers on his right hand, no thumb or little finger. Two years passed. People had seen a man in the woods with a hook wandering around. A boy disappeared from camp, never to be found. The same thing happened the next year. The children always disappeared on a moonlit night. The losses were attributed to Three-fingered Willy.

18. Did you ever hear about Bloody Joe? It's an old Girl Scout legend.

It's about when, I forget what camp it was, but the Girl Scouts used to go there for the summertime. They used to stay in this one cabin, and they had to wear stockings. And this man used to hang around at night. He used to get the stockings and he used to choke them with it and all the blood used to be on the stockings. And after that he used to throw the stockings away and the girls disappeared. And then another troop went and the same thing happened to them. And then finally, the last troop went, and they didn't go into that cabin anymore, but they still heard screams from Bloody Joe.

PLAYFUL HORROR TALES

The ubiquity of the horror legend among children is underscored by playful violations and manipulations of its form. These tales often appear more formulaic than the local ghost legends, although they can be filled with minute details. They take place in the institutional setting of large hotels or the haven of home and feature scary figures that come closer and closer, frightening people on the way. The suspense of the scary tale is often broken with a touch of humor by twisting the ending. Sharp contrasts to the supernatural of ghostly legends are ending lines from the mundane reality of television commercials ("Ivory Soap floats!"), matter-of-fact sayings ("I told you you'd be sorry"), or children's games ("Tag, you're it"). In many of the stories, the child ends up victorious over the scary figure after the failure of older family members.

Some of the other stories in this section can be told as seriously scary tales, but in those given below the teller plays on the suspense created by the approach of the scary figure in the story by reaching out and grabbing the listener. The telling serves then as a kind of prank, for it plays upon the fear of the listener; it makes the listener feel foolish and immature, at least compared to the teller.

19. There was this man who came into the hotel and he said to the clerk, "I want a room," and clerk said, "The only room we have is room 11. One man has already been killed there." The man said, "I'll take it." That night when he went to bed he heard a ghost call, "I am the ghost of the bloody fingers," and he killed the man. The next morning a lady came in and asked for a room. The clerk said, "The only room we have is room 11. Two men have already been killed there." The lady said, "I'll take it." That night when she went to bed she heard a ghost call, "I am the ghost of the bloody fingers," and he killed the lady. The next morning a boy came in and asked for a room. The clerk said, "The only room we have is room 11. Two men and a lady have already been killed there." The boy said, "I'll take it." That night he heard the ghost call, "I am the ghost of the bloody fingers." Then the boy said, "You'd better get a Band-aid then."

20. There were these three people and the one guy went up to the hotel manager and said, "I want a room." The hotel man said, "It's haunted." He said, "It's okay." The guy went and saw a dollar on the table and he heard this noise saying, "I'm the ghost of Mable Wable and that dollar belongs on the table." So he jumps out the window and dies. The next guy goes and says, "I'd like a room." "But it's haunted," the guy says, and he says, "I don't care." He saw a dollar on the table and heard a noise, "I'm the ghost of Mable Wable and that dollar belongs on the table." And he jumps out the window and dies. The next guy goes to the hotel manager and says, "I'd like a hotel room." The hotel manager says, "Okay, but two people have been killed in it because it's haunted." He goes, "I don't care." So he goes upstairs and sees a dollar on the table and then he hears this noise, "I'm the ghost of Mable Wable and that dollar belongs on the table." And the guy goes, "Shut up because I'm the ghost of Davey Crockett and that dollar there belongs in my pocket."

21a. Once there was a hotel and these three men came. They asked for a room. The clerk said, "There's one room and it is haunted." The men said, "We'll take it," and they did. One man went up in the room and heard, "Row, row your boat gently down the stream." He jumped out the window. The other man came up and he heard, "Row, row your boat gently down the stream." He jumped out the window. The other man came up in the room. He heard, "Row, row your boat gently down the stream." He jumped out the window. Then the maid came in because she had left her bucket in the room. There were three ants in the bucket with water in it. They were sitting on a toothpick singing.

21b. This lady, she comes walking into this place to this motel, and she goes, "I'd like a room." And he goes, "There's no more rooms left except this haunted one." And she goes, "I'll take it." So she goes up there and she hears, "If this log tips over, we'll all fall off." And she goes, "Where is it coming from?" It goes, "If this log tips over, we'll all fall off; if this log tips over, we'll all fall off." The lady says, "If I hear that one more time, I'm going to jump out the window." And it goes, "If this log tips over, we'll all fall off." And so, she jumps out the window. Then, this guy with a motorcycle comes in and goes, "I'd like to rent a room." He goes, "The only one left is the haunted one." And the guy goes, "I'll take it." He goes in the room and hears, "If this log tips over, we'll all fall off." And then he hears it again: "If this log tips over, we'll all fall off." He goes, "If I hear this one more time, I'm going to jump out the window." And so he jumps out the window. And then, this kid comes and goes, "I'd like to rent a room." "All I got is a haunted one." "That's all right, I'll take it." And he hears, "If this log tips over, we'll all fall off." And he hears it again: "If this log tips over, we'll all fall off." And so he goes into the bathroom and finds out that it's ants on a piece of poop.

22. There was this family, and this mother heard that a ghost was back in the back yard with a black eye. And the ghost was saying, "I'm the one with the black eye." And so she got so scared, she ran into the house and hid under the sofa. Then the father went outside to see what was the matter with her. So he didn't see her, and he heard the ghost saying, "I'm the ghost with the one black eye." And the father got so frightened that he hid behind the chair. Then the brother came outside to see what father was mad about. And so, he went outside and he heard the ghost saying, "I'm the ghost with the one black eye." And he was so frightened he ran under the sofa. And there was this little tiny girl about three or four, and she went outside to pick some flowers for her mom. So she heard the ghost saying, "I'm the ghost with the one black eye." And she said, "If you don't shut up, you'll be the ghost with the *two* black eyes."

23. There was a family of four living in a house. They heard a noise in the closet which they couldn't figure out. The mother went into the big closet and heard, "I got you where I want you, now I'm going to eat you." So she ran out of the house. Then the father went in and heard the same words. So he also ran from the house. Then the oldest child went into the closet and also heard the same words. He turned on the light and saw his little brother sitting in the corner with a booger.

24. There was this old lady and her daughter died in a car accident. And so, there is this coffin. And the old lady moved into her house. And at night she went to bed on the first floor and she woke up at the sound of "It flooooaats, it flooooaats, it flooooaats." At first she just ignored it and so she went to the second floor and she hears something go, "It

156

flooooaaats." So she goes to the third floor and she gets tired of the sound, you know. And so, something goes, "It floooooaats." Now she is really disgusted with it, and at the fourth floor, the last floor, she's so tired of it, and she just lays in bed and all of a sudden it goes, "It flooooaats." And so she wakes up and says, "What floats?" "It floats." And she says again, "What floats?" and she hears, "Ivory soap floats!"

25. There was this drunken sailor who, when he was walking home one night, heard this bumping noise behind him. He looked behind, and saw a white coffin bumping along down the road after him. Immediately, he became sober from fright and ran into his house. He locked the door. But the coffin bounced up on the porch, waited a few seconds, then, with a terrible crash, burst through the door. The man ran up the stairs, grabbed a chair, and threw it at the coffin. Something knocked it away, and it broke into a thousand pieces. Then the coffin started up the stairs: one step, two steps, three steps, more. Somehow the sailor knew that if it got all the way up, he would be doomed! Suddenly he got an idea. He ran into his bedroom, grabbed a small box, and ran back to the steps. He took out a cough drop, threw it at the coffin, and the coffin stopped.

26. There's this old house that no one wanted to live in because everybody that lived there was afraid. Because every night, about twelve midnight, there would be a rapping in the house that would echo all through the walls, and they couldn't sleep. Then no one would ever go into the house because of the rapping. Everybody that moved in there was afraid. Finally, someone wanted to investigate it. And so they went through all the doors. He checked all the woodwork and finally he came to a small closet. No one noticed it before. And there, he opened the door, really stiff, creeped over slowly, and inside *(pause),* he found *(pause)* a roll of brown wrapping paper!

27. There's this guy, and he's in love with this girl, and so they got married. This lady always wore this velvet ribbon around her neck. And every day and every night, the man would tell her to take off that ribbon. One night, he said it once more. And she said, "If I take it off you'll be very sorry." And that night, he was too curious to see it again. So he tiptoed to her bed and peeked over and snipped off the velvet ribbon. Off fell the velvet ribbon and off came her head. It rolled into the moonlight, and it yelled out, "I told you you'd be sorry!"

28. There was this guy and this lady, and they were laying in bed sleeping and this lady had a golden arm. And she always said the guy promised he wouldn't take the golden arm when she died. And the night she died it was raining and they buried her. And then the next night it was really raining, and he had an umbrella and all this junk, all these tools to dig with and everything. And so he dug the hole and got the lady and took the golden arm. Then when he got home, he put it under his pillow because it was really cold. And then when he was sleeping, he heard something. And then he heard these footsteps! Then all of a sudden he saw this lady and she said "I got ya!" *(teller grabs listener)*. Then the guy died.

29. This lady gave this boy named Johnny a dollar to go to the store to get some liver. But he spent it on something else before he got the liver, and he had to bring this lady her liver. So he saw this graveyard right next to the store. So he unburied a guy, and he got the guy's liver and brought it to the lady. The lady said, "This is real good liver." But that night they heard, "I want my liver back, I want my liver back, I want my liver back." Then they heard, "I'm on your first step, I want my liver back, I want my liver back, I want my liver back." Then "I'm on your porch, I want my liver back, I want my liver back. I'm in your living room, I want my liver back, I want my liver back. I'm in the bedroom, I want my liver back, I want my liver back" *(teller grabs listener in abdomen)*.

30. Once there was a little girl picking big ripe berries and she looked down and saw this ugly thing and it was a hairy toe. She picked up the hairy toe and she took it and set it in her room by her bed. She thought it was good luck. In the middle of the night she heard this "I want my hairy toe." Then she heard it in the courtyard, "I want my hairy toe." It was at the door. Then she heard it again and it was under her bed. And then she started screaming. Then it came up to her and it said, "I want my hairy toe" *(teller grabs listener's foot)*. Then he strangled her and she died.

31. There was this guy who owned a creepy house with 140 rooms and he also had a purple ape that weighed 999 pounds. He was 100 inches tall, 99 inches wide. And one day this guy went and bragged and bragged to his friends about this ape. And all of his friends ignored him except one and he said the only way they wouldn't ignore him is if he could see this ape. Anyway this friend went to this guy's house to see this ape and he went to this ape's room and the ape started chasing the guy all through every single room and the guy got very tired. So he sat down to rest by a table between two rooms and the ape said, "Tag, you're it" *(teller tags listener)*.

CHAPTER EIGHT

"Heavy, Heavy, Hangs Over Thy Head": Beliefs and Customs

TO CHILDREN, LIFE is full of mysteries. Childhood is a time of questioning and wondering. It is a time of testing the real and unreal, of finding one's place between the realms of nature and society and between the natural and the supernatural. Children call upon a host of beliefs and customs to make their way through an uncertain world. Many beliefs derive from parents and relatives who, realizing children's impressionability, plant ideas such as "If you play with matches, you'll wet the bed." There is also a store of popular tradition that children inherit and often test: opening up an umbrella in a house is bad luck, thirteen is an unlucky number. Beliefs about luck and signs are commonly shared among children and sorted out by the stories that children have to tell about their experiences.

The power of experience to interpret belief becomes ritualized in various customs familiar to children. The future holds many mysteries for those who view so much of their lives in front of them. Adding to their anxiety about the future are the tough questions asked by adults, like "What will you be when you grow up?" and "Who will you marry?" Playing with, as well as predicting, the future is the basis of several customs which divine the spouse one will have. And many others provide the child with "wishes" for the future. This is not to say that children expect these outcomes with certainty, but rather that the customs serve to focus their attention on roles expected of them and experiences that lie ahead.

Belief, custom, and experience come dramatically together in popular childhood experiments with raising spirits. Childhood versions of séances are among the typical activities of slumber parties and camp outings. Children, told of dangers and eerie sights in the dark, test their ability to control some of the forces beyond the natural world. "Concentrate! Concentrate!" is the order as children explore other-worldliness. They combine their spiritual energies to levitate someone among them and call on the dead to speak to them. One favorite spirit to call on is the legendary Mary Worth, or Mary Wolf, Mary Whales, Mary Walker, or Bloody Mary. Again challenging every-day beliefs, this custom requires children to recite "I believe in you" or else face dire consequences. These activities have a sense of play about them, to be sure, but tucked within them is serious questioning and exploration. There is a quest for the powers that lie within the child and beyond the child's immediate experience.

Often less spiritual in nature, but nonetheless focusing customary attention on the child, are rituals surrounding holidays. Children have great expectations of birthdays, Halloween, and Christmas in America, for they are filled with the exuberance of youth and the thrill of consumption. They are times when the child is at the center of atten-tion among other children, and gets to act out cultural priorities of her or his world. The small circles of children's culture also are acted out in private rituals unrelated to national holidays. Being stuck in the back seat of a car looking out on traffic, listening at dinner to two persons saying the same thing simultaneously, breaking the wishbone of a turkey — all these occasions offer children a chance to express themselves.

As children's culture stresses the goal of belonging and maturation, we find that belief and custom enter into several initiations. Children often seek the distinction of being part of an exclusive group, and submit to initiation customs which call upon them to show their matu-rity, courage, and self-control among those dangers and eerie sights of the dark. On occasion, initiations such as "snipe hunts" take the form of pranks played on unsuspecting campers or chums. They are reminders of the victims' novice status as well as their impression-ability — an impressionability associated with their willingness to take direction blindly from authority figures such as parents. So the lesson involved is for children to be more self-aware and self-assured, as befits people breaking away from home. It is a lesson that they will probably pass on one day when they are in the position of administer-ing the initiation.

The unknown, the future, society, then "heavy, heavy hangs" over children's heads, as their birthday ritual professes. The line is chanted by a gift-bearer with the present held above the birthday child's head out of his or her view. The child guesses the type of present offered or the person making the offering. In effect, the child realizes that the world and its rewards are uncertain but not unfathomable. With much that is out of children's sight in their world, beliefs and customs provide them with awareness, and serve as a guide to some of their experience.

BELIEFS

Beliefs are expressed in various ways — in legends, gestures, and speech. The beliefs found here are expressions of speech that children recounted as consequences of actions (step on a crack and you break your mother's back), predictive signs (your hand itches), preventative beliefs (if you burn hair off your comb, then you won't go crazy), signifiers of luck (it is good luck to carry a rabbit's foot), customary actions (lift your feet when someone tells a lie), and cures (to cure hiccups, drink from the wrong side of the cup). In the child's world, they can be guides to behavior, propositions to be tested, or notions to be recognized.

1. Step on the line, break your spine.
Step on a crack, break your mother's back.
Step on a crack, break the devil's back.
Step on a line, you look like Frankenstein.
Step on a line, your mom drinks wine.
Step on a line, break your father's spine.

2. If your hand itches, you're getting some money.
If your nose itches, someone is coming.
If your foot itches, you're going on a trip.
If your right ear burns, someone is talking good about you.
If your left ear burns, someone is speaking ill of you.

3. It is bad luck to open an umbrella in the house.
It is bad luck if a black cat crosses your path; turn around three times to
    ward off the bad luck.
It is bad luck to sneeze with food in your mouth.
It is bad luck to spill salt; throw some salt over your left shoulder to
    ward off the bad luck.
It is bad luck to walk under a ladder.
It is bad luck to wash clothes on New Year's.
If you break a mirror, you'll have seven years of bad luck.

4. It is good luck to keep a penny in your shoe.
It is good luck to find a penny on the ground.

It is good luck to find a four-leaf clover.

It is good luck to carry a rabbit's foot.

If you see a ladybug, and punch the person beside you, it is good luck.

For good luck, eat black-eyed peas on New Year's.

For good luck, eat sauerkraut and pork on New Year's.

5. If you play with matches, you will wet the bed.

If you go to bed singing, you will wake up crying.

If you let any limb of your body hang over the edge of your bed past midnight, the hairy hand will get you.

If you sit in a chair the same color of one a girl sits in, it means you're in love.

If you wear green on Thursday, you're queer.

If you cut your hair during a full moon, it will grow fast.

If you remove hair from a brush or comb and burn it, you won't go crazy.

6. Lift your feet off the ground when someone tells a lie.

While riding in a car, you must lift both feet off the floor while crossing a railroad track, or you will lose your friend.

7. To cure hiccups, hold your breath and swallow three times.

To cure hiccups, swallow three times and drink some water.

To cure hiccups, hold your breath and count to ten and have someone say "boo!"

To cure hiccups, drink from the wrong side of the cup.

To get rid of warts, on May 1, before talking to anybody, wash your face in the morning dew.

To get rid of warts, steal your mother's dishrag and bury it in the garden.

DIVINATIONS

Many customs revolve around foretelling the future, and girls, especially, possess ways of predicting their future husbands or offspring. Several customs call for taking plants and fruits to accomplish the divinatory task and others attach magic to the coincidence of letters in names.

8. You can find out the initial of the boy you will marry if you take an apple and repeat the alphabet giving the stem of the apple a turn with each letter. The letter the stem of the apple came loose on was the initial of the boy you will marry.

9. It is believed that if you can peel a complete apple with the skin in one piece and throw it over your shoulder, it will fall in the shape of the initial of your future husband's name.

10. To find out if a certain boy loves you, you take a straw and press with two fingers from one direction, saying "Loves me." And then use two fingers from the other direction, saying "Loves me not," and continue to the end of the straw. The last statement repeated will tell you if he loves you or not.

11. To find out how a certain person feels about you, repeat the phrase "He loves me, he loves me not" as you pluck the petals of a daisy. If you take the gold center from the daisy and throw it up in the air, the number of pieces that fall on the back of your hand as you hold it out tells the number of children that you will have.

12. If a person blows on a dandelion after it has gone to seed, she will know how many children she will have by the number of seeds left on the stem.

13. To find out what the future with a boy will be, write your name and the boy's name one on top of each other. Cross out all the letters that appear in both names. With the remaining letters, you say "Love, hate, marriage" repeatedly, one letter per word. What you end on will be what your future will be.

14. To find out how a boy feels about you, write your full name and a boy's full name that you like, and then you write T-R-U-E L-O-V-E A-L-W-A-Y-S A-N-D F-O-R-E-V-E-R. Count the number of letters from your names that match the letters in the list of letters from "True Love Always and Forever." Add them up and you'll get the probability of the two of you getting married.

15. If it is raining while the sun is shining, pick up a rock and look under it. You will find out what color of hair your husband is going to have.

SÉANCES

Wherever darkness lurks — at a slumber party, in the cellar, in the attic, or at a campout — children probe the spirits. These are not séances sanctioned by spiritualists, but rather an interpretation traditionally made by pre-adolescents and adolescents, which usually consists of lighting a candle, holding hands, chanting, and above all, concentrating. Testing their powers, participants levitate someone or call the spirits in to talk to them. Then they generally relate stories about the séance to others, inviting commentary on the experience.

16. There are some things you should know about doing a séance. It only works if it's all girls or all boys; it won't work if you mix them together. It also will only work if they're all virgins. And everyone has to believe in it, or else it won't work. You light a candle and four or five or six kids gather around it in a circle. Everyone holds hands. To warm up, someone says, "I'm concentrating, I'm concentrating." That person is the medium, she's the head of the séance, but it can be anyone in the group. That person leads it and asks all the questions. If someone else wants to say something, they have to make a signal, because if two people speak at once, that breaks it. If one person doesn't concentrate, that can also break it. You have to really concentrate, close your eyes tight and concentrate. The medium will ask, "Are there any spirits here?" The candle will give the signal. If it flickers up high, that means yes; if it goes low, you have to concentrate more; if it stays the same, ask the question again. Then you ask, "Do you like, or do you want to come in, by door, window, or vent?" If it's by the door, the door will shake; if it's by the vent, you'll feel a draft; if it's by the window the curtains will start blowing. If the candle starts flickering high, the spirits are in; they've come in the candle. Then you can ask questions, like "Can my great-grandma hear me when I talk to her?" You have to ask yes or no questions usually. The candle will give the signal. If it flickers up high, that means yes, if it stays the same, that means no. But if someone gets scared and breaks hands, that'll stop it, and something bad might happen. After ten or fifteen minutes, you should ask, "Are the spirits getting tired or angry?" Because you don't want to get them angry by keeping them. If the candle flickers, you tell the spirit that you're finished: you blow out the candle and break hands. But you have to make sure to blow the candle out first before you break hands. If someone breaks it, and the candle goes out by itself, that's bad luck! The spirits will get angry if you break it, because they'll think you don't want them. That happened once, the candle just went out.

17. We hold séances to talk to ghosts. One activity we would do was levitation. It has a leader and the chorus who chants:

> I think he's dead
> I know he's dead
> He feels dead
> He looks dead
> He looks deád
> He looks dead
> He is dead.

At this point everyone tries to pick the person up using only two fingers. You have to concentrate and it'll work.

18. My friends and I used to have lots of séances. One time my two girlfriends and I had a séance at my house in the bedroom. We were home alone and there were no lights on in the house. I lit a candle and we all went on my king-size bed and held hands. We were calling back Abraham Lincoln and we asked him to give us a sign of his presence. As soon as we said that my bed fell down and my dog started barking like crazy. The only time my dog barks is when there is a stranger in the house. And she was standing by the open door to my bedroom barking. I finally managed to turn on the lights and everything quieted down.

19. One time two of my girlfriends were over and they wanted to have a séance. One of my girlfriends wanted me to get a candle, but my mom didn't let me have one, so we used a flashlight. We went down into my cellar and we sat down. My girlfriend Diane said, "Hold each other's hands and concentrate." So we held each other's hand. Diane started saying, "If there are any spirits answer me." Diane said she heard a voice and it was a girl's voice. Its name was Debbie. Diane said, "Who are you?" It said, "I'm Debbie." My other girlfriend and me didn't hear nothing. Diane said, "Who killed you?" Diane said that Debbie didn't answer and that we weren't concentrating. So we tried it again. It didn't work, so we just stopped.

MARY WORTH RITUALS

Generally known as a girls' tradition common in elementary school, Mary Worth rituals invoke the atmosphere of the seance, but surround that custom in a particular legend. Mary, who has several alternate last names, is a spirit that can be seen in the mirror — if conditions are right, that is. How she died is a subject of much speculation among children, but it usually is described as an unnatural death. Huddled typically in a bathroom with the lights turned off, children insist that they have to really "believe" in her, or else she won't appear. And when she does, well, children offer several versions of what she looks like and what she's liable to do.

20. You can call back the spirit of this wolf-woman. Go into a bathroom with a few people and shut the lights out and close your eyes tight for about ten seconds. Then, open them up and stare into the mirror and say "Mary Wolf" or "I believe in you" slowly about five times. You're supposed to see her in the mirror.

21. You have a mess of kids lock themselves into a small room with a large mirror, usually a bathroom will do the job. Everyone is supposed to look at the mirror and concentrate on Mary Worth. If you want to call her just repeat that you believe in her. If she appears, she comes in the form of a blue light.

22. Mary Worth was a witch who had been burned at the stake. In order to call her you had to go in the bathroom alone at midnight and say "Mary Worth" ten times while looking in the mirror in complete darkness. She was supposed to appear and scratch the mirror while trying to get out.

23. Mary Worth had been an old maid who had died about 50 years ago. She was angry because she never married and as a result she hated everyone, especially little girls. If you went into a dark bathroom and stood in front of the mirror and chanted "I believe in Mary Worth" ten times, her image would appear in the mirror. If there was anyone in the group who did not believe, she would reach out and grab them.

24. Bloody Mary was a character who was murdered in the woods behind Pine Road Elementary School. To call her ghost, girls go in the bathroom and prick their fingers with a pin to draw a drop of blood.

Then they press the two droplets of blood together and say "We believe in Bloody Mary" ten times with their eyes shut. Then upon opening their eyes they look into the bathroom mirror. The image of Bloody Mary's face would appear in the mirror. She was said to have been a young girl with long hair, very pale skin, and blood running down her face from a large cut in her forehead.

INITIATIONS

The honors of membership in a group — especially one that signifies a growth in maturity, a rise in status, or an offer of protection — often involve initiation rituals. In these rituals, initiates are put through an ordeal, and typically taught a lesson about being a member of the group. Common, for example, is the lesson of sticking with the group, of not wandering off. In addition, the rituals often stress the importance of maturity interpreted as fearlessness (especially if other members of the group can be relied upon for help). To hear children tell it, these initiations not surprisingly are especially prevalent in isolated camps.

25. One day a troop of Boy Scouts were initiating some new members. One of the initiates was blindfolded and placed with his head in a guillotine. A noise was made which sounded like the blade of the guillotine being released, and at the same time a wet towel was slapped across the boy's neck. The troop members screamed to make the initiate think that something had gone wrong. The initiate, hearing the screams and feeling the towel, was shocked.

26. There's this legend about the Gullywompus that roams the camp. This legend is told by the older boy scouts to younger, first-year scouts (tenderfoots) at the camp. Older scouts would take some of the tenderfoots out looking for the Gullywompus at the far end of the camp. Older scouts would break up in groups leaving a group of tenderfoots out by themselves without a flashlight. Older scouts would then circle the tenderfoots running through the brush making wild animal sounds. This would scare the tenderfoots causing some to cry. This is when the older scouts would stop and reassure them that everything is all right and that it is just a legend. The Gullywompus is described as a large hairy creature that will get you if you don't watch out.

27. Do you know about the snipe hunt? It's a kind of initiation. The inexperienced and experienced scouts are divided into two groups. The inexperienced (those who don't know what a snipe is) will be sack men and the experienced hunters will be the drivers. Stories of snipes are told before the hunt takes place. The snipe is described as a ground bird that has a white spot on the middle of its back. They make a wonderful pie when you get enough of them. Each snipe is two to three inches long. The key, however, is having a cook who knows how to roast them. On the night of the hunt the sack men are stationed approximately 20 feet apart. This is done to separate and isolate each sack man and to limit noise and talking between members of the hunt. Frequently if the terrain is not accommodating to capturing snipes, fallen logs or rocks are placed to form a large funnel on the ground in front of each sack man. These funnels will direct the snipe into the sacks of the inexperienced sack men. The sack men are cautioned that they must be quiet, but are permitted to click two baseball-sized rocks together to lure in the snipe. This is performed because the clicking noise is similar to that of a male snipe in mating season. The female snipe is much easier to call in and is also known to be the tenderest of meats. A couple of experienced snipe men are stationed on each side of the funnels to prevent escape once the snipes enter the trap. Once the hunt gets under way, after dark, the drivers start driving toward the sack men, never quite making it the entire way. The hunting is so good (encouraged by shouts of "there goes one" and "I got him") that they keep actively after snipes out in front of the funnel area. The experienced scouts sometimes add to their own enjoyment by tying a small white cloth on the end of the stick. This, at night, looks like the white spot on the back of the alleged snipe. The white cloth is pushed in toward the sack, but one of the experienced scouts always manages to club it before it gets into the sack. On the way back to camp, there is always lots of talk about the good hunting and near misses by the sack men. Later, at the campfire, the inexperienced scouts can hardly believe it when the gag is revealed. Of course there are different finales. Sometimes the inexperienced scouts are left to go ahead in the woods, while the experienced scouts drop back, letting the inexperienced scouts think they're lost or alone. The inexperienced scouts were placed in the woods by the experienced scouts with a sack and a small bell. The sack man would tinkle his bell and be ready to capture the snipe as they appeared. After a respectable amount of time when the scouts started getting scared, usually one to one and a half hours, the hunt was cancelled for that evening and the new scouts welcomed into the troop. On one or two hunts flashlights were used to replace the white cloth on a stick. The experienced scouts would flicker their lights when they were sure they had seen or heard a snipe. Todd told of the "Bear in the Woods" that materialized during his most memorable snipe hunt. Todd was an inexperienced scout on this hunt; near the conclusion of the hunt one of the experienced scouts heard a bear noise in the woods. The experienced scout and an adult leader went up the hill to investigate. After a large amount of thrashing around, the adult leader's voice was heard to tell all scouts to get back to camp and lock themselves inside the vehicles. After at least a half of an hour of waiting, which seemed like hours, the adult leader had not returned. About this time one of the experienced scouts announced the presence of the bear in camp, and soon after the vehicle began to rock and the inexperienced scouts began to shake. The rear door to the vehicle was torn open and the adult leader's voice was heard to ask, "I didn't miss midnight snack did I?"

CUSTOMS

Among the private rituals and holiday customs that children practice are those that involve material gain or an expression of aggression. Sometimes, it's mainly a matter of your wish coming true. Some of these activities are localized to the child's family (especially with some Christmas traditions) while others are more national in scope (the tooth fairy, for example). Halloween, especially, encapsulates a host of children's customary traditions. It involves scary storytelling, trick-or-treating for the acquisition of sweet treasures, and pranks often for outlets of a combination of aggression, power, and playfulness. If this is the child's holiday, then Christmas in America is given over to the family as a whole, in which children are given a special place.

28. When you lose a tooth, you put it under your pillow before you go to bed. The tooth fairy comes in the middle of the night, and when you wake up you find money where the tooth was.

29. This is what you say as you are holding onto a wishbone with somebody and preparing to break it. You recite alternate lines:

Needles and

Pins.
Elephants.
Skins.
What goes up the chimney?
Smoke.
May your wish and my wish
Never be broke.

30. Ganie and Neil had a custom when people said the same thing at the dinner table. One person shouted out "jinx," and started to count until the other person said "stop." The person who said "jinx" got to slug the second person who said "stop" as many times as he counted.

31. This is something Ganie's family used to do on long trips. When they saw an ICX (Illinois California Express) truck, they would hit someone and say, "ICX." The ritual developed so that whoever saw the truck would say "ICX, no backs" (in other words, no one can hit me back), and later so that everyone else (Ganie had four or five little brothers and sisters) would answer as quickly as they could, "No givies" (i.e., you can't hit me). The final ritual went:

ICX no backs (attempts to hit someone)!
No givies, no nothings (response of other person).

32. Your friends catch the birthday person and either punch them on the arm, giving them their birthday whacks, or pull their earlobes according to how old they are plus one for good luck. You also get a cake with candles, one for each year of your age, plus one for good luck. You make a wish and then try to blow it out with one breath. If you do it, then your wish will come true.

33. This is a birthday party custom we know. As each present is brought out to be opened, it is held over the birthday person's head (so he can't see who it is from). This rhyme is repeated, and the birthday person makes a wish for the giver for the next year (e.g., "May you get your heart's desire," "May you have a hot romance," etc.):

Heavy, heavy hangs over thy head
What do you wish for this person, with a bump on the head? *(Bang present on person's head.)*

34a. On Halloween, the kids in our neighborhood pull various pranks on friends and neighbors such as soaping windows, corning houses, stealing others' candy, stealing jack-o'-lanterns off various porches, and transplanting them on others. Taking hubcaps was another specialty in which we would exchange these and put them on other vehicles and then apply toothpaste to the car handles.

34b. Around Halloween, we fill a stocking with flour and eggs and then hit others with it. You could also soap up car windows and shaving cream on car windows, and hang things from lamp posts. One prank was to get a friend to stand on one side of a street while you stood on the opposite side from him. As a car approached, you would both bend over and slowly stand up pretending to be pulling a rope taut between the two of you across the road. When the car would come to a screeching halt, you both would run away. This usually took place on "Mischief Night," the night before Halloween. On Halloween, we would go door to door in the neighborhood, and say, "Trick or treat," for which we got candies, nuts, and fruits.

35a. We decorate the tree on the Saturday closest to Dad's birthday (December 16). We leave cookies and milk for Santa Claus and carrots for the reindeer. Everyone opens one present Christmas Eve, and opens the rest on Christmas Day.

35b. On Christmas at our house we get the tree usually two weeks before and we spend those two weeks going berserk! Buying Christmas gifts, wrapping them, and decorating the tree. On Christmas Eve we deliver all the presents to people and we collect ours. We go home and open all the gifts we have so far and we get to stay up late.

35c. I am the youngest of my brother and two sisters. My brother is the second youngest. On Christmas morning, I would be the first one up, being the youngest of course. Before I could go out and open up my presents, I would have to wake up my one sister who was the oldest. She would then go wake up our mom and dad. They would then get their robes on and come out to the living room. After our parents got a cup of coffee, we could finally open our presents. This whole process seemed to take hours to me. If I got up too early (before 6:00 a.m.), my sister would tell me to go back to sleep. A couple of years I set the clocks ahead and almost got away with it.

36. At my house, we usually have two Christmas dinners spread out over a week. Each one is spent with different sides of the family. We decorate our house with a tree, wreaths, and other ornaments. We also pick names out of a box and whoever you pick, you must buy them a gift. Besides that you get gifts from your immediate family.

37. The second day of Christmas, 2 Juledag in Norwegian, is the beginning of the Christmas celebration. The previous two days focus on the immediate family and religion. On the second day, in the afternoon, the normal routine is to visit friends, family, and more distant relatives. Cakes, cookies, and coffee are offered. The night brings out another custom which is performed by the children of the community. This event is called *Julebukk* and is similar to our Halloween. The children get dressed up in different costumes and wear masks so they are not recognized by their neighbors. They walk around and knock on doors. In response, they are invited into houses for cookies and other goodies. The owner of the house tries to guess the identities of the masked paraders. Even if they guess the correct name, the idea is not to answer. The custom is not very satisfying for the adults involved, but the children are quite amused.

38. Hanukkah, usually held in December, is special for Jewish children. Hanukkah is celebrated with games, songs, special foods, and plays. We light the *menorah* (lamp with eight candles), on each day of the eight days, one candle for each day. There's usually a family party. At the party, the children get Hannukah *gelt* (money), usually in coins. The children use this to play with the *dreydl,* a top with Hebrew letters on it. Depending on which letter the top falls on, the spinner does nothing, takes everything in the pot, takes half of what is in the pot, or puts in two coins into the pot. The special foods served are potato *latkes;* they are like pancakes from shredded potatoes fried in oil. You have it with applesauce or sour cream on top. It is common to have riddles and puzzles told at Hanukkah; they are told by adults to the children and sometimes by the children to one another. They might ask: "It has four legs, but it is not an animal. What is it?" The answer is a bed. Riddles are also told on the other special holiday for Jewish children, Purim, usually held in February or March. Children wear costumes to Purim parties, and the costumes are usually of a Biblical character such as Queen Esther or Haman. The special food for this holiday is *Hamantashen,* three-sided pastries with a poppy-seed mixture in the center.

"Tag, You're It!": Nonsinging Games

WHETHER ON THE street or field, children find a way to play. Organizing play is not a simple matter, however, especially if newcomers to the play group are present. But new and old faces will likely unite when a traditional game is offered. "How about Hide and Go Seek?" someone might say, and that normally raises a howling chorus of "Not it." The drama of game begins.

Games bring children together. From the moment the game is organized, social awareness grows, and this expands still more with the addition of rules, boundaries, winners, and losers. Often involving an amount of fantasy, games offer children a chance to pretend for the moment, and to prepare for the future. In games, children learn to organize and legislate themselves. There's also the physical side of games, and especially in the nonsinging variety of game that involves running and chasing, children develop their bodies as well as certain ways of thinking.

Consider the early childhood game of Hide and Go Seek, one of the first and most common folk games that children play. An "it" is chosen who must find the scattered children and bring them back "home." It is a game that can involve a large number of children and can be played almost anywhere. Children especially like to play the game at dusk to add to the challenge, or to delay coming inside the house from outdoor play. But other things happen when the game is played. Under the shield of the game, children have the chance to explore new spaces. They familiarize themselves with their surroundings and develop their instincts. Still, what is the significance of the hiding and the "it"? One possible interpretation is that in early childhood, the "it" often takes on the role of a feared authority figure, yet the children also invite the "it" to chase them, to bring them back "home." In effect, the game plays out attitudes toward a parent. While the children look outward, the "it" looks to bring them back to the boundaries of "home."

As with other forms of folklore, traditional games such as Hide and Go Seek display variation in different locales and among different groups, while showing a consistency over time. What makes them traditional is the method of transmitting the rules. They are learned in customary ways, by demonstration and imitation within a social group, and not by formal or printed instruction. Despite the growing adult regulation of play in school centers and playgrounds, folk games thrive because they invite children's control.

HIDING AND BLINDFOLDING

Even before they can speak, American children engage in the hiding game of Peek-a-Boo. An adult masks a child's face temporarily with a hand, takes it away, and says, "Peek-a-boo, I see you." Children delight in the realization that someone can be there and not be there at the same time, and imitate the adult's actions when their own speech and motor skills allow. Once able to walk and run, children play with this concept in hiding and blindfolding games. In essence, these are the reverse of each other. In most hiding games, the "it" uses sight to search out concealed children. In blindfolding games, the "it" is kept in the dark while seeking out all-seeing children. Hiding games are often played outside and involve running, while blindfolding games adapt to smaller spaces indoors and more often involve walking.

1. Hide and Seek

One of the first games that I can remember playing in Levittown as a small boy was Hide and Go Seek. We played after supper and the game would usually last until after dark or even longer if we didn't have school the next day. When the time came around to deciding who was going to be it, we would usually get the whole group of players together and one of the older kids would say, "Let's play hide and go seek," and that person would usually initiate a counting-out rhyme. We did use "Engine, engine number nine" an awful lot and we also used "Eeny, meeny, miney, moe." When the unlucky person was finally chosen the game would begin. The boundaries would be set by all the streets in the Elderberry Pond section from our street, which was Edgewood Lane, to the swimming pool, which was about four streets away. The home base was always the mailbox in the middle of Edgewood Lane, and if during the game any person hiding could make it back to the base freely without being detected by the "it" person

Hide and Seek — The "it" counting (Harrisburg, Pennsylvania, 1987)

Hide and Seek — The race "home" (Harrisburg, Pennsylvania, 1987)

they would be in free. If the "it" person would give up during the round he could call everyone by saying "Ally Ally in free." Usually a person who was the last person to be "it" on a particular evening would have to be "it" on the next day the game was played if he decided to quit during the game and call everyone in and give up before the game was officially over.

2. Fifty-Two Scatter

Fifty-Two Scatter is like Hide and Seek, in that the rules are pretty much the same and the boundaries are also usually the same. But there is one important difference: in Fifty-two Scatter the person who is "it" has to catch everyone, because if he catches three people for example and there are still three people out, then one of them can run in and say "scatter" and everyone that had been caught is free to go, and the same person would be "it" again.

3. Kick the Can

Kick the Can is a close neighbor to Hide and Seek. The goal is two cans one on top of the other, and the person who is it has to count on his knees while hunched over the cans. If the one who is "it" doesn't catch everyone, then one of those that had not been caught can free those that had been caught. The freeing is accomplished by kicking over the two cans and then running like hell to get to a new hiding place before the person that was "it" can catch you. After the can had been kicked, and the people who had been caught have been set free, the person who is "it" then has to go get the cans, set them up, and count again.

4. Ghost in the Graveyard

In The Ghost in the Graveyard, there is one person who hides and everyone goes running around looking for the person. And after they find the person, they'll go running around trying to chase each other. And then, when the ghost catches someone, then they have to be the ghost that sits in the graveyard.

5. Blindman's Bluff

Blindman's Bluff is one we all know. One child is blindfolded and spun around three times. In the meantime all the children have scattered. The blindfolded child must try to catch someone. If he is successful, then that child becomes "it" and is blindfolded.

6. Marco Polo

In this game, played in the swimming pool, the object is for the "it" to catch another player while blindfolded. More often than not the person merely closes his eyes and promises not to peek. After the "it" has been led to the center, the other players assume a safe position away from "it." At this time, "it," who is trying to locate the other players, calls out "Marco." The players are now required to return the call by responding "Polo," thus giving away their position. If a player is finally caught, he must now assume the role of "it."

CHASING AND TAGGING

Games of tag organize children's running around. But in addition, these games also reveal some attitudes of American children, especially in the identity of the "it." In most American play groups, "it" is an undesirable position, which might be attached to an inferior status or frightening image. Most children want to be members of the larger group; they want to evade the authority of being "it." Another observation to be made is that games of tag are activities that integrate boys and girls. While other games often involve separate play groups by gender, tag literally brings boys and girls in touch with one another. Maybe that's part of the appeal.

7. Freeze Tag

One person is chosen to be "it." The other children run off and the person who is "it" chases them. If the person who is "it" tags a child then that child must freeze where he was tagged. For you to become free again, someone who has not been tagged has to touch you. The game is played in large open areas with usually many children. I usually played the game in my yard. There is a need for plenty of room for the children to scatter and then be chased. This game can continue for a long time and does not have a specific winner.

8. Cross Tag

The "it" must continue chasing his victim until another person crosses between the pursued and the pursuer. At this time, "it" must chase the person who crossed his path. No "safe" is necessary in this game. When a person is touched by "it," he becomes "it" and starts chasing someone else.

9. TV Tag

An "it" is chosen and everyone scatters to avoid being touched. Instead of a "safe," a person being chased can fall down or sit down to call out a TV program. He can only do this three times while one person is "it" and he can't say the same program more than once. If he goofs, he is automatically "it."

10. Chinese Tag

The person tagged must put his hand on the place where he has been tagged and he then becomes "it" and must try to tag the other players while in this position. The object of the game is to tag the person in a spot which will make it difficult to run.

11. Cooties Tag

In Cooties Tag, the girls who have the cooties chase the boys. You try not to let the girls touch you or you catch the cooties. If your fingers are crossed, you can't get them.

12. Pom Pom

Two boundaries about forty feet apart are picked. One person is chosen to be "it." All the other children line up by one boundary line. "It" screams "pom pom" and everyone runs to the other boundary line, while "it" tries to tag the children that are running. The people tagged stay in the middle of the boundaries with "it" and try to tag others when "pom pom" is called again. The game continues until the last person is tagged, and he is the winner.

13. Fox and Hounds

In Fox and Hounds half the kids are the foxes and the other half are the hounds. A home base is chosen where the foxes are safe. After the foxes get a head start, the hounds chase the foxes as they go off base. After being chased, the foxes try to return to the safe base. If the fox gets caught he is out of the game. Or sometimes we play that the fox that gets caught then becomes a hound. We play until all the foxes are caught. This usually takes all night until the game breaks up. We really don't have boundaries, we just use the usual playing area of the neighborhood.

14a. Pies

There's one game called Pies. There's this person who's the Baker, one person's the Wolf, and the other persons are the Pies. The Baker gives the Pies names like blueberry or strawberry or anything. And then the Wolf has to guess if they are blueberry, the Wolf has to try to chase the pies and if they catch the pies they are dead. But if he doesn't catch them they have to go back to the Baker and touch his hand.

14b. Pies
We play Pies. There's a Wolf, Mother, and the rest of the people that are playing are the Pies. And the Wolf, he comes knocking on our Mother's door and he answers the door and then he says he wants pies and all the other people are in the oven. And they all have these names like rhubarb or strawberry pies. And if the Wolf names that name, then the name that he calls, they have to run around the playground or wherever we are playing and if he catches them then they have to go in the Pickle Jar. But if he doesn't catch them they go back to their Mother.

15. Drop the Handkerchief
One person is chosen and he is given a handkerchief. The other children stand around in a circle with their hands clasped in back of them. They face the center of the circle. The chosen person walks around the circle and drops the hanky behind someone. That person must pick it up and tag him before he gets back to the position where it had been dropped. If he is successful in tagging him then the same person is "it." If he is not tagged then the chosen person takes the place of the one previously in the circle. This is continued several times. A group of ten or more is necessary.

STEPPING AND APPROACHING

Several folk games reverse the usual order of tag. Instead of children scattering away from the "it," the children approach the "it," who tries to ward them off or capture them. In several versions of this kind of game, practicing discipline or etiquette is the requirement for success. The child who doesn't say "Mother, may I?" is punished by being sent back to the start. The child who is caught moving when "red light" is yelled out is also sent back. In Old Lady Witch, when the children get close to the lady, they realize that the figure is evil and have to run back before being caught.

16. Mother May I?
The "mother" stands at one end of the playing area, and the

"children" at the other. She calls each of them in turn, saying they may take a certain number of giant, baby, or scissors steps. They must ask "Mother, may I?" to which she answers "Yes, you may." If they forget to ask, they must go back to the beginning. The first person to reach the "mother" is the winner.

17. Red Light

One person is chosen to be "it." All the children who wanted to play yell "not it." The last child to yell this is "it." This child stands about 25 yards from the other players with his back turned to them. The other players form a straight line behind him. The "it" closes his eyes and counts to ten to himself (or yells "green light" while the other players step or run toward him). Then he turns about quickly and yells "red light." When the other players hear him yell "red light," they must stop dead in their tracks. If the "it" sees any players moving when he turns to face them — that player must return to the starting line. The game is repeated until one player gets close enough to tap the "it" on the back while he is counting. The first player to tag the "it" becomes the new "it" and the game is begun again.

18. Old Lady Witch

In Old Lady Witch, you pick one person to be the witch and that person is called "Old Lady Witch." The rest of the kids go to one end of the playing area, and the witch goes to the other. The kids yell, "What time is it, Old Lady Witch?" The witch would yell out a time. This would keep going on until the witch yelled out, "Twelve o'clock." Each time they ask what time it is, the kids take one step forward. Then when "twelve o'clock" is said, the witch tries to catch one of the kids before they reach their safe area where they started. The person the witch catches is the witch.

TEAM PLAY

Children, especially as they get older, divide into teams in several of their favorite chasing games. In these games, children learn the qualities of leadership and camaraderie in addition to the organization and legislation that other games teach. Team games are especially useful when many children of various ages are present.

Mother May I? — Player taking a giant step toward "Mother"
(Harrisburg, Pennsylvania, 1987)

Red Light — Players approaching "it" during a green-light phase
(Harrisburg, Pennsylvania, 1987)

19. Red Rover

A large group of children and a large area to play are needed. The group is divided into two teams by chosen leaders who take turns picking from the children. All members of a certain team stand side by side and clasp hands. The teams stand on opposite sides of the playing area and face each other. It is then decided who will start. Then the leader of the starting group says "Red Rover, Red Rover, I send (name of teammate) right over." This person then runs to the other side between two members and tries to break their handclasp. If he is successful he can choose one of the two people that he went between to take back to his team. If he is unsuccessful he stays with that team. This is continued until only one person is left on one side and the other side is declared the winner.

20. Rolevo

Rolevo was the type of game that we used to play in the schoolyard during recess, because it required many kids to play. This game is played with teams, and the number varies from game to game. A "goal" is set up which is a fence of the yard. The game involves one team defending the goal, because this is where "prisoners" are kept, and the other team tries to free their prisoners and avoid getting captured. As soon as the team that is defending the goal has captured everyone from the other team, the roles will be reversed. To free the prisoners, you have to run in, touch the fence, and yell at the top of your lungs, "Rolevooo!" Then the defending team has to start all over again and re-catch all the players that are freed.

21. Prisoner Base

Two captains are appointed. The players are chosen by each captain until they are divided evenly. They set up bases on one side and prisons diagonally opposite from the base. At the signal of one of the captains, a player comes into the middle and taunts the other side to send out a player. When a player comes out, the taunter has to run back to his base. If he is caught, he is sent to prison. But the first player's captain can send someone out to capture the chaser. The captain can send someone out to release his players from prison by tagging them, but if the player gets caught, he too stays in prison. When all of one team is captured, the game is over, or else you just call the winner the one who has the most prisoners.

184

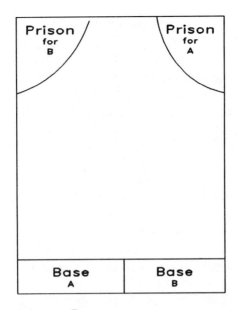

Prisoner Base

STREET AND SIDEWALK PLAY

The characteristic landscape of sidewalks, stoops, and walls common to America's cities and towns has inspired an assortment of folk games. In these games, one can see the adaptability of folk games to different settings. In addition to using the spaces for traditional play, some versions of sidewalk games, such as Box Baseball and Chinese Handball, show the adaptation of professional sports to folk variations.

22. Spud

Spud is played with a small ball. Everyone gets into a circle and one person is picked to be "it." The "it" stands in the middle of the circle and begins the game by tossing the ball up. When he does this, he yells out the name of one of the players.

That person has to run up and get the ball. When he gets the ball he yells out "spud" and the other players must freeze. The player who catches the ball then tries to hit a nearby person. This person can dodge the ball, but his feet must stay on the ground. If the thrower misses the person, the thrower gets the letter "S." If the dodger gets hit the letter "S" is scored against him. The game continues until one word "spud" is spelled out by one player. The person who gets the letter against him throws the ball next.

23. Hit the Coin

A quarter is placed on the "crack" between two boxes formed by the sidewalk. Each player tries to hit the coin by throwing the ball at it. Hitting the coin entitles the thrower to a point. If the coin turns over, the thrower receives two points. The first player to reach a designated number of points — usually eleven, fifteen, or twenty-one — wins. The winner keeps the quarter and the challenger must place down another coin.

24. Box Baseball

In this game, played on the sidewalk, a pitcher flicks the ball into the box closest to his opponent. Failure to do so is a "ball" as in regular baseball. The pitcher can manipulate the ball by shifting his middle finger which is spinning the ball. In this manner, the pitcher can make the ball "stop," "take off," or "curve." The opponent tries to slap the ball into the box closest to the pitcher. Failure to do so is an out. If the pitcher catches the ball before it lands, it is also an out. If the ball lands in the box closest to the pitcher, the number of bases awarded is determined by the number of bounces the ball takes. So if the ball lands in the box and the pitcher fumbles it so that it bounces twice more before it is caught, the result is a triple. After three outs, the players reverse roles until seven or nine innings are up.

25. Box Ball

A five-box sidewalk game is called Box Ball. The players stand opposite each other and try to throw the ball in the box closest to the opponent. If they are successful, they then try to throw it so that it bounces in both boxes closest to the opponent, then the three boxes closest, etc. The object is to throw the ball so that the ball bounces in each of the five boxes. This game sometimes ends in a reward for the winner that is common in the game "stickball" (a variation of baseball played in the street using broom handles for bats and a soft rubber ball in place of the hardball). The loser is forced to bend over and the winner is allowed one hard throw from a distance at the loser's buttocks.

26. Chinese Handball

The sidewalk boxes closest to a wall are often used for Chinese Handball. The players line up facing the wall in successive boxes. The lead box is the "Ace," the next is "King," the next is "Queen," etc. The ball is slapped against the wall on one bounce and is in play as long as this is done. Failure to hit the ball on one bounce results in a point for the player unless the player is the Ace. Players drop out when they receive too many points, usually five or seven. The Ace, like any other player, can be removed if he or she fails to return the ball. If this happens, the Ace goes to the last position. The Ace has the advantage of serving the ball. Just as the Ace can be removed, any lower player can move up when a higher player is forced out. Ploys in this game include spins on the ball to make it curve; "babies," which are soft taps on the ball resulting in a bounce very close to the wall; "killers," which are balls hit in the space where the wall meets the sidewalk usually making the ball roll out flat on the ground; and "slams," which are hard-hit, low-bouncing balls.

27. Half-Ball

Half-Ball was a popular game in my neighborhood. It is usually played in alleys, or in my case the front street. There is a fielding team and a batting team. The batter must hit half of a pimple ball to the field team in order to get a base hit. Anything that is caught on the ground or in the air is an out. Anyone who is batting gets only one strike for an out. Usually five or six half-balls are used in the game and are pitched in one after the other because the half-ball is difficult to hit.

28. Stoop Ball

In Stoop Ball, one player throws a ball off a stoop and another player tries to catch the rebound. Catching the rebound on the fly is an out. Balls that aren't caught are hits and it is a single, double, etc., depending on how far the ball travelled in the air. These distances are decided upon before the game. The game can also be played off a wall or curb.

29a. Skelly

In Skelly, you draw a large box with a circled "S" in the middle. One one end small boxes are numbered 1 and 5, on another end boxes are numbered 7 and 4, on another end boxes are numbered 8 and 2, and on the last end the boxes are numbered 3 and 6. Each player has a bottle cap which you place in box number 1. The idea is to flick the cap to the next numbered box until you get to the "S" and then you go backwards. You start over if you get on a line, and if you knock some guy's bottle cap out he starts over. The first person to complete the cycle wins.

29b. Skelly

The way we played Skelly, you shoot the bottlecap through the

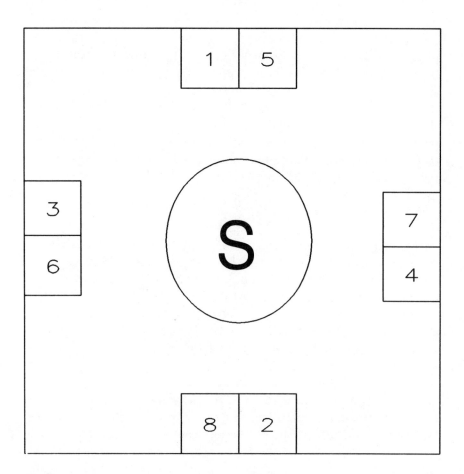

Skelly

course without "linies," shots that land on the line of the box. The bottlecap has to be completely in the box. There are some rules in the game that make it good for playing with several people shooting. The four boxes around the central "13" box are the "skels." When you put your bottlecap in there, you have to stay there until someone else shoots you out. When that player does, he can add the number of the box you're in to his total, and go directly there. So if a player is in the "3" box and hits you when you're in the "4" skel, then he can go directly to the box. But he doesn't have to knock you out if he doesn't want to; then you have to stay there, while everybody else goes through their turn. In games like this, usually you have to go through the cycle several times. Sometimes after completing a certain number

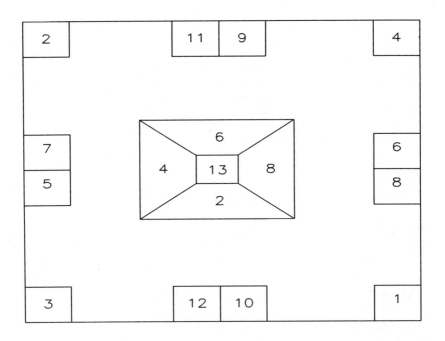

Skelly

of cycles, you can become a Killer, which means that you can knock somebody out of the game by hitting them.

30a. Hop Scotch

In Hop Scotch, you can use stones from the street as markers. You throw the stone into the first block and if it lands within it you hop over it, and not stepping on the lines, hop up landing on two feet, one in each, in a double block, and come back down. If you miss the block, you lose a turn and start in the same place in your next turn. In some places, they play that you pick up the marker up on your way up the board instead of on the way back. A top block, sometimes called "Sky Blue" or "Heaven" or "Home," is a rest block and you can put your feet any way there. If you feel you are going to fall when you pick up your stone on the way back, you can call "butterfingers" and put down two hands for support. Here's what the diagram looks like from Gary, Indiana, where this is played:

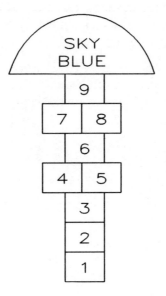

Hop Scotch — Gary, Indiana

And here are some examples of Hop Scotch diagrams from other places:

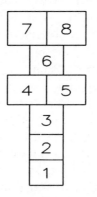

i. Hop Scotch — Arkport, New York

i. Learned in Arkport, New York. It is played the same as above except that players do not use butterfingers and if they do not get the stone in the block intended on the first throw, they get one free throw.

ii. New Albany, Indiana. Same as first version except players use no butterfingers. They use stones from the street and draw the board whenever they can with chalky stones.

iii. Peru, Indiana. Players draw the board with stones and use either stones from the street or buckeyes for markers. These players pick their markers up on their way up the board instead of on the way back.

iv. Quincy, Illinois. Players use stones from the street for markers. Same as first version except they have no butterfingers and they pick the stone up on the way up the board.

v. Hammond, Indiana. Same version as the first except they have no butterfingers.

vi. West Hartford, Connecticut. Same as first version; use stones and butterfingers.

vii. Owensboro, Kentucky. Players have no butterfingers. They use pennies or stones for markers.

viii-ix. Baltimore, Maryland. The procedure is the same as the first, using butterfingers. Players use chalk or stone to draw the board, and stones and rubber heels from the shoe repairman for markers.

30b. Hop Scotch

You play Hop Scotch by drawing the board with a stick in the ground. Someone takes a stone and throws it in the first box and jumps through the course, and on the way back, has to pick it up. You keep doing that until you've gone through all the numbers. But you have to be good at getting the marker in the right box, and not falling over when you pick up the marker, and not dropping it. There are special rules for this game. By calling out "Boardswalkies" (some kids say "Red, White, and Blue") you can walk on the lines of the board when going through the course. If you call out "Stretchies" you can lie full length upon the diagram before throwing your marker. "Butterfingers" is the most common call. It allows the player not to be out if she touches the line. Other calls are "Big Foot" which allows the player to take a giant step. "Lucky Seven" allows the player to put two feet in the "7" block of the diagram.

30c. Hop Scotch

A diagram is drawn on the sidewalk, with home base and a moon

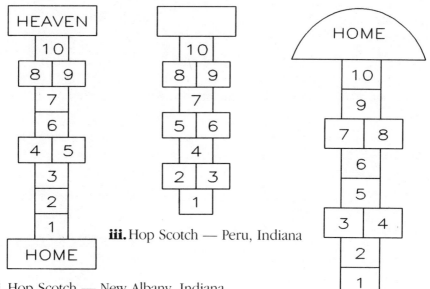

ii. Hop Scotch — New Albany, Indiana

iii. Hop Scotch — Peru, Indiana

iv. Hop Scotch — Quincy, Illinois

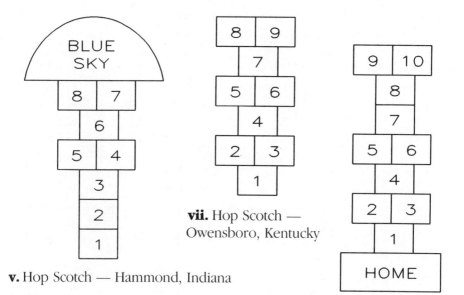

v. Hop Scotch — Hammond, Indiana

vii. Hop Scotch — Owensboro, Kentucky

vi. Hop Scotch — West Hartford, Connecticut

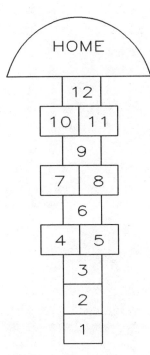

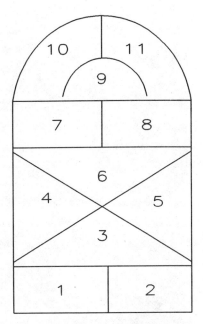

viii. Hop Scotch — Baltimore, Maryland

ix. Hop Scotch

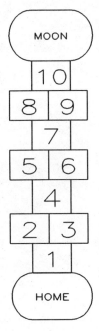

30c. Hop Scotch

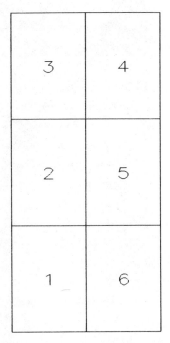

30d. May I? Hop Scotch

Players at Hop Scotch

Hop Scotch player demonstrating "boardswalkies" and "stretchies"

Hop Scotch played on a different diagram

4	5	12	13
3	6	11	14
2	7	10	15
1 Start	8	9	16 Stop

Movie Star Hop Scotch

base. One stands at home and tosses a stone to a number on the diagram. She then goes from home to the moon, jumping first with one foot, then with two feet on the squares, skipping the one with the stone. After reaching the moon, she must turn around and come home the same way, stopping only to pick up the stone.

30d. May I Hop Scotch

The player faces the diagram with eyes closed or looking skyward. She hops into square number six with the right foot while, at the same time, she hops into square number one with her left foot. The player then asks, "May I?" If the player hasn't stepped on a line or put her foot outside of the square, she is allowed to continue. These are called "misses"; if the player has "missed" her turn is ended. The player continues in like manner hopping with the right foot in number five while hopping with the left foot in number two; likewise for number four and three; turns around and proceeds back to start in same manner. Each time she has jumped asking, "May I?" When the player has "done frontwards" she turns backwards to the square, eyes closed, jumping in manner described above, but backwards, and asks "May I?"

30e. Movie Star Hop Scotch

The player hops on one foot, beginning at the box marked "start." She continues down one row and up the next, to the square marked "stop" and out. If the player completes her turn without a miss (hopping on line or hopping in someone else's square), she marks the initials of a movie star in a square. If the player misses she cannot mark a square. If the other players fail to guess for whom the initials stand,

the player has another turn. The players continue in the above manner, hopping over the squares with initials until all the squares have
been marked. The player marking the most squares wins. The number
of squares varies from 12 to 28 in rectangular form.

CHAPTER TEN

"We Made It Ourselves!": Toys and Constructions

CHILDREN, WHEN LEFT to their own devices, make elaborate things. Out of the work of their hands come toys and constructions suited to the spirit and imagination of youth. The creations, more often than not, are something personal, maybe understood only by the child. The child may be made to feel embarrassed about making playthings when toys supplied by Mom and Dad sit idly by, or may be discouraged from strange (by adult standards, anyway) flights of fancy. Adults often take the attitude that the child's world must spring from adult purses and tastes. But for many generations, following tradition, children have made things for themselves.

In these things children express the power to build, the same power that they see producing the houses, streets, and vehicles around them. Working in wood, paper, and sand, children demonstrate a fascination with how things are converted from nature to a contraption or edifice serving society. In making things, children express control; they figure out how to use tools and materials to make something meaningful to them. With ready-mades and consumer come-ons all around them, children find a world of their own making in folk crafts. A chain made of gum-wrappers for one's boyfriend is special because it was made by hand from tradition. Not from a store, it comes from the world of faith and belief, from the heart. The dark underside of childhood — its spit-ball shooters, bolas, spears, and slingshots — has its own social codes. In treehouses and cootie catchers, there is a purposefulness that builds up children's culture away from adult supervision.

The achievement of handwork can offer aesthetic rewards. Mothers like to tell me, for instance, of the amazing things children do with their food — mashed-potato mountains and string bean roads. Jonah is a boy I know in Pennsylvania who shaped a boat out of clay. It didn't resemble anything his mother could recognize, but Jonah worked and reworked the boat according to a blueprint he had in his head. His sisters shared the excitement he felt over the creation, and gave advice. Playing along the Susquehanna River days later, the children piled variously shaped rocks to make elaborate sculptures jutting out of the shallow water. "Sculptures" is the clinical adult view. To the children, they were castles, lighthouses, islands. Each child worked on an individual design, yet they carefully consulted one another on the form and function of the creations, and ultimately the things resembled one another. The children used the creations to express their ideas in material form.

Children rely on the materials familiar to them. To hear old-timers tell it, the playthings in a boy's arsenal were typically made from wood strewn along the countryside and a girl's treasure came from fabrics and plants around the community. With a pocketknife or needle in hand, children crafted marvelous toys and decorations from the surroundings. That spirit continues today, although the medium is often different. The old slingshot made from a forked stick and part of the inner tube of a tire today can be shaped from a wire hanger and rubber bands. An especially prevalent resource for children's folk industry is paper. Paper is a fact of school life, and provides an opportunity to turn a reminder of work into a plaything. On the beach children dig, scoop, and pile sand into shape; in winter landscapes they push, pack, and pat snow into imposing human figures.

It is easy to forget the prevalence of children's folk construction, because the things children make are often meant to be private and temporary. They are built for use and reconstruction. After they serve their purpose, they are often discarded, or the knowledge for making them is passed on to a younger child. Folk construction will continue to hold sway in children's lives because of the fascination that making things provides. Recent commercial influences add a powerful variable in the marketable world. In their advertising, toy companies persuade parents and children what they should have at a given age rather than answering what they might need. Commercial toys are more public and permanent, although not necessarily better. The mass culture stresses consumption and novelty. Folk culture values construction and reuse. Mass culture's products tend toward uniformity and faddism, folk culture's toward variation and long-standing tradition. In the mass culture you can be told what the fashion or standard is. And when the two cultures come into conflict, mass culture appears, at first glance, to dominate: folk products like the stickball bat, go-cart, and wooden puzzle, for example, are regularly usurped and repackaged. The stickball bat I made as a kid out of an old broom now sells for

$12.95 and comes in "official" and "professional" models. Still, children's folk crafts continue to thrive because they provide the feelings of "making it myself," mastering what came before, and "sharing with my group."

With sincerity, children's toy manufacturers claim educational, creative roles for products. Yet the same roles have been played in informal social exchange and self-production among children. Children show their ingenuity within the marketable world by altering factory-made products to suit their tastes. A deck of cards became to my childhood friends a marvelous thing with which to show off the patience and prowess needed to build a house or create a tower. These friends took Erector sets and communally figured out ways to use the steel rods and bolts on their homemade carts and boats. Such experiences emphasized their control, their personalizing of things around them.

Besides changing toys, children can change a community by leaving an imprint on their surroundings. It is not uncommon to find adult-designed playgrounds lying idle while the streets on which children live have chalked into them diagrams for Hop Scotch and Skelly and makeshift hoops for basketball. A parking lot becomes a daredevil course with the addition of bricks and boards to ride bicycles over. Such constructions integrate where children live with what they do, in the face of the modern tendency to separate the two.

In presenting children's folk crafts, I always have been inspired by the object lesson provided by novelist William Golding in *Lord of the Flies* (1954). He used the experience of children's constructions to make a point about social division. Shipwrecked and alone on an island, children created their own model of society with "littluns" and "biguns." The littluns

> had built castles in the sand at the bar of the little river. These castles were about one foot high and were decorated with shells, withered flowers, and interesting stones. Round the castles was a complex of marks, tracks, walls, railway lines, that were of significance only if inspected with the eye at beach level. The littluns played here, if not happily, at least with absorbed attention; and often as many as three of them would play the same game together.

The biguns mindlessly destroyed the castles, "kicking them over, burying the flowers, scattering the chosen stones." Yet they could not discern or destroy "the particular marks" in which the littluns were absorbed.

This chapter offers some overdue attention to the particular marks of the things children make for themselves. In these things, children are active and creative, expressive and revealing. Words alone do not adequately describe the things, so I have put together a portfolio of photographs I have taken over the years showing children's fabrications from wood, sand and snow, paper, and other materials. With these photos I intend to offer a "beach-level" view of children's handiwork.

WOOD

Americans are proud of what they can build in wood. In our society wood has been plentiful, mobile, and versatile, and because of these qualities it helped build our nation. Wood has also been well appreciated by generations of children, especially young boys. With pocketknife in hand, one could put together many toys to make music, movement, war, and home, which persisted in tradition because they delighted children and helped prepare them for the technical skills they needed later in rural life. Today, folk toys made out of wood frequently raise images of rural life, but children's traditional work in wood still remains popular in the city and suburbs. One national survey reported that 62 percent of nine-year-olds and 65 percent of thirteen-year-olds had "built something out of wood." Instead of collecting materials from nature, city children now collect scrap lumber and discarded boards from the curbside to construct their special objects. That feeling of building, shaping, controlling, continues to thrill and educate, even if the hillside has been paved over.

1. Slingshot

The slingshot is made from a forked stick. You can take your pocketknife and shave the stick down if you want to make it smooth. Take an elastic band (rubber from an old inner tube works real well) and tie it to the ends of the forked stick. You usually put a small stone in the elastic, pull back, and let it go. The force from the slingshot would cause the rocks to *zing,* making a loud noise.

2. Spring Gun

This gun is made from an elderberry bush. I've also seen it with reed or bamboo. Cut off a long, thin, flexible slice of the wood; hickory is good. Cut a hole at the bottom of the barrel and put the slice securely in the hole. Cut a slit in the top of the barrel and you should be

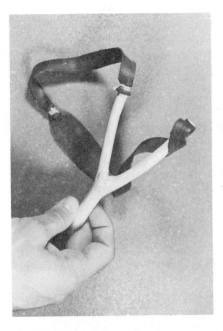

Slingshot

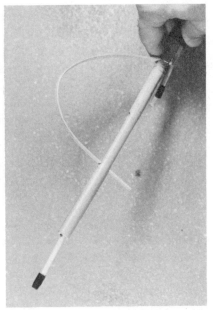

Spring gun

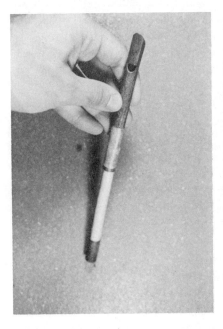

Whistle

Bull roarer

able to bend the end of the slice of wood into the top of the slit. You can make arrows by whittling wood to fit the barrel and putting tape on the end. Put the wooden arrows in the barrel and bend the slice of wood back. When you let it go, the arrow goes shooting out of the barrel.

3. Hickory Bark Whistle

Whistles can be made of other woods, like willow or box-elder, but hickory is the toughest. They have to be made in the spring when the sap is up. Cut in a hole at the tip and make a plug that adjusts the sound as you pull it in and out.

4. Bull Roarer

Hold the end of the stick, throw the paddle around fairly fast until it makes a loud roar. Don't let the string wrap around the end of the stick.

5. Whizzer

This toy makes a whizzing sound and you can also see colored lines on the wood twirl. You can find a big clothes button or you can make it out of wood. You can take a piece of wood and round it out and draw different colored lines on it. Put two holes near the middle. Put a string through two holes that are opposite each other, and loop the ends. The bigger the disk the longer the string should be. Hold the ends of the string apart. Twirl it so the string is wound up and the wooden disk is in the center. Pull and the string unwinds and the button whirls. If you lessen the pressure it winds up in the opposite direction and you can pull again and you can keep it whirling. It makes a whizzing or buzzing sound.

6. Spinning Top

I made this with a pocketknife from one half of a wooden sewing thread spool. Grasp the top end between the thumb and the second finger and start the top spinning.

7. Ball-in-Cage

This is a kind of puzzle. People want to know how you got that ball in the cage. Take a block of wood and mark out a center square and two rectangles above and below it. Take your pocketknife and work out the wood in the two rectangles, until all you have left is the center square. Then cut at the edges of the square until you form a sphere.

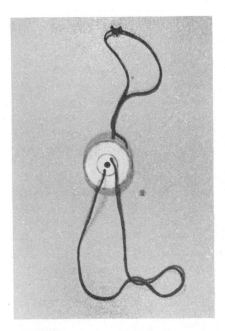

Whizzer

Spool top

Daredevil jump — A stuntsman and his admirers

Eventually all that should be keeping the ball in place should be a small spot where the sphere is attached to a pillar of the wooden block. Carefully cut down with your knife to release the ball. Smooth down the ball and the pillars to make it easier to slide the ball up and down in the cage.

8. Daredevil Jump
Take a board and put bricks under one end. Set up another one across from it. You can ride your bicycle over one board and land on the other board. Keep pushing the boards apart to make the jump more challenging.

9. Treehouse
The part where the branches of the tree comes together makes a good place to put the floor of the house. The walls can also rest against the branches, but you need to nail the boards firmly together. I put some old two-by-fours on the corners and nailed the boards against that.

SAND, SNOW, AND STONE

Rising from the flat surfaces of a still field, tranquil beach, or placid river, shapes of people, animals, towers, forts, canals, and castles announce children's activity, children's presence on the landscape. Often these kinds of objects are cooperative ventures, bringing many hands into the exercise of patting, pressing, and piling. These creations may vanish with a spring thaw or a rush of water, but for that glorious moment after the snowstorm or at the beach, they form a monument.

10. Sand Sculpture
The trick to making things out of sand is to keep the sand wet enough to shape, but not so wet that it pours. Use your bucket to set up the mounds of sand to shape. Use your shovel and hands to smooth and harden the sides of what you're going to make. Many people like castles; others form canals from the water to the beach; and others like to make animals like turtles.

11. Snow Men and Women
The snow men and women are made as if you're making three big

Ball-in-cage   Treehouse

Treehouse with tire swing

Tools for sand sculpture   Sand sculpture — Building a canal

Close-up of canal built by a child   Children shaping a turtle

Castles in the sand

Well-engineered fort at the beach

Sand turtle emerging

snowballs. The one at the bottom is the largest and the middle one is smaller, and the top one for the head is the smallest. Pile the snow and pat it to smooth and harden it into shape. You can take branches and things and use them for arms. Finally, you can pour water lightly over the surface to freeze it.

12. Rock Sculptures
We make castles and islands by piling rocks in the river. The trick is to balance the rocks just right so they'll stay up.

PAPER

Piles of paper lie everywhere around children today. They have notebooks to raid, wrappers to use, bags to tear. You can cut paper, fold it, paste it. Paper, free paper, is there for the taking, and the making. You can work the paper inside your room, at the desk while the teacher isn't looking, on the bus on the way home. And if you make a mistake, it's easy to start over. Folk toys and constructions from paper are the most common everyday expression of children's craft today. Small in scale, they often pass adult notice, but in their size is a reminder again of children's status in relation to adult standards. Isn't it an expression of creative control to bring play and art forth from that sheet of paper, which is the most conspicuous reminder of the work left to be done? And isn't it then part of that children's sense of community to display their efforts, amusing and amazing one another?

13. Puppet
You can make a puppet by taking a sheet of paper and folding it in half lengthwise. Fold it over again lengthwise. Then fold it in half across its width. You'll then have the paper with two ends. Take the end facing you and fold it in half across the width, folding downward. Turn the paper around and do the same with the other end. Put your fingers in the openings on the two ends and move them up and down to make the puppet "talk." You can draw eyes and a nose on the top, and a tongue, if you want, on the inside of the mouth.

14. Fortune-Teller
Take a sheet of paper and tear off the bottom so you form a square. Fold the corners inward toward the center so that you have a smaller square. Turn the paper over and fold the corners again toward the cen-

Snow man   Snow woman

Young sculptors intent on their creations

Child with rock sculptures

Folding a paper puppet

The puppet and its maker

ter. (Eight numbers will be written on the four flaps; four colors will be written on the blocks created on the other side.) Fold the now smaller square in half. There will be four blocks with spaces created to put your fingers. Put in your thumb and forefinger from one hand on one side and the thumb and forefinger from your other hand on the other. When you put your fingers in, the top will look like four blocks that come to a point in the middle like a cone. On these four blocks are the names of colors. When you spread your fingers back, two triangles will be formed on the inside of the paper. On each of these is a number. When you push you fingers in and out again, then another two triangles on the inside of the paper will. form and numbers are here also. On the other side of the flap where these numbers are, you write in a fortune like "You will be rich and famous," "You will marry a movie star," or "You will go to the poorhouse." You start telling someone else's fortune by having them pick a color. You then spread your fingers in and out according to the letters picked. For example, spelling out G-R-E-E-N means that you spread the paper in and out five times.

Then you have the person pick a number and you ask the person to pick a number. You spread the paper in and out that number of times. Then you ask the person to pick another number and spread the paper in and out that number of times. Then ask the person to pick a number and you read the fortune under that flap. You can also make this a "cootie catcher" by putting specks with your pen on the one set of the inside triangles and none on the others. With the blank side up, you scoop on someone's arm. When you spread the paper, the specks will show the cooties.

15. Box

Fold a sheet of paper at a diagonal. A portion of the sheet will be left over on the bottom; tear that off and you will have a square sheet of paper left. Fold the paper on a diagonal the other way. The paper will have folded lines showing an "x." Turn the paper over, crease it in the middle, hold it in the middle, and bend it in. Hold two sides in with your inside fingers while holding the outside with your thumb and middle fingers. Fold the paper so it makes a triangle. You'll have four corners. Take the top corner and fold it up to where the triangle comes to a point at the top. Do the same on the opposite side. Turn it over and do the same thing on the other side. You will end up with a diamond shape. Then you have four corners again. Take one of the corners on the right side and bend it over to the middle of the diamond and

Paper fortune-teller under construction

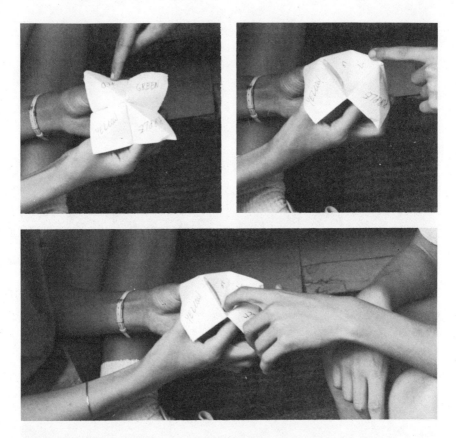

Child picking the fold of paper that will tell his fate

Listening as the oracle is read

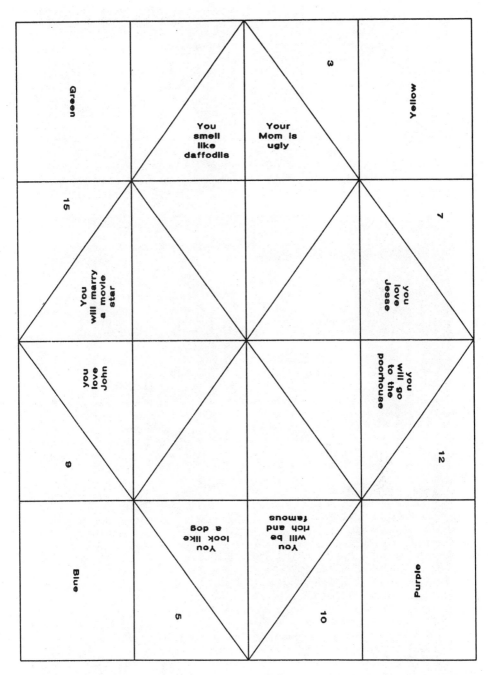

Fortune-teller

Paper box under construction

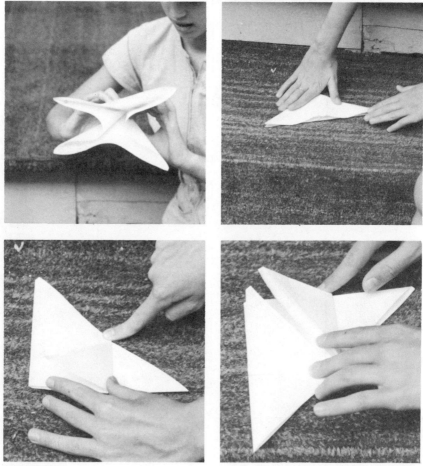

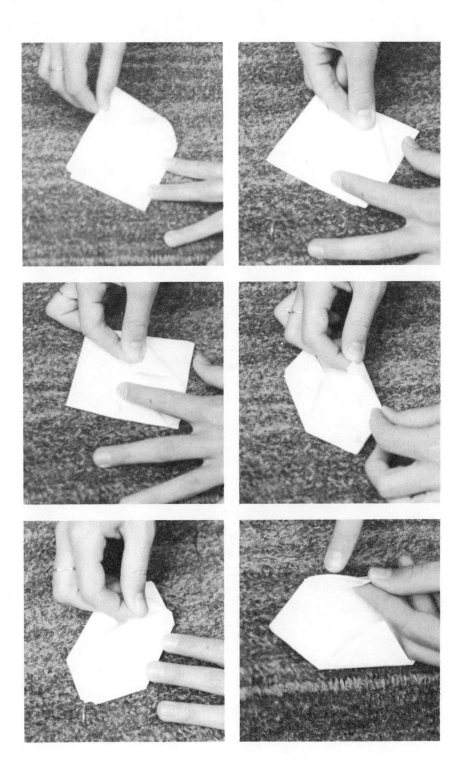

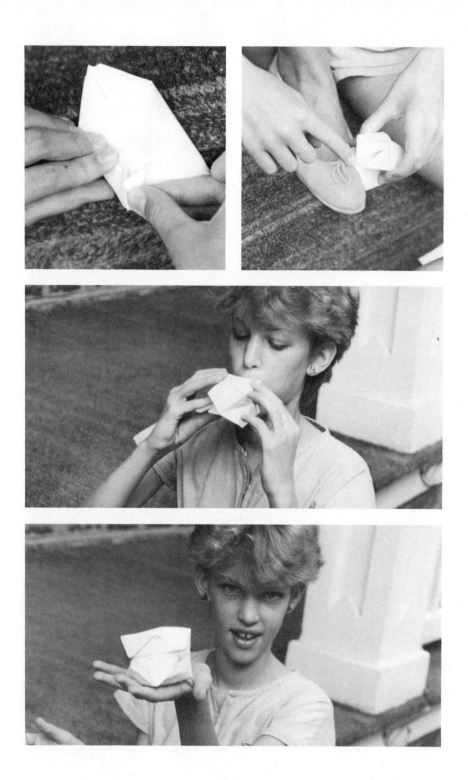

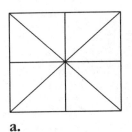

a.

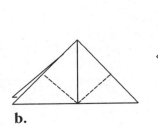

b.

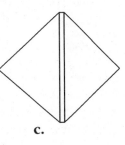

c.

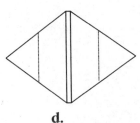

d.

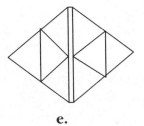

e.

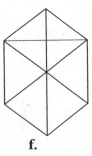

f.

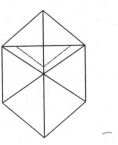

g.

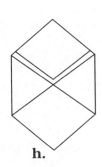

h.

i.

Box

crease it down. Fold the left side in the same way. Flip it over and do the same on the other side. You will end up with a hexagon. On the top of the hexagon you'll have a hole and on the bottom you'll have four flaps. Take the left flap and pick it up and fold it into the triangle. Fold this triangle into the slot above it formed by the flap on the left side of the hexagon. Take the right bottom flap and do the same thing for the right side. Turn it over and do the same thing on this side. At the top where the hole is, you blow into the hole until the box inflates. Then you have a box. You can draw designs on the box. You can write names or smiley faces on it.

16. Football

To make a football, you fold a sheet of paper in half lengthwise. Fold the paper in half lengthwise again. Start folding the strip of paper upwards from the bottom. The paper should be folded over from the left in a triangle. Fold the downward triangle up.

Keep folding up the paper in triangles until there is a little bit of paper remaining on the end. Tuck remaining paper in fold on top of the triangle. The game played with this football is played on top of a school desk. Players sit on adjacent ends. The football is laid flat. The game is started when the first player lays the football on the desk with one edge hanging over the desk. The player must push the football twice with his fingertips in hopes of getting the football to hang over the adjacent edge. After two hits, if the football does not hang over the adjacent edge, the player loses his turn. The second player has two chances from where the football landed to get it to hang over the opponent's edge. If the football falls off the desk, the player who pushed the football will lose his turn. Once the football hangs over the edge, six points are earned. After earning six points, an additional point-after is attempted. The opposing player makes a goal post with his hands by sticking his thumbs up and connecting the post by stretching out his forefingers together. The football is placed on its end and smacked in its middle with a finger. This is also the way a player can kick a field goal after one push of the football across the table.

17. Gum-Wrapper Love Chain

To make a love chain of gum wrappers, spread open the wrapper. Then fold both ends toward the middle forming a *V* shape. Make several this way, inserting one inside the other's flaps. After reaching the height of your boyfriend, hang the chain in your bedroom above or beside your bed. This process will bring your boyfriend to you. Some girls say that the longer you made it the greater your love.

18. Airplane

To make a paper airplane, fold the two top corners of a sheet of paper. Turn the paper over and fold the two top sections in toward each other, being careful to keep the sides even. Turn the paper over again and fold the two top sections to each other. Fold each side up

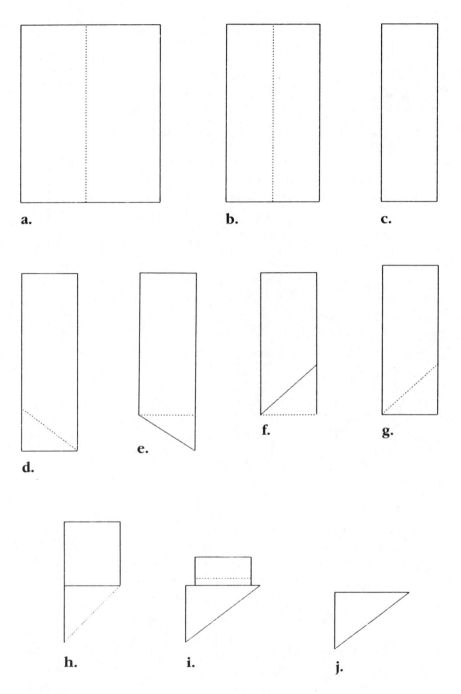

a.

b.

c.

d.

e.

f.

g.

h.

i.

j.

Football

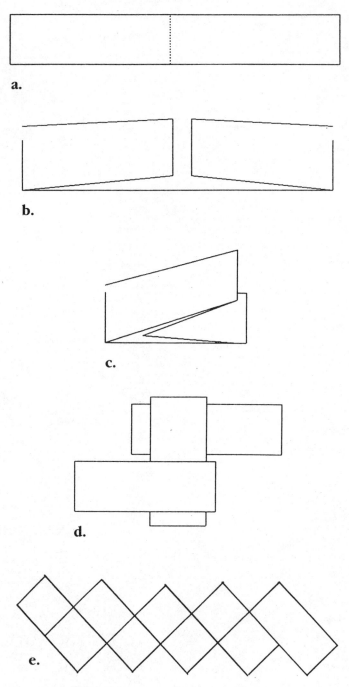

a.

b.

c.

d.

e.

Gum-wrapper love chain

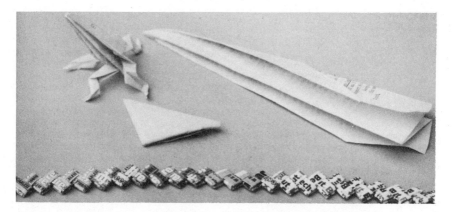

Paper frog, football, airplane, and gum-wrapper love chain

Displaying the gum-wrapper love chain

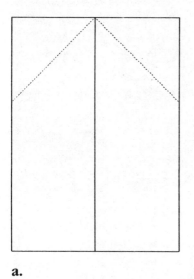

a.

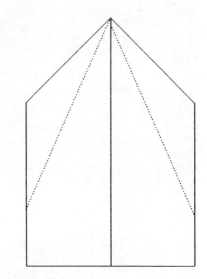

b.

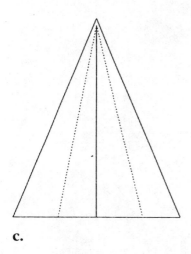

c.

d.

Airplane

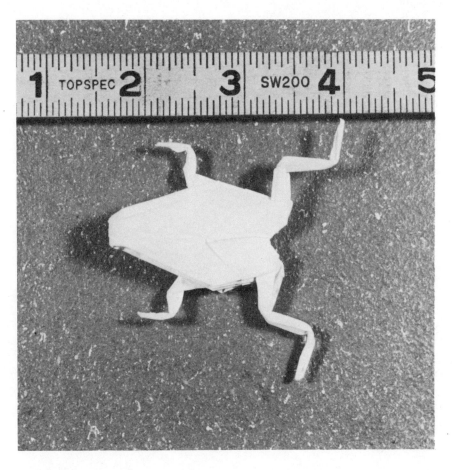

Handmade paper frog

and you will have a center section to hold the plane. With an easy motion, throw the plane up in the air and let it glide.

19. Frog

To make a frog, take a sheet of paper and fold it along a diagonal. You'll have a portion of the paper left on the bottom; tear that off and you'll have a square sheet of paper left. Fold the paper diagonally the other way. Undo the fold. Fold straight across in half once and undo and you have a paper divided into eight sections. Push up the center of the paper and set up like the box (item 15). Also like the box, you fold it down so you have a diamond. Fold the bottom of the diamond to form four triangles. You will then have a diamond with a long slender part at the bottom. The bottom parts can be bent to make the legs:.

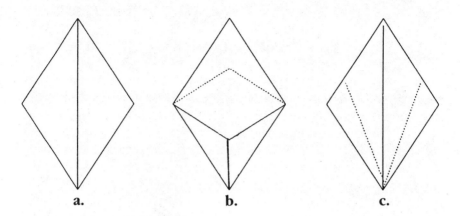

a.

b.

c.

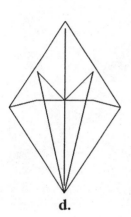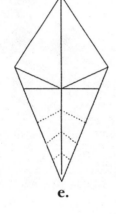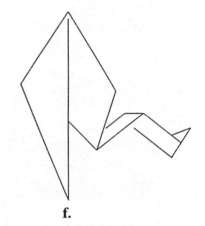

d.

e.

f.

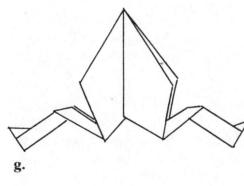

g.

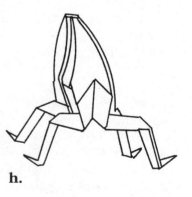

h.

Frog

STRING, CLOTHING, PLASTIC, AND OTHER MATERIALS

There's something about turning an ordinary length of string into a "cat's cradle" — something about turning socks into dolls, yarn into bracelets, or old clothes into porch figures. That something is the process of conversion. From the ordinary come new uses, unusual shapes; rather than throwing those everyday things out, we can use them to delight our minds, challenge our hands, and warm our hearts. Used as a tool for living, these pieces of cloth can appear circumstantial; used as an instrument for imagination, they seem cultural, communal, creative. In our plastic, disposable age, more is thrown out than ever before, and demonstrations of conversions, or performances of culture, are the delights of children. Plastic bleach bottles, egg packages, and trays become piggy banks, masks, and sleds. Milk crates have been long-time favorites. In an earlier generation, crates were made of wood and children converted them into wagons and go-carts. Today the back streets are lined with plastic milk crates converted into basketball hoops. When children put them up, their parents remember once when *they* did something like that.

20. String Figure

The string for this Jacob's Ladder came from sneaker laces tied together. You need two persons and one loop of string. One person holds the string and separates the hands with the strings around them. Pass each thumb away from you under all the strings, and take up from below with the back of the thumb the far — little finger — string, and return the thumb to its former position. Pass each thumb away from you over the near index string; take up, from below, with the back of the thumb, the far index string; and return the thumb to its former position. Release the loops from the little fingers and separate the hands.

Pass each little finger toward you over the near index string and take up from below on the back of the little finger the thumb string, and return the little finger to its former position. Release the loops from the thumbs. Pass each thumb away from you over the index loop, and take up from below, with the back of the thumb the near little finger string and return the thumb to its position. With the right thumb and index fingers, pick up the left near the index string, and put it over the left thumb. With the left thumb and index finger, pick up the right near index string and put it over the right thumb. Separate the hands. Bending each thumb toward the other hand and then up toward you, slip

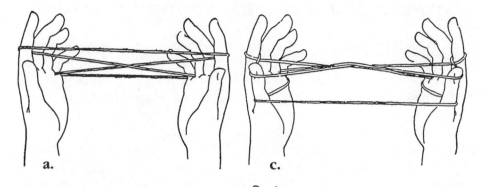

a.

c.

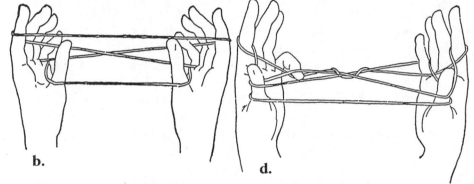

b.

d.

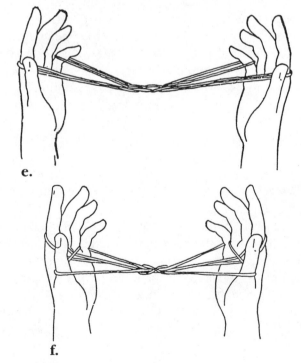

e.

f.

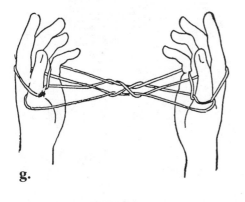

g.

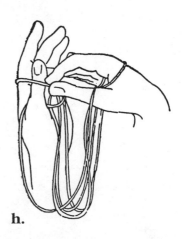

h.

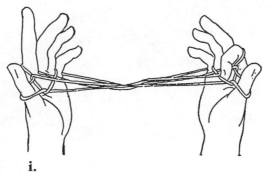

i.

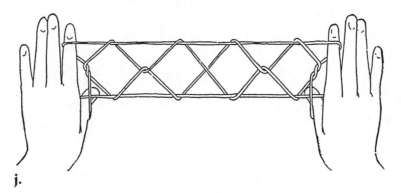

j.

Jacob's Ladder

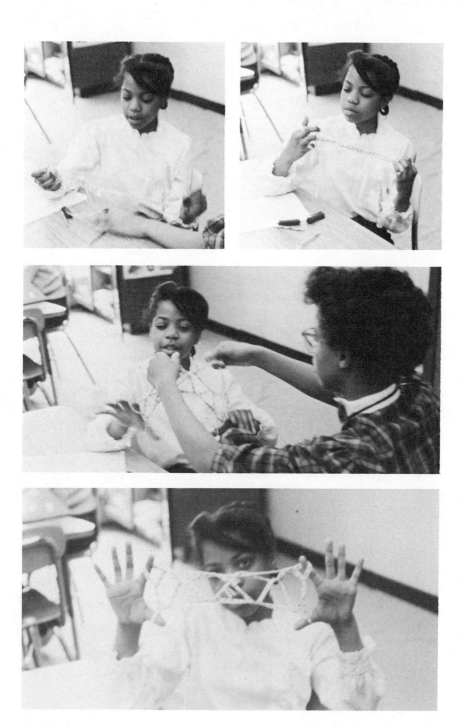

Forming a Jacob's Ladder

the lower near thumb string off the thumb, without disturbing the upper thumb loop. The other person can bend each index finger down, and pick up from below the far thumb strings and hold them up. That forms a "bridge" figure. When she releases the figure, insert each index from above into the small triangle formed by the string twisting around the thumb loop, and, turning the palms down, release the loop from the little fingers; then separate the hands, turn the palms away from you, and the Jacob's Ladder will appear.

21. Halloween Figures

Taking old clothes and stuffing them with hay or newspaper or some other filling is the way to make good Halloween figures. Putting sticks

Halloween figure waiting for nightfall

Scarecrow standing guard at Halloween

in the arms makes them stand better. Then we tied off the feet and hands together with strings. We used real pumpkins for the head, but some people use plastic. We took a fat stick and stuffed it in the neck of the figure. Then we cut out the pumpkin's face and stuck it on the stick. We sat the figure in a chair and set it out on the porch, or on top of the porch, and you can put straw or gourds around it.

A jack-o'-lantern is another Halloween decoration that kids make. Take a pumpkin and cut a circle around the stem. You want to make the hole big enough to put your hand in. You have to scrape out the seeds and pulp; a tablespoon works well for this. Then you can cut out features on the front for a face — nose, eyes, and mouth. To make it glow, burn candle wax to form a puddle on the bottom of the inside of the pumpkin. Put a candle in the puddle to hold it still and light it.

22. Basketball Hoops

For street basketball, you can take a plastic milk crate and nail it to a board on a garage, pole, or tree. Cut out the bottom to let the ball fall straight through. Some people try to shave down the top edge of the crate to make it more like a rim. The hoop is used mostly for one-on-one stuff.

Milk-crate basketball hoop   Milk-crate goal under defense

Close-up of milk-crate basketball hoop

23. Friendship Pins and Bracelets

You string beads on a pin and give them to your friends. And they give you theirs. The different colors of the beads make them nice. You can make some of the same color and mark that you're part of a group. It's similar with the bracelets that are braided from old yarn.

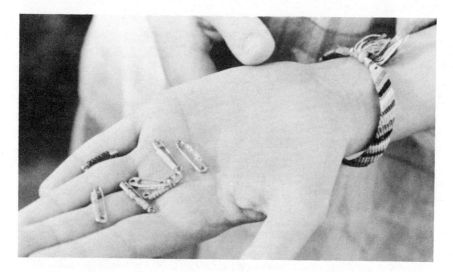

Friendship pins and bracelet

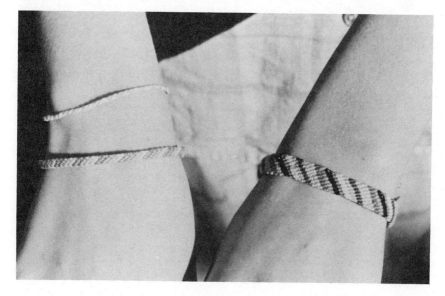

Friendship bracelets

Notes

All photographs are by Simon Bronner.

These notes are intended to provide the sources for the material that I present in this book. I provide as much contextual information about the informants and setting for the collection as is available to me. For extensive notes on the historical and cultural background of the lore, see the annotated edition of *American Children's Folklore,* also published by August House.

Chapter Two. Speech

1. This glossary has been compiled from a number of sources. The primary source is Gary Alan Fine's series of glossaries of "Pre-Adolescent Male Slang," *Children's Folklore Newsletter* 2.1 (Fall 1979) through 4.3 (Winter 1981). Fine's collection came from five different communities during the period 1975 to 1977: a suburb of Boston, an exurban township near Providence, Rhode Island, a professional suburb of St. Paul, Minnesota, a middle-to-lower-class suburb of Minneapolis, and an urban, upper-middle-class area of St. Paul. I also drew on a collection taken from pre-adolescent boys made by David E. Freed in 1981 entitled "Totally Different: A Further Study of PreAdolescent Slang" (typescript, Penn State Harrisburg Folklore Archives, 1982) and my own collection of vocabulary among middle-class boys and girls in Harrisburg, Pennsylvania.
2. Collected by Carolyn Henry from sixth-graders, Harrisburg, Pennsylvania (typescript, Penn State Harrisburg Folklore Archives, 1985).
3. Collected by Treva Lichti from fifth-graders in Nappanee, Indiana (typescript, Indiana University Folklore Archives, 1968).
4. Collected by Hannelore Wertz from junior high school students, York, Pennsylvania (typescript, Penn State Harrisburg Folklore Archives, 1982). For a comparable list of taunts to send an unwanted child away, see Knapp and Knapp, *One Potato,* p. 64.
5. Collected by Hannelore Wertz from junior high school students, York, Pennsylvania (typescript, Penn State Harrisburg Folklore Archives, 1982).
6. Collected by Simon Bronner from seventh-graders, Brooklyn, New York, 1976. The question of time often leads in children's culture to what the Opies in *Lore and Language* call "crooked answers" (pp. 42-45). The Opies write that these answers are repartee which "is a quick follow-on to a question or remark which just happens to crop up."
7. Collected by Carolyn Henry from sixth-graders, Harrisburg, Pennsylvania (typescript, Penn State Harrisburg Folklore Archives, 1985). The Knapps report the routines in *One Potato,* p. 70, with "John Brown" replacing Buster Brown. The "Pudding Tame" routine from North Carolina (c. 1923) is reported in Paul G. Brewster, ed., *Children's Games and Rhymes,* p. 195, with the follow-up, "Where do you live? In a sieve." For a version from Alabama, see Solomon and Solomon, *Zickary Zan,* p. 82. The Opies in *Lore and Language,* p. 157, record a version from Maryland, and comment: "The Maryland verse has previously been recorded in The Sussex Archaeological Collections, 1861, 'What's yer naüm? Pudden and taüm; Ax me agin, and I'll tell ye da saüm,' given as current 'thirty or forty years ago' (i.e., c. 1825). 'Pudding and Tame' seems to preserve the name of the fiend or devil, 'Pudding-of-Tame,' listed in Samuel Harsnet's *Popish Impostures* (1603). A number of similar formulas were collected in the nineteenth century."
8. Collected by Simon Bronner from seventh-graders, Brooklyn, New York, 1976. The Solomons in *Zickary Zan,* p. 85, offer the following variant: "None of your beeswax, cornbread, and shoe tacks."
9. Collected by Becky Townsend from Kathleen Hoeke, nine years old, Provo, Utah (typescript, Brigham Young University Collection at Fife Folklore Archives, Utah State University, 1971). These commonly collected replies are described by the Knapps in *One Potato,* pp. 68-69.
10. Collected by Elaine Chipko from grade-school children, Fort Wayne, Indiana (typescript, Brigham Young University Collection at Fife Folklore Archives, Utah State University, 1966). The Knapps in *One Potato* (p. 71) include "Drip's drop" in their collection, and offer it as a reply to the child who shouts "You're queer." "A playmate," they observe, "may be flattened by the syllogistic response: 'A queer is a drip, / A drip is a drop, / A drop is water, / Water's nature, / Nature's beautiful, / Thank you for the compliment!'"

11-12. Collected by Simon Bronner from sixth-graders, Harrisburg, Pennsylvania, 1982. For a comparable list of negative and positive replies, see Charles Clay Doyle, "Belaboring the Obvious: Sarcastic Interrogative Affirmatives and Negatives," Opie and Opie, *Lore and Language of Schoolchildren,* p. 43.

13-14. Collected by Simon Bronner from ten- to thirteen-year-old white boys in Clifton, New Jersey, and Brooklyn, New York, 1976. The collection was supplemented by collections from twelve-year-old white boys in the Harrisburg, Pennsylvania, area by Lyall J. Lehman (typescript, Penn State Harrisburg Folklore Archives, 1982), by Hannelore Wertz from twelve-year-old whites in York, Pennsylvania (Penn State Harrisburg Folklore Archives, 1982), and by Robert O'Keefe from white adolescent boys in Bloomington, Indiana (typescript, Indiana University Folklore Archives, 1976).

15. Collected by Simon Bronner from nine- to twelve-year-old black boys in Greenville, Mississippi, 1976. The ritual-insult tradition of Dozens among young blacks is documented in John Dollard, "The Dozens: Dialectic of Insult," and Roger Abrahams, "Playing the Dozens," in *Mother Wit from the Laughin' Barrel,* ed. Alan Dundes, pp. 277-94, 295-309; William Labov, "Rules for Ritual Insults," in *Rappin' and Stylin' Out: Communication in Urban Black America,* ed. Thomas Kochman, pp. 265-314.

16. Collected by Treva Lichti from Tracy Webb, ten-year-old girl (for "Rubber baby" and "How much would a woodchuck chuck") and Ken Kiester, eleven years old (for "Sally sells seashells"), July 13, 1968 (typescript, Indiana University Folklore Archives, 1968).

17. Collected by Treva Lechti from Susan Anglemeyer, twelve years old, Nappanee, Indiana (typescript, Indiana University Folklore Archives, 1968).

18. Collected by Dorothy Deal from Mary Ellen Manley, Cleveland, Ohio, January 4, 1968 (typescript, Indiana University Folklore Archives, 1968).

19-24. The transcripts of interviews come from Rochelle Berkovits, "Secret Languages of Schoolchildren," *New York Folklore Quarterly* 26 (1970): 127-52. Versions of "Pig Latin" and "Egg Talk" from Great Britain are documented in Iona and Peter Opie, *Lore and Language of Schoolchildren,* pp. 320-22. They suggest that some of the secret languages originated with adults hiding messages from children, which was followed by children learning the secret languages for their own purposes.

Chapter Three. Rhymes of Play

1. Collected by Simon Bronner from Sadie and Neva deWall, ten and eleven years old, respectively, Harrisburg, Pennsylvania, May 9, 1983. This counting-out rhyme was found in every collection of children's folklore I checked. The "potato" in this counting-out rhyme usually connotes the shape of the fist. The child thrusts it into a circle with the "potatoes" of other children to be counted out. Sometimes the first person to be counted "out" is "it"; on other occasions, including the one with the deWalls which I photographed for the book, the last person to be left in after counting out is "it." The counting-out is repeated first with five, then with four, and so on, until one person is left. The ubiquity of this rhyme is indicated by the listing of 35 published sources between 1916 and 1976 including sources from the United States, New Zealand, Australia, and England in Roger D. Abrahams and Lois Rankin, eds., *Counting-Out Rhymes: A Dictionary* (1980), pp. 164-65.

2. Collected by Clara Kathleen Bridgewater from Kirk Bridgewater, nine years old, Sharpsville, Tipton County, Indiana, January 1970 (typescript, Indiana University Folklore Archives, 1970). The informant is described as "American, white, Protestant, and in third grade," and his rhyme was learned "from classmates." The Knapps in *One Potato, Two Potato* mention it as a children's favorite with the alternate ending "T-W-O and you are Not It" (p. 26); see also the "bubble gum" version in Marice C. Brown, *Amen, Brother Ben* (1979), p. 9. Abrahams and Rankin in *Counting-Out Rhymes* list six published sources between 1927 and 1976, some of which list a common first line of "Ish, fish, codfish," or "Codfish, codfish" (p. 28).

3. Collected by Sandy Ballif from John Craig, Springville, Utah, February 1972 (typescript, Brigham Young University Collection at Fife Folklore Archives, Utah State University, 1972). The Knapps in *One Potato, Two Potato* list the "blue shoe" rhyme as a children's favorite (p. 27).

4. Collected by Sandy Ballif from John Craig, Springville, Utah, February 1972 (typescript, Brigham Young University Collection at the Fife Folklore Archives, Utah State University, 1972). This rhyme, using the coupling of "ink" and "stink," appears in various forms. Abrahams and Rankin in *Counting-Out Rhymes,* pp. 118-19, list 29 published sources between 1849 and 1976, some of which list the rhyme as a taunt as well as a counting-out rhyme.

5. Collected by Shannon England from Shelley England, nine years old, Kokomo, Indiana (typescript, Indiana University Folklore Archives, 1967). According to the collector, Shelley "and her friends say these rhymes at recess." The informant also knew another version which substitutes, "Some go up, and some go down, / And some go to the burying ground" for the last two lines. Indeed, the last two lines of this rhyme show great variation in the many published sources that include the counting-out rhyme. Abrahams and Rankin in *Counting-Out Rhymes,* pp. 176-77, list 39 sources between 1883 and 1969, beginning with collections from the 1880s.

6. This rhyme in various forms appeared in every collection of children's folklore I checked. This transcription comes from Lana Lassiter, 20 years old, Windfall, Indiana (typescript, Indiana University Folklore Archives, 1970). She remembered it from her school days in 1958. She also recalled a variant, "Eeeny, meeny, miny, moe, / Catch a nigger by the toe, / If he hollers, let him go, / Eeny, meeny, miny, moe." Other substitutions for "tiger" include "monkey," "rooster," "baby," "rabbit," "Tojo," and "piggy." As sensitivity to racial slurs has increased in the last two decades, "tiger" has generally replaced "nigger" as the common term.

7a. Collected by Sandy Ballif from Dennis Smith, Provo, Utah, February 1972 (typescript, Brigham Young University Collection at the Fife Folklore Archives, Utah State University, 1972). The rhyme sometimes appears with the alternate ending: "How she's polished, how she shines, / Engine, engine, number nine," although most modern archival collections most commonly include the "track" variant. "Engine, engine, number nine" has been widely reported since the 1880s on both sides of the Atlantic as well as in British colonies in the Pacific. Abrahams and Rankin in *Counting-Out Rhymes,* pp. 78-80, list 32 published sources between 1883 and 1976.

7b. Collected by Carolyn Henry from Jermica, an eleven-year-old black girl, Harrisburg, Pennsylvania (typescript, Penn State Harrisburg Folklore Archives, 1985). The monkey is a popular character in counting-out rhymes; Abrahams and Rankin in *Counting-Out Rhymes,* pp. 144-46, list six separate types of rhymes that feature the animal. See also item no. 8 in this chapter. This variant of the "Engine, engine, number nine" is apparently adapted from the traditional rhyme "Three, six, nine, / The goose drank wine, / The monkey chewed tobacco / On a streetcar line, / The line broke, / The monkey got choked, / And they all went to heaven / In a little row boat" (reported by Lana Lassiter, Indiana University Folklore Archives, 1970).

8. Collected by Cynthia Bough from Jonah Bough, Kokomo, Indiana, October 10, 1969 (typescript, Indiana University Folklore Archives, 1969). According to the report of this rhyme, "The people form a circle, placing one hand in. For each word in the rhyme, the counter taps the hand of each person going around the center of the circle. The one tapped on the word 'out' is it." The first two lines of this rhyme are widely reported in collections of children's folklore. Abrahams and Rankin, in *Counting-Out Rhymes,* pp. 145-56, list 29 published sources between 1883 and 1976.

9. Collected by Ann Kilgore from elementary school children, Conway, Arkansas (typescript, Arkansas Folklore Archives, Special Collections Department, David W. Mullins Library, University of Arkansas, 1962). In 1883, Williams Well Newell in *Games and Songs of American Children* reported a version from Massachusetts, dated 1820 (p. 201); in 1888, Bolton in *Counting-Out Rhymes of Children* reported this rhyme with "Little Freddy" (from England) and "Mary" (from Newport, Rhode Island, and Philadelphia, Pennsylvania) in the leading role (p. 93). As the listing of 30 other published sources between 1883 and 1972 in Abrahams and Rankin's *Counting-Out Rhymes,* pp. 178-80, shows, the rhyme has been prevalent in American folklore.

10. Collected by Ann Kilgore from Mrs. Kermit Dalton, Conway, Arkansas (typescript, Arkansas Folklore Archives, Special Collections Department, David W. Mullins Library, University of Arkansas, 1962). This rhyme was commonly reported on both sides of the Atlantic during the late nineteenth century and continues to be collected to the present; see the listing of 35 published sources between 1888 and 1969 in Abrahams and Rankin's *Counting-Out Rhymes,* pp. 122-24, and Brown, *Amen, Brother Ben,* p. 14.

11. Collected by Sandy Ballif from Ganie Bundy, Provo, Utah, February 1972 (typescript, Brigham Young University Collection at the Fife Folklore Archives, Utah State University, 1972).

12. Collected by Clara Kathleen Bridgewater from Kirk Bridgewater, nine years old, Sharpsville, Indiana, December 1969 (typescript, Indiana University Folklore Archives, 1970). The informant is described as "American, white Protestant, and in the third grade." The rhyme is one of several (see items 23, 26a, 26b) that refer to sibling rivalry; it is listed in this context by the Knapps in *One Potato, Two Potato,* p. 113. Although frequently reported as a jump-rope rhyme, this rhyme appeared in several archives as a counting-out rhyme.

13. Collected by Shannon England from Shelly England, nine years old, Kokomo, Indiana (typescript, Indiana University Folklore Archives, 1967). The report of this collection states that Shelly "and her friends say these rhymes at recess." This rhyme has been reported since the 1880s and continues to be heard today as both a counting-out rhyme and jump-rope rhyme; see Abrahams and Rankin, *Counting-Out Rhymes,* p. 174; Brown, *Amen, Brother Ben,* p. 12; Abrahams, *Jump-Rope Rhymes,* pp. 149-50.

14. Collected by Sandy Ballif from Christine Craig, Springville, Utah, February 1972 (typescript, Brigham Young University Collection at the Fife Folklore Archives, Utah State University, 1972). This rhyme and its many variants has been reported since the 1880s in Scotland, Denmark, Germany, and the United States.

15. Collected by Maria McCay from Rosemary McCay, Hammond, Indiana, April 1967 (typescript, Indiana University Folklore Archives, 1967). Although related to item 14, this distinct rhyme uses the sounds of "kinoba," "knabe," or "canaba" for its central feature. The derivation may again be from the German, since *Knabe* means *boy* and *Knobel* means *dice,* or *knuckles,* in the vernacular.

16a. Collected by Sandy Ballif from Ruth Craig, Springville, Utah, February 1972 (typescript, Brigham Young University Collection at the Fife Folklore Archives, Utah State University, 1972). This rhyme, often transcribed as "Acker backer, soda cracker, / Acker backer boo," has been reported since the 1880s to the present in the United States and Canada. See the listing of eighteen published sources between 1888 and 1976 in Abrahams and Rankin, *Counting-Out Rhymes,* pp. 8-9.

16b. Collected by Sandy Ballif from Dave Ruff, Springville, Utah, February 1972 (typescript, Brigham Young University Collection at the Fife Folklore Archives, Utah State University, 1972).

17. Collected by Kent Payne from Greg Cano, Logan, Utah (typescript, Fife Folklore Archives, Utah State University, 1979). The report of this collection states that the "chanter points to each player in sequence as he (she) says each word." This rhyme demonstrates the common play of making nonsense words out of the appealing sounds of rhyming syllables. One can hear, as Abrahams and Rankin point out in *Counting-Out Rhymes,* "Eeny, meeny, tipsy tee, / Delia, dahlia, dominee, / Hatcha, patcha, dominatcha" or "Eeny, meeny, mony, my, / Barcelony, bony sty, / Ara-wara, brown bear, / Acka-wacka, we wo, wack" (pp. 64-68).

18a. Collected by Carolyn Henry from Danielle, black, eleven years old, Harrisburg, Pennsylvania (typescript, Penn State Harrisburg Folklore Archives, 1985). The report of the collection states: "One person is in the middle on knees with hands over eyes, and pretending to cry. She rises and with eyes closed points to someone, the last one to be identified is it." This rhyme is usually reported as a singing game or a jump-rope rhyme, often with the title "Little Sally Water." The game has been reported since the nineteenth century in the British Isles as well as in America; Gomme in *Traditional Games of England,* vol. 2, pp. 149-79, gives 48 versions from the British Isles, and makes the claim that it is one of the oldest folk games in the Isles.

18b. Reported by Mary Kathy Clemmons, black, 22, New Castle, Delaware, from her memories of childhood (c. 1958) in Glen Jean, West Virginia, (typescript, University of Delaware Folklore Archives, 1973). Clemmons recalled this and "Punchie-nella" (see item no. 20) as the popular ring-game rhymes in her elementary school days. According to Clemmons, she and other black girls "used to play these games during lunch recess at school and after school."

19. Collected by Carolyn Henry from Eleanor, an eleven-year-old black girl, Harrisburg, Pennsylvania (typescript, Penn State Harrisburg Folklore Archives, 1985). The report of the collection states: "What you do is: someone stands in the middle of a circle, follow the directions in the rhyme. Then the person turns around with closed eyes and points at someone. . . . Then they go in the middle." Especially popular since the 1960s, this verse has been reported in the United States, Canada, Great Britain, and South Africa.

20. Collected by Carolyn Henry from Kyuati, twelve-year-old black girl, Harrisburg, Pennsylvania (typescript, Penn State Harrisburg Folklore Archives, 1985). This rhyme is an example of a verse designed for elementary school use which has become part of the spontaneous play of many children. The Opies in *The Singing Game,* pp. 412-13, trace the rhyme to a French instructor for singing and dancing rounds, c. 1910.

21a. Collected by Simon Bronner from Sara Gochnaur, five years old, white, Harrisburg, Pennsylvania, May 1987. The child reported learning the rhyme and hand-clapping routine from her kindergarten classmates. At the time, she claimed to have three boyfriends.

21b. Collected by Teresa Thoma from Jeannie High, Bloomington, Indiana, May 15, 1967 (typescript, Indiana University Folklore Archives, 1967). The identification of the boyfriend in the second verse demonstrates the variation possible in oral tradition. The chanter can use poetic license to localize the rhyme or to add drama.

21c. Collected by Teresa Thoma from Chris Kelly, Bloomington, Indiana, May 15, 1967 (typescript, Indiana University Folklore Archives, 1967). The last verse adds a divination rhyme frequently following the line "Who shall I marry?" (see item 39). See the variations listed in Abrahams, *Jump-Rope Rhymes,* pp. 168-69. The characters in this particular variation are silent-film-era cowboy star Tom Mix and 1940s and '50s bandleader Spike Jones. Other celebrities make their way into hand-clapping games, including Charlie Chaplin, Jack Benny, and Clark Gable; see Knapp and Knapp, *One Potato, Two Potato,* pp. 128-29; Opie and Opie, *Lore and Language of Schoolchildren,* pp. 115-17.

22. Collected by Nancy Dewald from Alison Dewald, seven years old, white, Camp Hill, Pennsylvania, May 27, 1986 (manuscript, Penn State Harrisburg Folklore Archives, 1986). The most widely reported part of this rhyme is the "I feel sick" section, which is commonly attached to the "alligator purse" rhyme (see item 44). Abrahams in *Jump-Rope Rhyme,* pp. 126-28, reports 50 published sources between 1927 and 1966.

23. Collected by Nancy Dewald from Alison Dewald, seven years old, white, Camp Hill, Pennsylvania, May 28, 1986 (manuscript, Penn State Folklore Archives, 1986). Abrahams in *Jump-Rope Rhymes,* pp. 79-80, lists 20 published sources for this rhyme between 1936 and 1966.

24. Collected by Deborah Turner from black third-graders, eight years old, Salisbury, Maryland, April 3, 1972 (typescript, University of Delaware Folklore Archives, 1972). "Miss Susie" (item 23) and this rhyme are often related together by children. As the Opies point out in *The Singing Game,* the character Lulu often appears in children's versions of old bawdy songs (pp. 472-73). The words to this verse are sometimes sung, but this version was performed as a hand-clapping game.

25a. Collected by Margaret Bedle from Debby Jascur, 21 years old, from her memories of childhood (c. 1960), September 29, 1973 (typescript, University of Delaware Folklore Archives, 1973). According to the report of this collection, Bedle learned the rhyme "from her girlfriends when she was about ten years old." Once she learned it, she didn't play it much unless it was to show off to younger girls. Opie and Opie in *The Singing Game,* pp. 474-75, point out that the rhyme is an adaptation of the popular song "Playmates," words and music by Saxie Dowell, 1940.

25b. Collected by Estelle K. Tullos from Kathy Spann, Morristown, New Jersey (typescript, University of Delaware Folklore Archives, 1973). Spann told Tullos that "all the songs I sing I just learned from my sisters or from my friends when I was young."

25c. Collected by Carolyn Henry from Aleatha, eleven years old, black, Harrisburg, Pennsylvania (typescript, Penn State Harrisburg Folklore Archives, 1985). This risqué parody continues the theme of female apprehension of sexuality found in many folk rhymes. It contains several commonplace rhyming formulas, such as "They gave me fifty cents" (see "My boyfriend gave me fifty cents" in item 26b) and "My father was disgusted" (see "How many men were disgusted?" in item 37b).

26a. Collected by Rebecca Wood from Mary Wood, fourteen years old, Kokomo, Indiana, February 27, 1968 (typescript, Indiana University Folklore Archives, 1968). A similar verse is reported by the Knapps in *One Potato, Two Potato,* p. 115. They cite it as an example of rhymes that "describe problems that women may face — being tied to an undesirable mate, being rejected — and these verses are in startling contrast to the lyrics of popular commercial songs. The unhappy or rejected girl in popular songs is usually forlorn and passive. The girls in the jump-rope rhymes are a pretty resilient lot" (p. 115).

26b. Collected by Rebecca Wood from Mary Wood, fourteen years old, Kokomo, Indiana, February 27, 1968 (typescript, Indiana University Folklore Archives, 1968). This is the common contemporary form of an old skipping rhyme: "Nine (or twelve, or seven) o'clock is striking, / Mother may I go out? / All the boys are waiting / For to take me out. / One will give me an apple, / One will give me a pear, / One will give me fifty cents / To kiss behind the stair."

26c. Collected by Teresa Thoma from Ann Carney, Bloomington, Indiana, May 19, 1967 (typescript, Indiana University Folklore Archives, 1967).

26d. Collected by Jerry Sechrist from Laurie Mizell, eleven years old, Bloomington, Indiana (typescript, Indiana University Folklore Archives, 1969).

27. Collected by Simon Bronner from Sadie and Neva deWall, ten and eleven years old, respectively, white, Harrisburg, Pennsylvania, May 9, 1983. These two girls are sisters who regularly play together. Sadie learned most of her material from Neva, who often is a leader in the neighborhood play group. This formulaic hand-clapping rhyme (also reported as a song and jump-rope rhyme) is more popular than the number of published sources would indicate; I collected it from children as young as six years old in Harrisburg, and it ranked only behind "Little Dutch Girl" (item 21a) in popularity as an easily remembered hand-clapping rhyme.

28. Collected by Simon Bronner from Sadie and Neva deWall, twelve and thirteen years old, respectively, white, Harrisburg, Pennsylvania, August 15, 1987. This clapping game has gained in popularity in the last decade. Children reported liking its variety of maneuvers and syncopated rhythm. The movements are first clapping, then snapping fingers, one hand up and the other down, hitting the other person, right-hand thumb over shoulder and then left, make a fist, hug the other person, imitate a gun with hand and point at other person (at "Pow"), hit hands with fist (at "Sock").

29. Collected by Teresa Thoma from Judy Parker, eight years old, Bloomington, Indiana, May 15, 1967 (typescript, Indiana University Folklore Archives, 1967). "Mary Mack, dressed in black, / Silver buttons all down her back" is an old riddle for "coffin"; see Archer Taylor, *English Riddles from Oral Tradition*, p. 234.

30. Reported by Dorothy Dwyer, Newport, Rhode Island, from her memories of childhood (typescript, Northeast Folklore Archives, University of Maine, 1971). She comments that "in this game, the idea is to keep bouncing the ball without stopping or breaking the rhythm and singing the following song. If the ball is dropped, then you must start the alphabet over. You continue through the alphabet with whatever names you want, as long as they begin with the same letter."

31. Reported by Renee McCoy, nineteen years old; Brooklyn, New York, from her memories of childhood (typescript, Northeast Folklore Archives, University of Maine, 1975). She comments that "what you do is get an old stocking, and put a ball (about the size of a tennis ball) in it. Stand against a wall and fling the ball. Catch it side to side and under your legs if you want to get fancy."

32. Collected by H.T. Reed from Shelley Reed, nine years old, Lewiston, Maine (typescript, Northeast Folklore Archives, University of Maine, 1960). According to the report of this collection, the actions that accompany the rhyme are: "Line one — toss ball in air and catch it. Line two — toss and catch ball without moving feet. Line three — toss ball, cover mouth with hand, catch ball. Line four — toss ball in air and catch it, keeping a 'straight' face (sober) while onlookers try to make player laugh. Line five — toss ball in air, using one hand and then the other. Line six — toss ball while lifting one foot and then the other foot. Line seven — toss ball in air, clap hands together in front of you; toss ball, clap hands together in back of you. Line eight — toss ball, clap hands together in front and in back, catch ball. Line nine — toss ball, clap hands together in back, in front, catch ball. Line ten — on 'tweedle' toss ball, right hand circles over left in fast forward movement while left hand circles over right; on 'twaddle,' toss ball, right hand circles over left in fast backward movement while left hand circles right. Line eleven — toss ball, curtsey, catch ball. Line twelve — toss ball, salute with right hand, catch ball. Line thirteen — toss ball, cross chest with hands pointing to opposite shoulders, catch ball. Line fourteen — toss ball, fling arms sideways, catch ball." This rhyme makes a social judgment on a secretary's work. This girl's rhyme uses the public performance of the secretary in the first four lines (No moving, no talking, no laughing), and then comments on the extraordinary actions that a secretary is expected to make (One hand, the other hand, / One foot, the other foot). Finally there is the expectation that after all this, she is still supposed to be gracious (**Curtsey**, / Salute-sy, / Cross your heart). This game-rhyme is an example of the ways that folk games comment on society's patterns. I have not seen this game played with "secretary" in the leading role in the last few years, which may indicate changes in attitudes toward sexual stereotyping. Fowke, for example, in *Sally Go Round the Sun* collected this ball-bouncing rhyme as "Ordinary movings," p. 76.

33. Collected by H.T. Reed from Jo and Shelley Reed, seven and nine years old, respectively, Lewiston, Maine (typescript, Northeast Folklore Archives, University of Maine, 1960). According to the report of this collection, the actions that accompany the rhyme are: "Line one — bounce ball and catch it. Line two — toss ball in air, arms up as if reaching for the stars, catch ball. Lines three and four — toss ball in air, swing arms from left to right, catch ball." This kind of play performance of bounce and catch to the accompaniment of simple rhymes is discussed in Howard, "Rhythms of Ball-Bouncing," pp. 166-69.

34. Collected by H.T. Reed from Bonnie Hinman, eight years old, Pittsfield, Massachusetts (typescript, Northeast Folklore Archives, University of Maine, 1960). According to the report of this collection, the actions accompanying the rhyme are: "Lines one to four — bounce and catch ball. Line five — bounce ball, touch toe, catch ball. Line six — bounce ball, touch knee, catch ball. Line seven — clap hands, catch ball. Line eight — bounce ball, swing hands out to sides, catch ball." In subsequent times, though, the player goes through these actions with "feet apart, no talking, no laughing, left hand, right hand, stand on left foot, stand on right foot, front clap, back clap."

35. Collected by Faye Somers from Lynne Forest, nine years old, Saint John, New Brunswick (typescript, Northeast Folklore Archives, University of Maine, 1963). According to the report of this collection, the rhyme "is said while bouncing a ball on a vertical surface." The rhyme, the report continues, can be frequently heard in the Maritime Provinces down through Maine.

36a. Collected by Elroy Baird from Christine Baird, ten years old, Provo, Utah, October 10, 1974 (typescript, Brigham Young University Collection at Fife Folklore Archives, Utah State University, 1974). According to the report of this collection, "When the jumper hops on one foot, she hops on one foot. When she is asked to jump on two, she jumps normally. When she jumps on three feet both feet and one hand must touch the ground. When she jumps on four feet both feet and both hands must touch the ground. The jumper crouches to achieve these last two positions. When the jumper is told to 'get out of town,' she must get away from the jumping rope." Abrahams in *Jump-Rope Rhymes* lists 27 published sources for this rhyme between 1934 and 1966 (pp. 110-11). The rhyme's circulation, however, dates at least to the mid-nineteenth century. The Opies in *Lore and Language of Schoolchildren* cite famed novelist Lewis Carroll's mention of it in 1866 and the Reverend Sabine Baring-Gould's collection of it in 1895.

36b. Collected by Deborah Turner from black third-graders, eight years old, Salisbury, Maryland, April 3, 1972 (typescript, University of Delaware Folklore Archives, 1972).

37a. Collected by Carolyn Henry from Dana, twelve-year-old black girl, Harrisburg, Pennsylvania (typescript, Penn State Harrisburg Folklore Archives, 1985). The popularity of this rhyme is indicated by the 50 published sources between 1926 and 1966 that Abrahams lists in *Jump-Rope Rhymes*, pp. 31-32. Brown in *Amen, Brother Ben*, p. 22, states that "this rhyme was the one most commonly cited by informants under twenty. It also had the widest regional spread."

37b. Collected by Deborah Lee Turner from black first- and second-grade girls, six and seven years old, Salisbury, Maryland, April 3, 1972 (typescript, University of Delaware Folklore Archives, 1972).

38. Collected by Mory Phillips from Leta Davis, Fort Worth, Texas (typescript, Arkansas Folklore Archives, Special Collections Department, David W. Mullins Library, University of Arkansas, 1971). This rhyme just might be the best known of traditional jump-rope rhymes. One indication is the whopping 72 published sources for the rhyme between 1926 and 1966 in Abrahams, *Jump-Rope Rhymes*, pp. 187-89. The rhyme has been reported in every corner of the United States as well as in Australia, New Zealand, the British Isles, Canada, Finland, and Germany.

39. Reported by Sandra Blakemore, 20 years old, Glendale, California, December 1970, from memories of her childhood (typescript, Brigham Young University Collection at the Fife Folklore Archives, Utah State University, 1970). This rhyme is one of several known to girls for divining their future husband. See Abrahams, *Jump-Rope Rhymes*, pp. 57-58, 168-69.

40a. Collected by H.T. Reed from Shelley Reed, nine years old, Lewiston, Maine (typescript, Northeast Folklore Archives, University of Maine, 1960). According to the report that accompanies this collection, "Two girls swinging rope, player 'jumps' in if she can, and continues jumping until she misses (i.e., stopping rope, stepping on rope, and doing the split — rope in between legs)." The report continues with an alternative: "Line one — pretend to hold bowl and stir fudge. Line two — pretend to dial with one hand, hold phone with other hand. Line three — cradle arms as if rocking baby and swing them from left to right. Line four — shake your head. Line five — cradle arms, same as line three." The action for the second verse is the same for all three lines: "Jump rope and then miss (this miss is called a split, one foot on one side of the rope, one foot on the other side). Each player repeats this until she misses." Abrahams in *Jump-Rope Rhymes* lists 33 published sources for this rhyme between 1926 and 1966 (pp. 51-52).

40b. Collected by Cynthia Gough from Kaye Bough, thirteen years old, Kokomo, Indiana, October 15, 1969 (typescript, Indiana University Folklore Archives, 1970). According to the report of this collection, the last line "should be repeated until a miss is made."

41a. Collected by H.T. Reed from Jo Ellen Reed, seven years old, Lewiston, Maine (typescript, Northeast Folklore Archives, University of Maine, 1960). According to the report of this collection, "this can be played by one child jumping and swinging by herself or by two girls swinging and one girl jumping. Lines one and two — jumps and salutes. Lines three and four — girl jumps in. Lines five and six — swing hips from left to right. Line seven — kick one foot. Lines eight and nine — jump with legs apart, rope between legs." Abrahams in *Jump-Rope Rhymes*, p. 161, lists ten published sources for this rhyme between 1947 and 1966. A nineteenth-century source can be found in the taunt "Blue-eyed beauty, / Do your mother's duty . . ." in Northall's *English Folk Rhyme*, p. 299.

41b. Collected by Deborah Turner from black third-graders, eight years old, Salisbury, Maryland, April 3, 1972 (typescript, University of Delaware Folklore Archives, 1972). The exhibitionistic flavor of this rhyme is indicated by the coupling of sexual and athletic performance in the first and second verse.

42. Collected by H.T. Reed from Shelley Reed, nine years old, Lewiston, Maine (typescript, Northeast Folklore Archives, University of Maine, 1960). According to the report of this collection, the actions that accompany this rhyme are: "Line one — jump rope. Line two — swing hips while jumping. Line three — jump on heels, jump on toes. Line four — do split (feet apart, both feet on same side of rope) and jump out." Although Shirley Temple has the leading role here, Charlie Chaplin, Betty Grable, Charlie McCarthy, Tommy Tucker, Donald Duck, and Marco Polo can also figure in the rhyme (Chaplin appears to be the most popular with Temple coming in second). The popularity of this rhyme is indicated by the 39 published sources between 1926 and 1966 listed by Abrahams in *Jump-Rope Rhymes,* pp. 26-27. The rhyme has been collected in every corner of the United States as well as in New Zealand, Australia, and the British Isles.

43. Collected by Carolyn Henry from Alethea, twelve-year-old black girl, Harrisburg, Pennsylvania (typescript, Penn State Harrisburg Folklore Archives, 1985). Abrahams lists thirteen published sources for this rhyme between 1937 and 1966 (p. 18), including one source from Canada. The rhyme has also been reported since in Australia in Turner, *Cinderella,* p. 20. Blondie and Dagwood are comic-strip characters created in 1930 by Murat Bernarch Young. Although Blondie and Dagwood are the most popular characters for this rhyme, some collections include Fred and Wilma (from the television cartoon show "The Flintstones"), Maggie and Jiggs (characters in the comic strip "Bringing Up Father," created by George McManus in 1911), and Jack and Jill (from the nursery rhyme). Sometimes Dagwood buys a pair of shoes rather than the evening news, and occasionally, Blondie and Dagwood's daughter Cookie buys the *Daily News* (a popular New York City newspaper that featured the strip in its Sunday color comic-strip section) in the last line. Some girls in the class from which Carolyn Henry took this collection also replaced the evening news with the "Patriot News," the Harrisburg morning newspaper. The use of comic characters in the rhyme can refer to the animated behavior demanded by the jump-rope activity (e.g., the second verse reported here: "Blondie jump on one foot," etc.).

44. Collected by Sandra Blakemore from Janet Jacobson, Delta, Utah, November 1970 (typescript, Brigham Young University Collection at the Fife Folklore Archives, Utah State University, 1970). This rhyme ranks among the most popular jump-rope rhymes, as indicated by the 50 published sources for the rhyme between 1927 and 1966 listed by Abrahams in *Jump-Rope Rhymes,* pp. 126-28. The rhyme has been collected in every corner of the United States as well as in Canada and the British Isles. Abrahams notes that "the lady with the alligator purse" is "the good fairy, deus ex machina, of Lucretia P. Haley's children's book, *The Peterkin Papers*" (p. 126).

45. Collected by Kevin S. Bender from Elsie Stouffer, Newburg, Pennsylvania (typescript, Mac E. Barrick Memorial Archives, Shippensburg University, 1983). Abrahams in *Jump-Rope Rhymes* lists 51 published sources for this rhyme between 1888 and 1966. In addition to having a long collecting history, the rhyme appears in a wide geographical expanse on both sides of the Atlantic. The jump-rope rhyme derives probably from the singing game "Down by the Riverside" which dates at least to the mid-nineteenth century: "Down by the riverside the green grass grows, / There stands Tracy hanging out her clothes; / She sang and she sang and she sang so sweet, / She sang for her true love across the street"; see Opie and Opie, *The Singing Game,* pp. 127-30.

46. Collected by Kevin S. Bender from Elsie Stouffer, Newburg, Pennsylvania (typescript, Mac E. Barrick Memorial Archives, Shippensburg University, 1983). Abrahams lists 29 published sources for this rhyme between 1916 and 1966, pp. 66-67. It has been reported in the United States and the British Isles, and Brian Sutton-Smith in *Folkgames of Children* cites this rhyme as the only generally known skipping rhyme around 1900 in New Zealand (p. 100); it also appears in England and Australia.

47. Collected by Ann Kilgore from Judy Garner, elementary school student, Conway, Arkansas (typescript, Arkansas Folklore Archives, Special Collections Department, David W. Mullins Library, University of Arkansas, 1962). "Bluebells, cockleshells, / Eevy, ivy over" is a commonplace prologue for many jump-rope rhyme performances; see Abrahams's *Jump-Rope Rhymes,* pp. 18-20.

48. Collected by Treva Lichti from Ken Kiester, eleven years old, Nappanee, Indiana, July 13, 1968 (typescript, Indiana University Folklore Archives, 1968).

49. Collected by Deborah Paruszewski from Susie Parsuzewski, eight years old, Wilmington, Delaware (typescript, University of Delaware Folklore Archives, 1975). Children are quick to point out the lack of maturity of other children, probably to emphasize their own maturity.

Calling someone a "baby" is a serious derision in the child's world.

50. Collected by Treva Lichti from Janet Sasaman, twelve years old, Nappanee, Indiana, July 13, 1968 (typescript, Indiana University Folklore Archives, 1968). This rhyme is one of the best-known traditional taunts.

51. Collected by Treva Lichti from Gerry Lichti, Nappanee, Indiana, July 13, 1968 (typescript, Indiana University Folklore Archives, 1968).`

52. Collected by Treva Lichti from Gerry Lichti, Nappanee, Indiana, July 4, 1968 (typescript, Indiana University Folklore Archives, 1968). The collector notes that "the first two lines of this rhyme were repeated by informants of all ages from Indiana, Nebraska, Kansas, and Texas. Sometimes 'bull's' was replaced with 'monkey's' tail."

53. Collected by Deborah Paruszewski from Susie Paruszewski, eight years old, Wilmington, Delaware (typescript, University of Delaware Folklore Archives, 1975). The rhyme as it is reported here is a taunt that involves pre-courtship behavior (see items 50-51).

54a. Collected by Dorothy Deal from Patricia Deal, fifteen years old, DeWitt, New York, December 28, 1967 (typescript, Indiana University Folklore Archives, 1968). According to the report of this collection, the informant learned the rhyme from "Baltimore, Md., neighbor children."

54b. Collected by Carolyn Fleck from Glenn Moore, nine years old, second-grade student, Fort Wayne, Indiana, April 17, 1970 (typescript, Indiana University Folklore Archives, 1970). According to the report of this collection, "This informant heard this the first time last year when she was in the first grade. This item is used to tease another child. This item's first two lines were heard before by the collector when she was a child so it has been around for some time." Sometimes this rhyme will appear as "Teacher, teacher, I declare, / I see someone's underwear. . . ."

55. Collected by Carolyn Fleck from Drew Armstrong, seven years old, second-grade student, Fort Wayne, Indiana, April 17, 1970 (typescript, Indiana University Folklore Archives, 1970). According to the report of this collection, the rhyme "is used to tease and make fun of someone and was first heard from his older sister when he was in first grade." The Knapps in *One Potato, Two Potato* report this rhyme and its various substitutions: "ten days" or "six months," "grizzly bear" or "polar bear" (pp. 90-91).

56. Collected by Deborah Paruszewski from Susie Paruszewski, eight years old, Wilmington, Delaware (typescript, University of Delaware Folklore Archives, 1975).

57. Collected by Carolyn Fleck from Glenn Moore, nine years old, second-grade student, Fort Wayne, Indiana, April 17, 1970 (typescript, Indiana University Folklore Archives, 1970). According to the report of this collection, "This item is used by the children to tease or make fun of another child. The informant heard it from another second-grader."

58. Collected by Carolyn Fleck from Julie Matson, nine years old, second-grade student, Fort Wayne, Indiana, April 17, 1970 (typescript, Indiana University Folklore Archives, 1970).

59. Collected by Carolyn Fleck from Julie Matson, nine years old, second-grade student, Fort Wayne, Indiana, April 17, 1970 (typescript, Indiana University Folklore Archives, 1970). According to the report of this collection, "The one about the 'Ump' is used by other second-graders when they are watching a game." Rhymes of derision against authority figures now include umpires and referees as competitive events have become more organized in the child's world.

60a. Collected by Carolyn Henry from Latosha, an eleven-year-old black girl, Harrisburg, Pennsylvania (typescript, Penn State Harrisburg Folklore Archives, 1985). This rhyme is a modern adaptation of older rhymes that follow from the cry "Made you look." The rhyme is often uttered as a "catch" — that is, it is sometimes used in play to make a child look at something that isn't there; see Eugenia Millard, "Sticks and Stones," p. 31; Roger D. Abrahams, "The 'Catch' in Negro Philadelphia," p. 109.

60b. Collected by Carolyn Henry from Jonathan, eleven years old, Harrisburg, Pennsylvania (typescript, Penn State Harrisburg Folklore Archives, 1985). This is another modern adaptation of "Made you look" catches (see item 60a).

61. Collected by Carolyn Henry from Nariah, ten years old, black girl, Harrisburg, Pennsylvania (typescript, Penn State Harrisburg Folklore Archives, 1985).

62a. Collected by Treva Lichti from Susie Pippen, seventeen years old, Nappanee, Indiana, July 13, 1968 (typescript, Indiana University Folklore Archives, 1968). According to the report of this collection, this rhyme was "learned from friends while in grade school in the late 1950s at Nappanee, Indiana. This rhyme was also repeated to me by children who are presently in fifth and sixth grades at Nappanee, Indiana." The Knapps in *One Potato Two Potato* offer this rhyme as traditional on the day the children are released for summer vacation. They list two variants on p. 224.

62b. Reported by Lana Lassiter, 20 years old, Windfall, Indiana, from memories of her childhood (typescript, Indiana University Folklore Archives, 1970). According to the report of this collection, she learned this rhyme in 1957 from schoolmates; along with this rhyme she also knew the rhyme listed here as item 62a. The first two lines of both rhymes are reported from oral tradition in Brown, *Amen, Brother Ben,* p. 91.

63a. Collected by Carolyn Fleck from Paul Holmquist, seven years old, second-grade student, Fort Wayne, Indiana, April 17, 1970 (typescript, Indiana University Folklore Archives, 1970). "Hi ho, hi ho" is the familiar first line of the dwarves' song from the Disney movie *Snow White.* Yet the parody verse appears in most collections as a chanted rhyme rather than a song, probably because of its similarity to other derisive rhymes about teachers; see Opie and Opie, *Lore and Language of Schoolchildren,* pp. 361-65.

63b. Collected by Mary Reynolds from Jimmy Reynolds, sixth-grade student, Wilmington, Delaware (typescript, University of Delaware Folklore Archives, 1973).

63c. Collected by Mary Ann Jackson from Steven Smith, ten years old, Wilmington, Delaware, September 22, 1973 (typescript, University of Delaware Folklore Archives, 1973). According to the report of this collection, "Steven repeats this chant with his friends while at Saturday morning religion classes. He learned it from friends while on a bus ride to a camp trip last summer. Reciters of this verse use it as a teasing phrase against their teachers the parochial nuns."

64a. Collected by Hannelore Wertz from a white ninth-grade boy, York, Pennsylvania (typescript, Penn State Harrisburg Folklore Archives, 1982). As the Opies point out in *Lore and Language of Schoolchildren,* "Quite commonly children . . . ape the flustered lecturer, not unknown in their school halls: Ladles and Jellyspoons, / I stand upon this speech to make a platform. / The train I arrive in has not yet come, / So I took a bus and walked. / I come before you / To stand behind you / And tell you something I know nothing about" (p. 25).

64b. Collected by Hannelore Wertz from a white ninth-grade boy, York, Pennsylvania (typescript, Penn State Harrisburg Folklore Archives, 1982). This rhyme combines two traditional recitations popular in the United States and England. The first is the parody of a formal lecture covered in item 64a. This particular variant is closely matched by a rhyme reported by Ord in "Ladies and Gentlemen," p. 1. The second is "Two boys got up to fight. . ." The two recitations are often collected together as one verse, although they have also been collected separately.

65a. Collected by Carolyn Fleck from Curt Lynch, eight years old, second-grade student, Fort Wayne, Indiana, April 17, 1970 (typescript, Indiana University Folklore Archives, 1970). According to the report of this collection, "This informant first heard this rhyme from his ten-year-old sister when he was in the first grade. The informant is usually quite shy, but he lost this shyness while telling this rhyme, so I would say that it has served its purpose, by giving this child momentary self-confidence."

65b. Collected by Carolyn Kramer from Mollie Kramer, eleven years old, Forest, Indiana, February 16, 1970 (typescript, Indiana University Folklore Archives, 1970). According to the report of this collection, "Mollie Kramer learned this rhyme while we were in Bloomington, Indiana, in 1968. The twelve-year-old boy who told her lived in the same apartment building with her."

66. Collected by Mary Reynolds from Jimmy Reynolds, sixth-grade student, Wilmington, Delaware, September 1973 (typescript, University of Delaware Folklore Archives, 1973). Sometimes this rhyme will simply be reported as "Tarzan the monkey man, / Swinging on a rubber band."

67a. Collected by Treva Lichti from Mabel M. Bontrager, Hutchinson, Kansas, July 15, 1968 (typescript, Indiana University Folklore Archives, 1968). This is a parody of the bedtime prayer dating to the eighteenth century, "Now I lay me down to sleep, / I pray the Lord my soul to keep, / And if I die before I wake, / I pray the Lord my soul to take"; see Opie and Opie, *Oxford Dictionary of Nursery Rhymes,* p. 221.

67b. Collected by Treva Lichti from Carl Bontrager, 22 years old, from his memories of childhood, Hutchinson, Kansas, July 16, 1968 (typescript, Indiana University Folklore Archives, 1968). According to the report of this collection, this parody was "learned when he was nine years old, 1954, from a friend at Kent School, a one-room country school near Hutchinson, Kansas."

67c. Collected by Treva Lichti from Kellie Curtis, ten years old, Nappanee, Indiana, July 11, 1968 (typescript, Indiana University Folklore Archives, 1968). According to the report of this collection, the parody was "learned from friends in 1966 when in the fourth grade at Central Grade School, Nappanee, Indiana."

67d. Collected by Treva Lichti from Kellie Curtis, ten years old, Nappanee, Indiana, July 11, 1968 (typescript, Indiana University Folklore Archives, 1968). According to the report of this collection, the parody was "learned from friends in 1966 when in the fourth grade at Central Grade

School, Nappanee, Indiana." Monteiro in "Parodies of Scripture, Prayer, and Hymn" offers this rhyme from oral tradition with peanuts being the precious commodity (p. 46).

68. Collected by Mary Ann Jackson from Steven Smith, ten years old, Wilmington, Delaware, September 22, 1973 (typescript, University of Delaware Folklore Archvies, 1973). According to the report of this collection, this is a parody of the Cub Scout Code. "Steven uses this saying on the playground with his friends. He picked it up from fellow cub scouts in his local den a few years ago. Participants consider it as an interesting variation of the traditional 'goody-goody' cub scout honor code."

69. Collected by Carolyn Henry from Tanisha, eleven-year-old black girl, Harrisburg, Pennsylvania (typescript, Penn State Harrisburg Folklore Archives, 1985). This is a verse often recited on Halloween.

70. Collected by Linda Craig from Kimberly Craig, eight years old, third-grade student, Kokomo, Indiana, September 29, 1969 (typescript, Indiana University Folklore Archives, 1969). This is a parody of a jingle for a popular bathroom cleanser.

71. Collected by Hannelore Wertz from a ninth-grade boy, York, Pennsylvania (typescript, Penn State Harrisburg Folklore Archives, 1982). The same verse was also collected from Mary Ann Jackson from Richard Jackson, 47 years old, Wilmington, Delaware, September 21, 1973 (typescript, University of Delaware Folklore Archives, 1973). According to the report of this collection, "My uncle recited this rhyme when he was a little boy outside playing with other children. He learned it as a child from playing with his friends. They all considered it as an amusing takeoff on the original nursery rhyme." The original rhyme is "Mary had a little lamb, / Its fleece was white as snow, / And everywhere that Mary went / The lamb was sure to go." The Opies in *Oxford Dictionary of Nursery Rhymes* iterate the belief that the "Mary had a little lamb" rhymes are "the best known four-line verse in the English language" (p. 300).

72. Collected by Mary Jackson from Steven Smith, ten years old, Wilmington, Delaware, September 22, 1973 (typescript, University of Delaware Folklore Archives, 1973). This is a parody of "Old Mother Hubbard / Went to the cupboard, / To fetch her poor dog a bone. / But when she came there / The cupboard was bare, / And so the poor dog had none."

73. Collected by Mac Barrick from a thirteen-year-old girl, Shippensburg, Pennsylvania, October 1986 (typescript, Mac Barrick Memorial Archives, Shippensburg University, 1986). This is a parody of the eighteenth-century nursery rhyme "Jack and Jill went up the hill, / To fetch a pail of water, / Jack fell down and broke his crown, / And Jill came tumbling after"; see Opie and Opie, *Oxford Dictionary of Nursery Rhymes,* pp. 224-26.

74. Collected by Susan I. Ralstin from Barbara Dunton, 24 years old, from her memories of childhood, Marion, Indiana, February 15, 1970 (typescript, Indiana University Folklore Archives, 1970). The Knapps in *One Potato, Two Potato* place this rhyme under the category of "bathroom shockers." They cite the verse as "The night was dark, a scream was heard, / A man got hit by a low-flying turd" (p. 184).

75a. Reported by Deborah Paruszewski, 20 years old, from her memories of childhood, Wilmington, Delaware (typescript, University of Delaware Folklore Archives, 1975). The Knapps in *One Potato, Two Potato* discuss rhymes such as this, which they categorize as "clean shockers." Often learned at summer camps, they argue, "by singing them, children assert a degree of control over their own squeamishness and immaturity" (p. 181).

75b. Reported by Greg Patterson, 25 years old, from his memories of childhood, Cedar City, Utah (typescript, Fife Folklore Archives, Utah State University, 1971). According to the report of this collection, Patterson "learned the rhyme on the playground at Cedar City Elementary School in Cedar City, Utah. He and his friends would tell the rhyme at dinner time to make people sick."

76a. Collected by Deborah Paruszewski from Cheryl Devine, twelve years old, Wilmington, Delaware (typescript, University of Delaware Folklore Archives, 1975).

76b. Collected by Linda Olsen from a white boy, Kearns, Utah, Fall 1978 (typescript, Fife Folklore Archives, Utah State University, 1980). According to the report of this collection, "this rhyme is used when school children are served lunch of which they don't approve. The rhyme makes fun of school lunch by comparing the food to animal parts that are unusual as well as gross."

76c. Collected by Linda Olsen from a white girl, Logan, Utah, fall 1978 (typescript, Fife Folklore Archives, Utah State University, 1980). This rhyme indicates the wide variation that this rhyme has undergone (see items 76a-b). In the rhyme reported here, part of the appeal for the expressive child is the alliteration as well as the images created.

Chapter Four. Autograph Album Inscriptions

1a. Collected by Ginger Gail Gillis from the fourth-grade autograph album of Linda Hallmark, 1955, Little Rock, Arkansas (typescript, University of Arkansas Folklore Archives, Special Collections Department, David W. Mullins Library, 1968). The collector reports that no signature accompanied the verse, and that it appeared in the same book three times.

1b. Collected by Ginger Gail Gillis from the fifth-grade autograph album of Sally Cline, 1960, Little Rock, Arkansas (typescript, University of Arkansas Folklore Archives, David W. Mullins Library, 1968).

2. Collected by Ginger Gail Gillis from the fifth-grade autograph album of Sally Cline, 1960, Little Rock, Arkansas (typescript, University of Arkansas Folklore Archives, David W. Mullins Library, 1968). According to the collector, the verse is signed by "Sharon J." The verse ranks as one of the most popular modern verses.

3. Collected by Ginger Gail Gillis from the fifth-grade autograph album of Sally Cline, 1960, Little Rock, Arkansas (typescript, University of Arkansas Folklore Archives, David W. Mullins Library, 1968). This verse is signed by "Peggy."

4. Collected by Ginger Gail Gillis from the fifth-grade autograph album of Sally Cline, 1960, Little Rock, Arkansas (typescript, University of Arkansas Folklore Archives, David W. Mullins Library, 1968). The verse is signed by "James."

5. Collected by Cynthia Bough from the autograph album of Mary Ashcraft, 1969, Kokomo, Indiana (typescript, Indiana University Folklore Archives, 1970). "This autograph," the collector comments, "should be written on a downhill slant." Like item 3, this one breaks norms to attract attention and to underscore the playful quality of the children's autograph album custom.

6. Collected by Treva Lichti from the autograph album of Tammy Hornish, twelve years old, 1968, Nappanee, Indiana (typescript, Indiana University Folklore Archives, 1968).

7. Collected by Simon Bronner from his sixth-grade autograph album, 1965, Brooklyn, New York (typescript, Penn State Harrisburg Folklore Archives, 1981). The verse is signed by "Gail." This popular verse is sometimes reported as "Remember the fights, remember the fun"; see Brown, *Amen, Brother Ben*, p. 91.

8. Collected by Annemarie O'Driscoll from the autograph albums of middle-class suburban girls, 1975, Wilmington, Delaware (typescript, University of Delaware Folklore Archives, 1975).

9. Collected by Ginger Gail Gillis from the fourth-grade autograph album of Linda Hallmark, 1955, Little Rock, Arkansas (typescript, University of Arkansas Folklore Archives, David W. Mullins Library, 1968). This verse is signed by "Julia E."; one sign of its popularity is that it appeared in the same book four times.

10. Collected by Carolyn Henry from the sixth-grade autograph album of Jason, eleven-year-old black boy, 1985, Harrisburg, Pennsylvania (typescript, Penn State Harrisburg Folklore Archives, 1985). A variant of this verse, "I was so glad to have a friend like you," appears in Knapp and Knapp, *One Potato, Two Potato*, p. 152; see also Wilson, "Yours Till," p. 249.

11. Collected by Carolyn Henry from the sixth-grade autograph album of Latosha, eleven-year-old black girl, 1985, Harrisburg, Pennsylvania (typescript, Penn State Harrisburg Folklore Archives, 1985).

12. Collected by Simon Bronner from his sixth-grade autograph album, 1965, Brooklyn, New York (typescript, Penn State Harrisburg Folklore Archives, 1981). "Dated till horseflies," this verse is signed by "Melodee."

13. Collected by Carolyn Kramer from the autograph album of Mollie Kramer, eleven years old, 1970, Forest, Indiana (typescript, Indiana University Folklore Archives, 1970). The verse is signed by "Mollie."

14. Collected by Ginger Gail Gillis from the fourth-grade autograph album of Linda Hallmark, 1955, Little Rock, Arkansas (typescript, University of Arkansas Folklore Archives, David W. Mullins Library, 1968). The verse is signed by "Cecelia."

15. Collected by Ginger Gail Gillis from the fifth-grade autograph album of Sally Cline, 1960, Little Rock, Arkansas (typescript, University of Arkansas Folklore Archives, David W. Mullins Library, 1968). The verse is signed by "Kay." The B-52 bomber is a large military airplane.

16a. Collected by Ginger Gail Gillis from the fourth-grade autograph album of Corky Ritchie, 1956, Little Rock, Arkansas (typescript, University of Arkansas Folklore Archives, David W. Mullins Library, 1968). The verse is signed by "Bill." The accusation of foul odor is the most common parody on the "sweet" sentiment of "Roses are red, violets are blue" (see item 9). In other versions, skunks, onions, stinkweeds, pig's feet, and the owner's mom stink.

16b. Collected by Rebecca Wood from the autograph album of Loretta Smith, Kokomo, Indiana (typescript, Indiana University Folklore Archives, 1968).

16c. Collected by Lana Lassiter from her sixth-grade autograph album, 1963, Windfall, Indiana (typescript, Indiana University Folklore Archives, 1970).

17. Collected by Simon Bronner from his sixth-grade autograph album, 1965, Brooklyn, New York (typescript, Penn State Harrisburg Folklore Archives, 1981). The verse is signed "Good Luck in 246, Robert Panzer" (the junior high school's number in the city school system is 246). A version of the verse appears in Knapp and Knapp, *One Potato,* p. 73.

18. Collected by Cynthia Bough from the sixth-grade autograph album of Nancy Bough, 1965, Springville, Indiana (typescript, Indiana University Folklore Archives, 1970).

19. Collected by Simon Bronner from his sixth-grade autograph album, 1965, Brooklyn, New York (typescript, Penn State Harrisburg Folklore Archives, 1981). This verse is signed by "Richie," who as I remember hadn't yet taken a drink. But this verse is not unique, and it is related to other references in autograph verse to drunkenness.

20. Collected by Simon Bronner from his eighth-grade autograph album, 1967, Brooklyn, New York (typescript, Penn State Harrisburg Folklore Archives, 1981). "Dated Till Hell Freezes Over and Little Devils Go Ice Skating" is signed by "Rochelle," who as I remember had a bit of a crush on me, or was it the other way around?

21. Collected by Ginger Gail Gillis from the fourth-grade autograph album of Linda Hallmark, 1955, Little Rock, Arkansas (typescript, University of Arkansas Folklore Archives, David W. Mullins Library, 1968).

22. Collected by Ginger Gail Gillis from the fourth-grade autograph album of Linda Hallmark, 1955, Little Rock, Arkansas (typescript, University of Arkansas Folklore Archives, David W. Mullins Library, 1968). This verse is signed by "Kay." Its popularity is indicated by the fact that the item appeared in the same book two more times, and in five of the six albums that Gillis collected. It also was reported in every other archival collection of autograph verse I checked.

23. Collected by Cynthia Bough from the autograph album of Mary Ashcraft, Kokomo, Indiana (typescript, Indiana·University Folklore Archives, 1969). The verse is signed "Jack Sims."

24. Collected by Cynthia Bough from the autograph album of Mary Ashcraft, Kokomo, Indiana (typescript, Indiana University Folklore Archives, 1969).

25. Collected by Ginger Gail Gillis from her seventh-grade autograph album, 1961, Fordyce, Arkansas (typescript, University of Arkansas Folklore Archives, David W. Mullins Library, 1968). The verse is signed by "Chip Cannon"; the verse also appeared in her sixth-grade album signed by "Louis Hunt."

26. Collected by Sandy Bailif from the autograph album of Ganie Gundy, 1972, Provo, Utah (typescript, Brigham Young University Collection at the Fife Folklore Archives, Utah State University, 1972).

27. Collected by Sandy Bailif from the autograph album of Ganie Bundy, 1972, Provo, Utah (typescript, Brigham Young University Collection at the Fife Folklore Archives, Utah State University, 1972).

28. Collected by Ginger Gail Gillis from her sixth-grade autograph album, 1959, Fordyce, Arkansas (typescript, University of Arkansas Folklore Archives, 1968). The verse is signed by "Ann." It is one of several verses that treats marriage and child-bearing as a separate state of being which puts limits on the married person's friendships (see items 27, 32).

29. Collected by Susan Jones from the autograph album of Debbie Robinson, Kokomo, Indiana (typescript, Indiana University Folklore Archives, 1970). Versions of this rhyme use the number "25," although sometimes they will use "four or five."

30. Collected by Ginger Gail Gillis from her seventh-grade autograph album, 1961, Fordyce, Arkansas (typescript, University of Arkansas Folklore Archives, David W. Mullins Library, 1968). The verse is signed by "Donna Gray." The collector comments in explanation of the verse that "Donna and I were cheerleaders."

31. Collected by Ginger Gail Gillis from her seventh-grade autograph album, 1961, Fordyce, Arkansas (typescript, University of Arkansas Folklore Archives, David W. Mullins Library, 1968). The verse is signed by "Shelbie Frazier."

32. Collected by Rebecca Wood from the autograph album of Loretta Smith, 1968, Kokomo, Indiana (typescript, Indiana University Folklore Archives, 1968).

33. Collected by Cynthia Bough from the autograph album of Nancy Bough, twelve years old, 1964, Springville, Indiana (typescript, Indiana University Folklore Archives, 1970).

34. Collected by Ginger Gail Gillis from her seventh-grade autograph album, 1961, Fordyce,

Arkansas (typescript, University of Arkansas Folklore Archives, David W. Mullins Library, 1968). The verse is signed by "Jerry"; the collector reports that the verse also appeared in another book she collected.

35. Collected by Rebecca Wood from the autograph album of Loretta Smith, 1968, Kokomo, Indiana (typescript, Indiana University Folklore Archives, 1968).

36. Collected by Cynthia Bough from the autograph album of Nancy Bough, twelve years old, 1964, Springville, Indiana (typescript, Indiana University Folklore Archives, 1970).

37. Collected by Rebecca Wood from the autograph album of Loretta Smith, 1968, Kokomo, Indiana (typescript, Indiana University Folklore Archives, 1968).

38. Collected by Cynthia Bough from the autograph album of Mary Ashcraft, 1969, Kokomo, Indiana (typescript, Indiana University Folklore Archives, 1970).

39. Collected by Ginger Gail Gillis from the fourth-grade autograph book of Linda Hallmark, 1955, Little Rock, Arkansas (typescript, University of Arkansas Folklore Archives, David W. Mullins Library, 1968). This inscription can be used alone or alongside a verse. In some versions the "U R" is omitted; many substitute "cute" or "sweet" or "nice" for "good."

40. Collected by Ginger Gail Gillis from the fifth-grade autograph album of Sally Cline, 1960, Little Rock, Arkansas (typescript, University of Arkansas Folklore Archives, 1968). The verse is signed by "Karen."

41. Collected by Ginger Gail Gillis from the eighth-grade autograph album of Linda Hallmark, 1961, Little Rock, Arkansas (typescript, University of Arkansas Folklore Archives, 1968). The verse is signed by "Suzanne Strickland."

42. Collected by Ginger Gail Gillis from the fifth-grade autograph album of Sally Cline, 1960, Little Rock, Arkansas (typescript, University of Arkansas Folklore Archives, David W. Mullins Library, 1968). The verse is signed by "Margie." Sometimes each line of the verse has a "2" preceding it. A common variant of this inscription is "Two in a hammock, / Ready to kiss, / When all of a sudden / They went like this," and "this" will be printed upside down.

43. Collected by Susan Jones from the autograph album of Debbie Robinson, Kokomo, Indiana (typescript, Indiana University Folklore Archives, 1970). "Four Roses" is the name of a popular whiskey.

44. Collected by Simon Bronner from his eighth-grade autograph album, 1967, Brooklyn, New York (typescript, Penn State Harrisburg Folklore Archives, 1981). "Dated till Herman marries Sherri," the inscription is signed "Love, Sherri" and is accompanied with the saying "Blessed is he who sits on a tack for he shall rise."

45. Collected by Cynthia Bough from her fourth-grade autograph album, 1959, Kokomo, Indiana (typescript, Indiana University Folklore Archives, 1970). This is translated as "Too wise you are, / Too wise you be, / I see you are / Too wise for me." This is the most frequently reported of the arithmetic inscriptions.

46. Collected by Carolyn Henry from the sixth-grade autograph album of Kyuati, twelve-year-old black girl, Harrisburg, Pennsylvania (typescript, Penn State Harrisburg Folklore Archives, 1985).

47. Collected by Ginger Gail Gillis from the fourth-grade autograph album of Linda Hallmark, 1955, Little Rock, Arkansas (typescript, University of Arkansas Folklore Archives, David W. Mullins Library, 1968). This verse is signed "Linda C." It is a common parody of the old sentimental verse with the last line "I love you as long as I live."

48. Collected by Ginger Gail Gillis from the fourth-grade autograph album of Linda Hallmark, 1955, Little Rock, Arkansas (typescript, University of Arkansas Folklore Archives, David W. Mullins Library, 1968). The verse is signed "Karen Millot" and appeared in three of the six books that Gillis collected.

49. Collected by Simon Bronner from his sixth-grade autograph album, 1965, Brooklyn, New York (typescript, Penn State Harrisburg Folklore Archives, 1981). This rhyme appears twice in the album. The first time it is signed "Terri" and "Dated till butter flies," and in the second instance it is signed "Jo Ann" and "Dated till Soupy Sales."

50. Collected by Simon Bronner from his sixth-grade autograph album, 1965, Brooklyn, New York (typescript, Penn State Harrisburg Folklore Archives, 1981). "Dated till butterflies" the verse is signed "Robert Rosen."

51. Collected by Simon Bronner from his eighth-grade autograph album, 1967, Brooklyn, New York (typescript, Penn State Harrisburg Folklore Archives, 1981). "Dated till bacon strips," the verse is signed "Your friend, Andrew." The verse is related to and may be an urban adaptation of one reported from 1956 in Ohio, in "Looking Through the Archives," p. 68: "Tulips in the garden, / Tulips in the park, / But the kind Joyce likes best / Are two lips in the dark."

52. Collected by Cynthia Bough from the autograph album of Mary Ashcraft, 1969, Kokomo, Indiana (typescript, Indiana University Folklore Archives, 1970).

53. Collected by Treva Lichti from the autograph album of Joan Young, 1968, Bourbon, Indiana (typescript, Indiana University Folklore Archives, 1968).

54. Collected by Susan Jones from the autograph album of Debbie Robinson, 1970, Kokomo, Indiana (typescript, Indiana University Folklore Archives, 1970).

55. Collected by Susan Jones from the autograph album of Brenda Manning, 1970, Kokomo, Indiana (typescript, Indiana University Folklore Archives, 1970). The verse reported here may be a takeoff on an older verse reported by Charles Francis Potter in "Round Went the Album," pp. 11-12: "May you always be happy / And live at your ease, / And have a kind husband / To tease when you please."

56. Collected by Susan Jones from the autograph album of Mary Manning, 1970, Kokomo, Indiana (typescript, Indiana University Folklore Archives, 1970).

57. Collected by Susan Jones from the autograph album of Debbie Robinson, 1970, Kokomo, Indiana (typescript, Indiana University Folklore Archives, 1970).

58. Collected by Simon Bronner from his sixth-grade autograph album, 1965, Brooklyn, New York (typescript, Penn State Harrisburg Folklore Archives, 1981). The most popular inscription of this list with seven pages was "Dated till toilet bowls." Appearing more than three times were "Dated till butterflies," "Dated till Catskill Mountains," "Dated till Bear Mountain gets dressed," and "Dated till the kitchen sinks." In other collections, they were prefaced by "Yours till."

Chapter Five. Song Parodies

1. Collected by Madeline Mongan from Dorin Day, eight-year-old girl, Heidi Rasmussen, eight years old, Henry Ackerman, eight years old, Sharon Harward, eight years old, Elizabeth Gray, eight years old, and Aaron Tovo, seven years old, Newark, Delaware, March 3, 1972 (typescript, University of Delaware Folklore Archives, 1972). According to the collector's report, "The informants said that they used the song when they really had a teacher they hated. Sharon said she sang often on the way home from school." The children offered the first two verses as the standard verses, and the last two as typical variations.

2. Collected by Linda Craig from Susan Bargerhuff, ten-year-old fifth-grader, Kokomo, Indiana, November 14, 1969 (typescript, Indiana University Folklore Archives, 1970).

3. Reported by Janell Thatcher from her childhood memories (c. 1957) of elementary school, Homedale, Idaho (typescript, Brigham Young University Collection at the Fife Folklore Archives, Utah State University, 1972). She explains her use of the song this way: "I learned this song from my older brother Roland the summer before I went to school. He was about eleven years old and I was six. I thought it was a terrible song but I sang it anyway. The most popular time to sing it was on the last day of school while we rode the school bus home for the last time before enjoying three months of freedom. The song emphasizes the victory of the students over the teachers."

4. Reported by Lana Lassiter from her childhood memories of elementary school (c. 1960), Windfall, Indiana (typescript, Indiana University Folklore Archives, 1970). According to Lassiter, the song was learned on the school bus. This version modifies the usually violent tone of the parodies by "tickling" the principal and offering that the tangerine's juice comes running down. The result in this song is embarrassment rather than annihilation.

5. Collected by Jeff Fisher from Joe Fisher, twelve years old, Benson, Utah (typescript, Fife Folklore Archives, Utah State University, 1983).

6. Collected by Becky Bradley from Mack Bradley, eight-year-old second-grader, Big Piney, Wyoming (typescript, Fife Folklore Archives, 1982). The inclusion of the first verse shows how children can manipulate texts in their performances. Children commonly know many parodies that they can call upon for creative ideas. In addition, children often know more than one parody of the "Battle Hymn" itself.

7. Collected by Paula Johnson from sixth-graders, Newark, Delaware, 1973. Paula Johnson was a student teacher who collected parodies from her students. In this song, the "aides" get into the act; they commonly supervise lunchrooms and provide other services in the school. They are usually considered at the bottom of the authoritarian hierarchy, just above the children. The rebellious act of writing in the books is sometimes replaced by writing on the walls in some versions.

8. Collected by H.T. Reed from Roubert Poulin and Paul Westleigh, twelve years old, Lewiston, Maine (typescript, Northeast Folklore Archives, University of Maine, 1960). Reed, a teacher, comments, "Before this was sung to me, it was prefaced with profuse statements that it didn't refer to me, but they knew I was collecting material and wondered if I could use this. There are various versions of this being sung in the elementary schools."

9. Collected by Beth Smith from two eleven-year-old girls, Columbus, Indiana, February 1973 (typescript, Indiana University Folklore Archives, 1973).

10. Collected by Madeline Mongan from William Mongan, thirteen years old, John Mongan, eleven years old, Daniel Mongan, eight years old, Newark, Delaware (typescript, University of Delaware Archives, 1972).

11. Collected by Carolyn Henry from Kyuati, twelve-year-old black girl, Harrisburg, Pennsylvania (typescript, Penn State Harrisburg Folklore Archives, 1985). Kyuati learned this song when she was five from her older brother. Although she learned it as a playful song, in other collections the song is recalled from summer camp. In 1963, words and music to "On Top of Spaghetti" were adapted and commercially recorded by Tom Glazer.

12. Collected by Paula Johnson from sixth-graders, Newark, Delaware (typescript, University of Delaware Folklore Archives, 1973).

13. Collected by Daphne Chu from Jennifer Chu, twelve years old, Wilmington, Delaware, September 29, 1980 (typescript, University of Delaware Folklore Archives, 1980). Daphne Chu collected this song from her younger sister while her sister was playing at home with a friend. According to the informant, she learned it on a bus coming home from a school trip during the fifth grade. It is a parody of a parody in a sense, for Jennifer thought it was a funny take-off on "On Top of Spaghetti" (see item 11). Having become so familiar, "On Top of Spaghetti" can itself be a target of parody, just as the original ballad has.

14. Collected by Andrea Ray from R. Fredrick Drake, twelve years old, Newark, Delaware, September 24, 1973 (typescript, University of Delaware Folklore Archives, 1973). According to the report of this collection, "The informant said that he learned this song in school when he was around eight years old. The first time he heard this parody it was sung by one boy from his class to a group of classmates during recess. It was also sung on class trips. It was sung mostly to impress the other kids, to show them how smart you were."

15. Reported by Vaughn Crawford from her memories of sixth grade at the Edith W. Fritch grammar school (c. 1963), Carson City, Nevada (typescript, Fife Folklore Archives, Utah State University, 1972). In his report of the collection, Crawford explains the background of this parody in his experience: "I learned this song in the sixth grade, at the Edith W. Fritch grammar school. The sixth grade is the highest grade there, and as such, the sixth graders feel it is actually their school and only by their permission and good graces are the faculty allowed to come and captivate them for a few hours each day. Each successive sixth grade class at E.W. Fritch, as far back as I can remember, sang a song like this, with a few minor corrections thrown in each year to prove that the new class was just as creative as the last. The song was usually sung during the all-too-infrequent recesses, and usually sung only by the boys. The girls would, however, stand and listen in a state of awe and admiration as the boys would sing of the brave deeds they were about to do."

16. Collected by Marian Schlange from Toni Johnson, ten-year-old girl, Ventura, California (typescript, Brigham Young University Collection at the Fife Folklore Archives, Utah State University, 1972). The collector reports: "During the summer of 1972, I was employed by the Recreation Department in Ventura, California, as the Playground Specialist in Music and Drama. I visited sixteen playgrounds weekly, leading children in recreational songs and games. However, I didn't do all the teaching. I quickly learned the songs that the children wanted to sing. Once I was recognized as a member in the 'Society of Children' the children were eager to teach me their favorite songs and chants. This song was among the Top Ten Favorites — Toni taught it to me, but all the children knew it." The parody twists the serene detachment of "Merrily, merrily, merrily, merrily, / Life is but a dream" around to the decisive involvement of "Throw your teacher overboard."

17. Reported by Larry Stewart from his memories of fourth grade (c. 1958) in Kailua, Oahu, Hawaii (typescript, Fife Folklore Archives, Utah State University, 1972). According to Stewart, he sang this song during school recess. The original song is itself a frolicking tune copyrighted as a comical minstrel song in 1891 and made famous by the turn-of-the-century music-hall singing of Lottie Collins in England, herself the subject of many a children's rhyme.

18. Collected by Madeline Monigan from William Monigan, thirteen, John Monigan, eleven, Daniel Monigan, eight, Newark, Delaware (typescript, University of Delaware Folklore Archives, 1972). This song parodies the eighteenth-century ditty that begins "Yankee Doodle went to town upon a little pony." By the early nineteenth century, the song with the comical lines "Yankee Doodle came to town riding on a pony, / He stuck a feather in his nose and called it macaroni" had entered the nursery; see Fuld, *Book of World-Famous Music,* pp. 659-60; Peter and Iona Opie, *Oxford Dictionary of Nursery Rhymes,* pp. 439-42.

19. Collected by Treva Lichti from Terry Eppley, twelve-year-old boy, Nappanee, Indiana, July 15, 1968 (typescript, Indiana University Folklore Archives, 1968). Lichti reports that the informant learned this verse from friends in grade school.

20. Collected by Linda Allen from Sandy Harnagel, 21 years old, who remembered the song from her childhood (typescript, Fife Folklore Archives, Utah State University, 1972). The original song "Bring Back My Bonnie to Me" was written in 1882 by Charles E. Pratt under the pseudonym H.J. Fulmer.

21. Collected by Cynthia Parrish from Judy Snyder, Payson Canyon, Utah (typescript, Fife Folklore Archives, 1978). According to the report of this collection, "It was during camp that I first remember Judy singing this song. She sang it around the campfire one night, and after that we would always ask her to sing it again. Other girls would join in when they knew the words. Most of the girls thought it was pretty gross, but no one really objected to it being sung." This parody combines a takeoff on "My Bonnie" with a spoken line from a gum commercial popular during the 1970s.

22. Collected by Mary Hetzel from Pam Mathews, Riverside, Illinois (typescript, Fife Folklore Archives, Utah State University, 1978). According to the report of this collection, "This is rather a blunt song, but none the less, Pam taught me this song when we were in the second or third grade. She sung it to me on the way home from school one day. She taught it to me later the same day when we were playing in my back yard."

23. Reported by Amy St. Clair, 21 years old, from her childhood memories (c. 1974), Dallas, Pennsylvania (typescript, Mac E. Barrick Memorial Folklore Archives, Shippensburg University, 1986). St. Clair states that she learned this song in elementary school and performed it during recess.

24. Collected by Mac E. Barrick, Carlisle, Pennsylvania, 1949-51 (typescript, Mac E. Barrick Memorial Folklore Archives, Shippensburg University, 1986).

25. Collected by Estelle Tulloss from Pauline Matt, 21 years old, from her childhood memories of elementary school, Ardmore, Pennsylvania (typescript, University of Delaware Folklore Archives, 1973). According to the report of this collection, the informant said, "I learned this song back when I was a little kid, probably in elementary school when we ran around singing songs that imitated any other songs we heard."

26. Reported by Patricia Ward, 24 years old, from her memories of childhood (c. 1971) in Albuquerque, New Mexico (typescript, Fife Folklore Archives, 1972). Ward states that "when I was in elementary school my friends taught me this song at Christmas time. I can't remember how old I was for sure, but I would guess about eight years old. My friends and I were goofing off, trying to top one another and this song came up." This religious song comes up of course at Christmas, and its conversion to a antischool parody bears a resemblance to what happens to "Battle Hymn of the Republic" (see item 1).

27. Collected by Eileen Black from Lydia McDaniel, 20 years old, from her childhood memories (c. 1962), Burnsflat, Oklahoma (typescript, Fife Folklore Archives, Utah State University, 1970). Gene Autry's version of this song, which was first published in 1949, is one of America's favorite Christmas songs and one of its all-time best-selling records; see Fuld, *Book of World-Famous Music,* p. 476. Gene Autry's popularity as a cowboy singer probably explains the rise of a parody about "Randolph the six-shooter cowpoke" or "Randolph the silver cowboy" or "Randolph the red gun cowboy" or "Roundoff the bull-legged cowboy" or "Rudolph the red-nosed gangster."

28. Reported by Thales Smith, Jr., 24 years old, from his memories of elementary school (c. 1962), Provo, Utah (typescript, Brigham Young University Collection at the Fife Folklore Archives, Utah State University, 1972).

29. Collected by Carolyn Henry from Robert, black twelve-year-old, Harrisburg, Pennsylvania (typescript, Penn State Harrisburg Folklore Archives, 1985).

30. Collected by Linda Craig from Kimberly·Craig, eight-year-old third-grader, Kokomo, Indiana, October 9, 1969 (typescript, Indiana University Folklore Archives, 1970). The collector comments that "Kim picked this song up at school and my kindergarten son also came home singing it." The references in this parody are to the comic-book, and later television, characters Batman and Robin.

31. Collected by Carolyn Henry from Danielle, black eleven-year-old, sixth grade, Harrisburg,

Pennsylvania (typescript, Penn State Harrisburg Folklore Archives, 1985).

32. Collected by Clara Kathleen Bridgewater from Kim Bridgewater, twelve-year-old seventh-grader, Sharpsville, Indiana, December 1969 (typescript, Indiana University Folklore Archives, 1970). The collector comments that the child learned the parody in elementary school. "We Three Kings of Orient Are" is one of the more frequently parodied carols, probably because it is so familiar to children's choirs and it has a spirit of pronouncement that appeals to the comrade-ship of children's play groups.

33. Reported by Melanie Hansen from her memories of camp (c. 1972), Brigham City, Utah (typescript, Fife Folklore Archives, Utah State University, 1981). According to the report of this collection, "This song is always sung in a large group. Sometimes if there aren't enough people then we just sing it while we are hiking or doing the daily camp chores. One year our ward picked this song to do on the Stake Skit Night. We all acted the song out. And then we taught it to the audience. It was a fun song. But the actions made the whole thing. Each year someone else thinks up a new action. Such as eating the oatmeal cookies. Or spraying on the mosquito repellant. The actions seem to have stuck. Because now the song is never sung without them. This song helps us make jokes about the awful camper's life." This carol is a natural for children's parody, because in its performance is a form of speech play. Children have to remember all the gifts in succession and be able to sing them at a good clip.

34. Collected by Treva Lichti from Colleen Phillips, eleven years old, Nappanee, Indiana, July 13, 1968 (typescript, Indiana University Folklore Archives, 1968). The original song is of relatively recent vintage, having been around since the 1920s. But the music had originally been composed for children in *Song Stories for the Kindergarten* (1893); see Fuld, *Book of World-Famous Music,* pp. 266-68. The acceptance of the song has been nothing short of remarkable, for it is now a part of every American birthday celebration, usually accompanying the bringing out of a birthday cake. In the spirit of play, children will often sing this parody. It teases the birthday child, heaping a reminder to stay humble on this day when he or she is in the spotlight.

35. Collected by Treva Lichti from Lois MacDonald, eleven years old, Nappanee, Indiana, July 13, 1968 (typescript, Indiana University Folklore Archives, 1968). The collector remarks that the informant learned this parody from her younger brother several years before. Besides physical appearance, children are sensitive to smells in both their taunts and songs (see item 30 in this chapter, and items 54, 56-58 in Chapter Three).

36. Collected by Claudia Williamson from Bill Williamson, twelve years old, Long Beach, California, November 1969 (typescript, Indiana University Folklore Archives, 1969).

37. Collected by Treva Lichti from David Kidwell, eleven years old, Nappanee, Indiana, July 13, 1968 (typescript, Indiana University Folklore Archives, 1968). The serious classical composition of Richard Wagner has been given rude treatment in this parody. Used today for countless weddings, the song often inspires restless children to offer this parody. The parody can also be used as a taunt to an amorous girl.

38. Collected by Peggy Durtschi from Alice Breckenridge, Provo, Utah, March 31, 1975 (typescript, Brigham Young University Collection at the Fife Folklore Archives, Utah State University, 1975). According to the report of this collection, "Alice first learned this song when she was in the 5th grade riding home from school on the bus. A seat full of 8th grade girls sang it loud enough so everyone on the bus could hear them. At first Alice was mortified to think that they would sing such a song, but after she thought about it for a little while, she decided it was pretty cute and wanted to learn it. She learned part of it by listening to the girls sing it, then she went home and her older sister filled her in on the rest of the words. Alice sang this song off and on through the years. She tried to teach it to her little sister, only to find out her sister already knew it. It made Alice feel important to sing it because it was just a little off-colored and because friends responded well to it." The parody plays on the definition of "dry" and "wet" in the original. For adults the song had a connection to drinking, but for children the meaning of "dry" and "wet" become a mark of urinary self-control, a matter of special concern in childhood.

39. Collected by Susan I. Ralstin from Mike Ralstin, six years old, Kokomo, Indiana, March 15, 1970 (typescript, Indiana University Folklore Archives, 1970). The collector remarks that "Mike heard this song from some of his kindergarten classmates." The theme to the popular television cartoon "Popeye" presents a scruff but tough sailor singing a boastful ditty. Children have extended the boast into verses that challenge taboos on socially respectable dining behavior. In this manner, the verses have a relation to the "gross" rhymes in Chapter Three (see items 74-76).

40. Collected by Madeline Mongan from William Mongan, thirteen years old, John Mongan, eleven years old, Daniel Mongan, eight years old, Newark, Delaware, March 3, 1972 (typescript,

University of Delaware Folklore Archives, 1972). This is a parody of the popular commercial jingle used by McDonald's, the fast-food corporation. Other overplayed jingles invite parody, but it is McDonald's, the biggest of the fast-food chains, which has attracted the most parody. Appealing as it did in its commercials and the design of its restaurants to children, McDonald's suggested a playful atmosphere in their restaurants which inspired a playful parody. Although of recent vintage, this parody spread quickly and took its place next to "On Top of Spaghetti" as among the best known food parodies.

41. Collected by Hannelore Wertz from an eleven-year-old girl, York, Pennsylvania (typescript, Penn State Harrisburg Folklore Archives, 1982). The staying power of this commercial parody and its variations are indicated by this collection; the first collection I found is from 1972 (see item 40).

42. Collected by Sheila Ann Marin from a white female, 20 years old, from her memories of elementary school (c. 1960) in southern California (typescript, Fife Folklore Archives, Utah State University, 1972). According to the report of this collection, "She learned this song in second grade. As she remembers, it was sung on bus rides, during recess, and at lunch, any time the students got together and wanted to talk about the teacher. She hasn't sung it since elementary school, however. After that students find bigger and better ways to taunt teachers."

43. Collected by Sue Fredrickson from Tina Fredrickson, thirteen years old, Hyrum, Utah (typescript, Fife Folklore Archives, Utah State University, 1981). According to the report of this collection, "Tina learned this song at Camp Porcupine, an L.D.S. (Latter Day Saints — the Mormons) Young Women's camp. The Big Sisters (those who had been at camp the previous three years) taught the girls the song. It brought a feeling of unity, of something shared, and it is a fun song. They sang it around campfires, and (I shudder to think of it) at flag ceremony, and on hikes. Tina has sung it often at home because her sister and brothers think it's fun. She is really excited for next summer because she'll be a Big Sister and it will be her turn to teach it." This camp song is found in many variations depending on the camp you remember. It is in essence a parody of a parody, the familiar "I Don't Like Navy Life" known also by its chorus, "Gee Mom, I Want to Go Home." The song was especially prevalent during the military mobilization of the 1940s and 1950s, and undoubtedly children and counselors picked up on the song back home.

Chapter Six. Riddles and Jokes.

1. Collected by Steven Dailey from Michael Dailey, eight years old, Altoona, Pennsylvania, September 1, 1987 (manuscript, Penn State Harrisburg Folklore Archives, 1987). Michael learned this riddle from his parents, who remembered hearing it from their grandparents. The custom in their households, which they have continued, was to pose riddles after dinner to the children, as a form of entertainment and education.

2. Collected by Ann Gardner Dunn from Jean Wright, eight years old, and Mary Ann Wright, fourteen years old, Russellville, Arkansas (typescript, University of Arkansas Folklore Archives, David W. Mullins Library, 1961). Taylor in *English Riddles* lists nine variants of this riddle with seven references (with all but one from the South) between 1922 and 1928 (nos. 910a-910i, pp. 339-41).

3. Collected by Ann Gardner Dunn from Jean Wright, eight years old, and Mary Ann Wright, fourteen years old, Russellville, Arkansas (typescript, University of Arkansas Folklore Archives, David W. Mullins Library, 1961). Taylor in *English Riddles* lists fifteen variants of this riddle and gives 30 references of collections in the British Isles, Canada, Caribbean, and United States between 1865 and 1935 (nos. 1315a-1325b, pp. 547-48).

4. Collected by Ann Gardner Dunn from Jean Wright, eight years old, and Mary Ann Wright, fourteen years old, Russellville, Arkansas (typescript, University of Arkansas Folklore Archives, David W. Mullins Library, 1961). Taylor in *English Riddles* suggests a seventeenth-century circulation for this riddle and lists nine variants of this riddle with 29 references of collections from Canada to the Caribbean between 1905 and 1943 (nos. 1309a-1313, pp. 545-46).

5. Collected by Simon Bronner from Paul Fennessey, eleven years old, black, Greenville, Mississippi, June 23, 1976 (typescript, Archive of New York State Folklife, 1977). Taylor in *English Riddles* lists this riddle as no. 174 (p. 63) and offers seventeen references from Canada to the Caribbean between 1902 and 1937. An alternate answer to the riddle, as Taylor notes, is "a snake."

6. Collected by Cheryl B. Derby from Valerie Williamson, ten years old, Houlton, Maine, April 15, 1972 (typescript, Northeast Folklore Archives, University of Maine, 1972).

7. Collected by Carolyn Kramer from Mollie Kramer, eleven years old, Forest, Indiana, March 4,

1970 (typescript, Indiana University Folklore Archives, 1970).

8. Collected by Ann Gardner Dunn from Jean Wright, eight years old, and Mary Ann Wright, fourteen years old, Russellville, Arkansas (typescript, University of Arkansas Folklore Archives, David W. Mullins Library, 1961). This riddle is listed by Archer Taylor in *English Riddles,* no. 867, p. 325, and he lists five related riddles with references to collections from the Caribbean and the southern United States during the 1920s.

9. Collected by Ann Gardner Dunn from Jean Wright, eight years old, and Mary Ann Wright, fourteen years old, Russellville, Arkansas (typescript, University of Arkansas Folklore Archives, David W. Mullins Library, 1961).

10. Collected by Susan I. Ralstin from David Ralstin, eleven years old, Kokomo, Indiana, March 15, 1970 (typescript, Indiana University Folklore Archives, 1970). According to the collector, "David heard this riddle at his Boy Scout meeting." This riddle is a "catch" form of the deductive riddle. Although the deductive riddle (see item 7) requires the listener to figure out the mystery from a series of clues, the "catch" is usually an obvious answer that the listener does not expect.

11. Collected by H.T. Reed from Robert Jalbert, twelve years old, Lewiston, Maine (typescript, Northeast Folklore Archives, 1960).

12. Collected by H.T. Reed from Robert Jalbert, elementary school student, Lewiston, Maine (typescript, Northeast Folklore Archives, 1960).

13. Collected by Carolyn Henry from Nariah, ten-year-old black girl in the sixth grade, Harrisburg, Pennsylvania (typescript, Penn State Harrisburg Folklore Archives, 1985).

14. The first seven riddles were collected by Ann Gardner Dunn from Jean Wright, eight years old, and Mary Ann Wright, fourteen years old, Russellville, Arkansas (typescript, University of Arkansas Folklore Archives, David W. Mullins Library, 1961); the next two were collected by H.T. Reed from elementary school students, Lewiston, Maine (typescript, Northeast Folklore Archives, 1960); the next three were collected by Alice L. Brown from elementary school children (manuscript, Ft. Hays State University Folklore Archives, 1967); and the next riddle was collected by Becky Townsend from Wendy Townsend, eight years old, Dunsmuir, California, November 1971 (typescript, Brigham Young University Collection at the Fife Folklore Archives, Utah State University, 1971); and the last riddle was collected by Simon Bronner from Milo Stewart, Jr., eight years old, Cooperstown, New York, February 28, 1976 (tape recording, Penn State Harrisburg Folklore Archives). Becky Townsend offers the following background on the riddle she collected: "Children love to entertain, especially loved-ones they haven't seen for a long time. Such were the circumstances surrounding the telling of this riddle. I am Wendy's aunt and we had just that evening arrived for Thanksgiving vacation. Wendy was so excited and part of her expression of this excitement and love for us is seen in her attempt to entertain. Without prompting, while I was standing in the kitchen, Wendy asked me the following riddle . . ." Taylor in *English Riddles* lists the following of these riddles: table (no. 305a, alternate answer — chair, bed, house), needle (no. 282), potato (no. 277b), Mississippi (no. 328a, alternate answer — stove), newspaper (nos. 1498a-1499), bed (no. 334), sidewalk (no. 200b, with the alternate answer — path), shoe (no. 296a), corn (no. 285). These riddling questions are found in most collections from oral tradition, and are the preferred riddling form today in the United States.

15. The first eight joking questions were collected by H.T. Reed from elementary school students, Lewiston, Maine (typescript, Northeast Folklore Archives, 1960); the next five were collected by Hannelore Wertz from junior high school students, York, Pennsylvania (typescript, Penn State Harrisburg Folklore Archives, 1982); the next seven were collected by Lola Plumley from Carl Plumley, eleven years old, Parsons, West Virginia, July 27, 1972 (typescript, Penn State Harrisburg Folklore Archives, 1984); the next two were collected by Simon Bronner from Milo Stewart, Jr., eight years old, Cooperstown, New York, February 28, 1976 (tape recording, Penn State Harrisburg Folklore Archives); the next three were collected by Hannelore Wertz from junior high school students, York, Pennsylvania, 1982); and the last joking question was collected by Judi McConkie from Kelly Crockett, nine years old, Provo, Utah (typescript, Brigham Young University collection at the Fife Folklore Archives, Utah State University, 1969).

16. Collected by Carolyn Henry from eleven- and twelve-year-old sixth-graders, Harrisburg, Pennsylvania (typescript, Penn State Harrrisburg Folklore Archives, 1985).

17. The moron jokes selected were ones that appeared in both the collections of H.T. Reed from elementary school students in Lewiston, Maine (typescript, Northeast Folklore Archives, University of Maine, 1960) and of Ann Kilgore from elementary school students in Conway, Arkansas (typescript, University of Arkansas Folklore Archives, David W. Mullins Library, 1962). The wide circulation of moron jokes was mainly reported by folklorists during the 1940s.

18. The first three jokes were collected by Chris Von Der Haar from Tom Von Der Haar, fourteen years old, Indianapolis, Indiana (typescript, Indiana University Folklore Archives, 1972) and the last joke was collected by Ann Kilgore from Sandy Beauchamp, elementary school student, in Conway, Arkansas (typescript, University of Arkansas Folklore Archives, David W. Mullins Library, 1962).

19. To give an idea of the range of ethnic jokes in the repertoire of children, I offer this collection made by Hannelore Wertz in 1982 from her ninth-grade class of 25 middle-class white students in York, Pennsylvania (typescript, Penn State Harrisburg Folklore Archives, 1982). The riddle-jokes are related to the widespread derisive ethnic humor about the Irish, Jews, and blacks that could be heard during the nineteenth century.

20. The first five jokes were collected by Hannelore Wertz from junior high school students, York, Pennsylvania.(typescript, Penn State Harrisburg Folklore Archives, 1982); the next seven were collected by Ann Kilgore from elementary school students in Conway, Arkansas (typescript, University of Arkansas Folklore Archives, David W. Mullins Library, 1962); and the last joke was collected by Judith W. Hansen from elementary school student Thea Hansen, Orem, Utah, December 7, 1977 (typescript, Brigham Young University Collection at the Fife Folklore Archives, Utah State University, 1977). Of the last joke, Hansen wrote, "Thea stated that this joke was told in the Cherry Hill lunchroom every time that spaghetti was served. The food in the lunchroom is usually good and well-cooked. Almost all of the children liked the spaghetti, but really enjoyed taunting the cooks and their teachers with this particular tale. Almost everyone within the Cherry Hill Elementary is aware of, and has told, this particular joke."

21. Collected by Ann Kilgore from elementary school students, Conway, Arkansas (typescript, University of Arkansas Folklore Archives, David W. Mullins Library, 1962).

22. The first three jokes were collected by Judith Hansen from Aleta Hansen, eleven-year-old sixth-grader, Orem, Utah, October 1977 (typescript, Brigham Young University Collection at the Fife Folklore Archives, Utah State University, 1977); the next joke was collected by Simon Bronner from Milo Stewart, Jr., eight years old, Cooperstown, New York, February 28, 1976 (tape recording, Penn State Harrisburg Folklore Archives); the next joke was collected by Cheryl Derby from John Sagar, Stow, Massachusetts, March 30, 1972 (typescript, Northeast Folklore Archives, University of Maine, 1972); the next joke was collected by Phyllis Peltier from Kim Peltier, white male, fifteen years old, December 1969 (typescript, Indiana University Folklore Archives, 1970); the next two jokes were collected by Linda Lea Williams from Mike Hegedus, ten years old, Richmond, Indiana, July 11, 1970 (typescript, Indiana University Folklore Archives, 1970); the next joke was collected by Judi McConkie from Kelly Crockett, nine years old, Provo, Utah (typescript, Brigham Young University Collection at the Fife Folklore Archives, 1969); the next eight jokes were collected by Carolyn Henry from sixth-graders, Harrisburg, Pennsylvania (typescript, Penn State Folklore Archives, 1985); and the remaining jokes were collected by Hannelore Wertz from ninth-graders, York, Pennsylvania (typescript, Penn State Harrisburg Folklore Archives, 1982). Notes on the telling of the elephant jokes are provided by Judith Hansen, who commented in 1977: "This joke and other elephant jokes are very popular with Aleta and her friends in the sixth grade. They tell them often and whenever they can get someone to listen to them. The elephant joke seems to be dying out in the junior high and high school in Orem, but still is very strong in the grade school, at least in the Cherry Hill grade school. Aleta's favorite is about the elephant wearing green toenail polish. It is probably the one I have heard told most often, every week or two all fall. Each time she tells it she finds it as funny as if it were the first time that she had shared the joke. The one about elephants having flat feet was also told by Aleta repeatedly. Her younger brother Jared, a third grader, and younger sister Karina, a first grader, also tell elephant jokes but usually only among the family as their friends do not often tell jokes. Their joke telling seems influenced more by wanting to be like their older brothers and sisters than to be like their peer group. Joke telling, again judging mostly from past observance of my own children, seems to be more typical of the 4-6th graders than the younger children. Jared and Karina like this joke because they can remember it and the mind picture it brings, that of an elephant jumping out of a tree, seems to them to be very hilarious. Although Aleta has told this joke many times this fall both to her family and to her friends she cannot remember where she first heard it."

23. Collected by Hannelore Wertz from junior high school students, York, Pennsylvania (typescript, Penn State Harrisburg Folklore Archives, 1982). Alan Dundes, in "The Dead Baby Joke Cycle" in *Cracking Jokes,* pp. 3-14, argues that the growth of the dead baby joke cycle in the last two decades is a response to concerns for abortion and the increased availability of improved contraceptives.

24. The first two jokes were collected by Carolyn Henry from Eleanor, eleven years old, Harrisburg, Pennsylvania (typescript, Penn State Harrisburg Folklore Archives, 1985); the next six were collected by Hannelore Wertz from junior high school students, York, Pennsylvania (typescript, Penn State Harrisburg Folklore Archives, 1982); the last three were collected by Robert O'Keefe from Ed Read, Beach Grove, Indiana, and Steve May, Columbus, Indiana (typescript, Indiana University Folklore Archives, 1976).

25. The first three jokes were collected by Kathryn Hobbs from Casey Crockett, elementary school student, Logan, Utah, February 24, 1983 (typescript, Fife Folklore Archives, Utah State University, 1983); the next two were collected by Hannelore Wertz from junior high school students, York, Pennsylvania (typescript, Penn State Harrisburg Folklore Archives, 1982); the remaining jokes were collected by Carolyn Henry from sixth-graders, Harrisburg, Pennsylvania (typescript, Penn State Harrisburg Folklore Archives, 1985). Kathryn Hobbs commented on her collection: "Casey Crockett says he likes Dolly Parton jokes best. He says he enjoys repeating these jokes in front of adults and giggles at their response. He says they act surprised and even a little embarrassed." A spate of celebrity jokes grew in popularity during the 1980s, which should come as no surprise in a society where the most personal facts of celebrities' lives increasingly blanketed the mass media.

26. Collected by Simon Bronner from sixth-graders, Harrisburg, Pennsylvania, February 1986 (manuscript, Penn State Harrisburg Folklore Archives, 1986). The Christa McAuliffe series of jokes emerged after the Challenger disaster in January 1986. There were seven astronauts on board, but McAuliffe, the first schoolteacher in space, attracted the most attention in humor.

27. Collected by Carolyn Henry from Giles Krill, eleven years old, and Angelea Heise, eleven years old, Harrisburg, Pennsylvania (typescript, Penn State Harrisburg Folklore Archives, 1985).

28. The second, fifth, and seventeenth to nineteenth jokes in this list were collected by Carolyn Henry from sixth-graders, Harrisburg, Pennsylvania (typescript, Penn State Harrisburg Folklore Archives, 1985); the last four jokes were collected by Simon Bronner from 4-H campers, twelve years old, East Lansing, Michigan, summer 1981 (typescript, Penn State Harrisburg Folklore Archives, 1981); the remaining jokes were collected by Hannelore Wertz from junior high school students, York, Pennsylvania (typescript, Penn State Harrisburg Folklore Archives, 1982). In Wertz's survey of her class, the "what's grosser than gross" series provided more items than any other joke collected. This joke series apparently comments on the variety of sick or "gross" jokes that had appeared by the 1980s (covered in the previous items).

29. Reported by Sally Lytle, nineteen years old, from her memories of childhood, Kokomo, Indiana (typescript, Indiana University Folklore Archives, 1970).

30. Collected by Linda Craig from Bob Upchurch, nine years old, New Castle, Indiana, November 29, 1969 (typescript, Indiana University Folklore Archives, 1970).

31. Reported by James M. Hodson, nineteen years old, from his memories of childhood, Wabash, Indiana, May 1970 (typescript, Indiana University).

32. Collected by Charles Spillar and Mark Cislo from Wendy, fourth-grader, Dupont, Pennsylvania (typescript, Penn State Harrisburg Folklore Archives, 1984).

33. Collected by Jerrold R. Stouder from Andy, nine-year-old fourth-grader, Middletown, Pennsylvania, November 1985 (typescript, Penn State Harrisburg Folklore Archives, 1986). This joke is a variant of "Johnny Fuckerfaster" collected from children by Sandra McCosh and reported in *Children's Humour*, p. 261.

34a. Reported by James M. Hodson, nineteen years old, from his memories of childhood, Wabash, Indiana, May 1970 (typescript, Indiana University Folklore Archives, 1970).

34b. Collected by Carolyn Kirkendall from Mary Kay Swander, twelve years old, Russiaville, Indiana, May 9, 1967 (typescript, Indiana University Folklore Archives, 1967).

35. Collected by Linda Craig from Dave Evans, Kokomo, Indiana, November 21, 1969 (typescript, Indiana University Folklore Archives, 1969).

36. Collected by Timothy Carroll from William Francis Carroll, twelve years old, Timonium, Maryland, July 15, 1977 (typescript, Indiana University Folklore Archives, 1977).

37. Collected by Joyce Halt from David, eleven years old, Bloomington, Indiana, July 12, 1969 (typescript, Indiana University Folklore Archives, 1969). The collector comments on the telling of the joke: "He thought the funniest thing about the joke was the punch line ''cause a peter tickles your innards only if you're married!' He added as an afterthought 'or else you don't hafta be married,' but thought that part shouldn't go in. David heard this joke in the bandroom of his elementary school 'where we always tell dirty jokes and hope the band teacher doesn't come in.' He heard the joke from a friend, Alex Balir, who told David the joke because David had told him one."

38a. Collected by Carolyn Henry from Gilles Carroll, eleven-year-old sixth-grader, Harrisburg, Pennsylvania (typescript, Penn State Harrisburg Folklore Archives, 1985). This joke is discussed in Rosemary Zumwalt, "Plain and Fancy: A Content Analysis of Children's Jokes Dealing with Adult Sexuality."

38b. Collected by Carolyn Henry from Robert Welsh, twelve-year-old sixth-grader, Harrisburg, Pennsylvania (typescript, Penn State Harrisburg Folklore Archives, 1985).

38c. Collected by Betty J. Belanus from Dirk Ewers, eleven-year-old sixth-grader, Bloomington, Indiana, September 14, 1977 (typescript, Indiana University Folklore Archives, 1977). The collector comments that Dirk learned this joke from "kids at school" and adds: "He was very adamant about not wanting his mother to know that he told the joke, since he knew he was not supposed to tell dirty jokes and that his mother probably didn't know he knew 'the facts of life.'"

39. Collected by Hannelore Wertz from junior high school student, York, Pennsylvania (typescript, Penn State Harrisburg Folklore Archives, 1982).

40. Reported by James M. Hodson, nineteen years old, from his memories of childhood, Wabash, Indiana, May 1970 (typescript, Indiana University Folklore Archives, 1970).

41. Collected by Linda Craig from Davie Allen, seven-year-old second-grader, Kokomo, Indiana, December 28, 1969 (typescript, Indiana University Folklore Archives, 1970).

42a. Collected by Susan E. Heberer from Nancy Brown, twelve years old, Clawson, Michigan, April 25, 1980 (typescript, Wayne State University Folklore Archives, 1980).

42b. Collected by Phyllis Peltier from Kim Peltier, fifteen years old, Kokomo, Indiana, January 1970 (typescript, Indiana University Folklore Archives, 1970).

43. Collected by Phyllis Peltier from Kim Peltier, fifteen years old, Kokomo, Indiana, February 1970 (typescript, Indiana University Folklore Archives, 1970).

44. Collected by Phyllis Peltier from Brian Lundin, fourteen years old, Kokomo, Indiana, February 14, 1970 (typescript, Indiana University Folklore Archives, 1970).

45. Collected by Janis Berlin from Jeni Bell, ten years old, Detroit, Michigan (typescript, Wayne State University Folklore Archives, 1975). According to the report of this collection, Jeni learned this joke from a ten-year-old friend, Stewart, who walks home with her from school. The collector adds: "Stewart let Jeni know, in a non-threatening way, that he knows that she too 'hasn't ripened yet.' It also provides a way for them to deal with their potential sexuality. And that Jeni shared it with me indicates her trust that she can share her sexual knowledge and fears with me, even though it's threatening."

46. Collected by Denise A. Kelso from a fourth-grader, Temple Christian School, Redford, Michigan, April 1, 1982 (typescript, Wayne State University Folklore Archives, 1982).

47. Collected by Carolyn Henry from Charmaine, eleven-year-old sixth-grader, Harrisburg, Pennsylvania (typescript, Penn State Harrisburg Folklore Archives, 1985).

48. Collected by Charles Spillar and Mark Cislo from fourth-grader, Dupont, Pennsylvania (typescript, Penn State Harrisburg Folklore Archives, 1984).

49a. Collected by Charles Spillar and Mark Cislo from fourth-grader, Dupont, Pennsylvania (typescript, Penn State Harrisburg Folklore Archives, 1984).

49b. Collected by Carolyn Henry from Jason, eleven-year-old sixth-grader, Harrisburg, Pennsylvania (typescript, Penn State Harrisburg Folklore Archives, 1985).

49c. Collected by Carolyn Henry from Tanisha, eleven-year-old sixth-grader, Harrisburg, Pennsylvania (typescript, Penn State Harrisburg Folklore Archives, 1985).

50. Collected by Charles Spillar and Mark Cislo from Brian, fourth-grader, Dupont, Pennsylvania (typescript, Penn State Harrisburg Folklore Archives, 1984).

51. Collected by Hannelore Wertz from junior high school boy, York, Pennsylvania (typescript, Penn State Harrisburg Folklore Archives, 1982). In a common variant of this joke, it is consistently the smell or dirt of a pig in the barn that forces the sleepers to come back into the house.

52. Collected by Carolyn Henry from Kelli, eleven-year-old sixth-grader, black girl, Harrisburg, Pennsylvania (typescript, Penn State Harrisburg Folklore Archives, 1985).

53. Collected by Hannelore Wertz from junior-high-school boy, York, Pennsylvania (typescript, Penn State Harrisburg Folklore Archives, 1982).

Chapter Seven. Tales and Legends

1a. Collected by Mary Muncie from James R. Muncie, eleven years old, Radcliff, Kentucky, April 1973 (typescript, Western Kentucky University Folklore Archives, 1973). The headless man is a popular theme in American ghostlore. This narrative, which appears to be in the process of developing into a firm plot, also incorporates the character of the "little man," who often plays the role of a mysterious character in folk legendry. Ernest Baughman in *Type and Motif Index of the Folktales of England and North America* lists E422.1.1(a), "Headless man," with ten references, and E422.3.1, "Revenant as small man," with two references.

1b. Collected by Rebecca Wood from Mary Wood, fourteen years old, Kokomo, Indiana, May 15, 1968 (typescript, Indiana University Folklore Archives, 1968). The teller heard this story told about the Mansfield Covered Bridge in southern Indiana. It is common for bridges (and tunnels) to inspire horror legends (see motif E332.la, "Ghost appears at bridge").

2. Collected by Cathy Ash from Mary Wood, eleven-year-old fifth-grader, Allen Park, Michigan, May 1975 (typescript, Wayne State University Folklore Archives, 1978). This story was collected at a Pathfinder camping trip for younger girls and boys. After dark, Ash went to a cabin filled with several girls and invited them to sit around a candle and offer stories they have heard. Ash then recorded a scary tale-telling session from which this story was taken. This story was the first full ghost story told at the session. Another girl responded to the story by saying, "Oh God!" and the teller added, "It's true too." In this story, the narrator is intentionally vague about whether it is the site that is cursed or whether the ghost of "the lady" had a hand in the events.

3a. Collected by Richard Goddard from Cathy Oke, twelve-year-old seventh-grader, Roseville, Michigan, March 1, 1971 (typescript, Wayne State University Folklore Archives, 1977). This modern legend known by children as the story of "Knock-Knock Street" is related to older legends about ghosts who produce knocking sounds at the site of their death. See Baughman motif E402.1.5, "Invisible ghost makes a rapping or knocking noise." The modern legend of "Knock-Knock Street" in Detroit (also told of Ann Arbor, Michigan, and Toledo, Ohio) is discussed by Richard Dorson in *American Folklore,* pp. 252-53.

3b. Collected by Richard Goddard from Rita Whit, Roseville, Michigan, February 16, 1971 (typescript, Wayne State University Folklore Archives, 1977). In this telling of the story, the cautionary message of the story is made explicit. It appears to be, on the one hand, a cautionary message to adults to watch out for children, and on the other hand, it warns children to be careful when playing in the street.

4. Reported by Rebecca Wood, nineteen years old, Kokomo, Indiana, May 15, 1968 (typescript, Indiana University Folklore Archives, 1968). Rather than a tale about ghosts, this story shifts attention to the believers. In my observations, it sometimes was offered as a commentary when discussions of ghosts come up, or as a follow-up to a tale dwelling on the reality of ghosts. The nonbeliever dies of fright thinking that a ghost was grabbing him or her, when a piece of clothing catches on the knife or fork. In *The Types of the Folktale* by Antti Aarne, translated and enlarged by Stith Thompson, p. 475, this tale is listed as type 1676B, "Clothing caught in graveyard (man thinks that something terrifying is holding him and dies of fright)," and located versions in Europe and South America in addition to the United States. Baughman in *Type and Motif Index of the Folktales of England and America,* p. 373, cites fifteen references between 1900 and 1959 to the tale in Anglo-American folklore. Among the variations are stakes, sticks, knives, forks, swords, and nails into a grave or coffin. The implement becomes stuck in the person's loose cuff or long coat tail. In more recent versions, the person dying of fright is typically a girl who gets the knife caught in her dress; see Ronald Baker, *Hoosier Folk Legends,* pp. 76-77.

5. Collected by Kathryn Johnson from Angie Sisson, fourteen-year-old ninth-grader, Logan, Utah, February 6, 1984 (typescript, Fife Folklore Archives, Utah State University, 1984). This story combines the themes of motifs E300, "Friendly return from the dead," from Stith Thompson, *Motif-Index of Folk-Literature,* and E452.1, "Dead quiescent during day." In addition, the tone of the story has the contrast of a real-life encounter with a closing realization of a ghostly experience typical of the "vanishing hitchhiker" story (E332.3.3.1, see items 6a-b).

6a. Collected by Rebecca Wood from Mary Wood, fourteen years old, Kokomo, Indiana, March 26, 1968 (typescript, Indiana University Folklore Archives, 1968). This story is a common variant among children and teens of the vanishing hitchhiker legend (motif E332.3.3.1); see Jan Harold Brunvand, *The Vanishing Hitchhiker,* pp. 24-46.

6b. Collected by Cathy Ash from Diane Boyd, nine-year-old fourth-grader, Trenton, Michigan, May 1975 (typescript, Wayne State University Folklore Archives, 1978). In this version, the girl disappears at the cemetery rather than nearer to home. The cemetery is where the ghost is "laid to rest," but the restless ghost is still seeking to return to the safety of home, a symbol of life in this story.

7. Reported by John M. Pekala, twenty years old, from his childhood memories, Altoona, Pennsylvania (typescript, Penn State Harrisburg Folklore Archives, 1982). Pekala added that the Buckhorn

Mountain area is often used for teenage "parking." Like many legends, this legend of the "lady in white" is localized around a specific place, usually a treacherous drive as well as adolescent "lover's lane."

8. Collected by Nellie Preston Davis from Dennis Wayne Sheppard, twelve years old, Simpson, West Virginia, 1972 (typescript, Penn State Harrisburg Folklore Archives, 1985). This legend combines two strong motifs in ghostlore: the jilted lover murdering the object of his affection, who then turns into a ghost (E21, "Dead lover's malevolent return"; E334.2.1, "Ghost of murdered person haunts burial spot"), and the headless revenant who haunts a house (E422.1.1.4, "Headless ghost carries head under arm"; E281.3f, "Ghost renders room where person has died uninhabitable").

9a. Collected by Simon Bronner from Roseanna Zamora, Mexican-American, ten years old, Stockbridge, Michigan, July 28, 1981 (typescript, The Museum, Michigan State University, 1981). This story is known as "the weeping woman" or, in Spanish, *La Llorona*. The narrative tradition about a sobbing female revenant in white searching for her dead children is evident in American ghostlore. See Baker, *Hoosier Folk Legends*, pp. 58-59, 67; Musick, *Coffin Hollow*, pp. 68-70, 94-96; Solomon and Solomon, *Ghosts and Goosebumps*, p. 40. But among Mexican-American children, and especially among girls, the story is particularly strong. When I interviewed a group of ten children of migrant workers at a school program in Stockbridge, Michigan, I heard variants of this story more than any other.

9b. Collected by Simon Bronner from Susan Medina, Mexican-American, ten years old, Stockbridge, Michigan, July 28, 1981 (typescript, The Museum, Michigan State University, 1981).

10. Collected by Carolyn Kramer from Mollie Kramer, eleven years old, Forest, Indiana, March 6, 1970 (typescript, Indiana University Folklore Archives, 1970). This modern legend usually goes by the name of "The Boyfriend's Death." See Brunvand, *The Vanishing Hitchhiker*, pp. 5-11.

11a. Collected by Kathryn Johnson from Heather Watson, fourteen years old, Logan, Utah, February 8, 1984 (typescript, Fife Folklore Archives, Utah State University, 1984). The collector, a ninth-grade English teacher, collected this story and others (see items 11b-15) by asking her classes to provide transcripts of stories they had been told by friends, that were not read to them or by them, and to tell them in front of the class. Johnson comments that "upon completion of a storytelling unit at Logan Junior High School, I had been 'grossed out' every period and every day. Stories of bloody murders, hanged lovers, unfortunate women of all description, and ghosts permeated their repertoires. Although other students told about embarassing moments or about heroic deeds of their relatives, those stories did not capture the attention of the listeners as did the bizarre. Most of these stories are rooted in the teenage traditional habits of slumber parites with no slumbering, camping trips into the unknown, and hall-talk. However introverted this age group may seem to be during class discussion requiring academic preparation, all one has to do is mention the above situations in relationship to storytelling, and the extrovert in all of them appears. Whatever reasons the ninth-graders have for circulating these stories, most of which they claim to be true stories and claim to believe, they relish in telling and retelling them and can clearly extrapolate and expound upon their function as cautionary tales."

11b. Collected by Kathryn Johnson from Owen Braker, fourteen years old, Logan, Utah, February 10, 1984 (typescript, Fife Folklore Archives, Utah State University, 1984).

12. Collected by Kathryn Johnson from Heather Watson, fourteen years old, Logan, Utah, February 8, 1984 (typescript, Fife Folklore Archives, Utah State University, 1984). This story is usually identified as the "Assailant (Killer) in the Back Seat." In 1968, Carlos Drake in "The Killer in the Back Seat" first reported the legend with the constant features found in the version reported here of a girl who drives alone and has a car following her; see also Brunvand, *The Vanishing Hitchhiker*, pp. 52-53.

13. Collected by Kathryn Johnson from Angie Wimmer, fourteen years old, Logan, Utah, February 9, 1984 (typescript, Fife Folklore Archives, Utah State University, 1984). Jan Brunvand in *The Choking Doberman* identifies this legend as "The Hairy-Armed Hitchhiker" because the owner of the car noticed the woman's hairy arms or back as the tipoff that the person in the car was an imposter (pp. 52-55), but tellers often identify it as "the old lady story." One difference is immediately evident: the girl in this story figures out the ruse rather than noticing the hairy arms. As with versions of the "Assailant in the Back Seat" (see item 11), the setting is typically a shopping area (often a large mall) and the victim is a girl or woman.

14a. Collected by Kathryn Johnson from Debby Warren, fourteen years old, Logan, Utah, February 7, 1984 (typescript, Fife Folklore Archives, Utah State University, 1984). The informant reported learning this story at a slumber party. Mary and Herbert Knapp report the story in *One*

Potato Two Potato, p. 243. "This is a cautionary tale," they comment, "reminding little girls to lock the house up tight."

14b. Collected by Kathryn Johnson from Laura Karren, fourteen years old, Logan, Utah, February 8, 1984 (typescript, Fife Folklore Archives, Utah State University, 1984). This story combines features of the "killer upstairs" story (see item 15b) and the "licked hand" story (see item 14a). The cautionary message of this legend is brought home by the man on the phone who reminds her to check the children. The moment that the sitter relaxes (eat a snack and watch TV) and lets her guard down is when dangers lurk.

15a. Collected by Kathryn Johnson from Debby Warren, fourteen years old, Logan, Utah, February 7, 1984 (typescript, Fife Folklore Archives, Utah State University, 1984). The informant reports learning this story at a slumber party. Sue Samuelson in "'The Man Upstairs': An Analysis of a Babysitting Legend," pp. 2-10, summarizes her survey of over a hundred texts from 26 states and five Canadian provinces, dating from 1960 to 1976. The story reported here is typical of one type of the complex in which the focus is the ax or hatchet murder of the children and the drama is provided by the threat on the sitter (see items 15b-c for a type in which the focus is on the sitter). The phone caller's message differs in many versions, such as saying, "I know you're home alone with the kids," but usually he asks, "Have you checked the children?" or implores her, "Check the children."

15b. Collected by Richard Goddard from Paula Zelinski, twelve-year-old seventh-grader, Roseville, Michigan, February 1971 (typescript, Wayne State University Folklore Archives, 1977). This story contains the typical features of the "killer upstairs" legend. Although similar to the "ax-murderer" story found in item 15a, this story adds the essential elements of the killer's calling from upstairs (in some versions the call comes from the basement), the call's being traced, and the babysitter's being told to escape the house (in some versions the police trace the call and tell her to leave). In this version of the story, the sexual overtones of the story are more apparent than the "murderer" story in item 15a; the caller, always a man, breathes heavily over the phone and focuses his attention on the girl rather than on the children.

15c. Collected by Jennifer Holmes from Allison Galanis, fifteen years old, Cincinnati, Ohio, 1974 (typescript, Indiana University Folklore Archives, 1974). According to the collector, "These stories were collected at about 9:30 p.m. in my parents' living room. There were candles lit in the room, and it was dark outside. My sister and her friends were there just to tell me stories they had heard at camp. I encouraged them to tell me stories, and they did most of the talking. I used a tape recorder that was located rather inconspicuously so that they would not notice it. Though none present really believed the stories, they all were scared, and told the stories as if they were true." The response from one girl to this telling was "Oh gee! Oh gross." Another then replied, "You've never heard that one?"

16. Collected by Jennifer Holmes from Nancy Holmes, sixteen years old, Cincinnati, Ohio, 1974 (typescript, Indiana University Folklore Archives, 1974). The setting for this telling was the same as the one for item 15c. One girl who listened to the story asked, "Is it real?" The teller responded: "They said it was real because, see like, he was a counselor for about five, uh, three or four years. And then he skipped a year. He didn't come back and he did leave, like, in the middle of the summer. He left camp, you know. And they said that was because he went a little loony, you know. And Perky, the owner of the camp, just wanted to make it kind of, you know, so that no one else found out about it except for, you know, the people who kind of told the kids, you know, it was just kind of a fake thing."

17a. Reported by Edward Martin, 22 years old, from his memories of childhood at camp (c. 1958-1959), Winthrop, Maine (typescript, Northeast Folklore Archives, 1964).

17b. Collected by Nancy Conant from Michael Holland, Skowhegan, Maine, July 26, 1964 (typescript, Northeast Folklore Archives, University of Maine, 1964). This story was collected as a legend about "Three-fingered Willy" (see items 17a-c). Unlike some camp figures which appear unique to a particular camp (see examples in the notes to item 16), Willy is known in camps throughout upper New England, and stories about him are among the most commonly collected camp legends in the Northeast Folklore Archives at the University of Maine.

17c. Collected by Nancy Conant from Keith Crockett, Skowhegan, Maine, July 26, 1964 (typescript, Northeast Folklore Archives, University of Maine, 1964).

18. Collected by Charles Spillar and Mark Cislo from a fourth-grade girl, Dupont, Pennsylvania, 1984 (typescript, Penn State Harrisburg Folklore Archives, 1984).

19. Collected by Linda Craig from Susan Bargerhuff, ten years old, Kokomo, Indiana, November 14, 1969 (typescript, Indiana University Folklore Archives, 1969). The collector commented that

"Susan really laughed when she told me this. She really enjoyed surprising the listener with a trick answer."

20. Collected by Jerrold Stouder from Cary Keytack, nine-year-old fourth-grader, Middletown, Pennsylvania, November 27, 1985 (manuscript, Penn State Harrisburg Folklore Archives, 1985). Following the formula of the hoax ghost story and having the appeal of several rhyming lines, this story has been collected from children as young as five years old; see Grider, "Supernatural Narratives," pp. 776-77.

21a. Collected by Jerrold Stouder from Elizabeth Ammon, nine-year-old fourth-grader, Middletown, Pennsylvania, November 27, 1985 (manuscript, Penn State Harrisburg Folklore Archives, 1985). Brunvand in "Classification for Shaggy Dog Stories" has a category for "Punch Line From a Song," but in this story, the expectation is reversed (similar to a technique used in the joking question, item 15, Chapter Six); the song provides the frightening circumstances and the nonsensical description is the punch line. In other versions of the story, the ants are singing in the toilet or bathtub.

21b. Collected by Susan Heberer from Mary Hill, eleven years old, Clawson, Michigan, April 25, 1980 (typescript, Wayne State University Folklore Archives, 1980). This story was collected in a joke-telling session at a Girl Scout campout. Eight girls from ten to thirteen were present at the session. The collector comments that "all attended a parochial school in a northern suburb of Detroit. Although they attend the same school, their homes are quite a far distance from each other. This limited the time in which they interacted socially. Because of this, there was usually someone who hadn't heard a particular joke before." One girl responded to Mary's telling by saying, "Oh, that's sick." The story differs from the nonsensical ending of item 21a by turning the expectation of supernatural imagery into a scatological metaphor common in children's humor and folk speech.

22. Collected by Simon Bronner from Sadie deWall, seven years old, Harrisburg, Pennsylvania, May 9, 1983 (typescript, Penn State Harrisburg Folklore Archives, 1983). Sadie heard this story from a girl one year older and then related it to her younger brother. "Shut up or I'll give you two black eyes" is the most popular ending line in this type. Other versions include the ghost's cry "bloody bones and butcher knives," to which the child replies, "Shut up or I'll give you bloody bones and butcher knives!" Still others identify the ghost as the "ghost of the white eyes" and then the ending line becomes "If you don't shut up you're gonna be the ghost with two black eyes."

23. Collected by Hannelore Wertz from an eleven-year-old boy, York, Pennsylvania (typescript, Penn State Harrisburg Folklore Archives, 1982).

24. Collected Susan Herberer from Alex Highland, ten-year-old girl, Clawson, Michigan, April 25, 1980 (typescript, Wayne State University Archives, 1980). The setting for this story is the same as for item 21b. One girl responded to this story by saying, "Oh how dumb." "Ivory floats" is a line from an advertising campaign for Ivory soap.

25. Collected by Hannelore Wertz from a twelve-year-old boy, York, Pennsylvania (typescript, Penn State Harrisburg Folklore Archives, 1982). Brunvand in "Classification for Shaggy Dog Stories" lists this story as C620, "The walking coffin."

26. Collected by Cathy Ash from Bobby Cain, fourteen years old, Allen Park, Michigan, May 2, 1975 (typescript, Wayne State University Folklore Archives, 1978). This story was recorded in a tale-telling session at a camp cabin with four other boys. According to the collector, Bobby's "voice was low and slow. Everyone sat quietly listening to him. His attitude filled the room with a spooky type of atmosphere." Bobby had preceded the telling of this hoax tale with "strange" ghost tales, according to the collector, but at the end of the telling of this story, his audience broke out in laughter. Brunvand in "Classification for Shaggy-Dog Stories" lists this story as C665, "The rapping paper: A man in a hotel (or haunted house) hears a rapping sound and searches for its source." After much running around and unlocking of doors, he finds a trunk from which the sound comes, and inside finds "a great big roll of rapping paper" (p. 64). Brunvand categorizes the story together with the "walking coffin" story (item 25) as stories that have "Punch Line with a Pun on a Word or Words — No Set Saying Involved."

27. Collected by Cathy Ash from Frank Ash, eight years old, Allen Park, Michigan, May 2, 1975 (typescript, Wayne State University Folklore Archives, 1978). This story was recorded in a tale-telling session at a camp (see item 6b) cabin of five boys, aged seven and eight. According to the collector, "Frank has got so much personality, and it came up very noticeably in his stories." This story can be told as a frightening story, but the matter-of-fact "catch" delivery of the last line produced giggling at this session. Indeed, it is included in Brunvand's "Classification for Shaggy Dog Stories" (B801, p. 58). Brunvand points out that "this is motif El2.1, "Red thread on neck of person who has been decapitated and resuscitated" and refers to Washington Irving's story "The Adventure of the German Student" in *Tales of a Traveller* (1824).

28. Collected by Cathy Ash from Julie, eleven years old, Dearborn, Michigan, May 2, 1975 (typescript, Wayne State University Folklore Archives, 1978). This item was collected in a tale-telling session at a camp cabin with five girls, aged ten and eleven. The performance was a convincing rendition of a scary story until the time when the teller grabbed the listener, at which point the audience giggled and realized the hoax. This popular story is related to an international tale type identified by Aarne and Thompson as type 366, "The man from the gallows: A man steals the heart (liver, stomach, clothing) of one who has been hanged (E235.4, E236.1). Gives it to his wife to eat. The ghost comes to claim his property and carries off the man" (p. 127). Thompson also recognized the "golden arm" variant of the story in international circulation and listed it as motif E235.4.1, "Return from dead to punish theft of golden arm from grave." Sylvia Grider in "From the Tale to the Telling: AT 366," in *Folklore on Two Continents,* ed. Nikolai Burlakoff and Carl Lindahl, pp. 49-56, identifes "The Golden Arm," the story reported here, as a distinct cycle of the tale in America.

29. Collected by Simon Bronner from Mary Wilson, nine years old, white, Bloomington, Indiana, April 14, 1978 (tape recording, Penn State Harrisburg Folklore Archives). I recorded this story at a tale-telling session with three girls and two boys in an after-school center. The story was preceded by a horror tale of "Hatchet Man Harry and his wife Mary," who according to legend chased after children around Fort Wayne, Indiana. There was a grave silence during Mary's telling, but members of the group giggled after Mary grabbed the abdomen of a girl during the last line and the girl shrieked. Grider in "From the Tale to the Telling" identifies this story as a distinctive American children's subtype of Aarne-Thompson tale type 366, "The man from the gallows" (see items 29-30 for the other major subtypes "The Golden Arm" and "The Big Toe").

30. Collected by Shannon Smith from Laura Smith, thirteen years old, Indianapolis, Indiana (typescript, Indiana University Folklore Archives, 1975). Grider in "From the Tale to the Telling," pp. 52-53, describes a subtype of Aarne-Thompson tale type 366, "The man from the gallows" (see items 28-29), which she calls "The Big Toe."

31. Collected by Jerrold Stouder from Amy Peters, ten-year-old fourth-grader, Middletown, Pennsylvania, December 1985 (manuscript, Penn State Harrisburg Folklore Archives, 1986). Brunvand in "Classification for Shaggy-Dog Stories" lists D1OO, "Encounter with a horrible monster," under the category "Hoax Stories told as Personal Experiences" (p. 66).

Chapter Eight. Beliefs and Customs

1. The first belief was collected by Irene Jacobs from Jill Walker, seven years old, New Castle, Delaware, September 25, 1973 (typescript, University of Delaware Folklore Archives, 1973); the second was collected by Phyllis Peltier from Kim Peltier, fifteen years old, Kokomo, Indiana, February 1970 (typescript, Indiana University Folklore Archives, 1970); the remaining beliefs were collected by Carolyn Henry from sixth-graders, Harrisburg, Pennsylvania (typescript, Penn State Harrisburg Folklore Archives, 1985).

2. Collected by Carolyn Henry from sixth-graders, Harrisburg, Pennsylvania (typescript, Penn State Harrisburg Folklore Archives, 1985). In traditional belief systems, unexplained tinglings on the body, such as itching or burning, can be taken as a sign of something to come. Itching and burning ears, eyes, hands, noses, and feet are obvious portents. Showing our bias toward right-handedness, burning or itching on the right side usually signifies good luck while that on the left signifies bad; also showing this bias is the oft-heard belief that itching on the right side means a man is coming or talking about you, while on the left means a woman. The beliefs for right or left ear burning commonly also hold for eyes; for example, if your right ear itches, someone is talking good about you. Although it is common to believe that an itching hand means "you're getting money" (because of the connection with clutching money), this result is also reported with itching eyes and noses.

3. Collected by Carolyn Henry from sixth-graders, Harrisburg, Pennsylvania (typescript, Penn State Harrisburg Folklore Archives, 1985). These bad luck signs and counteractants were the most commonly reported (each given by three or more children) by a single class, and thus offer a small sample of beliefs popular among children.

4. Collected by Carolyn Henry from sixth-graders, Harrisburg, Pennsylvania (typescript, Penn State Harrisburg Folklore Archives, 1985). To judge from a sample from this single class, there are as many good luck signs as bad luck signs (see item 3). The list shows some regional variations, at least in the case of New Year's foods. Eating black-eyed peas is a southern tradition; many of the children are black and have southern roots. Eating sauerkraut and pork is attached to Pennsylvania German tradition. These foods carry the symbolism of growth and abundance for the New Year: black-eyed peas swell in size when cooked, pork comes from a pig which increases its weight 150-fold during the first eight months of its life, and sauerkraut is made from cabbage which yields more produce per acre than any other vegetable.

5. The first five beliefs were collected by Hannelore Wertz from junior high school students, York, Pennsylvania (typescript, Penn State Harrisburg Folklore Archives, 1982); the remaining beliefs were collected by Carolyn Henry from sixth-graders, Harrisburg, Pennsylvania (typescript, Penn State Harrisburg Folklore Archives, 1985). In this form of belief, a condition is established by the phrase "if you . . ." and is followed by a result. The first three beliefs reported here are used as a form of social control over children (e.g., if you play with matches, you will wet the bed), while the others reflect traditional signs. The belief about wearing green seems to have arisen recently, especially as more public awareness of homosexuality has increased (see Chapter Two for children's derisive folk speech to identify homosexuals).

6. The first belief was collected by Hannelore Wertz from junior high school students, York, Pennsylvania (typescript, Penn State Harrisburg Folklore Archives, 1982); the second was collected by Phyllis Peltier from Linda Peltier, fourteen years old, Kokomo, Indiana (typescript, Indiana University Folklore Archives, 1970). In traditional belief systems, items such as those reported here might be called "imperative injunctions," according to the structure of superstitions outlined by Dundes in "Brown County Superstitions," pp. 25-56. In the child's world, lying is a serious crime, and it is often thought that one child's sin will become another's. Children can also protect themselves by crossing their fingers and putting them behind their backs and closing their eyes.

7. The cures for hiccups were collected by Carolyn Henry from sixth-graders, Harrisburg, Pennsylvania (typescript, Penn State Harrisburg Folklore Archives, 1982); the cures for warts were collected by Hannelore Wertz from junior high school students, York, Pennsylvania (typescript, Penn State Harrisburg Folklore Archives, 1982). Folk cures for hiccups and warts are among America's most lasting, and children can be emphatic about their preferred remedies.

8. Reported by Clara Kathleen Bridgewater from her memories of childhood, c. 1954, Sharpsville, Indiana (typescript, Indiana University Folklore Archives, 1970). This divinatory ritual is fairly uniform in American collections. The apple's vibrant color, sweetness, and biblical association with temptation has made it a compelling courtship symbol.

9. Reported by Clara Kathleen Bridgewater from her memories of childhood, c. 1954, Sharpsville, Indiana (typescript, Indiana University Folklore Archives, 1970). Apples seem to be the most popular fruit to try this out on, but some collections offer this ritual with pears, peaches, and oranges. Some informants call for observing this ritual during certain holidays, especially Halloween and May Day. In a common variant, the seeds of the apple will be counted and the number will match the letter in the alphabet which begins the future mate's name.

10. Reported by Clara Kathleen Bridgewater from her memories of childhood, c. 1954, Sharpsville, Indiana (typescript, Indiana University Folklore Archives, 1970).

11. Reported by Anita Hayes from her memories of childhood, c. 1956, Gardiner, Maine (typescript, Northeast Folklore Archives, University of Maine, 1966). Bergen in *Current Superstitions,* pp. 44-45 (nos. 211-19), collected this ritual during the nineteenth century from American children, and noted that the ritual appears ancient in form (p. 155).

12. Reported by Anita Hayes from her memories of childhood, c. 1956, Gardiner, Maine (typescript, Northeast Folklore Archives, University of Maine, 1966). Next to daisies (see item 12), dandelions are favorite plants on which to perform divinatory rituals; see Josephine Addison, *Love Potions,* p. 34.

13. Collected by Simon J. Bronner from Ginger Fetterhoff, eighth grade, Pillow, Pennsylvania (manuscript, Penn State Harrisburg Folklore Archives, 1987). Several variations of this divination ritual are found among folklore collections. Karen Carrera from Scranton, Pennsylvania, for example, told me that the words said after the letters are crossed out are "friendship, courtship, love, marriage, hatred, and divorce" (manuscript, Penn State Harrisburg Folklore Archives, 1987), and these extra words appear in other collections from Indiana and Delaware. Often the choices are "love, hate, friendship, marriage."

14. Collected by Simon Bronner from Laura Drawbaugh, 20 years old, York, Pennsylvania, September 16, 1987 (manuscript, Penn State Harrisburg Folklore Archives, 1987). Laura has a twin sister who knows the same custom but uses the short form of "T-R-U-E L-O-V-E" for her divination. Both remember practicing this custom around eighth grade.

15. Collected by Barbara Walker from Heidi Anderson, Logan, Utah, October 1979 (typescript, Fife Folklore Archives, Utah State University, 1979). The collector comments: "Heidi will be getting married in June. When I asked her to tell me any games, songs, rhymes, etc., that she could remember from her childhood, she told me this superstition."

16. Collected by Simon Bronner from Sadie deWall, eleven years old, and Neva deWall, thirteen years old, Harrisburg, Pennsylvania, September 19, 1987 (manuscript, Penn State Harrisburg Folklore Archives, 1987). The girls began participating in séances the year before I interviewed them. Typically, they told me, the séances were held at slumber parties or at summer camp in their cabins after lights out. Calling in the spirits of deceased family members was considered an especially scary session, and often media figures such as Dracula or Marilyn Monroe were called in.

17. Collected by Simon Bronner from Karen Connaghan, 29 years old, Harrisburg, Pennsylvania, September 16, 1987 (manuscript, Penn State Harrisburg Folklore Archives, 1987). Karen remembered engaging in this ritual from sixth to eighth grade.

18. Collected by Richard Goddard from Debra Pottet, twelve-year-old seventh-grader, Roseville, Michigan, February 16, 1971 (manuscript, Wayne State University Folklore Archives, 1977).

19. Collected by Richard Goddard from Karen Koch, twelve-year-old seventh-grader, Roseville, Michigan, February 16, 1971 (manuscript, Wayne State University Folklore Archives, 1977).

20. Collected by Simon Bronner from Laura Gerald, 21 years old, Chadds Ford, Pennsylvania, October 17, 1986 (manuscript, Penn State Harrisburg Folklore Archives, 1986). Laura remembered this custom from elementary school.

21. Collected by Claudia Williamson from Gary Wooten, 21 years old, Logansport, Indiana, October 1969 (typescript, Indiana University Folklore Archives, 1970).

22. Collected by Simon Bronner from Pamela Bromiley, Hazleton, Pennsylvania, October 17, 1986 (manuscript, Penn State Harrisburg Folklore Archives, 1986). Pamela, a college student, remembered this custom from elementary school. The custom is still active during the elementary school years: On May 27, 1988, seven-year-old Sara Gochnaur of Harrisburg, Pennsylvania, told me of sitting in a dark bathroom with several other girls. She said: "You touch the mirror five times in the dark, and a scary face will appear in the mirror."

23. Collected by Simon Bronner from Kim Baird, Reading, Pennsylvania, October 17, 1986 (manuscript, Penn State Harrisburg Folklore Archives, 1986). Kim, a college student, remembered this custom from her elementary school experience. The motif of an ugly or unmarried woman seeking revenge appears in a "Mary Worth" legend reported in Langlois, "Mary Whales," pp. 28-29.

24. Collected by Simon Bronner from Steve Roberts, Middletown, Pennsylvania, November 7, 1984 (manuscript, Penn State Harrisburg Folklore Archives, 1984). Steve, a college student, reported, "I remember hearing this story when I was in the second grade in the Lower Moreland School District in Huntingdon Valley, Pennsylvania. Lower Moreland is an upper-middle class WASPy township and a suburb of Philadelphia on the northeast side. The 'Bloody Mary' tale was popular with second- and third-grade girls. I remember walking by the girls' restroom and hearing some say 'I believe in . . .' I asked someone what it meant and that's how I found out what the legend was. I think the cut in Bloody Mary's forehead was from a knife, axe, or a club or whatever killed her." "Bloody Mary" is yet another name for variations of "Mary Worth" rituals (see items 20-23). The feature of Mary's blood appearing is found in other reports of the ritual; see Langlois, "Mary Whales," pp. 24.

25. Reported by Susan I. Ralstin, 21 years old, from her memories of childhood, Peru, Indiana, March 30, 1970 (typescript, Indiana University Folklore Archives, 1970). In this traditional prank, the initiate is reminded that he has to place complete trust in the group.

26. Collected by Wes Blakeley from Mick Peters, Columbus, Indiana, July 22, 1977 (typescript, Indiana University Folklore Archives, 1977). The collector reports that the "informant was a boy scout and actually had this done to him back in 1963 when he was twelve years old. He believed the story when it was told to him and while out in the woods he climbed a large rock to protect himself from the Gullywompus. As far as he knows they still do this to the tenderfoots every summer."

27. Collected by Clifford L. Horn from Kevin Sheriff, fifteen years old, Carlisle, Pennsylvania, May 1982 (typescript, Penn State Harrisburg Folklore Archives, 1982). The snipe hunt, Horn points out, is listed in the *Patrol and Troop Activities Handbook* (1979) published by the Boy Scouts of America, p. 110, although the tradition of the hunt predates official adoption and in its practice shows a variety of folk variations. Indeed, few scout leaders were aware that the hunt is described in any scout handbooks. The snipe itself as a mysterious, shy animal which prefers a swamp habitat was given legendary treatment in the nineteenth century; see Mary Alicia Owen, *Voodoo Tales,* pp. 261-65. The initiation trick also dates at least to the nineteenth century; Mac E. Barrick in *German-American Folklore,* pp. 137, 238, cites the earliest New World reference in Pennsylvania in an 1853 source; another source from the 1850s appears in Johana Smith, "In the Bag."

28. Collected by Simon Bronner from Sara Gochnaur, six years old, Harrisburg, Pennsylvania, September 7, 1987 (typescript, Penn State Harrisburg Folklore Archives, 1987). For her tooth, Sara received a quarter. The custom associated with losing baby teeth shows variation in the countries of the world. Marie-Noelle Chris Longe from France, for example, reports: "When a child loses its baby teeth, he puts them in a saucer in the living room for the tooth mouse to take. Sometimes the mouse leaves a gift instead of money. If the tooth is lost, the child substitutes a small nut for the tooth" (collected by Sally Lytle, Galveston, Indiana, March 26, 1970, Indiana University Folklore Archives, 1970). Other Europeans leave cake for the tooth left in the saucer. Japanese children report that the tooth, if it comes from the upper teeth, is thrown up in the air for good luck (collected by Simon Bronner from Motoko Sakai, Middletown, Pennsylvania, September 16, 1986).

29. Collected by Sandy Bailif from Byron Haws, Provo, Utah, February 1972 (typescript, Brigham Young University Collection at the Fife Folklore Archives, Utah State University, 1972). This traditional custom of reciting alternate lines often follows two people saying something in unison.

30. Collected by Sandy Bailif from Ganie Bundy and Neil Riddle, Provo, Utah, February 1972 (typescript, Brigham Young University Collection at the Fife Folklore Archives, Utah State University, 1972). Counting and touching (such as pinching) usually precede the granting of a wish when two people speak in unison, but in this adaptation, the children have made it into an aggressive game (see item 29 for other customs attached to people speaking in unison).

31. Collected by Sandy Bailif from Ganie Bundy, Provo, Utah, February 1972 (typescript, Brigham Young University Collection at the Fife Folklore Archives, Utah State University, 1972).

32. Collected by Simon Bronner from Bronwen H. Greathead, 21 years old, McConnellsburg, Pennsylvania, September 16, 1987 (manuscript, Penn State Harrisburg Folklore Archives, 1987). Bronwen remembered the custom of birthday whacks being done when she was between six and ten years old.

33. Collected by Sandy Bailif from Barbara Clyde, Provo, Utah, March 1972 (typescript, Brigham Young University Collection at the Fife Folklore Archives, Utah State University, 1972).

34a. Collected by Simon Bronner from William J. Rievel, 27 years old, Johnstown, Pennsylvania, September 16, 1987 (manuscript, Penn State Harrisburg Folklore Archives, 1987). William remembered practicing these customary pranks between the ages of eight and eleven years old. He reports that they still go on in his home town. With fears of tampered candy and public vandalism, Halloween has become in many places a tightly regulated holiday. But children still engage in many of these customs, especially "corning," i.e., throwing corn kernels (and in some cases, cobs) at one another and at houses.

34b. Collected by Simon Bronner from Eileen Franz, 36 years old, Dumont, New Jersey, September 16, 1987 (manuscript, Penn State Harrisburg Folklore Archives, 1987). Eileen remembered practicing these customary pranks between the ages of nine and eleven years old. Cohen and Coffin in *Folklore of American Holidays,* p. 309, observe that "Trick or treat," the Halloween threat of little children, is apparently a recent American phenomenon, as distinct from pranks and mischief long customary on the holiday. It seems to be related to the Gaelic practice of giving cakes to the poor at Samhuinn or 'summer-end,' a seasonal festival that coincides with All Souls' Day. They came to be called 'soul-cakes,' and in return recipients were obligated to pray for a good harvest.

35a. Collected by Simon Bronner from Michele Fink, 20 years old, West Lawn, Pennsylvania, September 16, 1987 (manuscript, Penn State Harrisburg Folklore Archives, 1987). Michele's family still practices the custom of opening one present on Christmas Eve and leaving the rest for Christmas Day. She practiced the custom of leaving food for Santa until she was about six years old.

35b. Collected by Carolyn Henry from Alethea, black twelve-year-old sixth-grader, Harrisburg, Pennsylvania (typescript, Penn State Harrisburg Folklore Archives, 1985).

35c. Collected by Simon Bronner from Gary Graham, 26 years old, Harrisburg, Pennsylvania,

September 16, 1987 (manuscript, Penn State Harrisburg Folklore Archives, 1987). Gary remembers this custom in his family occurring when he was between six and ten years old. As this account shows, Christmas has more and more become a children's holiday, especially enjoyed by younger children who tap into the mythology of the Santa Claus figure.

36. Collected by Carolyn Henry from Charmaine, black eleven-year-old sixth-grader, Harrisburg, Pennsylvania (typescript, Penn State Harrisburg Folklore Archives, 1985).

37. Reported by Laurie Samuelsen, 21 years old, from her childhood memories in Allentown, Pennsylvania (typescript, Penn State Harrisburg Folklore Archives, 1983). Showing some of the transitions that differences in such customs force, Laurie, who is American-born, commented: "I had my first American Christmas cookie two years ago and experienced part of an American Christmas just last year." She found many of the American Christmas customs were different from her Norwegian-American experience: "The main meal on Christmas Eve consists of boiled cod fish, *lefser* (similar to pita bread), potatoes, and vegetables with a lot of melted butter. For dessert, *risgrot* is served. This dish is rice cooked with milk for two to three hours. It is eaten with sugar and cinnamon."

38. Reported by Simon Bronner, 33, December 1987, from his memories of childhood in Brooklyn, New York (c. 1964). Hanukkah (the Festival of Lights) commemorates the successful revolt of Judah the Maccabee against the Hellenistic Syrians who occupied the land of Israel around 165 B.C.E. The term Hanukkah is a Hebrew term meaning "dedication." When the Temple was to be rededicated, oil that was only supposed to burn for one day burned miraculously for eight full days, hence the eight-day candlelighting ceremony. Like Christmas, however, Hanukkah has an earlier seasonal connection to the joyous lighting of fires to hasten bringing on light and warmth during the cold, dark season. Hanukkah traditions were strong in my Jewish neighborhood of Flatbush in Brooklyn, which had many East European immigrants. In more assimilated communities, such as the one I live in now within Harrisburg, Pennsylvania, these celebrations still thrive, but are organized and regulated by a Jewish Community Center.

Chapter Nine. Nonsinging Games

1. Reported by Charles Lorditch, 31 years old, from his memories of childhood (c. 1960) in Levittown, Pennsylvania (typescript, Penn State Harrisburg Folklore Archives, 1982). Lorditch offers the following background for his report: "The recollection of my childhood is filled with memories of hot summer nights playing tag and hide-and-go-seek, along with countless other variations of games that we just made up as we went along. This unique settlement of young families, more than 30,000 people in the first year of the community, brought together a blend of people from all parts of the United States. This sprawling community was mass produced and people would quickly build lasting friendships along with the children who developed common ties among their age groups. It seems that all of the children in my particular neighborhood of the Elderberry Pond section of Levittown all grew up together and shared many a night and long summer afternoon of games and adventure. Many of the children and their families migrated from the Philadelphia area, so many of the games that they learned had this influence."

2. Reported by Paul D. Morin, 20 years old, from his memories of childhood (c. 1962) in Amesbury, Massachusetts (typescript, Northeast Folklore Archives, 1973). Morin relates this game to the playing of Hide and Seek in his neighborhood. "Hide and Seek," he reports, "was one of our favorites. It was one of our main ploys against our parents. We used to play right in front of our house, well, we used the telephone pole in front of our house as the goal, so as far as my parents knew, it was all right for us to stay out late, because 'we'll only be right in front of the house.' What my parents did not know was that the boundaries extended for about three blocks. So for us, it was a big deal, because we got to stay out after dark, and we always felt that we were putting something over on our parents. Perhaps the best part about playing this game was that there was always someone different to be 'it' because we had a rule that the first one caught was 'it' next. The reason 'it' was not the last one caught was because everyone was afraid that they would get caught right off, because it would not matter. So the first-one-caught rule was just a method of keeping the game interesting." But in Fifty-Two Scatter, Morin reports, "it was important not to be 'it' first, because you could wind up being 'it' for the duration of the game. The 'it' power in Hide and Seek was greatly magnified to produce Fifty-Two Scatter."

3. Reported by Paul D. Morin, 20 years old, from his memories of childhood (c. 1962) in Amesbury, Massachusetts (typescript, Northeast Folklore Archives, 1973). Morin offers the following reflections on the game: "We always used to play this game at night, and through experience we learned a few unspoken rules to playing Kick the Can. (1) Never play Kick the Can near houses which contain little babies, because they go to bed earlier than you do, and the mothers of little babies get very upset when you wake up the little darlings. (2) Never play near people's new cars, because they (fathers especially) get very upset when they hear cans rolling around on their new cars, and tend to end the game on the spot. (3) Another very important rule to playing Kick the Can is that if the person that is 'it' knocks over the cans while counting, then he has to reset the cans and count again. (4) A final caution about kicking the cans, if you're playing near Mark Gosselin's garage, or anyone's for that matter, make sure that you always end up kicking the cans away from the garage. This is especially important if the garage door has windows in it like Mark's did, because I found out the hard way that windows in garages can be very expensive, especially when your allowance is only a dollar a week."

4. Collected by Mark Cislo and Charles Spillar from Wendy, a fourth-grader, Dupont, Pennsylvania, November 30, 1984 (typescript, Penn State Harrisburg Folklore Archives, 1984). Wendy mentioned in the interview that this game was a favorite to play around Halloween.

5. Collected by Susan May from Janet Marshall, 21 years old, from her memories of childhood (c. 1964), Hardinsburg, Indiana (typescript, Indiana University Folklore Archives, 1975). According to Brewster in *American Nonsinging Games,* p. 12-16, Blindman's Buff (or Bluff) is an ancient game. The term *buff,* he points out, is obsolete except for its use in reference to this game; it comes from an old French and Middle English word for *blow (n*; cf. a *buffet). Today the term *bluff,* referring roughly to the deception in the game, is generally used.

6. Collected by David Carr from observations made at a neighborhood pool, Bloomington, Indiana, November 1971 (typescript, Indiana University Folklore Archives, 1971). Carr adds the following remarks: "Unlike Tag, the 'it' is reduced to a blind, slow opponent who is easy to avoid. Since the 'it' has reduced power, the number of failures in tagging a player is greatly increased. And since the 'it' has a low-power role, the players combine forces against 'it' as well as use disparaging remarks at the 'it.' I find that this is a game which is played mostly by the girls, and not the boys. It is usually played in the pool, but at times when the pool is most vacant."

7. Reported by Susan May, 20 years old, from her memories of childhood (c. 1974) in Bloomington, Indiana (typescript, Indiana University Folklore Archives, 1975). Freeze Tag is the most common variation of tag I collected, especially in small groups of children. To be sure, tag can simply be played with children being chased by an "it"; when the "it" touches another child, the other child then becomes the "it." On occasion, if the chased child touches wood or iron, the child is immune from being tagged.

8. Collected by Alana Haws from first- and second-graders, Rigby, Idaho, 1972 (typescript, Brigham Young University Collection at Fife Folklore Archives, Utah State University, 1975). Haws observed this game at a Child Care Club where ten children engaged in the game. Cross Tag is among the oldest reported variations of tag.

9. Collected by Mark Cislo and Charles Spillar from fourth-graders, Dupont, Pennsylvania, November 30, 1984 (typescript, Penn State Harrisburg Folklore Archives, 1984). In TV Tag, features of the consumer society and electronic age that children live in are grafted onto an old game. The game described by these fourth-graders is directly related to the playing of Squat or Stoop Tag commonly reported in nineteenth- and twentieth-century collections.

10. Collected by Mark Cislo and Charles Spillar from fourth-graders, Dupont, Pennsylvania, November 30, 1984 (typescript, Penn State Harrisburg Folklore Archives, 1984). This game is referred to by other names. Renee McCoy collected a version called Hospital Tag in Brooklyn, New York, in 1975: "When you get tagged by whoever is it, you hold the part of the body that has been tagged. When you get tagged, you try and get someone else until everyone in the game has been touched" (typescript, Northeast Folklore Archives). Alana Haws also in 1975 collected a version called Japanese Tag in Provo, Utah: "The person touched must hold that part of his body until he tags someone else. There is a safe part of the territory that is agreed upon at the beginning of the game" (typescript, Brigham Young University Collection at the Fife Folklore Archives, Utah State University, 1975). In England, the game is usually called "French Touch" and less often "Hospital Touch" and "Poison Touch."

11. Collected by Hannelore Wertz from a male junior high school student, York, Pennsylvania (typescript, Penn State Harrisburg Folklore Archives, 1982). The term "cooties" in Cooties Tag stands for an imaginary lice-like insect or dirt. With the announcement that a child has cooties, there is the association of the child with an inferior social position or physical appearance. The idea of cooties, according to Sue Samuelson writing in "The Cooties Complex," pp. 198-210, was brought to the United States by returning servicemen after World War II who had likely picked up the term from an Indian or Malay word for lice *(kutu)*. The game became significant as a reminder of the fear of disease and contagion during the 1950s polio epidemic, and continued to reinforce the importance of cleanliness and appearance through the 1960s and 1970s.

12. Collected by Barbara Marroni from Dan, eight years old, South Bend, Indiana, March 1977 (typescript, Indiana University Folklore Archives, 1977). This game is also commonly called Pom Pom Pullaway. According to Brewster in *American Nonsinging Games,* p. 76, this game was often played on ice skates in New England and Canada.

13. Reported by Jenny Williams from her memories of childhood, Adams County, Pennsylvania (typescript, Mac E. Barrick Memorial Folklore Archives, Shippensburg University, 1980). References to this game, also going by the name Hare and Hounds and Hunt the Fox, have been traced by the Opies in *Children's Games in Street and Playground,* pp. 176-78, to the sixteenth century.

14a. Collected by Charles Spillar and Mark Cislo from fourth-graders, Dupont, Pennsylvania, November 30, 1984 (typescript, Penn State Harrisburg Folklore Archives, 1984). In the same class in which this game was collected, a similar game was played as Wolf Tag by a boy named Paul.

14b. Collected by Charles Spillar and Mark Cislo from Michelle, fourth-grader, Dupont, Pennsylvania, November 30, 1984 (typescript, Penn State Harrisburg Folklore Archives, 1984). After Michelle described the game, Spillar, a 22-year-old student from Scranton, Pennsylvania, commented on tape: "I remember that game. I used to play that game when I was younger." Closely attached to the games discussed in the notes to item 14a, this game substitutes a wolf for the witch and the addition of a base for the wolf (the pickle jar). This last feature makes this game resemble more closely the game of Colors in which there is a struggle (and sometimes its dramatization in the form of a tug of war) between good and evil; see Brewster, *American Nonsinging Games,* pp. 180-83.

15. Reported by Susan May, 20 years old, from her memories of childhood (c. 1966), Bloomington, Indiana (typescript, Indiana University Folklore Archives, 1975). May offers the following as background: "I remember playing this where large groups of children gather, such as a party, family dinner, in a large neighborhood, or at a playground. Since this game has to deal with chasing, it is necessary for the playing to be outside."

16. Reported by Lana Lassiter, 20 years old, from her memories of childhood (c. 1958), Windfall, Indiana (typescript, Indiana University Folklore Archives, 1970). This game is also called Steps or Giant Steps.

17. Collected by Charles Spillar and Mark Cislo from fourth-graders, Dupont, Pennsylvania, November 30, 1984 (typescript, Penn State Harrisburg Folklore Archives, 1984). Brewster in *American Nonsinging Games,* pp. 35-36, notes the international circulation of the game. This game is probably older than indicated by the name Red Light, referring to the twentieth-century invention of the traffic signal.

18. Collected by Carolyn Henry from Stephanie and Angela, eleven-year-old sixth-graders, Harrisburg, Pennsylvania (typescript, Penn State Harrisburg Folklore Archives, 1985). Although collected from sixth-graders who recounted their traditional pastimes, this game is commonly played among younger children, often as early as first grade. This game is variously reported as Old Witch, Old Lady, What's the Time Mr. Wolf, and Chicky My Chick My Craney Crow. Consistently, however, children in this game view the sign of old age in this game as a trait worthy of ridicule and fear. In effect, the children pester the Old Lady until she chases them back home.

19. Reported by Susan May, 20 years old, from her memories of childhood (c. 1966), Bloomington, Indiana (typescript, Indiana University Folklore Archives, 1975). Brewster in *American Nonsinging Games,* pp. 170-71, and the Opies in *Children's Games in Street and Playground,* pp. 239-41, note the international circulation of this game. Specific references to the name Red Rover associated with the game as it is reported by May are common in English-speaking countries of Canada, the United States, Australia, Scotland, England, and New Zealand.

20. Reported by Paul D. Morin, 20 years old, from his memories of childhood (c. 1962) in Amesbury, Massachusetts (typescript, Northeast Folklore Archives, 1973). Morin offers the following background to his report: "This game was a lot of fun, and was played at school during recess, because it took so many kids to have a decent game of it. The one thing about this game that made it such a rough game was the fact that it was played on hot top, you probably call it black top, and some of the kids took the game so seriously that they would think nothing of tackling someone on the hot top. Now if you've ever been tackled, or have fallen down on hot top, you will realize how bloody some of us got playing that game at times." Release, Rolevo, Relievo, Ringalario, and Ringolevio are common names for this game. It does not seem as popular today as it once was, but writing in 1969, the Opies in *Children's Games in Street and Playground,* pp. 172-74, reported that "in Scotland, Wales, and the northern half of England, 'Relievo' is the principal seeking game with two sides."

21. Collected by Pam Carter from Ruth Carter, Bloomington, Indiana, March 8, 1973 (typescript, Indiana University Folklore Archives, 1973). The collector notes that both boys and girls played the game, and played it often, during school recess. The Opies in *Children's Games in Street and Playground,* pp. 143-46, note the popularity of Prisoner's Base in England since the sixteenth century; up to the twentieth century, it was also known as Chevy Chase, and was "one of the most played schoolboy games."

22. Collected by Barbara Marroni from Dan, eight years old, South Bend, Indiana, March 1977 (typescript, Indiana University Folklore Archives, 1977). Some elaborations of the rules are common in this game. For example, in a version collected by Susan May from Nathan Abram, eleven years old, in Bloomington, Indiana, the child "can take three giant steps and try to hit somebody with the ball" after catching the ball. "If he doesn't catch the ball, he can still yell 'spud,' but he may not take three giant steps" (typescript, Indiana University Folklore Archives, 1975). This last version with the taking of steps, according to Ferretti in *Great American Book,* p. 57, in Philadelphia is called Baby in the Air; see also the description of Baby in the Hat in Barrick, "Games from the Little Red School House," p. 97. In this game, however, numbers are called out that correspond to numbers claimed by the players. Instead of spelling out "spud," the players are out when they spell out "baby."

23. Collected by Simon Bronner from sixth-graders, Brooklyn, New York, 1974 (typescript, Archive of New York State Folklife, 1975). According to Ferretti in *Great American Book,* p. 58, "sidewalk games that require more aim than brawn are Coin and Stick, also known as Hit the Coin and Hit the Stick." Collecting most of his material in New York City, Ferretti found the games played with pennies (and sometimes nickels or dimes) and ice-cream-pop sticks.

24. Collected by Simon Bronner from sixth-graders, Brooklyn, New York, 1974 (typescript, Archive of New York State Folklife, 1975). Ferretti in *Great American Book,* pp. 64-67, describes this game in New York City from at least the 1940s to the present. The game of Box Baseball corresponds to what he collected in the Bronx section of the city as Curves.

25. Collected by Simon Bronner from sixth-graders, Brooklyn, New York, 1974 (typescript, Archive of New York State Folklife, 1975). The five-box game is reported in Steinberg, "Sidewalks are for Playing," p. D25. He gives the following hints: "Make the first box a hard searing throw. A soft underhanded toss is suggested for boxes two-one and three-two-one, while a hard low toss, much like the kind used in skimming a stone over water, is suggested for the four and five through one boxes."

26. Collected by Simon Bronner from sixth-graders, Brooklyn, New York, 1974 (typescript, Archive of New York State Folklife, 1975). Because Chinese handball is bounced into the wall rather than hit up on the wall, it requires far less space, which makes it a popular urban game. It also is easier on the hands and can be played against any wall.

27. Reported by Charles Lorditch, 31 years old, from his memories of childhood (c. 1960), Levittown, Pennsylvania (typescript, Penn State Harrisburg Folklore Archives, 1982). The pimple ball is a commercial type of rubber ball that has small spheres on the surface. According to Lorditch, Half-Ball was brought to Levittown by the many children who had lived in Philadelphia, where the game was most common.

28. Collected by John McCague, John Tomik, and David Yeates from Bill Quinn, Westbury, Long Island, and John Romeo, Commack, Long Island, May 12, 1977 (typescript, Archive of New York State Folklife, 1977). According to the collectors, variations of this game were played as Curb Ball (throwing the ball against the curb of a sidewalk) and Wall Ball (played on the side wall of a house or a school playground wall). Besides baseball hits applied for the actions of the catcher, points can be applied, with different values given depending on whether the ball bounces off the point of the step or on the steps. Or as Brewster reports of a fastpaced version from Illinois in *American Nonsinging Games,* p. 89, the person who catches the ball then can throw it.

29a. Collected by Renee McCoy from Quano McCoy, fifteen years old, Brooklyn, New York (typescript, Northeast Folklore Archives, 1975). The Skelly board was drawn, according to the collector, with a piece of chalk on the street.

29b. Collected by Simon Bronner from sixth-graders, Brooklyn, New York, 1974 (typescript, Archive of New York State Folklife, 1975). The item that was flicked into the various boxes was a bottlecap, sometimes weighted down with wax or a coin. This design for the skelly board was the most common, although I also saw boards in which the middle square, which here is number 13, had diagonal lines crossed, the letter S, or even a skull and crossbones in it. Sometimes the squares around the center square have number values such as Sl, S2, S3, S4 (or 2, 4, 6, 8). As Ferretti explains in *Great American Book,* pp. 232-33, "If you land in any of them, you are forced to stay there for as long as the other players want you to. The only way you can leave is if another player shoots you out. This, however, entitles that player to the number of boxes indicated by the number of the skel. Thus, if you have gone through 12 and, in shooting for 13, land in the skel valued at 8, another player who is only at 5 can hit you out and automatically go into 13, which is the total of the number of boxes he had already moved through and the penalty value of the skel."

30a. Collected by Dorothy Deal from Frances Golinko, 21 years old, Gary, Indiana, November 24, 1967 (typescript, Indiana University Folklore Archives, 1967). Deal added the following notes on the other diagrams: "(i) informant is Mickey Wheeler, 20 years old, Moorestown, New Jersey, November 26, 1967; (ii) informant is Veda Stanfield, 20 years old, New Albany, Indiana, November 17, 1967; (iii) informant is Beth Ballard, 20 years old, Peru, Indiana, November 17, 1967; (iv) informant is Cherry Muse, 21 years old, St. Louis, Missouri, December 3, 1967; (v) informant is Donna Modjeski, 21 years old, Hammond, Indiana, November 23, 1967; (vi) informant is Sharon McBride, 21 years old, West Hartford, Connecticut, November 24, 1967; (vii) informant is Sharon Easley, 19 years old, Princeton, Indiana, November 23, 1967; (viii) informant is myself, I learned it in Baltimore, Maryland, about 1953; (ix) informant is myself, I learned it in Baltimore, Maryland, about 1953." The game of Hop Scotch is found in various forms around the globe, and although its origins are obscure, the game appears in English as early as 1667 in *Poor Robin's Almanac,* where it is called "Scotch-hoppers," according to J.W. Crombie in "History of the Game of Hop-Scotch," pp. 403-8. For the international circulation of the game and a report of American versions, see Brewster, *American Nonsinging Games,* pp. 107-15.

30b. Collected by Simon Bronner from Tajuana Green, eleven years old, black girl, Tynese Shadel, ten years old, black girl, Ayana Landon, eleven years old, black girl, Harrisburg, Pennsylvania, December 12, 1987. The girls played Hop Scotch in a field across from their homes on a single block. They are part of a play group made up of the older girls (to age twelve) and their younger siblings that included five- and six-year-old boys. In this group of ten children, the form of Hop Scotch that allows for an advantage to the quick-witted and quick-mouthed, as well as physically coordinated, is favored.

30c. Reported by Lana Lassiter, 20 years old, from her memories of childhood (c. 1961), Windfall, Indiana (typescript, Indiana University Folklore Archives, 1970). The top block, usually drawn in the form of a semicircle, is often referred to as the "moon" in collections of Hop Scotch.

30d. Collected by H.T. Reed from Delinda Reed, nine years old, Lewiston, Maine (typescript, Northeast Folklore Archives, 1960). This layout is called an "English" form by Bancroft in *Games,* p. 123. Because the layout is simple, the player's task becomes complex. In the version reported here, the player has to jump with eyes closed; Bancroft reports a version that requires the player to hold the stone between his or her legs.

30e. Collected by H.T. Reed from Delinda Reed, nine years old, Lewiston, Maine (typescript, Northeast Folklore Archives, 1960). Garrenton in "Children's Games," p. 30-31, describes a version of Movie Star Hop Scotch from North Carolina: "the player, after hopping through the pattern, writes the initials of a movie star in his block. The other players try to guess the identity. The one who correctly identifies the star is allowed to step in the block once." Brewster in "Some Unusual Forms of 'Hopscotch,'" p. 229, outlines a similar diagram, but instead of putting a movie star's initials in the block, the player puts in his or hers. "The next player then hops as did the first, but must not alight in the square containing the first player's initials."

Chapter Ten. Toys and Constructions

1. Collected by Simon Bronner from Earnest Bennett, Indianapolis, Indiana, May 31, 1987. Bennett, who was 82 years old when he recounted his memories of childhood whittling to me, recalled that a boy's life in the Kentucky hill country in southern Adair County was full of slingshots like this. "I guess I started whittling when I was three years old," he explained. Like those of many other rural boys, his pocketknife was a prized early possession. With this pocketknife, he made slingshots, whistles, and other toys out of the "daily supply of wood for heating the house and cooking the food." He also delighted in carving imitations of implements found on the farm. "My brother and I made a good-size wheel wagon. It looked very much like Dad's big-road wagon." Trying to explain his motives, Earnest said, "I guess it was to have things to play with. My only bought toy, aside from my knife, was a ten-cent cap pistol. At about age eight or ten, when I would see a new toy or a thing I wanted, I would go home and make one for myself." With the slingshot, he and other boys would take aim at targets such as cans or a tree; occasionally, they might take on rodents. If a forked stick was not available, Bennett recalled, a shot made from string and a rubber patch could also be used. Like the model used by the biblical David, the shot would be circled around the head until a flinging motion released the rock. Urban boys today still find the slingshot appealing, although it is as likely to be made from hanger wire as in wood.

2. Collected by Simon Bronner from Earnest Bennett, Indianapolis, Indiana, May 31, 1987.

3. Collected by Simon Bronner from Earnest Bennett, Indianapolis, Indiana, May 31, 1987. Whistles similar to the one made by Bennett appear in Page and Smith, *Foxfire Book of Toys and Games,* pp. 218-22. In these reports the whistles were made from hollow-core woods, such as bamboo, or slick-barked sticks, such as sourwood, willow, or maple.

4. Collected by Simon Bronner from Earnest Bennett, Indianapolis, Indiana, May 31, 1987. The name bull roarer has been recorded since the nineteenth century; it apparently takes its name from the bull-like sound it makes when whirled. The bull roarer in the United States also goes by the names dumb bull, noise maker, boomer, whizzer, swish, or buzzer. The making of the bull roarer is known throughout the world. Alan Dundes in his essay "A Psychoanalytic Study of the Bullroarer," published in his *Interpreting Folklore,* pp. 176-98, summarizes the bull roarer's international circulation and function. In the United States and Europe, the bull roarer was known as a boy's plaything admired for its noisemaking capabilities, but elsewhere it serves sacred and ritual purposes.

5. Collected by Simon Bronner from Earnest Bennett, Indianapolis, Indiana, May 31, 1987. This toy — also called a buzzer, spin-the-button, button-on-a-string, whirligig, and twirler — is probably the most common folk toy I ran across in my collection. The appeal of the toy comes from the noise it makes and often the color combinations or patterns caused by spinning the button. The other appeal of the toy is physical; children test themselves to see how long they can keep the button continuously spinning. Typically, children learn to make this toy in early childhood using spare buttons in the house. The use of wood is not uncommon, however, and is especially prevalent among rural boys. In most collections, girls favor making this toy more than boys. Michael Owen Jones in his collection for the Indiana University Folklore Archives, 1965, heard some aesthetic judgments from his informants on the operation of the button toy: "The size of the button makes a difference. The bigger the button is the harder it is to spin right good. 'Course the bigger the button the slower it'd go. If you had a smaller button, just reasonable size, why then it would really go fast." "The bigger button you could get the better it would sound. You could just make that thing fly and you couldn't tell but what it was one big wind going through there." "You can use any size but the bigger the button the longer the string should be." Folkloristic references to the toy have appeared since the nineteenth century and point to an international circulation for the toy.

6. Collected by Simon Bronner from Earnest Bennett, Indianapolis, Indiana, May 31, 1987. The spinning top has been pictured as a children's toy since the thirteenth century when it appeared in drawings in the Orient. References to the top, as Strutt points out in *Sports and Pastimes,* pp. 304-5, appear in ancient Greek and Roman manuscripts; for additional references to the top's antiquity, see also Alice Bertha Gomme, *The Traditional Games of England, Scotland, and Ireland,* vol. 2, pp. 299-303.

7. Collected by Simon Bronner from Charlie Savage, Bloomington, Indiana, May 30, 1980. In his twenties at the time he showed me this ball-in-cage, Charlie had saved it from the time he had made it when he was ten years old. And now, he reported, his younger brother had made one. Using the trick of cutting in the wood, rather than cutting out as one might expect, the carver can move on to other whittler tricks of the chain, pliers, and fan made out of one piece of wood. But the ball-in-cage usually stands out as the child carver's first work. For the boy, the trick offers him something to show off to his friends, and in the process of making it, besides problem solving, he learns the qualities of wood and the use of tools. Indeed, many men recalled how this toy helped prepare them for woodwork on the farm. But even in cities, balls-in-cages are made because of their visual and physical appeal. Typically, carving the ball-in-cage is left behind in childhood, but often whittlers will take up such tricks in old age. Below, for example, is a picture of Earnest Bennett holding a ball-in-cage attached to a linked chain made out of one piece of wood which he made as a boy in Kentucky. He stopped carving when he went to work as a man in Indianapolis, but resumed later in life. Now he demonstrates carving the items at the Indianapolis Children's Museum. The object draws attention to the maker and reminds others of the creativity that the maker, child or oldster, is capable of. See Bronner, *Chain Carvers,* especially pp. 59-72,

Earnest Bennett with ball-in-cage he made as a child in Kentucky

88-93. As I point out in this book, ball-in-cage making has an ancient lineage and international circulation.

8. Collected by Simon Bronner from Terence, Harrisburg, Pennsylvania, May 1983. The loose bricks and boards that litter the streets of our cities make building blocks for various children's constructions. Influenced by the daredevil exploits of Evel Knievel, children take bricks and boards and construct daredevil jumps and obstacle courses. The bicycle is no longer a contraption for getting from one place to another. In the hands of children, the bicycle becomes an acrobatic prop. The design of the bicycle since the 1960s has stressed thick wheels and a low-riding design that encourages rough handling. Children balance the bike on one wheel and perform other acrobatic tricks in addition to daredevil jumps over their home-made props.

9. Photographed by Simon Bronner in Middletown, Pennsylvania, July 1983, and Harrisburg, Pennsylvania, December 1987.

10. Collected by Simon Bronner in Cape May, New Jersey, July 1987. Using the tools of plastic shovels and buckets, children mold the sand of America's beaches for various constructions. The favorites from my observations at Cape May appear to be forts and canals. Some creative children, especially the girls, it seems, like to make sand sculptures, especially of turtles.

11. Collected by Simon Bronner, Bloomington, Indiana, March 2, 1979. Pictured here are a snow man and snow woman. An added decorative touch appears on the snow man; the bottom has been painted red and the top has been painted blue. An unpainted section on the top forms the outline of a necktie. The snow woman is identified by the triangular bottom in imitation of a dress and the broom placed in one hand. Most references to snow sculptures are to the making of male figures, but in the last decade, more snow women have appeared on front lawns. The other use of snow, especially among boys, is in making snow balls and snow forts for mock battles. Building snow men is found in other cultures as well. Culin in *Games of the Orient*, pp. 8-9, describes snow men and houses made by boys in Korea and Japan. For a guide to American snow sculpture, see Stein and Lottick, *Three, Four, Over the Door*, pp. 159-60.

12. Collected by Simon Bronner from Sadie and Neva deWall, Harrisburg, Pennsylvania, August 1983. While sand and snow provide the most conspicuous raw materials for children's imaginative play, rocks alongside rivers also provide abundant opportunities for creativity. You probably remember taking a stone and dropping it softly into the water to make concentric circles, and you may remember building mountains, forts, and castles out of rocks. In these examples, children play with form and display aesthetics, turning natural shapes into human-made constructions. In this artistic process, the child exercises more improvisation than with the technical play of paper-folding, for example. In the stone constructions pictured here, the older child, Neva, began the play with the rocks, and Neva soon followed suit. The children compared their constructions and discussed what they were: castles, islands, and volcanoes. After finishing one, they began arranging the constructions in rows, creating a neat landscape of forms. They stepped back to see if it looked "right" — right from their child's-eye sense of Western aesthetics. With this shared idea of what was being constructed, the girls began working together. Their little brother Jonah meanwhile worked off at a distance building a rectangular fort made of rocks. The forms themselves here are not necessarily traditional (although the Western tendency to arrange forms in rows and rectangles is), but the process involving informal learning, repetition, and variation shows the kind of conception and performance common to the folk art of children. The conventional tendency to arrange forms linearly and symmetrically in the deWalls' sculptures was balanced by an imaginative, almost magical, quality given the sculptures by their pyramidal shape.

13. Collected by Simon Bronner from Jonah deWall, ten years old, Harrisburg, Pennsylvania, August 15, 1987.

14. Collected by Simon Bronner from Neva deWall, fourteen years old, Harrisburg, Pennsylvania, August 15, 1987. This object is the most common folding-paper toy I collected from children. Usually made by girls, it sometimes went by the name of "cootie catcher," "whirlybird," or "fortune teller," but more often than not the maker had no name for it. In many versions, it is used as a divinatory device with predictions about future love, wealth, and careers, but often the messages are more related to the present. In the present-oriented version, the device is used to provide a kind of pranking humor. The person who picks the flap is embarrassed or insulted by the message written out by the maker of the device. Examples are "You love Mark" or "Your Mom is ugly."

15. Collected from Sadie deWall, twelve years old, Harrisburg, Pennsylvania, August 15, 1987. Perhaps related to the Japanese Origami tradition of paper-folding, this box has the special appeal to children of being blown into like a balloon to take its shape. The folding pattern of the hexagon is a basic foundation to make other paper toys such as a boat and hat. For Sadie, who had learned to make the box four years earlier, the appeal of the object was not it what it became, but rather its process of becoming. She impressed others by taking an ordinary sheet of paper and, after many folds that did not seem to lead to an identifiable object, turning out a three-dimensional box. The folk process then took shape as youngsters asked her how it was made, and she usually was more than willing to show them. For related comments on the appeal of paper folding in America, see Roger Dean Beatty and Yasuko Yamaguchi, "Origami: From Japanese Folk Art to American Popular Art," *Journal of Popular Culture* 9 (1976): 808-15.

16. Collected from sixth-graders, Harrisburg Middle School, Harrisburg, Pennsylvania, November 1982. This thick, folded object, makes a good playing object. The Knapps in *One Potato, Two Potato,* pp. 225-26, comment: "One of the most popular classroom toys is a fat, triangular football that the boys make by folding a piece of notebook paper. They flick it with their fingers, back and forth across a desk or table — sometimes from one table to another." It is also used to pass notes among children in a classroom.

17. Collected by Simon Bronner from sixth-graders, Harrisburg Middle School, Harrisburg, Pennsylvania, November 1982. The long chain was photographed in 1983. It is held up by its maker, Barbara Huber (now D'Arcy), a student at Penn State Harrisburg, who constructed it when she was twelve years old.

18. Collected by Simon Bronner from sixth-graders, Harrisburg Middle School, Harrisburg, Pennsylvania, November 1982. The appeal to children of flight and technological design is evident in the making of this paper folding. Sometimes called a glider or a paper jet, the design of the paper folding shown here is the most common type I collected, although many variations exist.

19. Collected by Simon Bronner from sixth-graders, Harrisburg Middle School, Harrisburg, Pennsylvania, November 1982. The photograph detailing the paper folding is a hooded frog; the nonhooded variety is pictured in the group shot of paper foldings.

20. Collected by Simon Bronner from sixth-graders, Harrisburg Middle School, Harrisburg, Pennsylvania, November 1982. Making string figures is an internationally known skill, usually performed by girls. This is a favorite figure to make, as the Knapps point out in *One Potato, Two Potato,* p. 229. When two players make different figures working off each other's designs, then the activity takes on the form of a game, often called cat's cradle, in which the object is to create many figures. The true cat's cradle is a specific string figure, but the term is often used generically for forming string patterns. In the sequence pictured here, for example, the girl with her back to the camera forms what she calls a "bridge" from the figure the girl facing the camera has.

21. Collected by Simon Bronner from Sadie deWall, twelve years old, Harrisburg, Pennsylvania, December 5, 1987. The photographs of the Halloween figures and pumpkins were taken in Harrisburg and Middletown, Pennsylvania, respectively, in October 1986.

22. Collected by Simon Bronner from sixth-graders, Harrisburg Middle School, Harrisburg, Pennsylvania, November 1982. The streets of Harrisburg, as in other cities, are lined with homemade basketball hoops, varying block by block, while "official" playgrounds lie idle. Partly responsible for the proliferation of these homemade hoops are the strong neighborhood feelings in Harrisburg. Playgrounds do not answer to neighborhood lines or needs. The localized hoops allow small groups of children, especially younger children, to engage each other regularly close to home. The most popular hoop is the plastic milk crate, but in 1987, as a result of milk company losses of the crates, Pennsylvania made it illegal for private citizens to own the crates. Still, that didn't stop the communally owned hoops from going up.

23. Collected by Simon Bronner from Sadie deWall, twelve years old, Harrisburg, Pennsylvania, December 5, 1987. For several years during the 1980s, beaded safety pins were the rage. Children made them carefully from combinations of different colored beads. They were worn on sneaker laces or on clothes, or just collected and exchanged among groups of friends. In the last two years, I have collected many more friendship bracelets woven from yarn, using colorful combinations reminiscent of the friendship pins. They appear similar to friendship bracelets made from telephone wire which I remember from my childhood.

References

Here I list the books, articles, theses, and dissertations cited in my notes. For the sources of unpublished folklore collections, check the list of archives which follows.

Aarne, Antti. *The Types of the Folktale: A Classification and Bibliography,* translated and enlarged by Stith Thompson. Second revision, Helsinki: Academia Scientiarium Fennica, Folklore Fellows Communications No. 184, 1964.

Abrahams, Roger D., "The 'Catch in Negro Philadelphia." *Keystone Folklore Quarterly* 8 (1963): 107-11.

———, ed. *Jump-Rope Rhymes: A Dictionary.* Austin: University of Texas Press, 1969.

———. "Playing the Dozens." In *Mother Wit from the Laughing Barrel: Readings in the Interpretation of Afro-American Folklore,* ed. Alan Dundes, pp. 295-309. Englewood Cliffs, New Jersey: Prentice-Hall, 1973.

——— and Lois Rankin, eds. *Counting-Out Rhymes: A Dictionary.* Austin: University of Texas Press, 1980.

Addison, Josephine. *Love Potions: A Book of Charms and Omens.* Topsfield, Massachusetts: Salem House, 1987.

Baker, Ronald L. *Hoosier Folk Legends.* Bloomington: Indiana University Press, 1982.

———. *Jokelore: Humorous Folktales from Indiana.* Bloomington: Indiana University Press, 1986.

Bancroft, Jesse H. *Games.* 1909; revised and enlarged edition, New York: Macmillan, 1937.

Barrick, Mac E., ed. *German-American Folklore.* Little Rock, Arkansas: August House, 1987.

———. "Games from the Little Red School House." In *Two Penny Ballads and Four Dollar Whiskey: A Pennsylvania Folklore Miscellany,* ed. Kenneth S. Goldstein and Robert Byington, pp. 95-120. Hatboro, Pennsylvania: Folklore Associates, 1966.

Baughman, Ernest W. *Type and Motif Index of the Folktales of England and North America.* The Hague: Mouton, 1966.

Bergen, Fanny D. *Current Superstitions: Collected from the Oral Tradition of English Speaking Folk.* New York: Houghton, Mifflin, Memoirs of the American Folklore Society, No. 7, 1896.

Berkovits, Rochelle. "Secret Languages of Schoolchildren." *New York Folklore Quarterly* 26 (1970): 127-52.

Bolton, Henry Carrington. *The Counting-Out Rhymes of Children: Their Antiquity, Origin, and Wide Distribution.* 1888; reprint, Detroit: Singing Tree Press, 1969.

Brewster, Paul G. *American Nonsinging Games.* Norman: University of Oklahoma Press, 1953.

———. "Some Unusual Forms of 'Hopscotch.'" *Southern Folklore Quarterly* 9 (1945): 239-40.

———, ed. *Children's Games and Rhymes.* 1952; reprint, New York: Arno Press, 1976.

Bronner, Simon J. *Chain Carvers: Old Men Crafting Meaning.* Lexington: University Press of Kentucky, 1985.

Brown, Marice C. *Amen, Brother Ben: A Mississippi Collection of Children's Rhymes.* Jackson: University Press of Mississippi, 1979.

Brunvand, Jan Harold. "Classification for Shaggy Dog Stories." *Journal of American Folklore* 76 (1963): 42-68.

———. *The Vanishing Hitchhiker: American Urban Legends and Their Meaning.* New York: W.W. Norton, 1981.

———. *The Choking Doberman and Other 'New' Urban Legends.* New York: W.W. Norton, 1984.

Cohen, Hennig, and Tristram Potter Coffin, eds. *The Folklore of American Holidays.* Detroit: Gale Research, 1987.

Crombie, J.W. "History of the Game of Hop-Scotch." *Journal of the Anthropological Institute of Great Britain and Ireland* 15 (1886): 403-8.

Culin, Stewart. *Games of the Orient.* 1895; reprint, Rutland, Vermont: Charles E. Tuttle, 1958.

Dorson, Richard M. *American Folklore.* 1959; reprint, Chicago: University of Chicago Press, 1977.

Doyle, Charles Clay. "Belaboring the Obvious: Sarcastic Interrogative Affirmatives and Negatives." *Maledicta* 1 (1977): 77-82.

Drake, Carlos. "The Killer in the Back Seat." *Indiana Folklore* 1.1 (1968): 187-9.

Dundes, Alan. "Brown County Superstitions." *Midwest Folklore* 11 (1961): 25-56.

————, ed. *Mother Wit from the Laughing Barrel: Readings in the Interpretation of Afro-American Folklore.* Englewood Cliffs, New Jersey: Prentice-Hall, 1973.

————. *Interpreting Folklore.* Bloomington: Indiana University Press, 1980.

————. *Cracking Jokes: Studies of Sick Humor Cycles and Stereotypes.* Berkeley, California: Ten Speed Press, 1987.

Ferretti, Fred. *The Great American Book of Sidewalk, Stoop, Dirt, Curb, and Alley Games.* New York: Workman Publishing, 1975.

Fine, Gary Alan. "Pre-Adolescent Male Slang." *Children's Folklore Newsletter* 2 (Fall 1979): 2-3; 2 (Winter 1979): 2-3; 3 (Spring 1980): 3-4; 3 (Winter 1980): 3; 4 (Spring 1981): 3- 4; 4 (Fall 1981): 3; 4 (Winter 1981): 4-5.

Fowke, Edith. *Sally Go Round the Sun: Three Hundred Children's Songs, Rhymes and Games.* Garden City, New York: Doubleday, 1969.

Fuld, James J. *The Book of World-Famous Music: Classical, Popular and Folk.* 3rd edition, New York: Dover, 1985.

Garrenton, Valerie. "Children's Games." *North Carolina Folklore Journal* 21 (1973): 27-31.

Gomme, Alice Bertha. *The Traditional Games of England, Scotland, and Ireland,* 2 vols. 1894, 1898; reprint, New York: Dover, 1964.

Grider, Sylvia. "The Supernatural Narratives of Children." Ph.D. dissertation, Indiana University, 1976.

————. "From the Tale to the Telling: AT 366." In *Folklore on Two Continents: Essays in Honor of Linda Dégh,* ed. Nikolai Burlakoff and Carl Lindahl, pp. 49-56. Bloomington, Indiana: Trickster Press, 1980.

Hale, Lucretia. *The Complete Peterkin Papers,* 1880; reprint, Boston: Houghton, Mifflin, 1960.

Howard, Dorothy. "The Rhythms of Ball-Bouncing and Ball-Bouncing Rhymes." *Journal of American Folklore* 62 (1949): 166-72.

Knapp, Mary, and Herbert Knapp. *One Potato. Two Potato: The Secret Education of American Children.* New York: W.W. Norton, 1976.

Kochman, Thomas, ed. *Rappin' and Stylin' Out: Communication in Urban Black America.* Urbana: University of Illinois Press, 1972.

Labov, William. "Rules for Ritual Insults." In *Rappin' and Stylin' Out: Communication in Urban Black America,* ed. Thomas Kochman, pp. 265-314. Urbana: University of Illinois Press, 1972.

Langlois, Janet. "'Mary Whales, I Believe in You: Myth and Ritual Subdued.'" *Indiana Folklore* 11 (1978): 5-33.

McCosh, Sandra. *Children's Humour.* London: Granada Publishing Panther Books, 1979.

Monteiro, George. "Parodies of Scripture, Prayer, and Hymn." *Journal of American Folklore* 77 (1964): 45-52.

————. "Religious and Scriptural Parodies." *New York Folklore* 2 (1976): 150-66.

Musick, Ruth Ann. *The Telltale Lilac Bush and Other West Virginia Ghost Tales.* Lexington: University of Kentucky Press, 1965.

————. *Coffin Hollow and Other Ghost Tales.* Lexington: University Press of Kentucky, 1977.

Newell, William Wells. *Games and Songs of American Children.* 1883; reprint, New York: Dover, 1963.

Northall, G.F. *English Folk Rhymes: A Collection of Traditional Verses Relating to Places and Persons, Customs, Superstitions, Etc.* 1892; reprint, Detroit: Singing Tree Press, 1968.

Opie, Iona, and Peter Opie, eds. *I Saw Esau: Traditional Rhymes of Youth.* London: Williams and Norgate, 1947.

————. *The Oxford Dictionary of Nursery Rhymes.* 1951; corrected edition, Oxford: Clarendon Press, 1952.

————. *The Lore and Language of Schoolchildren.* Oxford: Clarendon Press, 1959.

————. *Children's Games in Street and Playground.* Oxford: Clarendon Press, 1969.

————. *The Singing Game.* Oxford: Oxford University Press, 1985.

Owen, Mary Alicia. *Voodoo Tales — As Told Among the Negroes of the Southwest.* 1894; reprint, New York: Negro University Press, 1969.

Page, Linda Garland, and Hilton Smith, eds. *The Foxfire Book of Toys and Games: Reminiscences and Instructions from Appalachia.* New York: E.P. Dutton, 1985.

Potter, Charles Francis. "Round Went the Album." *New York Folklore Quarterly* 4 (1948): 5-14.

Samuelson, Sue. "The Cooties Complex." *Western Folklore* 39 (1980): 198-210.

————. "'The Man Upstairs': An Analysis of a Babysitting Legend." *Mid-America Folklore* 12 (1984): 2-10.

For information about other titles in

THE AMERICAN FOLKLORE SERIES

please send a self-addressed stamped envelope to:

August House Publishers, Inc.

P.O. Box 3223

Little Rock, AR 72203

Smith, Johana H. "In the Bag: A Study of Snipe Hunting." *Western Folklore* 16 (1957): 107-10.

Solomon, Jack, and Olivia Solomon. *Zickary Zan: Childhood Folklore*. University: University of Alabama Press, 1982.

————. *Ghosts and Goosebumps: Ghost Stories, Tall Tales, and Superstitions from Alabama*. University: University of Alabama Press, 1981.

Stein, Susan, and Sarah T. Lottick. *Three, Four, Open the Door*. Chicago: Follett Publishing, 1971.

Steinberg, Harvey. "Sidewalks Are for Playing." *New York Times* (July 18, 1976): D23, 25.

Strutt, Joseph. *The Sports and Pastimes of the People of England*. Enlarged and corrected edition by J. Charles Cox. 1903; reprint, Detroit: Singing Tree Press, 1968.

Sutton-Smith, Brian. *The Folkgames of Children*. Austin: University of Texas Press, 1972.

————, ed. *A Children's Games Anthology: Studies in Folklore and Anthropology*. New York: Arno Press, 1976.

Taylor, Archer. *English Riddles from Oral Tradition*. Berkeley: University of California Press, 1951.

Thompson, Stith. *Motif-Index of Folk-Literature,* 6 vols. Revised edition, Bloomington: Indiana University Press 1975.

Tucker, Elizabeth. "Tradition and Creativity in the Storytelling of Pre-Adolescent Girls." Ph.D. dissertation, Indiana University, 1977.

Turner, Ian. *Cinderella Dressed in Yella*. 1969; reprint, New York: Taplinger, 1972.

Zumwalt, Rosemary. "Plain and Fancy: A Content Analysis of Children's Jokes Dealing with Adult Sexuality." *Western Folklore* 35 (1976): 258-67.

Archives Consulted

Archive of Folk Culture, Library of Congress, Washington, D.C. 20540.

Archive of New York State Folklife, Library Special Collections, New York State Historical Association, Cooperstown, NY 13326.

Center for the Study of Comparative Folklore and Mythology, University of California, Los Angeles, CA 90024.

Fife Folklore Archives, Utah State University, Logan, UT 84321.

Folklore Archive, Department of English, Wayne State University, Detroit, Michigan 48202.

Folklore Archives, English Department, Brigham Young University, Provo, Utah 84602.

Folklore Archives, English Department, Western Oregon State University, Monmouth, OR 97361.

Folklore and Folklife Collection, Helms-Cravens Library, Western Kentucky University, Bowling Green, KY 42101.

Folklore Archives, Library, Fort Hays State University, Hays, KS 67602.

Indiana State University Folklore Archives, English Department, Indiana State University, Terre Haute, IN 47809.

Indiana University Folklore Archives, Folklore Institute, Indiana University, Bloomington, IN 47405.

Mac E. Barrick Memorial Archive of Central Pennsylvania Folk Cultures, Shippensburg University, Shippensburg, PA 17257.

Michigan Folk Arts Archives, The Museum, Michigan State University, East Lansing, MI 48824.

Northeast Archives of Folklore and Oral History, Department of Anthropology, University of Maine, Orono, ME 04469-0158.

Penn State Harrisburg Folklore Archives, Humanities Division, Pennsylvania State University at Harrisburg, The Capital College, Middletown, PA 17057.

University of Arkansas Folklore Archives, Special Collections Department, David W. Muslins Library, University of Arkansas, Fayetteville, Arkansas 72701.

University of Delaware Folklore Archive, Folklore and Ethnic Art Center, University of Delaware, Newark, DE 19735.

University of Pennsylvania Folklore and Folklife Archives, Folklore and Folklife Department, University of Pennsylvania, Philadelphia, PA 19104-6304.

SIMON J. BRONNER is professor of folklore and American studies and coordinator of the American Studies Program at the Pennsylvania State University at Harrisburg. He has served as president of the Pennsylvania Folklore Society and the Children's Folklore Section of the American Folklore Society. He has written four other books on folklore — *Grasping Things: Folk Material Culture and Mass Society in America, Chain Carvers: Old Men Crafting Meaning, American Folklore Studies: An Intellectual History,* and *Old-Time Music Makers of New York State* — and is the editor of *American Material Culture and Folklife, Folk Art and Art Worlds,* and *Folklife Studies from the Gilded Age.*

W.K. McNEIL, General Editor of the American Folklore Series, is the folklorist at the Ozark Folk Center at Mountain View, Arkansas. He has written many studies in American folklore and has edited two anthologies. McNeil holds a Ph.D. in Folklore from Indiana University.